THEY CAME FROM

GHANA

(The Two Worlds of Kwame and Kwabena Boaten)

A historical novel

by

Noel Smith

T0329287

Sub-Saharan Publishers - Accra

First published in 2012 by
SUB-SAHARAN PUBLISHERS
P. O. BOX LG 358,
LEGON, ACCRA, GHANA

Email: saharanp@africaonline.com.gh

Copyright: Noel Smith 2012

ISBN 978-9988-647-40-7

Design & typesetting by Phillip Dawson.
Cover design by Kwabena Agyepong.

Contents

Foreword and Acknowledgments

I have defined this book as a historical novel. It is a formula that novelists have used with success ever since Sir Walter Scott wrote his romance *Waverley* in 1814. Factual historical events, great and small, are presented as they occurred and persons, real and imagined, who were living at the time, describe the effect that these events had upon them or what they thought about them. The novelist seeks to enter into the thoughts and emotions of the characters, real or imagined, who played a part in these events.

In the fascinating history of the former Gold Coast and the present day Ghana, there are many occasions when young men were assigned by chiefs to traders or to European missionaries or government officers as surety for an agreement. Often these youths were taken to Europe to be trained and educated there. Philip Quaque, a son of Chief Kojo of Cape Coast was taken by Rev. Thomas Thompson, a Church of England missionary, to England and returned in 1765 to work in the school at Cape Coast until his death in 1816. Fifty years of faithful service! From the mulatto school in Christiansborg, the chaplains sent youths to Holland and Denmark. Rev. T. B. Freeman, the pioneer Wesleyan missionary took two Asante princes to England and returned with them in 1831. In 1837, two more Asante princes were taken to Holland as pledge for a treaty with the Dutch.

My interest was aroused by the fact that as part of the treaty made by the Asantehene and the Juabenhene with Bowdich and Tedlie, one each of their sons was allocated to the Britons who would personally be responsible for their education, first in Cape Coast and then in England. I could find no further references to them. As a result I have constructed their careers as they would most likely have developed. Like many Ghanaians, before and since, they worked responsibly and diligently outside their homeland. Kwame died of malaria in the ill-fated Niger Expedition of 1841 while Kwabena passed away in his Juaben village, exact date unknown.

I acknowledge gratefully the help I have gained from the books I have listed, especially from those of more recent Ghanaian writers like Akosua Perbi, J. K. Adjaye, R. E. Obeng and Kari Dako, but I also owe my thanks to former colleagues at P.T.C. Akropong who stimulated my interest in Ghana history and who clarified my understanding of Akan life and beliefs. I name here only a few: L.S.G. Agyemfra, F. Agyeman, C.A. Akrofi, H.T. Dako, H. Debrunner, R.O. Danso, S.T. Akunor, J. H. Nketia, F. A.Gyampo, O. A. Boateng, A. L.Kwansa and E. Kobler. I add the name of the late Rev. J.H. Keteku who was my mentor and friend for many years.

I am deeply indebted to Dr. Margot Schantz for her constant interest and encouragement. Finally, thanks to Sub-Saharan Publishers for their care and counsel in the publication.

The responsibility for any errors or omissions and for all expressions of opinion is mine.

Noel Smith

Chapter 1

Bowdich's Mission to Asante 1817

"The Kings agree to commit their children to the care of the Governor in-Chief for education at Cape Coast Castle, in the full confidence of the good intentions of the British Government, and of the benefits to be derived therefrom." Clause 9 of the Treaty 1817 between Thomas Edward Bowdich and Sai Tootoo Quamina, King of Ashantee and its Dependencies and Boitinnee Quama, King of Dwabin and its Dependencies".
Bowdich, Mission to Ashantee, 2nd ed. London, 1873. pp143

Thomas Edward Bowdich paused to wipe the sweat off his brow and to give his aching feet a rest; they had been walking all day along a bush path made slippery by recent rains and had not made the progress that he had hoped. It was clear to him now that he had made a serious blunder in rejecting the advice not to press on to Akrofrom given to him by the group of soldiers appointed by the Asantehene to accompany him on the return to Cape Coast. He had given them permission to return but they had followed at a distance behind Henry Tedlie and Kwame Owusu Boaten. Now here he was alone with Kwame's cousin Kwabena Apia Boaten at the head of the returning mission with the baggage carriers, and everyone else was out of sight. When it began to grow dark they had tried shouting but had received no answer. It was too late to retrace their steps even if they could have done so; there was no alternative but to press on. Suddenly Kwabena called to him and pointed urgently at the sky in the west which had become pitch-black, beckoning vigorously with both arms that he should come up to him. Almost without warning the wind grew in intensity and violence, seeming to come from all directions at once, while out of the black cloud came fierce stabs of lightning and menacing rolls of thunder.

He half-ran to join Kwabena who pointed up a hill-slope; they must try to reach higher ground. He tried to keep pace with the young man, but they were now in the bush; thorns ripped his jacket; one of his boots came off and he discarded the other, his hat blew away and branches lashed at his head and body. When he caught up with him, Kwabena had twisted his cover cloth to make a sort of rope which he tied firmly round his body and gave Bowdich the other knotted end. The hiss of the torrential rain became louder and louder and then it was upon them; drenched to the skin Kwabena pulled him along in the darkness through gullies and bogs formed by the rush of water, always a bit higher until he halted below a group of large boulders. Bowdich let go of the cloth and fell to the ground utterly exhausted but after a few minutes Kwabena pressed the cloth into his hand and made it clear that they should go further.

There was another flooded gully to wade through where the water was waist deep and only then Kwabena indicated that they could sit down and wait until the storm had abated. Bowdich fell into a sleep of sheer exhaustion and when he awoke he found himself covered with banana leaves. Kwabena helped him to his feet but Bowdich felt so weak that Kwabena took him on his back and in about an hour, with frequent stops, they reached Akrofrom. It was still dark but the violence of the storm had passed. Kwabena called for help and the villagers came out, lit torches, brought them to a dry hut, gave them water in a brass pan to wash in, some fruit to eat and palm wine to drink. Then they stripped him, dried him, swaddled him in many cloths and laid him on a mat to sleep. But before he slept his conscience troubled him with the thoughts of his failure. Thanks to Kwabena he was still alive, but when the disaster of the return journey became known he could only merit complete condemnation.

At first everything that he had done had been successful: he had been appointed as scientific research officer to the first official embassy to Kumasi under the leadership of Frederick James, the Governor of the English fort at Accra. He had been lucky at the age of 26 to have been chosen for such a good post; his father had wanted him to enter his export-import business in London but his interest had been directed to Africa and three years ago,through the help of his uncle, Mr. Hope Smith, then Governor-in-Chief of the British forts and trading posts of the African Company, he had obtained a writership in that Company, and had taken up residence in the Cape Coast fort. The expedition had been warmly welcomed in Kumasi with a tremendous display from a mass of warriors, a large number of chiefs, a deafening tumult of drums and horns, after which they had approached to shake the hand of Osei Tutu Kwamina, the Asantehene and had been conducted to their quarters. On the following days they had delivered the presents from England and had received gifts in return. He still puzzled over the attitude of their leader, Mr. James, who, when the Asantehene expressed his irritation over the fact that, although he possessed a number of Notes of European castles on the coast he had not received the rental monies, put the responsibility on the shoulders of the Governor of Cape Coast and thus caused the entire purpose of the embassy to be at risk. He had consulted with his colleagues, the surgeon Henry Tedlie, and William Hutchison the writer, before reporting to Cape Coast that, contrary to their view, Mr James was prepared to give up the mission and return to Cape Coast. They had informed Mr. James of their action, the Asantehene had been apprised and both had written to Cape Coast. As a result, after a wait of a month, a letter had come from Cape Coast ordering Mr James to return and appointing him, Edward Bowdich, as leader of the expedition. Of course, James had been ill with fever, but had seemed obsessed by the notion that if the Notes were not discussed, their lives would be at risk. On the contrary, he had found the Asantehene to be amenable in discussion and the business of the Notes for Cape Coast and Accra had been resolved smoothly. He seemed to have found favour with the Chief and his elders and when he had asked Quashie, the interpreter, what the Asantehene had said, he could still remember almost the exact words:

"The King likes you; you speak a proper good palaver; you speak like a man; the King wishes to be a friend to white men; he thinks white men next to God."

He had led the discussions to a successful signing of a treaty and his colleague William Hutchison had been left in Kumasi as Resident English officer. He had made copious notes: for the first time the Company and the British Government in London had a full record of Asante life and beliefs, its political organisation and military power as well as its dominant trading position in West Africa. But why had James seemed so indifferent to the success of the mission? He had, after all, volunteered to lead it. Had he been annoyed that the choice of personnel had been made by his uncle, John Hope Smith, Governor-in-Chief of all the Company's work on the Coast, and had included his nephew as scientific officer? At any rate, on the trip north James had always lagged behind and had never fraternised with them; a few times they had had to stay two nights in a village because of his lateness; once he had insisted on stopping overnight in the forest and twice he had rested a whole day. He seemed often indisposed and once had had a fever. But he, Bowdich, personally had retrieved the situation, had achieved all the aims of the mission and they had left Kumasi with honour.Now he had thrown it all away in a fit of arrogance and had put the lives of all the members of the expedition at risk! Again and again his own stupidity reproached him until at last merciful sleep took over.

At first light he awoke to see Tedlie and Kwame standing over him looking weary and dishevelled. Tedlie said: "I'm glad to see you alive and well, Edward. You know, we owe our lives to these two young men. During the worst of the storm Kwame climbed a tree and pulled me up after him, then he supported me the rest of the way here, I'd lost my boots and my feet are badly cut and bruised. One of the Asante soldiers caught up with us; he had found your torn jacket in thorn bush; we didn't know whether it was an encouraging sign or not."

"And I'm happy to see you two. Kwabena showed great presence of mind and literally pulled me through. They have been entrusted to us and have already shown their worth. We must reward them later, all we can do now is to say thank you. Can you recall the phrase we learned?"

They both turned to the young men with hands outstretched and a smile on their faces and said together: *"Meda w'ase pii"*. Then they all laughed and the boys clapped their hands.

"Have we any news of the rest of the group?"

"Some of them took refuge in a shed on a farm. The baggage is safe and no one has been injured."

The news lifted a great load from Bowdich's mind and as during the day all the party reported in, they were able to organise themselves for the march to Asharaman the following day. A week later they were in Payntree's town (Dunkwa) where they were warmly welcomed and well-fed, and a day's march after that brought them once again to Cape Coast.

They had taken a direct track through the forest and on the outskirts of the town Bowdich grouped them in marching order: the Asante soldier-escort in the lead, then the baggage carriers and himself, Tedlie with the young men in the rear. They marched in step through Oguaa and got their first glimpse of the sea, then halted at attention before the castle gate. A messenger had been sent on ahead the previous day and they were received in style in the courtyard: the Company soldiers, smart as paint in their red coats and peaked caps, had formed a semicircle around the seated Governor dressed formally in his velveteen coat, knee-breeches, silk stockings and silver-buckled shoes, accompanied by his senior officers in their best clothes. Bowdich took a few steps forward, shook the Governor's outstretched hand, presented his report and diary of the mission, saluted and walked back to his place.

The Governor stood up and said: "I am very pleased to welcome you all back. You have accomplished the task given to you and you have returned today bringing with you a treaty of friendship between the Asantehene and the Company which will be forwarded to the Government of the King of England. You have also brought with you two young men from Asante, one is a son of the Asantehene called Kwame Owusu Boaten; the other is a son of the Juabenhene called Kwabena Apia Boaten. These young men have been entrusted to Mr Tedlie and to Mr Bowdich who will look after their interests." He beckoned to the youths to come forward which they did proudly; they had had time to put on their gleaming *kente* cloths while the gold chains around their necks clearly indicated their status. They bowed their heads as they shook hands. Then he continued:

"Accompanying the party and ensuring their safety were six Asante warriors and I thank them personally." Hope Smith walked up to them and shook hands with each one. It was all quite impressive and the implications were not lost on the crowd of spectators who applauded generously; he had welcomed his nephew back from a successful visit to Kumasi and had thanked the Asante in a cordial manner. They would report back every detail to the Asantehene.

"Finally, I have to inform you that Mr. Hutchison has remained in Kumasi as the first Resident English Officer; we wish him well. Last of all I have to tell you of the sad death of one of the party, Quamina Bwa, the guide, who passed away in Kumasi after a serious illness. Mr Tedlie did all that was possible for him. I request you to keep silent for one minute in his memory." After the silence the band played 'God save the King' and the ceremony was over.

Kwame and Kwabena had been put in the care of a Company soldier who led them up a flight of stone steps to a balcony that went round the entire fort building. He took them to a place on the south side where they could see the black rocks on which the fort was built, the vast expanse of sea with its constantly breaking waves, the canoes of the fishermen, the masted ships of the Europeans at anchor, and on the left, the Oguaa township. Out of a basket their guide brought balls of *kenkey*, fried plantain, European bread and sweet milky tea in a bottle.

"I have to look after you for an hour, then I must take you to the Quartermaster to get your kit and show you your room. Do you understand me?" He had spoken in Fante.

"Yes. Not every word, but we understand. We come from Juaben, the language is the same only with some different pronunciations."

"I come from Anomabu, a fishing village just along the coast."

The Asante boys looked round in amazement at the size of the massive fortress while their guide explained:

"It's all built of bricks brought out as ballast in the holds of ships, the English captured it from the Dutch and rebuilt it after 1664. There are many rooms inside built of brick on two floors, and underneath are cellar rooms for more than 1000 slaves. We don't buy or sell slaves any more, the Dutch buy them in Elmina and sell them to the Americans. About 200 soldiers and employees of the Company live here and we receive supplies by ship on the landing-pier down there on the beach. There are apartments for the Governor-in-Chief, for the Director-General and for factors, writers and soldiers. There are storehouses and warehouses for all kinds of equipment, granaries, guard rooms and two huge water cisterns, workshops for carpenters and smiths. In addition, there are gardens growing fruit and vegetables and we have a chapel where you can pray to God." Their soldier-guide spoke proudly.

Kwabena asked: "What is ballast? We don't know that word". "Ballast is heavy material like iron, rock or sand loaded into the bottom of a ship to keep it steady."

"We have never seen the sea before. How far does it go?"

"You see those sailing ships? They have to sail twenty days or more to reach Europe or America."

"How do the ships stay in one place on the water and how do they move?"

"They are held by an anchor at the end of a long chain; the anchor has two great flukes at the end like claws that stick into the sea bed. The ships are moved by the wind blowing into the large canvas sails; see, like that one on the horizon." He pointed far out to sea. "The ship is steered by the rudder at the back of the ship just under the surface of the sea."

"Do people live on the ships?"

"Of course. On a large ship you need a crew of at least 20 sailors and then you have maybe 100 passengers."

"What is the name of the town where we are?"

"They call it Oguaa; the sea crab is a kind of totem for the locals. Nowadays everybody calls it Cape Coast."

Then the sergeant led them to the Quartermaster who was found in charge of the large store of clothing; a tailor and three seamstresses were busy cutting out and sewing.

The sergeant announced authoritatively: "Full kit for two protégés of the Governor to be ready tomorrow". He fumbled in his breast pocket for the order form and handed it over. 'Navy blue jackets, fustian trousers, waistcoat, two pairs drawers, buckle shoes, peaked caps, two good quality shirts, soap and towels,' read the Quartermaster aloud and then said: "You are lucky, I had a good delivery of ready-mades only last week." They tried on the garments for size and laughed when they saw themselves in the cracked pier-glass which reflected them from head to toe. He made chalk marks for the alterations by the seamstresses and admired their kente cloths. "You are easy to fit and your outfits will be ready in the morning."

The sergeant led them to a room on the second floor with two beds, a large table, two chairs and a cupboard. On the mattresses a white sheet was folded and underneath one of the beds was a chamber pot; only for urine he explained, the privy he would show them later. Food was brought to them and after they had eaten they talked by the light of the candle, rolled themselves in the sheets and fell asleep listening to the unusual sound of the surf.

On the following day they put on the new clothes and were taken by Quashie the interpreter from Accra that Bowdich had kept, to an interview with the Governor at which Tedlie and Bowdich were present. He was also dressed in the same way as they were except that he wore a cravat and there was an embroidered design on the sleeves of the jacket. He smiled, showed them where they could sit and called Quashie to his side to interpret.

"Mr. Bowdich has given me a good report of you both of how you rescued him and Mr. Tedlie on the return journey. Now, tell me about yourselves: how old are you and where were you brought up?"

He nodded to Kwabena to speak.

"Honourable Sir, we don't know exactly how old we are but from what our mothers tell us we were born soon after the present Asantehene was enstooled. He is Kwame's father and my father is the present Juabenhene. Our mothers are twin sisters who belong to the Aduana clan, that is why we both have the name Boaten. Our mothers are very beautiful and were chosen as favourite wives, we live together in Juaben; we think that we could be about 16 years old. For very important matters the Juabenhene takes his court to Kumasi so when we were called to present ourselves there we knew that the affair concerned us. We had heard quite a lot about the visit of the English from Cape Coast."

Hope Smith turned to Kwame to continue.

"We were presented to the two chiefs, the elders and to the three white men. Then the Asantehene told us of a possible treaty of trade and friendship with the English and that as a pledge of his serious intention he would send us to Cape Coast Castle to be educated. We would come back equipped to help our people. I would belong to Mr. Tedlie and Kwabena to Mr. Bowdich."

"Were you pleased to be so honoured?"

"Yes, Sir."

"Why?"

"Among our people, to be chosen by the Asantehene for a special duty means that he has favoured you and if you succeed you would be rewarded."

"Are you both prepared to go to school here in Cape Coast to learn English and then to study in England if it should be so arranged?"

"Yes, Sir, we are. We have spoken together; Kwabena would like to be a scientific officer like Mr. Bowdich and I should like to be a medical doctor like Mr. Tedlie."

"You would need to work very hard. The Company will give you sixty guineas a year each when you are in England and I hereby place you in the custody of these two gentlemen who are prepared to take responsibility for your future welfare."

The young men thanked him and left the room with Quashie. When they had gone Hope Smith turned to Bowdich and Tedlie:

"What do you think of the two boys?" Bowdich answered: "We have been convinced from the start that the choice was a good one. We had a number of opportunities to observe them closely and they kept close to us: for example, whenever Tedlie was treating the sick and especially when he demonstrated his instruments and botanical engravings to the King, and whenever I discussed matters of Asante custom and law with any of the elders. It became clear to me that they were both intelligent and curious, always polite and well-behaved, and as we learned on the return journey, capable and resourceful. They will profit by their schooling and training and Tedlie and I look forward to taking them to England. What will happen to the other children that Osei Bonsu has sent?"

"The boy and girl he sent to me in August have been placed with a good family and they will go to school. In your letter of Sept. 26th about your last audience with the Asantehene and the Juabenhene you report that a boy and a girl were presented to me, to be brought up in my service, a boy and a girl to you, Edward, and a boy to you, Tedlie. I am assuming that the two girls will arrive later and they will remain here in Cape Coast. Now, on the matter of The Treaty, let me say first that I am delighted with your reports and comprehensive letters; for the first time we have a factual picture of Asante, unique in its detail and wide-ranging in every respect. I congratulate you both and I hope that you can get it soon in print. I fear, however, that when our lords and masters in Government in London read that the Company has presumed to make a political treaty between the King of England and the Asantehene they may react unfavourably."

"But isn't that exactly what Osei Bonsu wanted? He spoke on many occasions of the 'permanent union of the English and the Ashantees' as he put it, and in The Treaty this was expressed as 'perpetual peace and harmony between the British subjects in this country, and the subjects of the Kings of Asante and Dwabin."

"That is true, but the preamble says clearly that the treaty was entered into by you, 'in the name of the Governor and Council at Cape Coast Castle, on the Gold Coast of Africa, and on behalf of the British Government, with Sai Tootoo Quamina, King of Ashantee and its Dependencies, and Boitinee Quama, King of Dwabin and its Dependencies.' There's the rub. The Government criticised us for not having made proper contact with Asante in the past and then sent us supplies and presents for our expedition, now there will be annoyance at the Company for having had the temerity to enter into the political sphere. The problem is the phrase: 'on behalf of the British Government'; Companies like ours under Royal Warrant get involved in local affairs and then when things become difficult the London Government hesitates and repudiates what the Company has done. We must wait and see how the Government will react and that will take a year or two. Even if I had taken over from James the result would have been the same. What you have achieved will be vindicated by posterity. Get your book published as soon as you get back to England so that the facts of the situation in Asante may be truly known. I am to blame, not you; I gave James the draft of a treaty which he passed on to you, so my head will roll. It seemed to me that a treaty would achieve more than a trade agreement to stabilise relations between Kumasi and Cape Coast. Maybe I am being unduly pessimistic, time will tell. Say nothing to any of your colleagues. Perhaps I should have spoken to you like this before but I thought that it would hamper you. The Company Committee had agreed on the Embassy and that was enough, although for some time I have thought that the whole future of the Company is in the melting pot. Ever since 1807 and the abolition of the Slave Trade, we have not earned enough by other export goods to justify our existence and we are in no position to solve the question of whether Britain will take political power on the Gold Coast or not. The main thing is that thanks to you the Company has once again pioneered; yours is the best and fullest report about Asante that has ever been made and I am proud of you both and of Hutchison."

It saddened them to listen to a probable unfortunate outcome of their endeavours but they felt honoured to receive the confidence of the Governor. They knew him as a sympathetic, reasonable man who loved his country and who at the same time had a special regard for African customs and beliefs. They were also aware how difficult the job of Governor had become. After 1807 there had been no trade in slaves by the British forts but the trade still continued through Elmina and other forts belonging to other nations. If the Company had to justify its existence other exports had to be found like palm oil. Many believed that great riches lay in the interior but that meant making a treaty with Asante so that the new 'legitimate' trade could take the place of slaves. They also knew from previous conversations with him that fresh ideas about the future of European trade with Africa were being proposed that included the introduction of plantation crops in conjunction with training, schooling and missionary enterprise.

The Governor asked Tedlie: "Tedlie, you are a shrewd observer, how would you describe the Asantehene, Osei Tutu?"

"I had ample opportunity to observe him and I got to like him. He is a mixture of dignity and affability, of authority and paternalism. He speaks clearly and logically, asks shrewd questions and is always courteous. My firm impression was that he was personally trustworthy but that the constant pressures from his elders, from his army captains, even from the leader of the Moors from the north, were so great that he was led into decisions against his own preferences. For example, a number of states are always ready to break away from the federation, like Denkyera, Akim, Gyaman, and then he comes under pressure to punish these 'wayward' members by war, although, in my view, he is not a warlike man. His main aim is to trade directly with us and with the Dutch and cut out the Fante middlemen. He has to sell his slaves at Manso to the Fante slave handlers who bring them in turn to Elmina or to other forts although he holds the Notes for many forts and the rents are paid directly to him by the Europeans. You can imagine his frustration and that is why when we negotiated The Treaty there was so much palaver about the Notes.

"The relationship with Juaben seems to be strong, I suspect

because of their wives, you recall that the boys called their mothers 'beautiful'. Everyone knows the story of Osei Kwamina, the eldest brother of Osei Tutu, who was Asantehene from 1781 to 1797. He was a young boy so the Adontenhene acted as ruler until he was older. But then he was so infatuated by the beauty of Gyawa, the Juabenhene's daughter that he spent an entire year with her in Juaben and neglected his duties in Kumasi. On that account he was destooled. Whether the royal women of Juaben are particularly attractive I can't say. I sensed that the bond between the two chiefs was not so durable, Osei Tutu is much the stronger character. I got the best information from Agyei, one of the king's spokesmen; he was the most objective and the preferred *okyeame* when a case presented problems or when tact was required; he had suggested Kwame and Kwabena to the Asantehene. Agyei once told me how as a boy he worked for a salt trader who had been falsely accused of fraud and brought to trial. He listened to the lies until he could stand it no longer, stood up suddenly in the court and called out to the Asantehene: 'You have people to wash you, to feed you, to serve you, but you have no people to speak the truth to you, and tell you when God does not like your palaver.' He showed up the false witnesses and his employer was acquitted. He was kept at court after that and rose to become the chief's confidant."

Hope Smith thanked them both for all that they had achieved and suggested that they accompany the boys to greet the Chief of Cape Coast and then organise English lessons for them but first speak with the headteacher at the school.

"They are too old to sit with the young children. The statement in the treaty that they should be educated in Cape Coast Castle is not possible and in any case they have been entrusted to me and to you both personally. Teach them as much English as you can so that when they leave for England they are reasonably fluent in our language."

The following morning King Aggrey had been forewarned of their visit and the four of them, accompanied by Tom Quashie, the Cape Coast interpreter, strode out of the main gate where a group of women were selling foodstuffs: nuts, limes,maize cobs, plantains, bananas, *kenkey* and dried fish, then westwards along the beach. Fishermen had unloaded their catch, heaps of silvery herring separated from larger fish by which women stood ready to buy. The boys, in their European clothes which they had begun to get used to, matched Bowdich and Tedlie stride for stride as they had done on the long march from Kumasi. It wasn't far from the beach, through the huddle of African houses to the imposing brick-built, straw-thatched residence of the Chief, made up of two parallel blocks, each with five rooms above and a number of rooms on the ground floor, joined at the ends by a wall and entrance doors. It was erected on a small rise with a good view of the fort. The Chief sat in the centre of a semi-circle of elders whom they greeted from right to left with open palm and then presented their 'dashes' of two bottles of rum. They were then seated on stools and formally welcomed. King Aggrey was tall, strongly-built and studiously polite to his friends from England and Asante, as he slipped his *ntama* from his left shoulder, a special mark of honour. All four were bidden to speak in turn after which he pronounced a formal welcome to the young men from Asante.

On their return they paid a courtesy call to the school, the first one to be founded on the Coast. It was teeming with children of all ages and when they announced themselves at the gate there was a sudden silence and a hundred curious eyes gazed at them. The boys were fascinated and listened eagerly to the answers to their questions given by the head teacher.

"What is the purpose of the school?" Kwabena asked.

"The children learn to read , write and speak English first, then they learn to use numbers. After that they learn about the Bible and about the religion of the white man."

"Who started the school?"

"Over fifty years ago a white man, Rev. Thomas Thompson, came to Cape Coast and stayed here for four years. He tried to start a school but he was forced by ill-health to return to England. He took three boys with him to be educated but two of them unfortunately died, but the third, Philip Quaque, the son of Chief Kojo, returned in 1765 as a minister of the Church of England to us and worked as schoolmaster and catechist until he passed away only last year, after fifty years of faithful service.

"How old was Philip Quaque when he went to England?"

"He was a bit older than you. Will you also travel there?"

Bowdich told the Headmaster about the boys and he in turn informed the children who clapped their hands in welcome. The visitors made a donation of a golden guinea and made a request to borrow primers and an English grammar; books which the head took from his own small collection. As they said goodbye, two senior girls gave the boys a ball of *kenkey* each and said: "*Nantsew yie*" (Goodbye) with typical Fante courtesy.

On their way back Kwabena wanted more information.

Some of the children had pale skins and faces like Europeans. Where have they come from?" It was Tedlie who replied:

"These are the children of white men, traders, employees and soldiers of the Company who work in the castle; it is a rule of the Company that these people must support the mothers and pay for the children to go to school."

"What do the children, black or white, do when they leave school?"

"If they have learned to read and write English well, they can find employment by traders, or by chiefs, as letter-writers. If they have learned arithmetic, as bookkeepers."

Bowdich and Tedlie led the way back to a large room on the second floor of the fort with two large tables and four chairs. There were dusty wooden shelves along the whole of one side and it had the air of a disused storeroom. Bowdich said: "Will this room do for us, Henry? We can work together here; I have my report to finalise and my book to organise in which a section of the history and all the medical stuff will be yours. It seems to me that we both should take the schooling of the boys in hand, we have the primers and the English grammar from the Headmaster; if I am responsible for the Arithmetic can you manage the English?"

"Yes, I agree Edward. They should work with us so that no time is lost. They will learn quickly; Africans seem to learn languages more easily than we do, I think because they learn by ear and by heart. Can we get hold of pictures of things, places, buildings, anything that we can describe? You have lots of plant pictures and you can also draw. There are some old musty books in the mess-room, we must look through them. I'm going to bring my sextant, thermometer and compass along: both chiefs and the boys were fascinated by them and you have your plants so that we have a mutual interest. We have to get them reading and writing and speaking English as soon as we can; it will be slow going at first but they are both intelligent and once they reach a certain stage they will be strongly motivated."

During this conversation the boys sat silent and wondering; they had turned once to Tom Quashie for enlightenment but he had placed his forefinger on his lips. Kwame and Kwabena were sure that the exchange of views concerned them but they were content to wait. The boys were so much alike: both slender in build, almost six feet tall, slim-waisted and poised easily on their feet; only their faces and facial expressions distinguished them: Kwame's nose was slightly aquiline, Kwabena's was broader; Kwame's eyes were deeper set and a lighter brown than his cousin's. Both had a confident, capable and alert look; both possessed an open, genial disposition; their eyes lit up eagerly when they were interested in anything or anyone and both smiled readily. Bowdich thought how lucky they had been to have the two entrusted to their care.

He nodded to Tom Quashie: "You are the interpreter, Tom, tell them what we have decided about their education!"

As he did so the boys' smiles and shining eyes showed their appreciation and gratitude; what could be better than to have two white men like Bowdich and Tedlie as personal teachers!

"Let's get this room swept and cleaned and the materials ready so that we can start tomorrow, all four of us. One day should be given to English and the next to Arithmetic while on alternate days each one of us will be free to work on our own tasks. What am I going to call my book, Henry?"

"The Company Committee used the word 'embassy' for our undertaking but I would just call it 'Mission to Ashantee'. It's less official in view of what the Governor told us."

"Will you write the last chapter on medical matters; the main diseases you encountered in Asante and your list of herbal plant remedies you found?"

"Certainly. I've also got some historical notes to give you."

The education of the boys and their initiation into the European world began with Tedlie on the following day. Both men responded to the challenge; they had never taught before but they learned by doing and soon a pattern emerged: lists and tables to learn by heart, new words each day, writing practice in sand trays, pictures and sketches were pinned to the walls and described. Early on, Tom Quashie sat in to help out when communication broke down but after a few weeks his presence was no longer necessary. The boys messed with the soldiers and in the evenings dined with the Governor and the white men so that their ears soon became accustomed to the sound of English even if they understood little of what was said. Sergeant Koomson taught them to play draughts which they found more exciting than *owari,* and they watched the soldiers gambling at the card games of nap and poker. What interested them most then were the ways in which the character and temperament of the players were revealed. Their instruction in western ways was cumulative: the more they learned and experienced the more they built on them; they snapped up everything. After two months they had mastered many of the phrases that were used every day in the daily round and could repeat much of what they had learned by heart, for example, descriptions of Asante life and custom. On Sundays the majority attended a Christian church service led by the white man who was called Padre. He wore a black gown, a white collar with white cotton tabs was round his neck. They stood up when he prayed to God and sat when he read from the Christians' holy book called the Bible and a few times there was singing from another book; then they stood and recited a creed, the padre gave them a lecture, prayed over them and the service was over. Kwame was full of questions afterwards: "Why don't the Christians kneel and bow their heads to the ground like the Moors do?" Is our God, *Onyame*, the same as your God? Is the Bible different from the Koran, I mean the Bible I have seen you reading? Who is Jesus Christ? Are all white people Christians?" Tedlie replied: "Wait until you know more English, I will try to explain then."

Henry Tedlie was a Methodist, a follower of John Wesley. He carried his Bible always with him and read in it daily and the boys had often seen him on his knees praying to God. On Christmas day they awoke to the boom of the fort bell at daybreak. Normally it was only rung in times of fog or storm to warn ships or when there was an emergency but this morning it was ringing to celebrate the birth of Jesus. Their bedroom seemed to hum with the reverberations as they hurriedly dressed and then ran to the great hall. Everybody was wishing everyone else a 'Merry Christmas' and when they were gathered together the padre led them in the singing of well-known hymns: 'O come, all ye faithful', 'While shepherds watched their flocks by night', and 'The first Noel'. There were many sailors present from two Preventive Squadron ships who joined in lustily and ended the singing with the British Navy's special song in which everyone joined:

'Rule Britannia, Britannia rules the waves,

Britons never, never, never shall be slaves'

It was another puzzling experience for Kwame and Kwabena! It meant yet many more questions for Tedlie and Bowdich to try to answer!

The traditional Christmas dinner with roast and stuffed fowls, roast beef and pork served with vegetables, followed by huge helpings of Christmas pudding topped with cream sauce or vanilla custard all washed down with beer, punch and tots of rum, took place in the fort courtyard in the afternoon. All Company employees, soldiers and sailors, white, black and mulattos sat down together at trestle-tables and feasted and drank; the only day in the year when colour and rank were disregarded except that the Governor and a few of the seniors sat at a 'high' table.

As distinguished, high-ranking guests, Kwabena and Kwame, sat with them. Speeches and toasts were deliberately kept short, interspersed with 'Hear! Hear!' of approval or choruses of 'For he's a jolly good fellow, and so say all of us',for those who had earned special praise. At a nod from an officer rowdies were removed, discipline in the navy was notoriously strict, and good order was maintained. Late in the afternoon, when the Governor had withdrawn, guests could then leave and at a fixed time the sailors were marched back to their boats and returned to their ships that lay at anchor.

Everything had gone well for the boys during the first three months: they were pleased at the progress they had made, each day afforded fresh experiences of the white man's world and they had become closely attached to Bowdich and Tedlie who treated them as favoured sons. The persistent dysentery of Tedlie distressed them; he had suffered from it in Kumasi but he had never complained or allowed it to interfere with his duties. He could cure others but not himself! Sometimes he would take a day's rest and sit on the beach in the shade; finally it had been decided that Bowdich and the boys would take a ship to England about the middle of January and Tedlie would follow later when he was better.

Just after Christmas an unpleasant episode took place as the boys were returning from a walk on the beach and had reached the gate of the fort. A noisy argument between the Fante soldiers on guard and an Asante man was in progress; the visitor had been asked for his credentials but he had neither messenger's cane nor written letters and he had refused to take his cloth off his left shoulder as a sign of courtesy while he had used insulting words to the Fante soldiers. The captain of the guard had placed him under arrest, at which he had become increasingly abusive. When Kwabena heard him so speak he said sharply in Asante:

"Why are you shouting in this rude way? Have you no respect for the Governor, the representative of the King of England, with whom the Asantehene has made a treaty of friendship? You put shame on the face of the Asantehene and on mine." As he heard the unmistakable accents of a high-born Asante, the man was immediately subdued and muttered something about being cheated in the market and that he had come for redress. The arrested man was taken to prison to await a decision by the Governor. The following morning the captain of the guard reported that the man had committed suicide. He had twisted his cloth into a rope which he had attached to a low beam and had drawn the end very tightly round his throat; part of his body was lying on the ground and it was only by the most determined resolution that he had succeeded in strangling himself. Hope Smith complimented Kwabena on the part he played in the affair and reported to the Asantehene.

One day, they were taken by a small sailing boat, called a cutter, the short distance along the coast to the harbour of Elmina from where they could visit the Dutch fort, the oldest and the largest of all the forts on the Guinea coast. It was their first experience of the power of the sea, of the tremendous surge of the breaking surf through which they had to fight their way; one moment they were in a long hollow between two waves, in the next the boat was riding high surrounded by hissing foam. They admired the calm and assured way that the two sailors navigated the small craft and steered it to a smooth landing in an inlet where many brightly-coloured fishing boats lay at rest. Tom Quashie was their guide and interpreter who led them to the entrance gate of the fort through which they were allowed into the courtyards but not into the buildings. Tom explained: "For a long time the Dutch have had a close relationship with the Asantehene: the Dutch got slaves and gold dust in exchange for goods from Europe especially guns and gunpowder from Rotterdam and Birmingham. Every ship included guns and gunpowder in their cargo; three guns bought a slave, that's how the Asantehene could equip his army. There are not many slaves sold from here since the British abolished the trade; the slaves are sold secretly from smaller places like Apam and Axim and that is arranged by one or other of the middlemen, Jacob Rhule and Jan Niezer, both have Fanti mothers. The British Naval Squadron catch a number of slave ships of other nations but not all because the demand for slaves in the West Indies, Brazil and Cuba is very great and slaves from this area are preferred."

"How do you know all this?" the boys asked and Tom Quashie smiled as he answered:

"I am a well-known interpreter for the English and often I hear information when I interpret for ship's captains and traders."

"Can you speak the language of the Hollanders?"

"No, only a few words but the sea-captains and traders usually speak some English."

"Do you think that the slave trade will ever stop?"

"No, because the demand is too big. The whites want more and more sugar, more and more cotton, more and more coffee, more and more tobacco and only blacks can handle the heavy work on the plantations. We Kormantins know all about these things: we have contact with our people in Jamaica, they are called Maroons there, runaway slaves who formed their own towns in the mountains under their own chiefs. The British accepted their existence and even shipped a shipload of them to Freetown, Sierra Leone, to help to organise the colony. Recently, some of our people landed back from Brazil in South America where they had taken over a plantation and made a deal with the owner to pay the cost of their passages!"

Tom had spoken with some pride: the ingenuity and industry of his people had overcome the hardships and miseries of slavery and had turned it to their advantage! His knowledge impressed the boys and they understood more clearly why their fathers had been perplexed by the action of the British in abolishing the slave trade, and why the Asantehene held so firmly on to the Note for Elmina, and why they were so annoyed at having to deal with Fante middlemen. They thanked Tom and the sailors at the end of their return trip to Cape Coast and retired to their quarters with minds still full of unanswered questions about slavery.

When their departure from Cape Coast had been arranged the boys decided to write a letter to their fathers not only to inform them of their departure for England in the near future but also to prove that they had learned to write in English. They knew that their letter would be read aloud by Adoocee and translated by him in the presence of all the elders and that their mothers would be informed. This is what they wrote, corrected by Tedlie.

Cape Coast Castle,
January, 20th,1818.

To Sai Tootoo Quamina, King of Ashantee, and
Boitinee Quama, King of Dwabin.

Dear Honoured Sirs,
We, your sons, wish you long life and great success in all your endeavours. We write to inform you that we shall soon travel in a ship of the navy of the English King on a long sea voyage to England. We thank you that you have agreed that we should be sent to England for our education so that on our return we shall be able better to serve you.

We have been obedient and we have already learned and experienced much. We have been treated with kindness by all the people here and by the Governor who has promised that the Company will pay each of us five gold guineas for every month that we are in England. Mr. Bowdich and Mr. Tedlie have cared for us like their own sons and they have taught us personally every day, English speaking, writing and reading, as well as Arithmetic and Measuring. As you see by this letter, we are now able to write in English. The Governor, Mr. Hope Smith, has also given us European clothes to wear.

Because Mr. Tedlie is unwell, we shall travel with Mr. Bowdich who will care for us both. As soon as he is fit to travel he will follow us. We beg you to let our mothers read this letter and to convey our greetings to them. We shall write to you again when we are in England.

We remain,
Your dutiful and faithful sons,
Kwame Owusu Boaten and Kwabena Apia Boaten.

The letter was wrapped and sealed to be sent by the next official messenger to Kumasi. Enclosed as gifts to their mothers were two sketches of a mimosa shrub with clusters of yellow flowers which they had coloured.

The day of their departure came and the ship that was to bring them to England lay at anchor beyond the breakers; she was a Royal Navy vessel, a two-masted brig with ten large, rectangular sails called the Phoenix. Her slim hull and extra sails fore and aft gave her added speed and she was used by the naval patrols as a messenger and supply ship between Lagos and Freetown. The boys had packed their gear in canvas kitbags which were loaded in the ship's cutter then they turned to say goodbye to Tedlie who had got up from his sick-bed and had come down to the small jetty. He embraced his three comrades, as he called them, and wished them a good voyage: "Reach England safely; I shall follow you as soon as I can."

They wished him a speedy recovery and took their places in the boat and the sailors steered at an angle into the surf and rowed powerfully through the waves into the open sea. Kwame spoke sadly:

"I'm sorry that Tedlie is not coming with us. You know, Kwabena, I have come to love him like a father or an elder brother. He is a true man. I mean, he always speaks the truth and never pretends; he wishes only to help other people. Do you remember how he treated our guide, Quamina Bwa, when he was sick, although Bwa had secretly cheated us over payment for provisions to local people; how he treated the illness of my aunt; how he tried to heal anyone who came to us in the villages we stayed in or in Kumasi where people came to him every day, how he gave them medicines and bandaged their ulcers and wounds himself? Do you remember how he healed my grandfather who couldn't properly urinate and who was in great pain? And the elder who had an ulcer on the roof of his mouth and couldn't talk clearly? And Opanyin Opoku who had a rupture that Tedlie pushed back and held it in place with a wide cotton belt? I mean, he never refused anybody; he never asked for money or a dash or any reward; it didn't matter whether they were poor or rich, black or white, children or adults; if they were ill, he just did his best to make them better. If he succeeded, he was modest, and if he failed, he was sorry. I can only say to you, that if he had stayed in Kumasi, he would have been famous; you recall how popular he had become? You remember that occasion when my father asked him to show him his equipment and Tedlie showed him his plant pictures of herbal remedies as well? I shall never forget the impression he made on my father; I think that from that moment any prejudice he might have had against the British was removed."

"I understand exactly, Kwame. I remember when we were in Salaga he treated the Moors also. On one occasion, he was writing in his notebook and I was sitting by his side and I coughed. Immediately he stopped writing and asked me if I was feeling ill. He opened the black bag which he always had with him, remember? Took out his thermometer to measure my temperature, looked into my throat with his spatula, listened to my heart and chest with his stethoscope, just to make sure that I was alright. What I mean is, he attended to me like I was an important person; I never met anyone like that before. Do you think that all white doctors are the same?"

"I don't know, but Bowdich once told me that Tedlie had a very good name. During the expedition to Ceylon he had operated on the head of an Indian who had been wounded and had taken a piece of bone from it; the man lived and was restored to health."

"I've seen that bone , he showed it to my father. He was proud of that success. You know, Kwabena, my mind is quite made up; in England I want to study to be a surgeon like Tedlie."

When they and their baggage had been hauled on board by a hoist, they were shown to a cabin by an officer who introduced himself as the purser. It was in the stern of the ship and consisted of two compartments, a small one with two hammocks for the boys and a larger one with a hammock for Bowdich, a large cupboard for clothes, and a corner screened off by a curtain where they could wash. They shared the privy with the officers. On one side was a porthole with a glass window through which they had a view of the sea and the castle that they had just left. Bowdich showed them how to get into and out of a hammock and then they were called to a welcome meeting by the captain and a few of the officers and crew who had assembled in the officers' mess.

"Welcome aboard!," the captain said as he shook hands. "I was signalled to stop at Cape Coast to pick up three important passengers bound for England and we are curious to know who you are." Bowdich presented himself:

"Edward Bowdich, Sir, Writer and Scientific Officer, Leader of the African Company's Expedition to Kumasi, Asante, from which I am returned three months ago." He turned to Kwame and Kwabena:

"My companions on the return trip through the forest who have been entrusted to me and Mr. Tedlie, the surgeon on the expedition, as surety for the treaty which we have signed with the kings of Ashanti and Juaben. We have undertaken to give them an education in England and we are grateful to you for taking us on board." The boys had stepped forward as Bowdich had told them.

"Allow me to introduce Kwame Owusu Boaten, son of Osei Tootoo Quamina, King of Asante and Kwabena Apia Boaten, son of Boitinnee Quama, King of Juaben. They will thank you in English."

First Kwame and then Kwabena delivered the short speeches that Tedlie had taught them and which they had learned by heart:

"Honourable Sir, I am deeply obliged to you for taking us on board your ship for the long voyage to England. This is the first time that we have sailed on the sea in a large European ship but we know that the British are very good seamen and that you will bring us safely to our destination." To this Kwabena added: "Honourable Captain and Gentlemen, I should also like to add my grateful thanks to you and your crew. I look forward to the voyage; there are so many things I have to learn and experience and my cousin and I hope that some of you will talk to us from time to time so that our English can improve."

There was utter astonishment on all the sailors' faces, first that these young men were princes of the most powerful state in West Africa and secondly, that they had spoken with the accent of educated Englishmen! All eyes were turned to Captain Isaac Manley; like James Cook, he was a native of Whitby in Yorkshire, and had retained his north-country accent.

"Well, messmates, I never thought that I could be so flummoxed! We have two young Africans who speak the King's English with a better accent than me! Let's give them a good round of applause as welcome and congratulation." He led the clapping and they all came forward to shake the boys' hands. The noon rum ration had already been poured out; the boys accepted but, as Bowdich had advised them, they called for water to dilute their portion. Their shrewdness was not lost on the captain.

"These two lads will go far," he remarked to Bowdich.

Afterwards as the anchor was weighed, the sails unfurled and the ship was steered into the open sea, the boys stood in wonderment at the starboard railing and watched the palm-fringed shore and the castle recede and sink out of sight while now they saw only the masts of the other ships still at anchor, Kwabena said: "I know now why our people say that the white men came up out of the sea. It seems now that the castle is sinking into the sea. You remember, Kwame, when Bowdich was trying to teach us that the world was a round ball circling the sun? But what keeps the water from flowing away?" Edward had just joined them at the rail and had heard Kwabena's question.

"There's a law of nature which explains that; it was discovered by Sir Isaac Newton about a hundred years ago; the moon, the stars and planets that you see in the sky all exercise a power according to their size by which they pull everything near them to them. The earth pulls the clouds, the rain, the sea to itself; anything loose falls to the earth, human beings can't jump up more than a few feet. All the stars and the planets are the same but the influence they have on other stars and planets, including the earth, weakens with distance so that they are all kept in place. It's called the Law of Gravitation. That's why the sea can't fall off the earth, nor can we."

"What about the birds?" asked Kwame. "They fly up."

"But they fly up only so far, even the strongest birds can't break free from the pull of the earth."

The ship's bell with its piercing resonant sound rang four times stridently; it was 6 p.m. and the evening meal would be served to those not on duty. There had to be sailors on duty at all hours of the day and night, these periods of duty, Edward explained, are called 'Watches' and last four hours, those on watch now eat earlier or later. A ship is organised to the last detail: every member of the crew has his own special task in which he must never fail otherwise the life of the crew and the ship are in danger. The British have a phrase to describe when everything is in order, they call it 'ship-shape'.

In the cramped officers's mess the three passengers were assigned to a small table in an alcove under the only window; at a large oblong table sat the Captain and the commissioned officers in order of rank including the Surgeon and the midshipmen in training at the foot.

"Where do the other sailors eat?" enquired Kwabena, ever curious.

"They have their mess in the front of the ship which is called the 'bow' or forecastle (pronounced 'fokesel'). All the men possess special skills: the boatswain is the senior who controls the work of the other seamen and has charge of the ship's ropes, sails, masts, and small boats; he can be a warrant officer but he is always a Leading Seaman. There will be a quartermaster who steers the ship, a signalman who sends and receives messages by semaphore or by hoisting flags, a cook, a carpenter and gunners who man the cannons you see on deck. All these have 'mates', that is, a helper and assistant, and all of them are called 'able seamen', that means they are capable and skilled in things to do with ships. In the navy, of course, they must be always ready to fight an enemy; and the sailors who fire the cannons are called 'gunners'."

"That's many new words we have to learn quickly," they said laughing.

"You have made great progress in English so far and during the voyage your learning must continue. Tomorrow we start lessons on the sextant which I have brought with me. You remember how on the journey to Cape Coast I used to stop to take measurements from the sun to find out our position? You will see one of the officers do that tomorrow. Look round you now, can you see anything except water? The sextant will show us the right way. To prepare for tomorrow make a sketch of a ship and write the names of the parts of it on the paper."

"What is that sailor doing at the front of the ship? Is he fishing?" "No. He is letting down a weighted line to find out how deep the sea is under the ship, the line is marked every six feet. That is called a fathom, another new word for you."

There was no end of the basic things that the boys had to learn, that was the problem, thought Bowdich. But he himself had learned much about teaching from Tedlie. Always start from what they know, he had said, and lead on to what they don't know, even if they don't absorb the detail they'll remember the basic principle or the reason behind it. And, whenever possible, draw a diagram, that's how we all learn best. So Bowdich had thought through a scheme for using the sextant: teach them the compass first and about finding your way by the sun and stars, then making maps and measuring distance. One thing would lead to another. It never failed to astonish him how much progress they had made in such a short time; he hoped that he would be able to find a suitable school for them in England. Meanwhile there had to be an enforced pause in the learning, the motion of the ship had brought on sea-sickness and they were both vomiting over the ship's railing! He postponed the lesson till the afternoon and when, about midday, he went to find them, they were sitting on deck at the bow with the two young midshipmen, all four eagerly exchanging information about themselves. Kwame introduced them as Will and Thomas and said: "They want to know about our life in Asante, they said if we were sons of kings we would be kings one day and we have tried to tell them that we inherit through our mothers but we don't have enough words to explain."

"I didn't know about that until I came to the Gold Coast. Among the Akan people the right of succession and inheritance runs through the female line not the male line, so that the successor of a king will be his brother or his nephew. So they may be 'princes' but they will never be kings."

"They asked us why we were going to England but we couldn't really make it clear to them." So Bowdich explained:

"You see, I signed a treaty with the Asante King on behalf of the Company and the British Government and as a pledge that he would honour the treaty he gave these two boys to me and my colleague. We promised to educate them in England, the Company will pay the costs."

"Phew! Golly! You mean that they are your prisoners?"

"Not at all, they are perfectly free; they came of their own free-will; they wanted to come. It was only because of the treaty that they got the chance to be educated in England, they can go back then to serve their country. The point is, they are not just any two young men, they are kings' sons, one from Kumasi and one from Juaben. If, for any reason, the treaty is repealed or broken, they will still be free of any obligation to us."

Kwabena interrupted with a question: "What is that black, oily liquid with the strong smell that the sailors are painting the wood with?"

"It's called creosote, we get it from coal-tar, in the Navy it is used for preserving wood, as a disinfectant against disease germs and as a killer of pests. I think that's why sometimes sailors are called 'tars." The entire voyage was an exciting time for the young men from Asante: there was the constant learning while each day something new in their experience took place. One day the swell of the ocean was so strong that waves broke over the bows and drenched them with spray, another day the wind strengthened and the seamen had to go aloft on the yard-arms, to furl some of the sails; the boys were amazed at the agility of Will and Thomas and the precise way they all worked together poised precariously on the masts and the rigging. It was almost uncanny how, day or night, an order would come from the officer on duty or from the bo'sun, and automatically one or more of the crew whose job it was went about their task with the customary 'Aye-aye,Sir'. Whenever they could they chatted with members of the crew without understanding all that they were told. The accents varied: the British were made up of Englishmen, Scotsmen, Welshmen and Irishmen who had their own intonation, but they all shared the very special naval vocabulary like. 'ahoy','belay', 'to be on her beam ends', 'chart', 'buoy', 'capstan', 'helm', 'tiller', knot and knots', 'astern', 'prow', 'poop', 'bilge', 'reef', 'splice' and many others, some of which even Bowdich didn't know.

It was an invigorating time for Bowdich, too. He had time to put the finishing touches to his book and have it ready for the printer soon after they landed but whenever he showed his face on deck or in the wardroom the officers pressed him for information about the interior of West Africa. They knew practically every inch of the coast but no one had ever been more than a mile inland, so they were full of questions: were the Asante warriors really as fearsome as they had heard? Had they ever been in danger of their lives? How had they travelled? How had they been received in Kumasi? They accorded to him greater prestige than he really deserved, reflected Bowdich, but it was pleasant to be listened to and praised. He tried as hard as he could to be absolutely factual and not to embellish what he had already written, even so, the telling of his experiences held their closest attention. It was naval officers and men who had opened up the wider world to the British, like Martin Frobisher, Francis Drake, James Cook and many others; they had pioneered the sea routes across the oceans, it had become part of the naval tradition to enlarge the knowledge of distant lands, so it was a special pleasure to get first-hand information from a man like Bowdich.

At the same time, it was a privilege for Bowdich to learn about the task of the British naval patrols which, ever since the abolition of the slave trade in British ships in 1807, had stopped ships of other nations that were carrying slaves and brought them as free persons back to Africa. He heard that the patrols had intercepted over 1500 ships and had freed more than 150,000 slaves landing many at Freetown and some in the West Indies. But during this period still more slaves were taken to America, to Brazil and to Cuba. The profits from trading in slaves, explained Captain Manley, were so great that an illicit trade had grown up and the British Parliament was being pressured to make the trade an act of piracy, and thus punishable by death. But the trade was still continued by Spain, Portugal and the United States and it seemed impossible to stop them all. Captain Manley summed up the situation:

"What we have been able to do is to shift the trade further south to the Congo and Angola; they tend now to avoid our ships between Sierra Leone and Lagos. Sometimes the odd ship will steal into port to trade, and under cover of darkness, take a few slaves aboard. In theory the Dutch have abolished the trade, but quite a number of blacks embark at Elmina, we've watched them by telescope. We believe that the Dutch recruit them as 'volunteer soldiers'; some kind of payment takes place but we have no proof. What is interesting is that they go on board Dutch ships bound for the East Indies, Java or Sumatra. Our Lords of the Admiralty don't react to our reports." His expression was resigned.

One night the movement of the ship stopped and when they looked out of the brass porthole at first light they saw mangrove trees growing in the water at the coast and when they looked upwards there was tropical forest like in Asante and then a high mountain, higher than any they had ever seen before. The ship circled at anchor and gave them a view of a huge bay in which a dozen masted ships were anchored. On shore, half-hidden by the mist, were the houses and buildings of Freetown which rose up a hill to a more level area. Between the ships and the shore many small boats went to and fro loaded with goods or passengers. When they left the cabin they felt the moisture in the air like a damp blanket around them and suddenly there were flies everywhere; as they had reached the coast the cool, dry harmattan wind from the north-east had been lost. European clothes were hot and sticky and jackets superfluous. Bowdich gave them a description:

"This is Freetown, the capital of the British Colony of Sierra Leone. The Portuguese gave it the name, Lion Mountain, that you see in the distance. It has an interesting history: in 1772 a planter in Virginia visited London with his slave; the slave was mistreated and ran away but was caught and the planter decided to sell him. An Englishman called Granville Sharp, who was strongly opposed to slavery, took up his case and argued that if a person set foot on English soil he became automatically a free man. He won his case and then acquired twenty square miles from the Temne chief in Sierra Leone and repatriated to Africa four hundred freed slaves who had gathered in London. In 1808 it became a Crown Colony, so when any slaves landed in Freetown, they became free."

"Why could they not be taken back to their own homes?"

"It was much too difficult: the slaves had come from many different places in the interior but the main reason was that they would probably have been made slaves again, only in British territory were they really free."

"What happens to them here in Freetown?"

"At first they are given a piece of land on which they can build a house, they are given provisions and then organised into the community. But the problems are many; a man called Zachary Macaulay is in charge who has encouraged Christian missions to start schools and clinics, he has started food plantations and had given every facility to merchants and traders. The British Government has established its headquarters here in Freetown for all its interests in West Africa, the buildings with red roofs you see up there is where we all have to report. So you see how the former slaves are building up a new country."

"We never thought about slaves in Asante at all. You could go to Salaga and buy one at any time; we never thought of them as being equal with us, most families had one or two. We thought of all the tribes in the north as being in a slave class, you could pawn or sell them for money," declared Kwabena. And Kwame added:

"My father was always puzzled by the fact that having sold

slaves to the English for so long, they suddenly refused to buy them."

Bowdich tried to explain as simply as he could: "Many European countries continue to make big profits by trading in slaves from West Africa: there are colonists in North America, South America, Jamaica, the Caribbean Islands and Cuba who have established plantations for sugar-cane, coffee, cocoa, cotton,tobacco and spices which are exported to Europe and who need labourers to clear the forest, plant and harvest the crops. The work is very strenuous but these black slaves can be trained to do it. So all along the Guinea Coast traders have always bought slaves, kept them in the forts, sold them to the owners of the ships who took them to the plantations where they were sold. With the money crops were bought and brought to Europe to be sold. The merchants in slaves made huge profits, at least 100% each successful voyage. Then English people began to hear of the cruelties of the trade especially of the way they were transported in the holds of ships, chained side by side as they lay down with no room to move; many died after suffering intense misery from illnesses. *The Zong* case was a turning-point: she was a slave-ship trading from Liverpool on which dysentery had broken out, many slaves had died and more were likely to die, so that the voyage would be a financial loss. The captain ordered 132 sick slaves to be thrown overboard and deliberately drowned. The owners of *the Zong* then claimed the full value of the jettisoned slaves from the insurance company! The slaves had ceased to be human beings, they were treated worse than cattle. Many reports were made about the harsh cruelties and flogging that the slaves suffered on the plantations, so that the people petitioned Parliament to pass a law against the trade in slaves but because of the long war with France it was only in 1807 that the law was passed."

Bowdich felt that he had spoken long enough on the subject. The boys were clearly interested but there would be lots of time later for their questions; it was a theme these days that no one could avoid. During his few years with the Company he had seen enough of the worst effects of the slave-trade system to make him a supporter of complete abolition but what would you put in its place? The farms needed workers; how would they be paid without a great increase in the prices of the crops in Europe? Now, in Freetown, they were about to be confronted by another unpleasant British problem. A message had come from Captain Manley that they should accompany him and the Surgeon on a visit to Freetown and just then the longboat drew up to the ship's side; a rope-ladder was attached to the rail down which they clambered into the boat and when they were seated Manley explained:

"I've arranged a get-together with two of my fellow-captains; we were trained at Osborne together, we were in the battles of the Nile together and then met in Malta. That was twenty years ago, then we met in Lisbon, bringing supplies to Wellington's army about ten years since, and now here we are in Freetown! You see that brig on the port side, she's *H.M.S. Baring*, captained by Thomas Johnson, one of the Preventive Squadron like us, who has just delivered fifty slaves on shore from a Spanish vessel which he has towed into the bay. He is already on shore attending to them. The three-master ahead of us is *The Huguenot*, under the command of Captain Henry Harwood, with a ship-load of convicts from Britain on their way to exile in Australia. We shall collect him off the ship."

Bowdich suddenly felt uneasy in mind: there would certainly be more searching questions from the boys, questions to which he had no easy answers. He was a loyal patriot but what was the Government in London really doing: shipping black slaves to freedom but at the same time transporting white Britons to seven years hard labour to an unknown land fifteen thousand miles away in conditions similar to those of the blacks, except that the voyage would take four or five months? Fate had played him a nice trick: he was the one earmarked to do the explaining! You could call it an unusual coincidence, the way in which these two activities of his Government were present together on a tropical shore in Africa, good intentions mixed with injustice, idealism linked with exploitation; while for him personally, his patriotism became infected with mistrust. Blind Fate, in the shape of the British Government, pulled the strings, and here in Freetown harbour this morning are blacks and whites existing in the utmost misery! Here were two man-made catastrophes bringing untold distress and despair!

As they approached *The Huguenot* they saw the red and white pennant which proclaimed her as a convict ship; the decks were full of bedraggled and dishevelled white human beings, some were standing in line with tin cups in their hands receiving something to drink ladled out from a barrel by a sailor; some were washing clothes and blankets in tubs; some were scrubbing the decks with holystone which others swabbed with water and at the ship's sides was an unbroken line of people drinking from tin cups and gazing all around them. Kwame said:

"I never saw so many white people before, they look poor. What are they drinking?" Captain Manley replied:

"It's lemon juice to prevent scurvy, a disease of the skin, the gums and the stomach; you can die of scurvy on a long voyage."

"Who are they? Where are they going?"

"They are convicts from Britain who have been sentenced to seven years' hard labour in Australia, they are thieves who have stolen money and other things from people, from their employers and from shops. Some of them have assaulted others with weapons, some have plotted against the King, some have committed murder but have been pardoned by the King. The prisons are full in Britain so they are being transported to far-away Australia."

"Will they be sold in Australia?"

"No; they are not slaves, they are criminals, they will be fed, clothed and housed; they will work making roads, clearing land, building houses and other premises, or loaned out to farmers. After seven years, if their conduct has been good they will be free; they can stay in the colony or return home."

"Do many return to Britain?"

"No. Over 90% stay in Australia."

Bowdich detected that Manley had had enough of being

questioned and nudged Kwame to be silent. Just then, Captain Harwood joined them, to be greeted heartily by Captain Manley, while the boys and Bowdich were introduced. In a short time they were at the jetty and then on land again. About fifty yards away they could see a huddled group of freed slaves sitting round two sailors who were doling out bread and water. Standing nearby was Captain Johnson who waved and called out a cheerful greeting to his messmates. The blacks looked dejected and miserable; you could see marks of scars on some of their backs, many had sores on their legs where the chains had galled; their hair was matted and filthy, their eyes dull and apathetic. Yet they ate and drank cheerfully enough as if now their rescue had given them fresh hope. The quick eyes and ears of the boys picked out a young woman clutching a whimpering baby to her breasts while trying to soothe it with comforting words. Kwabena spoke to her in Asante:

"Where have you come from?" To everyone's surprise she answered in the same language:

"I come from Salaga but I was a slave of an Asante family in Sampa who sold me to a slave dealer in Abidjan in payment for a debt. When we were on the Spanish ship an English ship released us; they took the iron fetters from our feet and threw them in the sea, then they gave us clothes to cover our naked bodies, opened the water casks so that we could drink all the water we wanted and we also ate food till we had enough. What will happen to us now? My baby needs milk and my breasts are dry. Perhaps there is a woman in this town who can be a wet-nurse for her?"

Captain Johnson had listened to the conversation and asked Kwabena to translate into English and when he had done so, he said:

"Tell her that she and all the others will be given somewhere to live and given food until they are able to work. We shall certainly find a wet-nurse for her baby. Thank you for your help, please stay with us until someone comes from comissioner's office to take care of them. You have solved a permanent problem that we have in communicating." He shook Kwabena and Kwame warmly by the hand. Both had been enlisted into service as interpreters and the spirits of the freed slaves rose in response: Kwame and Kwabena spoke to the young woman in Asante and she, in turn, managed to make clear to most of them what had been said. The majority were from the Gonja and Dagomba districts and the rest from Togoland across the Volta river.

They all made their way up the red laterite track to the top of the hill; by now, the warmth of the sun had lifted the mist upwards and they could see how the central part of Freetown was taking shape: the Secretariat was the largest building which housed all the Government offices. Not far away was the huge,old silk-cotton tree where the earliest traders had put up houses. Nearby there was a building which did duty as a court of law as well as a police station; the beginnings of a main street could be seen along which stores and shops were being built and which led to the market. Below stretched the sea, the large Sherbro island, mangrove swamps and the great extent of the bay in which the European masted ships were at anchor. Inland, on an undulating low range of hills, the white officials had begun to erect bungalows and to the right and left were the new settlements of the freed slaves while further inland was the backdrop of forest-clad mountain ranges.

The captains, the surgeon, Bowdich and the young men had duly reported their presence and it was then agreed that the white men would spend an hour or two yarning over drinks in the Secretariat canteen while Kwame and Kwabena wandered round the town.

They would all meet again for curry and rice in the canteen, the only dish the canteen offered, and return together to their ships.

When the seven of them sat down together, the Ashanti young men had aroused considerable interest. The naval officers had already heard from Bowdich the details of his mission, he had become, in their eyes, something of a hero, as the first white man to go so far inland and to return safely, and to lead an important expedition at the age of 26. He had done his best to depreciate his achievements but it was pleasant to receive praise from men who themselves carried great responsibility. Now, here he was with two protégés on their way to England to be educated! The only Africans they had ever met had been slaves with whom they could not converse, here were two young Asantes who were quite well-dressed and at ease in the company of whites; not only that, they could express themselves in real English! So far as the captains were concerned, it was an encounter to be savoured!

"How did you get chosen to go to England?" asked Manley.

"We were lucky. When an important agreement is made among us, a pledge is normally given on both sides, often an expensive gift. In this case our fathers gave us as guarantee," replied Kwabena.

"Where will you go to school in England?"

"We don't know yet, but Mr. Bowdich will arrange it for us, or Mr. Tedlie."

"What do you want to study?"

"My cousin, Kwame, was greatly impressed by Mr. Tedlie who was the Surgeon on the expedition; he wants to become a surgeon. I think that I could study to become a lawyer, our people know nothing about European law."

"Did you meet anyone on your walk round Freetown?"

"Yes. We spoke with a few people at the market place. There were many people there, a few were in African dress but most were wearing European dress, all of them could speak a kind of English so we could understand one another. Those dressed like Europeans are called Creoles, they told us. What are Creoles?" Captain Johnson answered:

"It is a name given to persons of mixed blood, one parent African and the other European who have come to Freetown from London, and over a thousand refugee slaves from North America, while the Preventive Squadron has brought nearly 40,000 others to date, and small groups are coming all the time from the Caribbean islands. But many thousands more are being sold into slavery from West Africa at the same time that we can't catch. The population of Freetown must be now about 50,000 and growing. The original people inland, the Mende, Temne and those on Sherbro Island want to have the same status as the Creoles, but the Creoles consider themselves to be superior because they are familiar with Europeans and can comunicate with them. The kind of English they speak is a bit like pidgin English with many words from other European and African languages. The Creoles dominate because they who are literate take posts with the Government, with the Christian Missions or with the traders. A number of them are trading on their own.They are all living in two worlds at the same time, which you both are now learning to do."

The two young men were listening intently. Kwame took up their tale:

"One man told us that the Temne chief, Nembana, had sold twenty square miles of land to a white Englishman called Sharp but that he had no right to do that, so the next chief had attacked the first settlers and had destroyed their houses but they started to rebuild. Some years later, a slave-trader, some of whose slaves had escaped to Freetown, had in revenge guided a French ship there. That was during the war. The French looted and partly destroyed the settlement but then the British government took it over and made it a colony. Another man we talked to was from Kormantin, near Cape Coast, where the Dutch had built a fort. His father was shipped as a slave from there to Jamaica. Some of the Kormantins escaped from their farms and set up their own village in the Blue Mountains called Accompong under a chief called Kodjo. They called themselves Maroons. He had been allowed to go to Freetown,and now he was working for a Fante trader."

"You have both learned a lot in a very short time," commented Manley, "We all wish you every success in England." They made their slow way to the landing stage after a last round of drinks, farewells were said and they were rowed back to their ships.

The last section of the voyage was also full of incidents: there was a short stop at Las Palmas in the Canary Islands to buy bananas, oranges, lemons and fresh fish from canoes that came alongside but no shore leave was given. As the ship sailed further and further north into the track of the south-west winds everyone felt colder, the hours of daylight were fewer, the sky was cloudier and it rained oftener. They were each given a thick, navy-blue second-hand jersey with sleeves by the petty officer in charge of stores and equipment as well as a sou'wester oilskin cap to wear in the rain. The jerseys were loose on their bodies and they laughed at each other: "You look like a baboon," Kwame teased his cousin, who retorted: "And you resemble a well-fed witch!" With a belt round the middle they looked better and more like the midshipmen.

With the wind behind them, the *Phoenix* leaped into the heaving sea, the bird carved on the bow looked like a guinea-fowl but it rose up bravely over the wave-crests and then pitched resolutely down into the troughs. In rough weather the cousins admired the skill of the helmsman who kept the swaying ship on a straight course as well as the agility and dexterity of the sailors who climbed the masts aloft to furl or trim the sails according the the wind. The command came from the officer on the bridge, and were repeated by the bo'sun; the sailors were so drilled that the sails were adjusted competently, even in a strong wind. As the ship entered the Bay of Biscay, they were battered by a violent storm of wind and rain; the entire sky became threatening and then all the top and mainsails were furled to prevent the ship capsizing while the helmsman relied on the foresail and the rudder to keep the ship on an even keel and to keep it moving forwards. No one went on deck then except those on duty; somehow, even in these conditions, the cook provided meals!

In foul weather and in fine, Bowdich adhered to his educational programme: he was proud of his skill with the sextant to teach the boys artithmetic. First they learned the compass bearings and the degrees of a circle, then he called in the young mishipmen, Thomas and Will, whenever they were off duty, to help him to demonstrate the use of the sextant and how to find their position on a chart by using lines of latitude and longitude. The navy lads were in their element showing off their skills and in helping Kwame and Kwabena to draw maps and diagrams. In addition, Surgeon Marsh joined them to give basic information about the circulation of the blood; the heart, liver, lungs, kidneys, bones and brain functions. They talked with him about Tedlie and copied diagrams from the book that Tedlie had given to Kwame.

One day they discussed with Bowdich the question of slavery and the transportation of white people to Australia.

"We can't understand the difference: you stop buying and selling black slaves but you start again with white people from England!"

"Listen carefully. The British have been transporting convicts since 1787, over 20 years ago, because all the prisons are full."

"Why have you so many criminals?" Kwabena was puzzled.

"Because great changes are taking place in Britain brought about by the invention of the steam engine and the building of huge factories in the towns and cities. Many people have left the land to work in them. The number of people in the country has grown very fast; there is not work for them all, thousands of young men and women have drifted to the cities, some get work for poor pay, some start to steal just to live. We have no police to keep order; London swarms with rascals and thieves. Many old ships in the river Thames and other ports are used as prisons; 'hulks' they are called, and from them they are transported to Australia."

"How long is the voyage to that country?"

"About five or six months, it is quite on the other side of the world. Because of the crowded conditions on the lower decks some of the convicts die of illnesses, they are allowed on deck only once a day for exercise. The food is poor, while in the tropics the heat is almost unbearable."

"What happens to them in Australia? Are there people already there to welcome them like in Freetown?"

"Yes, there are some white people already there trying to start a colony. The black people, the aborigines, are very few and Australia is very large, half the size of all Africa. Each fresh shipload of convicts has to be fed, clothed and housed; then they have to work for the government clearing land for crops, building houses, making roads. It is very hard work."

"Are they paid wages for this work?"

"Yes, not much, ten pounds a year. For that they must work six days a week, nine hours a day. Many of them are loaned out to farmers. They have to work for seven years and after that they get a ticket-of-leave by which they are no longer compelled to work for the government or for a farmer; they can work for whom they wish and where they wish. They are not slaves; slaves have no rights at all: they are slaves till death, they are the owner's property, they can be bought and sold, their children are slaves. The convicts who are shipped to Australia serve a fixed term of years as punishment and they can get a grant of land and become a free citizen of the colony. It is a harsh, I would say, often unjust punishment but, what is important to know, is that out of the thousands of convicts only six out of every hundred decide to return to England. They prefer to stay in the new colony of Australia. There are also a growing number of ordinary people who emigrate to Australia."

The young men listened carefully but sometimes explanations of the ways of the English were hard to grasp; there were slaves and criminals in Ashanti, no one ever questioned or discussed the fact. Prisoners of war could be made slaves and sold, criminals were different. Stealing was often dealt with by two families: the family of the thief had to pay, but for more serious matters like stealing a wife of the chief or swearing an oath against him you could lose your life. Quite a number of slaves could be killed just to accompany on the journey to the other world somebody important who had died. Kwame recalled that at rituals and festivals criminals and captives were killed but the bloodshed was just taken for granted by everybody, no one spoke against it. In any case, they were all going to join their ancestors, and moreover, many of them were foreigners who were quite different and less important than the Asante.

One morning they were still in their hammocks when the motion of the ship ceased; it was still dark but there were some lights to be seen and they could see that the ship was tied up to a dock. In the darkness the ship had been steered safely into the great harbour of Portsmouth, the chief naval station of England.

As it became light, farewells were said and the three were put on shore at the Troopship Jetty accompanied by Captain Manley and the two midshipmen, Thomas and Will, who had offered to carry the boys' kitbags. When they reached a sailors' canteen, the captain asked them to wait until he returned.

"A very distinguished person has come specially to meet us."

During his absence Will and Thomas pointed out Nelson's ship at anchor, the Navigation School and Admiralty House and soon afterwards Captain Manley returned with a sturdy, grey-haired, ruddy-faced elderly, naval officer in uniform who was introduced to them by Manley as Admiral Isaac Smith:

"We were together for three years on the famous voyage of the Endeavour in 1768 when we discovered Tahiti, Australia and New Zealand! I was 12 years old then, and Isaac Smith was 16! His uncle, James Cook, was captain of the ship. Isaac Smith was the first Englishman to set foot in Australia; he later had a brilliant career ending as Admiral in the war against the French. Now he is retired in Southsea where next year I am going to be!"

He turned to Bowdich and explained:

"I never told you that this was my last voyage in the *Phoenix*, next year I shall be retired."

There was hand-shaking all round and the two Isaacs were exuberant at meeting again; both were full of talk as they led the group along Queen Street to an inn much frequented by naval officers where they all sat round a large mahogany table and were invited by the Admiral to enjoy a traditional English breakfast.

"What are your plans for these young men from Asante?" he asked Bowdich.

"They were entrusted to me and my colleague, Surgeon Tedlie, who will follow us later, to give them an education in England. We shall make contact with my father at his office and warehouse in Poplar, then we shall proceed to my family home in Hampstead village. Afterwards we shall have to make decisions about their schooling. They are intelligent and highly-motivated and have made astonishing progress in English and other subjects in the last three months."

"Will they be living with your family in Hampstead?"

"Yes."

"Have any contacts with possible schools already been made?"

"No."

"Then may I give you some good advice; I am a Governor of Highfield Free Grammar School. Highfield is quite near Hampstead, half-an-hour's walk across Fenton House Park. I know the Headmaster, Mr. Forster, who has earned a good reputation for the school. There are about 50 or 60 boys and four teachers, so classes are small. It gets grant from the Charity Commission and was founded about fifty years ago when a vicar of Highfield discovered that funds to be used for education from the sale of Waltham Abbey lands could be used for a school in Highfield because Highfield is situated on former Abbey grounds. When the boys have reached a level for entry, get in touch with me."

Edward Bowdich expressed his gratitude especially since a small school would suit the boys better and moreover they could live in Hampstead with the family while the allowance from the Company would go further. Most of all, to have as sponsor a Governor who was a retired Admiral of the Fleet was an added bonus.

The rest of the day was spent in a post-chaise between Southsea and London, a roomy coach on four wheels drawn by four horses under the control of a coachman who sat at the front on top of the coach and cracked his whip from time to time or flicked the flanks of a fractious horse. The day was fine but cold and wrapped in a horse blanket, Kwabena and Kwame sat on one side of the coachman enjoying their first view of England. There were other passengers on top behind them with the heavy luggage, as well as inside the coach where they sat facing one another. At the entrance to a village or town the driver would blow his horn and sometimes they would halt for the sake of passengers and once, about half-way, to change horses. In large towns, the mail bag was given into the waiting hands of a messenger. It was late in the afternoon when they were finally set down near the Mansion

House from where a London cab took them to the Bowdich office in Poplar. After warm greetings and introductions, they made their way on foot to the Cutty Sark tavern where accommodation for the night had been booked for them. From their room windows they looked over the busy Thames river and the docks and Mr Bowdich explained:

"That's where the goods from overseas are landed: the tea from China, the spices from the East Indies, the sugar and the coffee from the West Indies, the palm oil from the west coast of Africa. I store them in my warehouse and the merchants come and buy. This tavern has the name of the fastest clipper ever built, the *Cutty Sark*, which brought tea from China in 107 days; round the Cape of Good Hope on the outward trip and round Cape Horn homewards. I deal in these luxury items mainly and other importers deal in cotton, tobacco and cereals. We live by trading with the rest of the world which buys our manufactured goods. My son, Edward, wanted to travel and ended up in Cape Coast as writer with the African Company, made a great journey to Kumasi and brought you two young men back with him! Tomorrow I'll take you to my home in Hampstead where you will be welcome guests of the family so long as you remain in England."

The following day, after a breakfast of bacon and fried eggs washed down with strong, sweet milky-tea they set off along the north bank of the Thames, through Shoreditch and Camden to Hampstead village. The Bowdich family house, called Heath View, stood in grounds of about four acres on East Heath Road directly on the edge of the open heathland with its woodlands and lakes. On the side facing the road were decorated railings and an imposing entrance gate leading to a lawn and a gravelled area in front of the main door of the house. Built in the Georgian style beloved by the English, square, solid, roomy and robust, such homes reflected the character of the wealthy manufacturers, tradesmen and merchants who lived in them. At each side of the main door, sheltered by a porch on two pillars, were the windows of the living rooms, on the first floor were the bedrooms and in the roof attic space two dormers. From the wide hall a large staircase led upwards to the first floor and a winding stair connected with the attic rooms. At the side and rear of the house you could see stables for the horses and a coach, a grassed area and a walled garden.

Standing in a group at the front door to welcome them were Mrs. Harriet Bowdich (Edward's mother), Eleanor Morier (Edward's fiancee), Fanny the cook-housekeeper, Amy, the young maidservant and Jack, the gardener and coachman. Mrs. Bowdich was a tall, grey-haired lady with kind eyes and a ready smile; as she clasped her son to herself and exchanged kisses you could see how proud she was of him and how fond of her he was.

"So you have come back to us from Africa and brought with you these two fine-looking Ashanti young men. We are all proud, Edward, at what you have achieved."

It pleased her that her son had a heart for Africans and she would do all she could to help them; she smiled as she shook their hands. Eleanor was about the same age as Edward, fair-haired and blue-eyed, radiant that her betrothed had returned in good health with his mission to Kumasi successfully accomplished; now they could marry without further delay!

The young men were led up to the attic rooms: in each was a bed, a table, two chairs, a chest of drawers and a wardrobe while the remaining space held a washstand with a large basin and a jug on it, a cupboard under it contained a chamber pot. At the side were towels on a rail and nearby two full pails of water stood ready.

"The attic rooms will be all yours," explained Mrs. Bowdich. "When it is cold, Amy will bring coals and make a fire in the grate for you;" she pointed to the small fireplace in the north wall. "You will take your meals with us downstairs either in the kitchen or in the dining-room; also downstairs is the privy, my son will show you. At night you will use the commode." She smiled at them and their hearts were warmed by such a friendly welcome. "A meal will be ready for you in about an hour," she concluded, and left them to unpack. They stood together gazing out of the windows; on one side they viewed the Heath landscape with its trees and lakes; on the other was a distant glimpse of the great city of London. Kwabena spoke first:

"This is our new home, Kwame, I never thought that we should be treated so well. This house is bigger than the Juaben *ahemfie* and the Bowdich family is so friendly. Our fathers chose well to put us in the charge of Tedlie and Bowdich."

"I think the same. We have heard nothing of Mr. Tedlie, I hope that he has recovered his health and is already on his way to us."

"I hope so too but it is certain that this will be our home for some time especially if places can be found for us in the Highfield school."

In the dining-room the head of the large mahogany table was taken by Mr. Bowdich with his son on his right and the African visitors on his left and after a short prayer of thanks to God the meal began. He welcomed them as new members of the household:

"We want you to feel at home with us, so long as you are with us we consider you to be members of the family." The boys stood up to express their thanks and Mr. Bowdich said:

"There is no need to stand up when you speak to me; within the family we are all equals. Let me tell you a bit about Hampstead Village where we are: people who can afford it like to live here, the heath is the largest open stretch of country within reach of the city. We have artists and architects, writers and poets as well as the Fenton Manor House and merchants like myself who can travel daily to and from the city. The Heath is at our doorstep to wander in away from the hustle and bustle of the city. Edward has told me of your fortunate meeting with Admiral Isaac Smith who happens to be a member of the Governors of Highfield Grammar School which is situated only about two miles away across the Heath. Edward will speak with the Headmaster about possible places at the school for you when you have reached the required standard in Latin. Latin was once the language of all Europe and all the professions demand it but Edward tells me that you both are very intelligent and what I suggest is that we find a tutor for you here in the village. There is a former member of staff of the school retired here called Mr. Dawson who earns a bit as a crammer. I think he would relish the challenge of bringing you up to scratch in Latin and English in a year. Your allowance from the Company will easily pay his fees. If you agree I will send a note to him to call on us. Meanwhile, during the next few days, you may wander around the neigbourhood and make yourselves familiar with your new home."

Later, when they were alone, Kwame said: "Now we have to learn Latin before we have had time to learn more English! Tedlie told me once about that when I asked him about becoming a doctor, how all the plants had Latin names and how Latin was a kind of international language among educated men in Europe. I think that when we learn Latin our English will improve."

"In any case, if we attend the Grammar School in Highfield, we must learn it. I think that the prospect of having a private tutor during the next year will be a great advantage to us; he will speak English with us too and help us in different ways to meet the school requirements. It's all part of the process of becoming Europeans with black skins!"

"How do you feel, Kwabena, I begin to feel more like an *Oburoni* every day!"

"It's not only the language, it's the clothes and the food!" Kwabena responded, and they laughed together, and he asked: "What would we be doing now in Juaben if we had never left?"

"Clearing the bush for the farm, weeding and planting, cutting firewood and the usual chores around the house. You know, white people seem to have so many more varied things to do than we have. Think of all that we have learned during the last months, what we have seen and experienced, and what we still have to learn in school. We are living in a completely different world but it's a world that I begin to enjoy much more than in Asante. I wonder, if we are educated like Europeans, whether we would ever want to go back home, and, if we did, whether we could fit in."

"It's the same with me: I begin to forget some of the words in Asante. Here we are in England speaking to each other in English. I begin to feel used to European food and clothes but I still prefer my *ntama* to sleep in rather than the night-shirt!"

Chapter 2

The School Years in England

*"And what is a liberal education? That which draws forth
and trains up the germ of free-agency in the individual."*
(From a letter of Samuel Taylor Coleridge).

Their first year in Hampstead under the tutelage of Mr. Andrew Dawson was strenuous: he arrived at the house punctually at 9 and was shown into a little-used sitting room with a large table which had been allocated as their classroom. He was small in build, simply-dressed, polite and modest but everything he did and said was exact and meticulous. His life as a teacher of Latin and English had ingrained in him deep respect for the logic of grammar and for method and system in learning. He spoke exactly and precisely so that the young men from Ashanti understood him and each lesson was arranged in steps to a definite conclusion. He gave them each a dog-eared copy of the Latin primer in use in the school at Highfield as well as a copy of a book of readings in English Literature from Chaucer to Wordsworth with copious notes and comments. For him the task was a special challenge: not only were the African boys well-motivated and intelligent but their minds were, as he put it, a tabula rasa, a clean slate on which nothing was already written; the responsibility was completely his to make sure that what was inscribed there was correct and in order. At the end of each lesson they were required to repeat in summary what they had learned. In addition to learning they shared in other experiences; there was Edward's marriage to Eleanor in the Parish Church, for example, which they discussed afterwards.

"It must cost a great deal of money to marry in England," declared Kwame, "when you think of the fine clothes, the reception for so many guests, the honeymoon and all the other expenses."

"I suppose that there is no financial payment to the bride's family and remember that the bride's money belongs to the husband after the wedding. The wealthier the bride's family the greater the dowry she brings to the marriage. But what puzzles me most is the oath they both swear to God to remain together for life whatever the circumstances, one man, one wife, for life. What happens if the man takes another woman or is cruel to the wife that he has or vice versa?" Kwabena relished using the Latin phrase he had learned. "Is there no possibility of divorce?"

"I don't know and we can't ask Edward; maybe Tedlie can explain to us when he comes."

Then there was the mystery of Edward's cool reception at the Foreign Office: a formal letter had arrived from the Secretary of State for the Colonies requesting his attendance at his office but Edward had returned with all his high hopes dashed to the ground.

"I was received courteously but not cordially; I was thanked for my report of the expedition to Kumasi and for my book which My Lord Bathurst had read. An Under-Secretary who was introduced to me as Mr. Joseph Dupuis, was present. He referred to the letter of Mr. Hope Smith and to a so-called treaty which had been signed by me and asked, who had authorised me to sign? I could only reply that I had been given the authority of the Governor at Cape Coast upon which he turned to the Secretary of State and murmured words about the arrogance of the Company. I was then informed that the Government had completely other plans for dealing with the situation on the West African coast and I was politely dismissed with a supercilious smile from Dupuis. It was abundantly clear to me that not only was the Company in disfavour but also that I had been singled out by Mr. Dupuis as a personal antagonist because he had earlier suggested himself to Lord Bathurst as the leader of an official government mission to Kumasi."

"Was there then no hint that there might be further employment for you in one of the colonies?" queried his mother anxiously.

"Nothing like that was mentioned. Lord Bathurst is a sincere man but I gained the impression that he was totally uncertain how to deal with the problem of the future of the company's presence on the Coast. You see, after 1807 the profitable trade in slaves is over; the Company is losing money because no real substitute for the trade has been found and the many forts must be staffed and maintained; now the Asante are threatening to dominate the coastlands and the Fante don't want that. Should we sell our forts to the Dutch and the Danes, abolish the Company, and give up our interest in the Coast? Now, in the shape of my Treaty, the Governor has taken an initiative which commits the Government and that they are too proud to concede. My uncle hinted to me of that possibility. So everything is in the melting-pot and I suspect that Under-Secretary Dupuis is stirring the mixture. I'll just have to wait for news from Cape Coast."

In fact, as a result of Bowdich's visit, Lord Bathurst consulted Lord Castlereagh at the Foreign Office; they had been at Oxford together and Castlereagh had twice been Secretary of State for the Colonies before him, and they met as old friends. At the end of a wearisome Cabinet meeting they sat over a welcome glass of Madeira and Bathurst remarked: "It's the old problem on the Gold Coast that has now come to a head: the Asante are threatening and the Company has made some kind of treaty with the Asante King that we can't accept."

"Why not wait a bit longer; these matters often solve themselves in time. You and I have had a long experience in waiting for a solution to problems for which there was no precedent, our maritime and trading interests have led to protectorates and colonies all over the world, each one demanding from you and me complex decisions on situations that have never happened before. Why can't you accept the treaty?"

"As it stands it is quite reasonable and fully expresses our views but it was entered into by a young writer in the service of the Africa Company on behalf of the Government! The King of Asante is under the impression that he has made an agreement with the King of England. The Company has gone too far and must be brought into line at once."

"That you must do. Why not send someone out there, a diplomatic agent in rank, call him His Majesty's Envoy, to give him status, with the task of sorting things out to your satisfaction? Who have you available on your staff?"

"The only possible person is Dupuis, the Under-secretary; you sent him to me some years ago, remember? He is ambitious and efficient and would relish the task but he can be tactless and impatient with subordinates. His presence would almost certainly antagonise the Governor and Company officials."

"You must give him the full credentials as Government agent to safeguard your own reputation, otherwise Cabinet would give you a roasting."

Then in April, 1819, two letters arrived for Edward Bowdich from Cape Coast; the first one read:

Dear Edward,

You will be truly sorry to read of the death of your dear friend and comrade, Henry Tedlie, who passed away in his room in Cape Coast Castle on March 9th, 1819. It had seemed that he was making a recovery from the severe dysentery which had so long troubled him but suddenly the illness took a turn for the worse and the medicaments no longer had any effect. His end was peaceful and he passed away quietly in Christian hope. The day before he died he spoke with me of you and the Asante boys and the wonderful comradeship during your expedition to Kumasi. He is buried in the cemetery here.

According to his instructions all his possessions are to be sent to his widowed mother but all his books and medical instruments are to go to Kwame Boaten. I am therefore forwarding by the next ship bound for London, two chests, one to be delivered to his mother in Camden, the other to be given to Kwame. He has also given the sum of five pounds to Kwabena Boaten.

Kindly convey my condolences to the two boys and assure Kwame that you will care for him.

Yours most sincerely,
John Hope Smith

The second letter, dated a few days later on March 30th,1819, read:

Dear Edward,

I hasten to convey to you the disturbing news that the Secretary of State for the Colonies has informed me by letter that a Royal Envoy, Mr. Joseph Dupuis, has been despatched to Cape Coast to resolve the problem of the treaty with the King of Asante. This is a severe shock to my authority. According to private information from Company sources, the Government is seriously considering taking over the Company forts and vesting them in the Crown under the authority of the Governor of Sierra Leone, Sir Charles McCarthy.

If this should happen,I would be dismissed from my post as Governor as the Company would no longer exist; its officers would be dismissed or replaced. This could not take place in a shorter time than two years but I apprise you of the eventuality now because the provisions of the treaty that you signed will come into question as well as the custody of the Asante boys. I will make every endeavour to ensure that funds are laid aside for their education. I do not think that the two chiefs would request their repatriation.

Convey my regards to my sister, your esteemed mother.

Yours sincerely,
John Hope Smith

Edward Bowdich felt a sudden pang of irretrievable loss; his life had become so closely bound up with that of Henry. They had shared so many experiences together, without his unwavering support he could never have achieved the aims of the mission to Kumasi. Henry, the ideal comrade, modest, reliable, totally loyal, self-effacing, only eager to serve and help! He called the young men to him and read the letter slowly to them and watched their eyes fill with tears; their grief was so great that they seemed suddenly older. He took them both into his arms and then they sat looking sadly at one another. At last Kwame spoke: "Dr. Henry Tedlie was my European father, as you, Mr. Bowdich, have become

Kwabena's European father. Now that he has passed away from us and he has given to me his medical books and instruments it means that he wished for me to follow in his career; these books and instruments are meant to be further used. I wish, therefore, to become a medical doctor like him. Will you, Edward, take me now under your wing and help me to achieve my aim? I am sure that Henry, your closest friend, would have wished it."

Edward grasped his hand and declared: "Of course, Kwame, I will do everything in my power to help you to become a true successor to Henry. I shall be European father to you both." Their sorrow had bound them together in a fresh way and they were using first names. Kwame thanked him and then asked: "Was Henry Tedlie laid to rest according to Christian funeral custom, I mean, buried in the earth?"

"Yes; in the Castle cemetery at Cape Coast."

"Then Kwabena and I would like to honour his life and to remember his passing also in the traditional Asante manner. Today is Tuesday and on Thursday, the day of *Asase Yaa* or Mother Earth, we should like to do that with a short ceremony in a corner of the garden. We shall fast on that day and remember him."

So on the following Thursday morning, at first light before breakfast, the household met together with the servants in a secluded, wooded corner of the garden which was bounded by rhododendron bushes and a hawthorn tree. Kwame had borrowed a bowl from the kitchen in which he had poured apple cider. Both boys were wearing their *ntama* and were bare-footed; all solemnly drank a little wine from the bowl and then Kwame poured out the rest on a spot where a square of turf had been taken while he said in Asante:

"Asase Yaa, gye nsa nom.
Wo ba, Henry Tedlie, na wawu.
Oburoni, Barima Henry Tedlie, oduruyefo kese.
Wosre no ade a, ode rema wo.
Yen Agya a ne nsa ye no fakye-fakye
Owuo yi afu me mu; owuo yi anhye m'ase na maboa me ho.
Asase Yaa, gye nsa nom."

Kwabena stepped forward and gave the English translation:

"Mother Earth, take this wine and drink. Your child, Henry Tedlie has passed away. An honourable white man, famous doctor, if you asked anything from him he gave it to you; our father whose hand was always tempting him to give. This death has taken me by surprise; this death gave me no warning that I might prepare myself. Mother Earth, take this wine and drink."

Then they recited together the talking drum stanza each taking a line:

"Spirit of Earth, you grieve, Spirit of Earth you suffer.
Earth and the dust within you, as long as I am dead I shall be
 at your mercy.
O Earth, as long as I live I will put my trust in you;
O Earth who will receive my body.
We appeal to you and you will understand,
We appeal to you and you will understand."

The bowl was put down on the square of turf and a creeper of ivy was laid in front and Kwame said: The funeral is finished, let us go home in peace." They crossed their hands over their breast and walked slowly back to the house followed by the others. Mrs. Bowdich asked them if they would come to breakfast and Kwabena answered:

"No thank you; today we walk on the Heath and return this evening." When they had gone she said to Edward:

"You know, these Asante young men are more naturally religious than we Westerners; they are much more instinctively aware of the world of the spirit. The returning of the body to Mother Earth is only a version of our 'ashes to ashes, dust to dust'; the earth takes the body back to itself while the soul joins the ancestors in the other world. Whenever I hear missionaries talking about preaching to the heathen I wonder if they had never met people like Kwame and Kwabena. I'm so glad that you put Kwame`s mind at rest, there will be a home for them here as long as they need it. What your uncle has written in his second letter should stay private. There is no point is causing the boys unnecessary uneasiness, it may be years before the government takes any action about the Company."

The second letter from his uncle made it quite clear to Edward that Under-secretary Dupuis had played a leading role in planning the future of the British presence on the Guinea Coast but there was nothing that he could do. By pure chance he had been given the leadership of the mission to Kumasi but it did not mean, as he had hoped, a promotion to an important post in the colonial service; on the contrary, the initiative lay in the hands of Joseph Dupuis and he could only wait on further developments. He did not have to wait long. In the summer of 1819, Dupuis was gazetted as His Majesty's Envoy to the Guinea Coast and landed at Cape Coast in July where he took up residence in the Castle pending his visit to Kumasi. In the following October a private letter from Mr. Hope Smith informed his nephew as follows:

Dear Edward,

I am writing privately to inform you of the disastrous consequences of the arrival of Mr. J. Dupuis. He has proclaimed himself as the plenipotentiary of the British Government to bring all the Africa Company forts and trading posts under the authority of the Governor of Sierra Leone, to visit Kumasi to abrogate the Treaty signed by you and to replace it with a new 'official' treaty.

I and my senior colleagues have reasoned with him in vain; so far as he is concerned the matter is not open to discussion and it is clear that he foresees for himself a leading role in the future plans of Government for the Guinea Coast. We are all quite upset by his arrogant manner and superior air. I have appointed Mr William Hutton to accompany him to Kumasi. Suddenly the entire enterprise of the Company has been placed in jeopardy and the entire staff in a state of turmoil.

I shall inform you of further developments. Say nothing to the Asante young men at this stage; I shall do my utmost to ensure that the promise by the Company to pay for their education in the treaty

*signed by you is continued by Government. In any case, I am personally
prepared to contribute to the costs of their education.*

Yours most sincerely,
John Hope Smith

Edward Bowdich later learned that Dupuis and Hutton had
reached Kumasi where they received a warm welcome. Dupuis did
not hesitate to derogate the authority of Governor Hope Smith
and to place the Asantehene under the impression the he had
been deliberately deceived. The situation was made worse when
it was discovered that the copy of the treaty that Osei Bonsu had
made with Bowdich differed in important respects from the copy
at Cape Coast. The first treaty was torn up and a new one was
signed by the Asantehene and Dupuis which Hope Smith refused
to ratify because it gave Ashanti explicit power over Fanti country!
Dupuis returned to London alone, indignant and highly offended,
to put the matter before Lord Bathurst. Osei Bonsu was utterly
bewildered by the vacillations of the British and after waiting ten
months in vain for a reply he turned deliberately to the Dutch
and the Danish forts for trade. A year later a report in the *Times*
confirmed that the British Government would take over the
British forts and trading posts and place them under the authority
of Sir Charles McCarthy, the Governor of Sierra Leone.

Already after his uncle had been relieved of his post and had
returned to England, Edward knew that there would be no chance
of further employment on the Gold Coast so long as Dupuis
was at the Colonial Office but his interest in West Africa and its
people was still strong and he longed for another outlet there for
his interests and energies. His father encouraged him to equip
himself further for colonial service and Edward had introductions
to the German explorer, Alexander von Humboldt, and to the
French Natural Scientist, Baron Georges Cuvier, both in Paris; he
learned French and Portuguese and made researches in Lisbon
and Madeira in the hope that a post in Sierra Leone might come
his way. For the next few years Kwame and Kwabena were without

his direct guidance but by the time of their admission to Highfield Grammar School they had profited greatly by the patient, skilful teaching of their tutor, Mr. Andrew Dawson. Their motivation and their ability to learn Latin by ear endeared them to him and in the summer of 1819 he proudly announced that the two young men were fit to be admitted to the Highfield Free Grammar School in the 4th form! The Headmaster, Mr. Forster, had agreed with Edward to accept a reduced fee for tuition so that the grant from the Company would cover all their expenses.

The school was small: it was housed in two converted villas whose combined large gardens and outbuildings formed a private quadrangle and a staff of seven taught about 60 boys aged between 13 and 18 in 5 classes or 'forms.' The Asante were admitted into Form 4, the year before the attempt at matriculation in one of the Universities. Most of the boys attended daily from their homes in the district but a few were boarded with local families. On the appointed day Kwame and Kwabena presented themselves and were introduced at the school assembly and afterwards to their class-master, Mr. Ferguson, a young man recently appointed from Scotland. He showed them to a wooden desk, scarred with the initials and names of previous occupants, on the front row of the classroom. Behind them were the desks of ten other boys who gazed at them warily; no one spoke or greeted them, they were not only foreigners but also black-skinned negroes from darkest Africa and they had no precedent for dealing with them. Up to this point in their sojourn in England, Kwame and Kwabena had encountered friendliness and kindness but now they were to encounter one of the seamier sides of English public-school life.

Bullying, as it was called, was always present in all public and Grammar schools and took the form of the intimidation of new boys or 'freshers' or of the younger and smaller boys in the class by bigger and stronger boys. The bully was the most powerful boy in the class who imposed his will on the others by force, by arm-twisting, skull-scrubbing, shin-kicking, slapping, punching and similar cruelties; if he lost a pen or pencil, he took yours, if his homework had not been done,he copied from yours, if you possessed anything that he coveted, you gave it to him. The bully was usually supported by a small group of cronies who flattered him and egged him on. The bully made sure that any newcomers were quickly 'brought into line.'

The 4th form at Highfield had its bully in the shape of the red-haired, thick-bodied, heavy-handed Alexander Hardwick; 'Sandy' to his cronies. He was the 'boss' of the class: at 17 he was as tall as or taller than the masters who knew him as a duffer who would never pass a matriculation examination and they had succeeded in forcing him to repeat a year but he was tolerated only because his father, the owner of a plantation in Jamaica, had made a useful donation to the school with which to purchase an adjoining meadow for a playing field. The Headmaster had introduced the game of rugby of which Hardwick had grown very fond. He played scrum-half and if the ball came out on his side he would clutch it and run like a mad bull forwards, without feinting or swerving or passing the ball, handing off with his free arm any defender who had the courage to try to tackle him, stopping only when in triumph he had grounded the ball over the line for a 'try', the right to carry the ball in front of the goal and kick the ball between the posts for a further points score.

So on the first appearance of the boys from Ashanti in class, all were waiting for Alex Hardwick to show his hand. The opportunity came quite soon: it was a Latin lesson for which they were using a book of selected extracts from Latin writers. Mr Ferguson had thought to show to the others that the African boys had attained their level, he knew from Mr. Dawson that they were acquainted with the particular Tacitus passage that he had chosen, but he had not reckoned with Hardwick's astuteness. He turned to Kwabena:

"Boaten, please construe the first paragraph."

Kwabena had translated the first few sentences into quite good English, when suddenly the authoritative voice of Hardwick rang out:

"Are you aware, Sir, that these blackamoors sitting in front of us come from a warlike, cruel and bloodthirsty tribe on the west coast of Africa which constantly makes attacks on our people trading on the coast? What are they doing in a school like ours? When I informed my father of the fact he was quite indignant and said that they would be better to be learning to be slaves on a plantation in Jamaica."

The scholars grinned in delight. This was wonderful stuff! Hardwick may be stupid in class but when he wanted, he could speak with power. No one else but Hardwick would have dared to speak to a master in this manner! There was dead silence in the classroom and Ferguson knew that he had to deal with the situation with the utmost tact; a sharp rebuke would serve no purpose at all. He let a tolerant tone come into his voice as he answered:

"It is thought, Hardwick, by many of our people, that the people of Africa, would benefit by schooling and that young men like Kwame and Kwabena Boaten would profit by an education in a school like ours so that they could return to help their own people to make progress in civilisation."

"My father, Sir, is in favour of schools for white children but not for blacks. He is of the firm opinion that blacks should always be kept in their place as slaves and labourers for the whites".

"Does your father mean that Africans should be denied an education? Not even to learn to read and write?"

"Yes, Sir, he means just that; they don't need any school learning to work on the sugar plantations. It is their destiny to work as slaves and labourers for the white man."

Hardwick so clearly relished this statement that he regarded the teacher with a derisive smile and in a stern tone of voice Mr. Ferguson brought the discussion to a close: "That is quite enough on this topic, Hardwick. It is a source of disappointment to me that you have not seen fit to welcome our new scholars from Africa. I should remind you that the Head and the Governors of this school unanimously decided to admit them as fit and proper scholars on the same terms as all the other pupils. Now, Hardwick, you will continue to construe the passage from Tacitus that Boaten began."

There was a pause while Hardwick fumbled uncertainly with a small book in his hands; it was a crib, a word-for-word translation into English, from which he read unashamedly aloud much to the amusement of the boys. How far would Hardwick's cheek go?

"I think that you are reading from a crib?" Ferguson questioned and Hardwick responded with a sneer:

"Why do we need to construe, Sir, when we have a perfectly good crib?" He waved the book aloft and said:

"In any case, Sir, English is better than Latin!"

Too late, Hardwick realised that he had gone too far in his impudence but he could not back down and he stayed sullen and silent when the reprimand came.

"May I remind you, Hardwick, that is my duty to ascertain the extent of your ability in Latin, and if you seek to make a public mockery of my efforts you give me reason to doubt whether you are a fit and proper person to be a scholar in this school. Your insolence in class today will not be forgotten."

For the remainder of the lesson the boys in the class wrote out in silence their own, unaided translation of the Tacitus and when the bell rang, Ferguson motioned to Kwame and Kwabena to accompany him out of the room. When they were alone he said earnestly:

" As your form-master I much regret the behaviour of Hardwick towards you but you should know that the opinions of his father are shared by many people in England but most of us wish to see a complete end to slavery and racial prejudice. We also wish to see an end to bullying in our schools. I counsel you to be patient and modest, in course of time the other boys will accept you fully as one of themselves. Should you experience anything nasty, however, from Hardwick or any other boys, you may inform me."

For the rest of the day Hardwick seethed with anger that he had been put down by Ferguson,a young teacher new to the school, since he knew that the opinions of his father were shared by many. If the niggers were to stay at the school and in his class they should be taught soon enough to respect and fear him, he and his pals would see to that. Their life would be made a misery!

As Kwame and Kwabena walked home from school that day they did so in a dismal frame of mind. It was the first time that they had met open hostility on grounds of their race and colour and it was particularly unpleasant because it came from youths no older than they were. It was comforting that their class-master had promised his support but what was this 'bullying' that he had spoken about? They were soon to know. When they reached the footpath round the Fenton House lake, Hardwick and four of his cronies stepped out from behind a group of shrubs to confront them. They knew instinctively that it was a hostile encounter but they remained outwardly calm.

"Where might you be going?" demanded Hardwick.

"We are going home to Hampstead village." replied Kwame.

"Are you not aware that this is private land and that there is no right of way for foreigners, especially niggers?"

"Then we shall walk round by the road."

"But first you will pay your deepest respects to me and to my pals: you will both kneel down and kiss our boots and say each time, "I am a dirty, negro bastard".

"This we cannot do: we are not dirty nor are we bastards," declared Kwabena, "we are negroes but we belong to one of the greatest people of West Africa."

"Did you hear that , you fellows? For your arrogance and your showing off in class today and your toadying to Ferguson, you must be seasoned."

Hardwick loved the word 'seasoned' which he had heard his father use to describe the brutal and harsh discipline of work on his plantations without rest together with starvation rations and whippings which was used to beat recalcitrant slaves into submission. He raised his hand and slapped Kwabena a stinging blow on the cheek with the palm of his hand but as he drew back to give a second slap on the other cheek with the back of his hand, to his great surprise his wrist was seized and as he was spun round, both boys quickly pushed past him and ran off.

Hardwick gave chase to cries of "Give 'em hell, Sandy!" from his comrades, but he slipped on the wet ground and fell face forward on the earth. In the next few moments the cousins had flown out of reach and when they could see that they were not followed, they paused for breath.

It was Kwame who spoke first:"They will wait somewhere else for us tomorrow and we shall have to fight them all. Should we report what has happened to Mr. Ferguson?"

"I think not. A slap on the face and insulting words among young men are quite common; we can't complain. And it is our first day, remember.What Hardwick said in class will certainly be reported and for what has happened now we have no witnesses. If they attack us tomorrow we shall be forced to submit, there may be more of them, but we can bear rough handling. They cannot break our spirit; we are Asante men, remember; and afterwards we shall carefully plan our revenge." He smiled at Kwame, they embraced and walked on. "Not a word to anyone at home." Kwabena added. "This is something that we have to solve ourselves."

The following day was nerve-racking for the cousins but nothing unusual happened in class. As they walked home, however, in a sheltered corner of the Heath, they were seized by the same four and held tightly from behind by the arms and brought before Hardwick who ordered: "De-bag the black buggers, and take their jackets and shirts off ! They are not fit to wear European clothes. Then they will kneel and kiss my boots and repeat, "I am a dirty negro bastard."

They were forced to do Hardwick's bidding ; it was useless to struggle. They were compelled to lie face down on the ground and their faces were rubbed in the earth. Suddenly, at a signal, they were released and their attackers fled leaving them sitting in their underwear. In silence the boys put on their clothes which had been thrown in a heap, wiped their faces with a handkerchief and looked ruefully at each other.

"How are we to explain our dirty clothes when we get home?" asked Kwame."Tell them that we as new boys, have been 'ragged'. Just that, no details, no names. They know that such things happen in boys' schools, Edward told us. The clothes are not damaged," replied Kwabena. For the next few days in school they moved around quietly, spoke only when spoken to, and gave the other boys the impression that they had been duly 'subdued'. It was on Wednesday afternoon at rugby-football practice that a way of revenge occurred to Kwabena. He explained to Kwame: "You know how Hardwick waits for the ball coming out from a scrum, he grabs it and runs straight for the try-line; if anyone has the courage to tackle him he hands them off with great force. On Saturday we must make sure that we are on the opposing side, ask the prefect in charge to do us a favour. Then every time Hardwick runs with the ball we attack him and bring him down hard, really hard.

When the day came, they found themselves in the back three-quarter line of the 'B' side and the first time that Hardwick ran with the ball they failed to reach him before he had scored a try. The sides were evenly balanced and they had to wait a while for a second chance; there was a scrum on their wing and as soon as Hardwick began to run with the ball the cousins positioned themselves to intercept him from both sides. Hardwick saw the move but disdained to swerve; as Kwame approached he tried to hand him off but Kwame held fast on to the arm and in the next moment Kwabena dived at Hardwick's knees and brought him down. Hardwick did not release the ball and the Asante boys piled on top of him, grinding his face in the mud and kneeling on his back while two of their classmates, with scores to settle, added their weight to the heap. By the time the referee blew his whistle, Hardwick had been mauled as never before in his life. In the second half this process was repeated; each time Hardwick had the ball he was tackled and brought down and it became clear that the stuffing was being knocked out of him. Shortly before the final whistle after such a tackle he failed to stand up; he was turned over, the mud wiped from his face and hauled to his feet by players nearby. He looked at the players around him with disdain and contempt and made his way slowly off the field. His mortification was complete.

In class, on the following Monday, his seat in class was vacant and eventually the news filtered down that without informing anyone, Hardwick had packed up and had gone home to London.

Meanwhile, at Moreton House in Highfield, Dr. James Gillman, the father of two boys at the preparatory department of the Grammar School, was sitting after dinner chatting with his paying-guest, the famous poet and philosopher, Samuel Taylor Coleridge. "My boys have just told me an extraordinary happening that they witnessed on the Heath a few days ago. Would you like to hear it?"

"Of course, the most interesting things happen to youngsters." Gillman called the boys in from the garden: James, the elder, about 10 years old with his brother, Henry, clearly two or three years younger. "James, tell Mr Coleridge what you witnessed last Monday on the Heath." "We were out by the elms lying doggo in the long grass watching two weasels feeding off a rat. We had spotted them once before in the same place. Then, on the other side of the path five fellows from the upper school sneaked in behind some elder-flower and rhododendron bushes like they were waiting for somebody but didn't want to be seen. Well, after about five minutes, along came two black boys, also from the upper school, and as they passed they were grabbed from behind by four of the first group and held fast. The leader gave the orders."

Their father interrupted: "How did you know that all the boys were from the upper school?"

"They were all dressed in school uniform and all grown up, as tall as you, father."

"Did they see you?"

"No. We were in a hollow and quite hidden by the long grass. I put my finger to my lips to warn Henry to keep mum."

"Could you recognise any of the youths?"

"No. We never meet upper school boys. But the leader had ginger hair and they called him 'Sandy'."

"And one of the four was trying to grow a moustache." Henry interjected.

"What happened next? Could you hear what the leader said?"

"Yes. He said: 'Debag the black buggers! They are not fit to wear European clothes.' So they took the jackets, shirts and pants off the black boys in spite of their struggles and when they were in their underwear the leader slapped them with his hand backwards and forwards repeatedly. The black boys winced but never cried out. Then the leader ordered them to kiss his boots and they were forced on their knees and their heads were pushed down. They had to repeat the words: ' I am a dirty nigger bastard', which they did. Then suddenly the leader gave the black boys a kick and they all ran off. We kept still. The boys picked themselves up and dressed themselves and held each other close; then they slowly walked off in the direction of Hampstead Village. We got up and went the other way."

"What do you think was happening?" their father asked. "It was a kind of bullying, but rough and cruel; the white boys seemed to be out for revenge for something, they seemed to hate the blacks."

"Thank you both for telling us all this. You can leave us now. Mr. Coleridge and I would like to discuss it privately." When the boys had left, Gillman asked: "What do you think, Coleridge?"

"It is clear to me that the bullying of the boys from Africa has more than normal significance, it has its roots in racialism. The school would not have accepted these young men from Africa if there was any prejudice against colour, on the contrary, these scholars must have been responsibly sponsored. We can assume that this racial prejudice stems from a group in the upper school and it is right and proper that the Head is made aware of the matter."

"I agree entirely. One reason for my move to Highfield was that the school has a good reputation and I could send my boys there. As a parent I have every right to speak with the Head about such behaviour in public."

"Another consideration, Gillman, is that the scale of bullying in our public schools often reaches disgraceful proportions.

Thomas Arnold has expressed in public his deep disquiet over the matter."

"Thank you, Coleridge. As a parent with two boys in the school and who resides in Highfield I shall speak with the Headmaster about the occurrence."

Before Dr. Gillman had the opportunity to contact the Headmaster, however, the absence of Hardwick without leave together with the disquieting report of the 4th Year Form-master, Mr.Ferguson, regarding Hardwick's arrogant outburst in class against the presence of the African boys, prompted Mr. Forster, the Headmaster, to call a meeting to enquire into the affair. Present were: the prefect who had been referee at the rugby game, the Form-master, and Kwabena and Kwame. "You have no doubt heard of the absence without leave of Alexander Hardwick. I have spoken with his landlady who reported to me that he limped back to his rooms after the rugby game and complained to her that he had been attacked by the Boaten boys during the game and that his face, ribs and back had been injured by their ferocity. He bathed and changed and left by coach to London to report to his father. You will agree that I had no alternative but to enquire into the matter. Anderson, you, as senior prefect, were referee at the game, had you any reason to suppose that the African boys played unfairly and deliberately sought to hurt Hardwick by their tackling?"

"On the contrary, Sir, Hardwick is one of the biggest boys in the school who takes great delight in tackling others when they have the ball and bringing them down by reason of his size and weight. Whenever he has the ball he enjoys handing off would-be tacklers with great sweeps of his free arm; not with the fist, Sir, but with an open hand. Many boys are afraid to tackle him but on Saturday last, the African boys showed great courage and speed; the two of them defended as a pair and grounded him almost every time he ran with the ball. They played according to the rules and the players applauded them afterwards. You understand, Sir, that rugby is not a game for faint hearts, you can receive minor injuries when you are tackled if you do not release the ball or pass it which Hardwick rarely did. So the other players piled in when Hardwick was down; we had a few loose mauls with Hardwick at the bottom of the heap. Near the end of the match, when he saw that he was beaten, he walked off the field in silence."

"Thank you, Anderson, for your succint explanation." Turning to the Form-master the Head asked: "As Form-master, Mr. Ferguson, you know the 4th Form scholars as well as any of us; you felt properly obliged to report to me a serious breach of classroom discipline committed by Hardwick during a Latin class. Kindly inform me of the circumstances and if he has seen fit to apologise."

"Hardwick openly objected to the presence of the Boaten boys in the school. He had not been invited to speak but did so in an arrogant tone asserting that black-skinned people had no need of education because their destiny was to be slaves and labourers for the white man. He further read openly from a crib when asked to construe and declared that English was better than Latin. He has not been to me to apologise."

The Head thanked Mr Ferguson and looked at the Asante boys with a smile: "Your presence seems to have annoyed Alexander Hardwick. Had you previously given him any reason for his annoyance?"

They had agreed that Kwabena would speak, if requested, but that they would say nothing of their humiliation on the Heath. Kwabena had argued that they had had their revenge on the football field and that Hardwick had left the school of his own accord. If any, or all, of his four cronies dared to assume his role, they would be in a position to threaten to reveal their support of Hardwick. The four would know, however, that Kwame and Kwabena had kept silent at the interview with the Head.

"No, Sir, we had never met him before our first lesson in school."

"Have you a private explanation for his hostility?"

"We think that he is echoing his father's opinion of black people, although he has never spoken personally with either of us."

The Head thanked them and remarked that he was now better equipped to deal with the matter.

During the evening of the following day, Dr. Gillman called on Mr. Forster at his residence in the High Street. They took a seat in the parlour and the Headmaster poured out a glass of Madeira for them both: "Your good health, Sir, a glass of wine after a tiring day is to be recommended!"

"Indeed it is," responded the doctor, sipping gratefully.

"It is always good to see you but I take it that you have a special reason this evening for your call."

"A disquieting report reached my ears recently of flagrant behaviour on the Heath of a number of senior boys from the school, so serious that I felt obliged to inform you personally and privately."

Dr. Gillman related the incident to which the Head listened gravely. "I am most grateful to you for taking the trouble to acquaint me of this incident. You are assured of the veracity of your informant? Sometimes members of the public complain of minor cases of boisterous behaviour on the part of high-spirited boys. Forgive my putting this question."

"My informants are members of my family, my two boys at the preparatory school. I and Mr. Coleridge, who is a paying guest at Moreton House, questioned them closely. I have complete faith in their veracity otherwise I would not have come to you."

"Who knows of this incident apart from your sons, yourself and Mr. Coleridge?"

"No one. And I have instructed my boys to say nothing of it to anyone."

"From what your boys observed of the appearance of the scholars concerned we should be able to identify them but you will appreciate that in such serious cases I have to move carefully in making my enquiries. What is especially important is that the affair concerns the two African boys who are sponsored by the Royal African Company and by a retired Admiral of the Fleet who is a member of our Board of Governors. I can assure you, Dr. Gillman, that this matter will not be taken lightly. Bullying, as you know, takes place in our public schools, sometimes to excess. I deplore it and I shall endeavour to root it out in Highfield."

Mr. Forster lost no time in calling on Edward Bowdich and apprising him of the hostility of Hardwick in class, of the events on the rugby field, the absence of Hardwick from the school and, as it now seemed, the involvement of Hardwick and four others in the affair on the Heath. He stressed the necessity of hearing directly from Kwame and Kwabena their account of what had happened on the Heath, with the assurance that no one would ever know that they had revealed their secret. They should speak privately with Bowdich, and he would privately confirm the facts to the Headmaster.

That was how the episode was settled: Alexander Hardwick was 'sent down' for indiscipline in class, for being absent without leave and for failure to meet the required academic standards. So far as the members of Form 4 were concerned it was good riddance; only four felt uneasy and found it difficult to look the Boaten boys in the eye. No mention had ever been made of the humiliation on the Heath; it seemed clear that the blacks had not blabbed to the Head but all the same they had the guilty feeling that one day the story would become known.

Although Hardwick had gone, it still took time before the members of the class learned to accept Kwame and Kwabena as one of themselves. Their speed and agility at rugby won them friends because English boys always admire those who are 'good at games' much more than those who excel at learning and slowly they were accepted as 'good sports' and 'decent types'. Another peculiarity of English schoolboys, the Asante cousins discovered, was their inexplicable attitude to hard learning and study. If you got good marks in a subject and were congratulated, you showed no pride but rather spoke so modestly about the achievement as if it were hardly worth the mention. In general, their classmates were casual and nonchalant about academic success and the hard learning necessary to achieve it. Hard learning normally took place in the period before examinations; it was called 'swotting', but only eggheads or highbrows swotted all the time! Of course, their black classmates had to work hard all the time, as they had so much to catch up, but it soon became evident in class discussions and in question and answer, that their intelligence and understanding were as good as, if not better than that of the native British boys. It was the innate modesty and sincerity of the Africans that won an equal place for them and the prejudice of skin colour ceased to have any significance. Kwame and Kwabena had picked up much information from their voyage, like knowing about a sextant and plotting a ship's course from charts; hoisting and reefing sails; knowing what the life of the crew of a frigate involved, which fascinated their classmates. But more than that their curiosity about life in Asante was unbounded and the cousins were always in demand for descriptions and explanations.

"Why were the reports of travellers full of references to human sacrifice, for example at festivals and deaths of chiefs?" In Bowdich's recent book, which some of them had read, there were many accounts of the sacrifice of men and women, they were once asked.

Kwame nodded to Kwabena to answer; they had agreed that he was best at speaking about ideas, so he had to try his best. They were all in the classroom after morning break waiting for the English teacher and sometimes then someone would put a question but never as difficult as this one. Kwabena started slowly:

"You need to know that we Asante are always conscious of our ancestors who are in the other spirit world; they are always there watching what we do. When we die or are killed our soul goes automatically to join them, so death is for us a transition to another kind of life, it's not hell, it's not paradise, but it's a continuation: I mean, we're not afraid to die, we don't wish to die but we're not afraid of death."

He was just getting into his stride when the door opened and the teacher walked in. Kwabena began to explain:

"They asked me about human sacrifice in my country, Sir, and I'm trying to explain." The teacher nodded his agreement and said:

"Go on, I'd like to hear too."

"Well, if a chief or someone important dies, we think it to be necessary that they should be accompanied on their journey to the ancestors by servants befitting the status that they had in this life. Many of those killed are war prisoners but not all; close friends and relatives may lose their lives. At a funeral there can be deep mourning but also dancing, drumming and rejoicing that everything has been done in order and that the ancestors will be pleased."

Someone interrupted: "Do the ancestors ever communicate with the living?"

"Yes, they do. Sometimes they send someone back. For example, when a child is born, the relatives look at it keenly and if it shows a clear resemblance to a former living person, the child is given the name, *Ababio*, meaning he or she has come again. We expect that the one bearing that name will, in due course, make a special contribution to the community. May I mention one other aspect of human sacrifice which has just occurred to me; you must excuse my mentioning it, but since coming to England we have been reading about recent European history and what has amazed us is the great number of lives lost in the French Revolution and in the battles against the French. There seemed to be nothing but wars from one end of Europe to the other, bloody fighting on land and on the sea! I mean, in France a machine was invented just to cut peoples' heads off in public; they beheaded the king first, then 1200 persons who remained loyal to him, and after that, under the tyrant Robespierre over 40,000 lost their heads as so-called 'enemies of the people'. In a battle near Leipzig, there were 330,000 allies against 200,000 French, in which 120,000 were killed and the same number wounded. In Russia, Napoleon lost half of his Grand Army of 450,000 men. In the book we are reading this vast human sacrifice of human life in war just seems to be accepted. In comparison, the number beheaded in Asante is very small, and our battles are ended on the same day because we wish to give the dead a fitting burial."

Kwabena thought that it was time he stopped and as his voice died away, there was dead silence, a silence of amazement that their black classmate could so hold their attention. The teacher began to clap his hands and they all joined in.

On another occasion they asked Kwabena about slavery because in Britain there had been nation-wide agitation for Parliament to abolish the slave trade in British territories and this had been achieved in 1807, but it was now becoming evident that the practice of slavery itself must be abolished. What was the Asante opinion on this topic? This time, the English teacher arranged the lesson formally and Kwabena spoke from the front.

"For as long as anyone can remember, the Ashanti King has sold slaves to the English traders in exchange for European goods that we didn't have: like muskets, ammunition, gunpowder, hardware of all kinds, cheap cloth, drinkables like whiskey and gin and many other things. We could also pay in gold which the traders liked, this was after all the Guinea coast. The slaves were mostly war prisoners but criminals were also sold. Many Asante families possessed a domestic slave or two, foreigners from the north and east, and we could pawn them or sell them if we needed the money. These slaves were sold to the whites through Fante middlemen, the Asante could not sell direct to the Europeans and this fact was one of the main reasons for the Asante wars. When the English stopped buying slaves after 1807 we had to sell them to the Dutch or the Danes instead. It was very disappointing. We never knew why the English had changed their minds. We never gave a thought to the question of whether selling slaves was good or bad, it had gone on for as long as anyone could remember, and it still goes on. It was only when we were being shown around the Castle in Cape Coast and we went down to the cellars, the huge, dismal dungeons where the slaves were kept until they were shipped, that then, for the first time, I began to realise what the slaves suffered. There were two dank and dark cellars, one for men and one for women; the one for men could hold up to a thousand and the captives had to sit or lie on the stone floor. Whenever they were fed, the food came in basins and because they were in chains they were forced to scramble for it as best they could. There was an open drain where they could relieve themselves but the stench was appalling.

The only light came through slits high in the wall. Over the women's prison there was a small gallery from which white officers and men could feast their lust on naked women.

If a particular girl was fancied, a rope ladder was lowered down for her to be taken to bed by the white man and afterwards she would be lowered back into the prison. We were told that if the passage was delayed or she was pregnant, her departure was postponed; if she bore a healthy child, she could be set free and the father had to pay a set sum for her support and to pay for the child in the fort school. Often the child would be baptised as Christian and the mother would perhaps give the name of the father to the child. She would be one of the lucky ones!

Then, when we sailed to England in a naval preventive ship we saw a group of slaves on shore at Freetown, Sierra Leone, who had been freed from a slaving ship, and once again Kwame and I began to realise what miseries they had endured and we began to understand the reason for the English giving up the trade in slaves. They looked so wretched and had a bewildered, hopeless look in their eyes, completely apathetic as though they had lost their souls. We could see the scars on their backs from whipping and the sores on their legs from the chains. There was a woman from Salaga whose baby was sucking in vain at her breasts; she could speak a little Asante and could tell us of her experiences. We were able to find a wet-nurse for her in Freetown. The town was full of slaves rescued by British naval ships who could speak to us in a kind of English; all of them were grateful to be free. In this way we experienced the slave trade and we began to understand better why the English had given it up.

That's what puzzled the Asante King; after centuries of profitable business they had suddenly abandoned it.

Then, anchored in the harbour not far from us was a ship full of white men and women, all on deck or leaning on the rail, all from Britain, all convicted criminals being transported as punishment to Australia on the other side of the world. I thought that the English had stopped buying our slaves and had begun selling their own people because it was cheaper!" There was some amusement at that idea and Mr. Ferguson remarked: "That was a transportation ship; we have been sending convicts to Australia since 1787."

"Thank you, Sir. I didn't know that then. I asked the Captain what evil deeds they had committed, he told me that most of them were petty thieves, burglars and robbers, a few were swindlers and forgers. When I further enquired what the petty thieves had stolen, he informed me anything worth less than 40 shillings, like stealing food, clothing, domestic animals; this surprised me because in my country such thefts would be dealt with by the families concerned. He wasn't pleased when I suggested that they could be sold as slaves and sternly informed me that these convicts were not slaves, they would be punished for their crimes by working for the government and, after seven years, with a clean record they could return to England. Only very few go back, they prefer to stay in Australia. Most of them, men and women, were young: between 15 and 35.

I conclude, Sir, by saying that my mind is still not clear about slavery but I think that every human being should have the right to freedom but then we must pay for the work they do. And if we do not pay, the work will not be done. Abolition of slavery will bring with it many problems for those who grow sugar, cotton, and other crops on the plantation system, as well as for my people who still trade in slaves!"

They applauded Kwabena and the rest of the class time was given up to discussion. Mr. Ferguson put the question: "Are you inferring, Kwabena, that the transportation system is a kind of slavery?"

"Not really, Sir. I can understand the difference. But when I saw the conditions below decks in which the white convicts travelled they were not much better than in the slave ships. My other feeling was: why such harsh punishment? Why should you have to leave your native land and work as a labourer for seven years for stealing a loaf of bread and a pound of cheese to feed your children with? Couldn't they just as well work on farms in England?" The Form-master turned to the class: "That's a challenge for you. Who is going to explain how and why the penal colony in Australia was started?"

In this way, because of the presence of the young men from Africa, the pattern of the English lessons changed. To interest teenage boys in English poetry and drama is never easy, now the short talks of Kwabena had aroused their curiosity and had led to spontaneous discussion which he could guide. They were now each set a topic to prepare and introduce in good English to the class and be prepared to answer questions raised in discussion. Mr. Ferguson chose themes of topical, sporting or historical interest which concerned them all but in particular widened the understanding of Kwame and Kwabena of British life and custom. Ferguson was a shrewd teacher: the success of Kwabena in his short talks was so evident that he didn't want them to be over-praised, let the Gold Coast boys show what they could do. In this way, the English classes of the Form-master became popular, the spirit of the class was raised, they were all contributing to the topic under discussion and learning to express themselves cogently. Ferguson was pleased; he felt that most of them would reach matriculation level in the following year, but what pleased him most was the way in which the Asante boys had been accepted as equals in the class, the school had truly initiated them into the world of the white man.

Other factors also played a large part in their initiation: their total assimilation into the Bowdich household in Hampstead village, and their acceptance as regular visitors to Moreton House in Highfield. Mrs. Bowdich was their foster-mother and Eleanor, Mrs. Edward Bowdich, was like an older sister, both of whom felt a special maternal interest in their welfare. They were given specific duties: they helped Fanny with fetching and carrying heavy loads, chopping wood for fires, beating carpets and rugs; they assisted Amy in carrying coals and cleaning footwear; above all they worked with Jack in the garden and in the stables. It was a real boon to have the help of two cheerful young men! At first the servants called them both Mr. Boaten and pronounced it like 'Boating' until one day they insisted on first names but they were still called Mr. Kwame and Mr. Kwabena! On top of that they made their own beds and swept the attic.At meals they talked together like old friends, patricularly in the evenings they recounted events at the school and what they had learned or experienced but not a word of the bullying.

Edward Bowdich grew more dispirited: the lack of success of his book together with his cool reception at the Foreign Office made it clear that there would be no prospect of employment for him in the Gold Coast. Yet he still yearned for further work in West Africa and encouraged both by his father and his uncle he had taken steps to equip himself further for colonial service by studying in Paris and later in Lisbon. Towards the end of the year 1819 he and his wife took up residence in Paris where their daughter was born and was given the name Harriet together with the names of his two comrades Tedlie and Hutchison, on the Kumasi expedition. They had been away more than two years and on their return there was great rejoicing, the family was re-united with a contented baby as the new member.

During this period Kwabena and Kwame became regular visitors at Moreton House in Highfield. Both Dr. Gillman and his paying-guest S.T.Coleridge, one of the leading literary personalities in England, had had their curiosity aroused by the Hardwick affair and were eager to get to know the two Ashanti boys who had suffered from such harassment; how appropriate, therefore, to invite all three to dine with the family and to give an account of their adventures! Coleridge had come to Moreton House to be cured of his opium addiction. He was then 45 years old, a man of wide sympathies and interests, an inveterate talker who, out of his encyclopaedic mind could speak on any topic with gusto and exuberance. By the time he came to Highfield, he had a reputation as a poet, an essayist and a lecturer on literary, philosophical and scientific themes, while his deep concern for social justice was widely known. He bitterly criticised the rich landowners and manufacturers who exploited their workers, he singled out the sufferings of child-workers in the factories in England, and he had written against the Slave Trade and slavery. In particular, any kind of child-exploitation roused his anger whether it was "the poor little white slaves in the cotton factories" or "the black slaves on the plantations in America and the West Indies". James Gillman, at 34, a tall, intelligent, humane and compassionate man, already had a growing reputation as a doctor and when Coleridge was referred to him, they got on so well together that they had become close friends.

That first invitation to the Gillmans was a huge success: Edward gave a concise account of the expedition to Kumasi and when questions began, handed over to one or other of the Asante boys. Gillman was profoundly interested in the last chapter of Edward's book and was sorry to hear of Tedlie's death. He asked:

"What follow-up have you been able to arrange for the list of plants used in diseases in Asante?"

" I supplied a list to Kew Gardens and about half of them could be given their Latin name and classification."

"I think that we can do better than that. I will contact the Curator. You know that Sir Joseph Banks and Carl Solander, who were on the *Endeavour* with Cook, and since 1772 have enriched and developed the tropical plant collection at Kew Botanic Garden. They have research facilities there." Turning to Kwame, he questioned:

"Why have you the wish to become a medical doctor?"

"Because of Mr. Tedlie. He impressed me by the way in which he worked: if any one was sick, male or female, old or young, black or white, he tried immediately to help them. Sometimes he stayed with them for quite a long time. He performed some serious operations with great success like hernia. He never turned anyone away and always tried to help them although he himself was sick with a dysentery which he couldn't cure. Above all, he never asked for money. I never admired a man so much and whenever he had a little spare time he took us with him to collect medicinal plants.

On the return journey he talked to me about diseases and how to relieve them or cure them. When he passed away he left his books and instruments to me as though he knew that I would want to follow in his footsteps. He was like a father to me and I loved him." Addressing Kwabena Gillman queried:

"Have you a specific career in mind?"

"Not yet, Sir. But I have given the matter much thought. If and when I return to West Africa what kind of knowledge would help my people most? It seems that, in the days to come, we shall come more and more in contact with Europeans, for example, the British government has announced its intention of taking over the coastal forts from the trading company and putting them under the control of the Governor of Sierra Leone. In such a case, although we possess our own customs and traditions, we should need to know the way in which the Europeans regulate their affairs especially as their way of life is so much more complicated than ours. Therefore I think that it would be very useful if I studied English law."

Edward Bowdich was congratulated on his achievement and asked about his future plans.

"My efforts received a cool reception by the Secretary of State for the Colonies. I was not offered a post either at home or in West Africa probably on account of my youth and because I had not studied at a University. So in the near future, I plan to study in Paris and Lisbon. Later there could be opportunities in Sierra Leone for someone with my experience. I still have an aspiration to work in Africa and do research there."

After the guests had departed, Coleridge remarked:

"You know, Gillman, I was deeply impressed by both these African young men; their intelligence and the concise, coherent manner in which they spoke, in splendid English, mark you. They are more articulate than most English boys of their age. Is it not quite amazing that the notion of the inherent inferiority of the dark-skinned races is so widespread among our people? They still have a year or more at school, I take it? I should like to do something to help them."

"I too, was deeply interested in the wish of the one called Kwame to study medicine. The associate of Bowdich, Tedlie, could not have been given a more fitting epitaph than the one he gave. I have thought that in the days to come, I might invite them to the house on a regular basis; my young medical assistant, John Williams, is keen on medicinal plants and he can work with them with the plants from Africa. My two youngsters could join in; they call him 'Wiz', the laboratory wizard! How would it seem to you if we introduced Kwame to your close friend, Dr. J.H. Green?

If he can, in course of time, matriculate, and Green and I believe that he possesses the ability to study medicine and surgery, he could be supported at the Royal College of Surgeons. If you approve I will speak with Bowdich about the finance involved."

"I approve entirely. What could be done to help the other boy, Kwabena, who said that he would like to study law? Green must have friends at Lincoln's Inn, I must sound him about getting a place there. As they were speaking I thought of inviting them eventually to my seminar. What do think of that? Wouldn't it be an eye-opener for some of my undergraduates?"

"It would certainly be important for them to realise that Africans can profit from education quite as much as Europeans. With regard to Kwabena, I agree that Dr. Green could advise us but you know, Coleridge, that Lord Mansfield is a near neighbour at Kenwood House. He has been long in retirement but he became famous when as Lord Chief Justice, he gave the celebrated verdict in the case of James Somerset, a negro from Virginia, who had accompanied his owner, Charles Stewart, to England. Somerset ran away but was recaptured and the owner arranged to have him shipped to Jamaica to be sold there. Granville Sharp brought the case and argued that by setting foot in England, Somerset had become a free man. In 1772, Mansfield decided that no man in England could be a slave, and no slave who had set foot on English soil could be forced to leave England against his will. You may recall, Coleridge, Mansfield presided over the *Zong* case when the owners of the slave-ship *Zong* claimed under their insurance, the full value of 132 slaves who had been thrown overboard and deliberately drowned! Dysentery had broken out, many slaves had died and many more were sick and likely to die. The captain had decided to jettison the cargo of slaves so that the financial loss would not fall on the owners but could be claimed from the insurers! It was again Sharp who argued that the men who had thrown the negroes overboard should be brought to trial for murder. The Government took no action but the people were shocked and it marked the beginning of the campaign to abolish the slave trade. Mansfield is an old man now but I feel sure that he would be interested to meet the Boaten young men."

"What a splendid idea! These youths from West Africa should also meet William Blake, the engraver who has also composed fine poems. You remember how passionately he has written against the inhumanity of the Slave Trade and against the unbridled materialism of our time. I must also tell them of the work of my friend Thomas Clarkson who battled all his life against the iniquities of the trade in slaves and who died only a few years ago. Thank you, Gillman, for this evening."

"Good night, Coleridge. We shall keep in close touch with these two remarkable young men and help them all we can."

From this time forwards Moreton House was open to them; they were popular with the Gillman boys, Henry and James, who initiated them into the mysteries of the game of cricket and schoolboy slang; they worked with young John Williams on making a catalogue of medicinal plants, Dr. Gillman talked with them about medical problems while Coleridge questioned them unceasingly about Asante life and beliefs. And on one memorable afternoon they were taken to visit the old Lord Chief Justice Mansfield in Kenwood House, the beautiful and imposing, pillared mansion that looked like a classical Greek Temple.

"Is the Judge some kind of King, to live in such a palace?" asked Kwabena in astonishment.

"No. The Lord Chief Justice is one of the highest ranking judges in the English legal system but the house is privately owned," explained Gillman. They were received by a footman in livery and led into a huge tiled hall with wood-panelled walls and a curved, painted ceiling, and followed him up a wide staircase to a room on the first floor where His Lordship welcomed them cordially and waved them to seats. The boys remained standing out of politeness on which he remarked:

"They shall sit on each side of me on the sofa, then I can see and hear them clearly!"

They did not sit, however, until they had paid their respects to the Chief Justice and had shaken hands.

"You young men from West Africa should know, that by my decision over thirty years ago all slaves who set foot in British territory had the benefit of English law and ipso facto become automatically free men!" Kwame replied:

"Yes, Your Honour, we have been informed of that important decision, but we Asante have never been slaves. Our people have sold many people to the English traders as slaves in the past but now we must sell them to the Dutch and the Danes. My father, the Ashanti King, is quite unable to understand why the English no longer wish to trade in slaves. Since we left Kumasi the King of England has sent another officer, Mr. Dupuis, to confirm the decision."

"The English Parliament decided not to trade in slaves any longer because it was cruel and wrong to deprive human beings of their liberty, to sell them for profit like cattle and to force them to work on the plantations. We are now seeking to abolish slavery completely. What do you young men think about that? Let your friend answer," Lord Mansfield responded.

Kwabena felt uneasy; since they had seen the freed slaves in Freetown and had listened to their miserable stories, both he and Kwame had been forced to accept the fact that Ashanti was not the centre of the world and that all other human beings had a right to exist. But in Asante no one thought like that; all the other tribes were held to be inferior and it was accepted that it was the right of conquerers to enslave prisoners and others taken in a battle. It was also clear that other European nations still traded in slaves, like the Dutch, the Portuguese, the Spanish and the

Americans. A further reason for his uneasiness was that among his people such serious matters were never discussed; what the King and the Elders had decided was the law. How could he now possibly speak openly to a Lord? He glanced at Dr. Gillman who nodded and smiled reassuringly as if to say that he need have no anxiety and thus encouraged Kwabena answered: "Your Honour, excuse me to say, that my cousin and I have not had the time to study this matter and we are not yet able to make a proper judgment. There has been so much to learn since we left Africa to enter into the completely different European world that we dare not presume to reach a decision on such important issues. But we can say that since our stay in England we have come to value highly the opportunities in school in Highfield that have been given to us so that in such important matters like slavery we learn to examine the question from all sides!"

The Judge laughed appreciatively at Kwabena's reply.

"If this young man studies law, he will go far! The first rubric in law: reserve judgment until you have assembled all the facts!"

He beckoned to his footman who brought to him a leather pouch from which he took two coins and gave one to each of them with the words: "A golden guinea made from Guinea gold. It is worth 21 shillings but had been recently replaced by the sovereign worth only 20 shillings! Keep it in memory of your visit to an old English judge!"

They thanked him warmly and took their leave.

It was not long afterwards that fate struck the Bowdich family a terrible blow and which also deeply affected Kwame and Kwabena. On a cold, frosty afternoon in the middle of February 1824, as the cousins came home from school, they saw that the blinds had been drawn at all the windows although it was not yet dark and when they were in the hall there was complete silence in the house. They opened the sitting room door quietly where all the members of the family, David Morier and all the servants sitting together, the women crying and the men with a fatalistic, despairing look on their faces. Mr. Bowdich looked up as they entered and said in a distressed tone of voice: "My dear boys, our family and both of you have been dealt a terrible blow; our son Edward has been taken from us, he passed away from malarial fever in Gambia six weeks ago."

His face showed his deep distress as he handed the letter to them to read. It was from the Governor's office in Freetown and read:

Dear Mr. and Mrs. Bowdich,
I deeply regret to inform you that your son, Edward Bowdich, died on January 10th, 1824, near Bathurst in Gambia territory. He had been making surveys when he was stricken with malarial fever and was brought to the clinic in Bathurst but it was not possible to save his life. He was buried in the Christian cemetery according to the Church of England practice. Should you wish a memorial stone to be erected kindly write to me. All his personal effects have been laid in a packing case which has been dispatched to you.

All those who knew of him are saddened by his loss and we send our deepest condolences.

I remain, yours faithfully,
Acting Governor

They handed back the letter, shook hands with all the mourners and sat down miserably. What could they say? All those present felt utterly bereft: the Bowdiches had lost their only son, Eleanor and her infant had been deprived of husband and father, David Morier mourned his closest friend while they had had their English foster-father taken away from them. What comfort could there be? All during the following week they all, including the servants, went about their household duties silently, their thoughts on Edward whom they would never meet again in this life. On the Thursday, they assembled in the garden as they had done for his comrade, Henry Tedlie, and the boys from Africa said a prayer and poured libation in Asante fashion. Slowly, their mutual grief became less distressing and they were able to think of the future without Edward.

A week later, as they all sat round the dining table, the family solicitor read Edward's will: everything that he possessed was left to his wife Eleanor but in a codicil Edward had left his sextant, his silver pocket watch,microscope and all his books to Kwabena as well as gift of five guineas to both young men; his journals and manuscript of his book, *Mission to Ashantee*, were left to David Morier. David and Edward's father were executors of the will and they were bidden to have special regard for the future career of the Asante boys.

It seemed that the last letter that Edward had written had been to them and Mr. Bowdich asked:

"What had Edward written about his future plans?"

"Mainly to express his frustration that he had had no reply from Freetown," replied Kwabena.

"He had spent many months in Madeira and then in October he had taken a ship to Bathurst, Gambia, hoping to do some research there and to obtain a post in the government of Sierra Leone. But his letters to Freetown had either gone astray or had been ignored. He wrote in his letter that he was beginning to suspect that his wish to obtain a post in West Africa was being deliberately frustrated by someone."

"Who could that possibly be?" queried Mr. Bowdich.

"We think that the Under Secretary at the Colonial Office, a man called Joseph Dupuis, who was sent officially to Kumasi shortly after Edward's visit to abrogate the treaty that Edward had made and to make a fresh one with the Asantehene, is responsible. You remember that he told us of his cool reception at the Colonial Office by the Earl of Bathurst."

"Yes, Edward told me about that, it was a great disappointment for him because he had thought that after his achievement in Kumasi a place would be found for him in Government service. But his uncle had already intimated to me that the Secretary of State might resent the fact that a treaty had been entered into by the Company which had political consequences."

"But why should Dupuis have such an enmity against Edward?" Kwame asked.

"Because he felt that Edward had frustrated his own ambitious personal plans. It is clear to me now that the future presence of the British on the Coast after 1807 had long been debated; there was now very little trading profit and there was the threat of Asante control of Fante territory. The other factor was the fact that Sierra Leone had become a British Colony, there was an existing British government there.

I feel sure that tentative plans had already been made, possibly by Dupuis, and that was the reason why he was sent out to Kumasi so quickly after Edward had been there. But he had not reckoned with Hope Smith's determined opposition and his refusal to accept the new treaty that Dupuis had made. Don't forget that Governor Hope Smith was Edward's uncle so Dupuis suspected a personal motive. That is why he didn't want Edward in Sierra Leone at any price! It was part of his revenge!"

"Do you think, Sir, that Kwabena and I might be included in his revenge programme?"

"Yes, in so much that he has written a letter to the Company to say that the financial support for you will cease when you leave school. The letter was signed personally by him. I had not yet informed you of the fact because I wished to check first with Mr Hope Smith about future financial arrangements for you, but in any case, have no fear, you will be provided for; in my son's will he has asked David and me to look after you both and I know that Mr. Hope Smith will also help if necessary."

Joseph Dupuis' personal advancement was duly announced in the Gazette in the following year when he was appointed Comptroller of Accounts in the Crown Colony of Sierra Leone whose Governor had responsibility also for the Gold Coast forts. It represented for him an important step forward, it could mean that one day he could aspire to become Assistant Governor and later Governor. His forbears had left France when non-Catholics were forced into exile and thousands of Huguenots, as they were called, settled in the East End of London. His parents had prospered as timber importers and producers of high quality household furniture and had been able to send him to St. Paul's

School and to Cambridge University. He was the first in his family to enter the Government service and when he had been appointed to a clerkship at the Exchequer he had felt that he was on the first rung of a ladder to high office.

He possessed many advantages and good qualities: in appearance he looked to belong to the upper class of society; he was tall, dark-haired, an aquiline nose, high forehead and shrewd eyes, full lips and a prominent chin while he spoke with the accent of the ruling class. He dressed well but not showy and took pains to be agreeably respectful to his superiors. He had remained single because he felt that marriage and a family would interfere with his ambition but he had, in any case, a semi-permanent liaison with Sarah Ridley, a second cousin, who was teaching in a school in Chelsea and was betrothed by her family to a naval officer whom she disliked. Dupuis was hard-working, orderly and meticulous; his accounting was always correct and exact to the last halfpenny and whenever he was asked to comment, he did so with precision and pertinence. His overpowering ambition he took care to conceal. Now with his appointment as Comptroller in Sierra Leone he felt convinced that he was at last on his way to even greater advancement.

But the Government Gazette brought further news: in March 1824 was published the almost unbelievable dispatch that in the Gold Coast on January 21st British troops, commanded by the Governor, Sir Charles McCarthy, had been utterly defeated by an Asante army. He, and a number of officers, had been beheaded and their heads sent to Kumasi, a disastrous piece of news for the English! At the same time the additional information was given that the Asante King had passed away on the same day and that he had been succeeded by his young brother Osei Yaw Akoto. In class, the Asante boys were bombarded with questions by their classmates: "Why, if you are the King's son, will you not be made King?"

Kwame explained: "In Ashanti, succession to the stool goes in the female line, brother can succeed brother or nephew can succeed his uncle; none of the sons has any claim."

"Would your father have been in the battle at Nsamankow?"

"I don't know but I think he might have been ill. Normally he would be there with the stool and if the battle should be lost he would take his own life."

"If you had stayed at home would you have had to serve in the army?"

"Almost certainly because in time of war all the states in the federation had to send a contingent to the Ashanti army and we would have been in the Juaben group."

"What was the war about?"

"For a long time Asante people have resented the fact that they could not trade directly with the Europeans on the coast, the Fantis operated as middlemen and, of course, took a commission for doing so.Even the Europeans in their forts at Cape Coast and Elmina, had to deal through Fante agents although the Ashanti King held the rental notes for the forts. My father was delighted to have direct contact for the first time with Mr. Bowdich. The matter is not yet settled and the war will go on. If the Europeans want to continue to trade on the coast they will have to reckon in the future with Asante military power or else withdraw from the coast altogether."

That evening the cousins discussed the situation and Kwabena said: "We seem now to be completely isolated from Africa. I don't suppose that Osei Yaw Akoto will have any interest in us; the Bowdich treaty that sponsored us no longer applies, we have no news of my father or from our mothers. Is it possible that they have forgotten us?"

"Our mothers will have remembered but they cannot write, maybe no one could write for them and, in any case, who would deliver a letter to Cape Coast and arrange for it to be sent by ship to England? It is unlikely that we shall ever get a letter from Kumasi or from Juaben. Are you sorry, Kwabena, that you came to England?"

"No, emphatically No! Think of what we have learned and experienced. What would we be doing now if we had stayed in Juaben? In the army fighting the Fantis and the English!

By chance we are on the way to becoming well-educated black Englishmen with the ability to live in two worlds and to belong to neither! But if we go on studying perhaps we shall be able to return to Africa in a completely new role."

"Henry Tedlie told us that, you remember. If I return as a doctor and you as a lawyer we can then play a useful part in helping the transition forward in our country. I mean, the change by which we adopt ideas from Europe."

It was about this time that their life took a new turn: they were in the top class at school and it seemed certain that they would matriculate while at Moreton House they came increasingly under the influence of the poet and philosopher, S.T.Coleridge and of William Blake, poet and engraver. Coleridge had already met them in connection with the bullying affair, he loved to speak with young men but he found in Kwabena and Kwame a special interest not only because they came from the Guinea Coast and could speak at first hand about the burning question of slavery, but also because he could discuss with them the topic of 'natural' religion which fascinated him. He always questioned them with sympathy and humility and they found it stimulating to try to give a realistic account of the way in which Asante regarded the world in which they lived and their religious outlook. Coleridge asked them once:

"Do you have a belief in a supreme god?" and Kwabena explained:

"Yes. We all believe in *Nyame* but he's somewhat remote; my mother used to tell a tale of the first old woman, *Aberewa,* who, when she was pounding with the pestle, preparing food for the children, knocked against *Nyame* and in anger he withdrew farther away in the sky. So that our religion has more to do with ancestors and spirits. Some of these spirits are powerful and belong closely to our nation, like the Tano river and Lake Bosomtwe. Other spirits dwell in great rocks or trees and possess a shrine in the forest served by a priest and people go to him or her for advice and help in sickness and in adversity. The priest goes into a trance and utters 'explanations' which the assistant priest translates. The petitioners pay with eggs, fowls, goats, sheep or money. You see, Sir, for us Africans, the world is a spiritual arena; these powerful spirits can do good or bring disaster or misfortune; life for most of our people is insecure and full of unknown dangers and they try to get the help of the spirits. You have always to take care not to offend any of the powers in nature, large or small."

"How do you do that?" This time Kwame explained: "You must always enlist the co-operation of Mother Earth because she has the power to sustain or to destroy life, so that if you are getting the use of land or leasing it, or making a farm in the forest, or building a house, or digging a grave, or felling trees and using the wood for any purpose whatever, you must placate Mother Earth for the disturbance."

"How can you soothe the Earth Mother?" Coleridge questioned.

"We pour a libation of palm wine or strong drink onto the earth, then we sacrifice an animal, a fowl, a sheep or a goat and let the blood run out, and finally we invoke the Earth Spirit and pray for her consent ending with the words: 'We are addressing you, and you will understand.' In addition, as all plants and shrubs have souls you have to pacify them if you take them for medicinal purposes and you should make sure that their future growth is assured."

"How do you know that the Earth Mother has been placated?"

"We wait a short time and if nothing bad happens, we know that the Earth Mother or the ancestors are in agreement. In general, we have to be careful all the time to keep the taboos and traditional customs in the family when a child is born, when a girl first menstruates, when we marry and of course, when we die. Also at festival time or travelling or making a trading agreement with anyone. If you break any of these rules you can put yourself and your family in danger; we live in a spirit-filled world and when rules are broken the spirits can send misfortune or disater on all of us. It's like in your poem, 'The Ancient Mariner', about the old sailor killing the albatross for no reason, especially when the bird was guiding the ship through the ice and fog to safety but the crew had hung the bird from his neck. They all suffered from a terrible thirst and then a skeleton ship approaches on which the Death and the Death-in-Life Spirits are playing dice, and when the ship vanishes all the crew except the old mariner die and he is surrounded by rotting corpses. We really appreciated that story, Sir, our people would immediately understand it. Is the albatross a sacred bird among the English?"

"No. The crime of the mariner, which was followed by such disaster, was the wilful and wanton killing of a creature that was leading the ship to safety. Such cruelty and indifference makes the spirits weep. Where did you read the poem?"

"In class, Sir. We found Shakespeare and Milton difficult so Mr. Ferguson lent us a copy of the Lyrical Ballads that you wrote with Mr. Wordsworth."

"Which other poems in that book did you read?"

"We liked the one called 'Frost at Midnight' when you spoke to your son, and Wordsworth's 'The Idiot Boy,' the son of a poor peasant woman who made night-time adventures."

Coleridge was truly pleased that the Asante young men had been able to respond instinctively to the poems which fused ideas, thoughts and feelings in simple, imaginative language. He said with enthusiasm: "The next time we meet I am going to introduce you to William Blake who has written wonderful poems that will stir your hearts and minds."

In fact, Coleridge had only recently got to know Blake and to read his poems which had impressed him and he knew how much Blake would enjoy meeting the young men from Asante. Late one afternoon Blake arrived at Moreton House with a much-worn copy of his 'Songs of Innocence and Experience' which he offered to them and said:

"Here are poems for you to read and think about, but one of them is specially for you!"

William Blake was an elderly man but he possessed a vigorous and animated manner. Unlike Coleridge he was not a public figure; neither his poems nor his engravings had attracted much attention and at this time he was living in poverty with his wife Catherine in two small rooms in Fountain Court in the Strand in London. But Coleridge had instantly recognised that Blake shared many similar ideas with him, especially Blake's mystical view, expressed in symbol, of the opposing elements of good and bad in the world of nature and in man, but also Blake's radical opposition to the social evils of child labour in the cotton factories in the north of England, which he called 'Satanic mills', and his hatred of the black slave-system in the plantations. So, for both Coleridge and Blake, the opportunity to talk with Kwame and Kwabena was a challenge and a privilege; here were two well-educated Africans who could speak excellent English and who could clearly expound the beliefs and customary usages of their people. It was a unique chance to obtain, at first hand, an understanding of African religion and life-style, which was so different from the stereotyped utterances of many missionaries. They both became new 'fathers' to the Ashanti young men and until their deaths, Blake in 1827 and Coleridge in 1834, they did their utmost to further their careers.

Later, when they read some of Blake's poems together the cousins were caught up into a new thought-world: the English was deceptively easy but the meaning was profound because everything was symbolic, for example, the meekest and mildest domestic animal, the lamb, gives its name to Jesus, the Lamb of God. For example:

"Little Lamb, who made thee?
Little Lamb, I'll tell thee
He is called by thy name,
For He calls Himself a Lamb."

By contrast, the feared but beautiful tiger was created by the same God who made the lamb:

"Tiger! Tiger! burning bright, in the forests of the night,

What immortal hand or eye could frame thy fearful symmetry?
Did He who made the Lamb make thee?"

Everything in creation spoke of God's creative power:

"To see a World in a Grain of Sand and Heaven in a Wild
Flower".

Above all in his poems, Blake expressed his deepest sympathy
for all human beings who suffer in any way through no fault of
their own:

"Can I see another's woe, and not be in sorrow too?
Can I see a falling tear, and not feel my sorrow's share?"

But it was the poem called 'The Little Black Boy' that riveted
their attention. It began:

"My mother bore me in the southern wild,
And I am black, but O, my soul is white!
White as an angel is the English child,
But I am black, as if bereaved of light."

and continued to tell how his mother taught him that at death
all skin colour vanishes, so that now he is encouraged to say:

"And thus I say to little English boy,
When I from black and he from white cloud free,
And round the tent of God like lambs we joy,
I'll shade him from the heat till he can bear
To lean in joy upon our Father's knee;
And then I'll stand and stroke his silver hair,
And be like him, and he will then love me".

Kwabena and Kwame never forgot the discussions they had

afterwards with their two new mentors who with great skill, with their poems as a base, opened up new ways of thinking to them.

"What impressions have you gained from those of our poems that you have read?" they were asked, and they often took turns in replying and helping each other out.

"We were helped by Mr. Ferguson; for example, in the '*Ancient Mariner*' he told us to read the last few verses first and then we understood that wanton cruelty to any living creatures is hateful to God. We found it difficult to accept that a flying insect has the same value as a human being but we realised that if all living things are created by God then we must respect them."

"What did you think of the Tiger and the Lamb?" asked Blake.

"I never thought about this problem before," Kwabena spoke hesitantly, " but there are some beautiful animals which are always dangerous; they kill other creatures for food, they feed on blood and flesh; there are also other beautiful animals which feed on grass and leaves, which we human beings kill for food, like sheep and goats and antelopes. All living creatures feed on other living creatures too. So I think that our Creator must have allowed for that: he created both Lamb and Tiger; I mean, through all creation, plants, animals, human beings, there is this double aspect, some plants are thorny and poisonous, others are good to eat or make good medicine. Why the Creator made things like that I can't begin to think of an answer. When Jesus, as I understand it, called himself the Lamb of God, I think he did so because he allowed himself to be killed. But that is another problem!"

Kwame added: "In Ashanti our language is not written, but we have oral praise poetry performed for our kings and a lot of proverbs about the best way to behave and about God. One proverb speaks of the Death Spirit, it states, "The Creator god created Death and Death killed him!"

"What does that mean for your people?" enquired Blake.

"I think it means that everything created on earth, plants, animals and human beings must die; they can reproduce themselves, of course, but that is not creation. Creation by God is finished on this earth, the Death Spirit has taken the place of the Creator god."

"Do you think that death is the end of life?"

"On earth, yes. But the soul lives on in the unseen world where our ancestors are."

"Even the souls of people who have committed great crimes on earth?"

"It must be so, Sir. Death is a transition not a destruction, nobody is completely good or completely bad. What death brings to an end is our sojourn on this earth. In your beautiful story of the Little Black Boy you make it quite clear that after death blacks and whites rejoice together round God's golden tent. We don't know where that is but the proverb shows that the Creator god has left this earth probably in order to create life again elsewhere in the universe. That is how our people would explain this proverb. We seem to have a stronger belief in the next world than Europeans have."

Blake nodded as if in complete agreement. What never ceased to amaze him and his friends, Gillman and Coleridge, was the utterly sincere way in which these young Africans could relate to the poems.

"What did you think about the 'Sick Rose' verses?" It was Kwabena's turn again.

"We think that you mean that all beautiful things suffer from decay and death. The worm eats the rose away until it decays and dies. It is an example of all created life, even human life. When we are happy there is always some sadness with it and there is always sickness and pain and misfortune to trouble us. Without noticing it, we are moving towards bodily decay and death. Am I right, Sir?"

"Yes, of course, you are right. It is an example of what I call the 'opposing forces' in all created life. Tell me now, since your long stay in England, what have you learned about European religion? What do your people think about Christianity?" He turned to Kwame.

"Our people tend to think that the religion of the Europeans must be good because their god has given them so many things that we don't have like ships, guns, books, medicines, tools, clothing as well as knowledge of reading and writing, and that their god must be powerful. But most of the white men that we met in Africa did not seem to have much interest in religion or in the book they call the Bible, only a very few, like Mr Tedlie; all I know about European religion started with him."

"Who was he?"

"He was the surgeon who came to Kumasi with the Bowdich expedition and who unfortunately died on his return to Cape Coast. My father entrusted me to him. He read out of the Bible every day; he didn't ever get angry and swear at blacks, in fact, he liked Africans and got on well with them, he was modest and never regarded himself as superior. He treated sick people whether they were black or white, whether they paid him or not. We often went together in the bush looking for medicinal plants and he used to talk with me about his beliefs. My English was poor then but I learned quickly in Cape Coast and I understood most of what he said.

'He told me that everything about the Christian religion is in the Bible where Moses and many different men called prophets, had written down God's words, and later God had sent His own son, called Jesus Christ, to speak personally to people on earth his final message how exactly they should live and behave. That message is also written down in the Bible. But people didn't listen and they even killed Jesus on a cross yet he came alive again so people knew that everything that he had said and done was true. Since that time, all followers of Jesus Christ can have a personal relationship with God by professing their belief in him, they have a friend at God's court who pleads for them if they have broken any of God's laws, so God forgives them. All these forgiven people, called Christians, gather on a Sunday in a building called a church to pray and praise God. They then have to serve and love their fellow men. Tedlie said that if I became a Christian and studied to be a surgeon that would be pleasing to

God. The Europeans want to send people called missionaries to convert all Africans to this religion."

"Do you think that the missionaries will be successful ?"

"Yes, to some extent. Our people will accept the Christian religion just as many in the north have accepted Islam. A written book, like the Koran and the Bible, is a great argument, and the motivation to learn to read and write, is very strong. Yes, our people will accept the Christian religion but without giving up the parts of their own religion that they consider to be important."

"What will be most difficult for your people to accept?"

"It is hard to be certain but the aim of the missionaries seems to be to establish a new group separated from the main body of the people. Now no one ever contemplated such a step before; to separate yourself from your clan and tribe is unthinkable. Religion for us is a community affair, it has nothing to do with individual conversion to a different belief, so what I think will happen in Ashanti will be similar to what we saw in Cape Coast, namely that the separated Christian church will consist at first of outcasts from the community, like abandoned women and children, half-European bastards, detribalised slaves and prisoners of war; then, as soon as a proper school is organised some parents will accept baptism for one or two children so that later these children will get paid jobs with trading firms or with the ruling authority. If a chief became Christian then the whole tribe would convert, but then he would have to give up or modify some of the traditional customs which hold the nation together. The children coming out of the schools will form a kind of elite group within, but separated from the community."

These and similar discussions helped Kwame and Kwabena greatly not only to express traditional African life and thought but also better to appreciate and understand how Europeans formed their opinions and made decisions. In their own minds, the two worlds of Africa and Europe, so alien before, began to come together.

Chapter 3

London 1825–1835

*He who is tired of London, is tired of life; in London
is everything that life can offer".*
Dr. Samuel Johnson, 1709 – 1784.

There had been long and exciting discussions about the future of
the two young men from Asante during their last year at Highfield
School. The first problem to be settled was whether they should
return to Kumasi, and if they were to stay in England for further
study how this would be paid for. They had both performed
creditably in the Cambridge Matriculation examination and for
this reason the Free Grammar School had offered them both
the sum of 10 pounds a year; Mr. Bowdich, Edward's father
promised to pay for their board and lodging at college, while Dr.
Gillman, Coleridge and his close friend, Dr. J.H. Green, agreed
to take responsibility for their tuition costs. Neither Kwame nor
Kwabena had ever deviated from their desire to study medicine
and law respectively, now all that remained to be determined
was where this should take place. Dr.J.H.Green who had become
Professor of Anatomy at the Royal College of Surgeons in 1825,
sponsored Kwame to a studentship there, while, after a discussion
with Lord Mansfield, it was decided to enrol Kwabena at Lincoln's
Inn and then apprentice him to a lawyer who was a magistrate's
clerk so that he would gain a first-hand knowledge of English
legal practice and procedure.

These arrangements were the result of a letter to Mr. Hope
Smith from the Secretary of State for the Colonies informing him
that the stipend to the two Asante boys would cease and that they
should be returned to their own land. The Government would be
prepared to refund half of the costs of the passage. The letter was

signed by Joseph Dupuis and it was clear that his resentment against the boys had not ceased. Strong representations were made to Lord Bathurst, together with a personal letter from Lord Mansfield, that the young men should stay in England to complete their education and after some delay, the request had been granted. The Headmaster of the school, Mr. Forster, and Dr. Gillman took the responsibility of organising the finances and the courses of study, while William Blake begged for the privilege of looking after their welfare in London.

Kwame and Kwabena were delighted at this new turn in their fortunes; the prospect of a return to Asante at this stage had not been so agreeable.

"Why are they taking all this trouble over us?" asked Kwame one summer evening as they sat in the garden, and Kwabena replied: "It's difficult to say, I can only speculate."

"You're beginning to use 'Coleridge' words again! What's this word 'speculate' mean?"

"It means forming an opinion, guessing, if you like, when you don't have complete information. You ask me a question which I can only try partly to answer. We have been many years in England now and we have learned a lot but we really don't know for certain what motivates them. Think of Hardwick and his cronies with their hatred for us blacks, think of Dupuis who hates us because we were in the care of Edward Bowdich and Henry Tedlie, yet, at the same time, our classmates, our form master, our Headmaster and all the adults we know have treated us in a specially friendly way."

"That's what interests me, why have they been so kind to us? After all, we are foreigners and our two countries are at war or so it seems."

"Well, let me try to speculate. You know that there is a very strong movement among the English, led by evangelical Christians, who deplore slavery and want to abolish it. They feel ashamed that their countrymen have made a lot of money out of the Slave Trade so they made it illegal in 1807. That was what puzzled your father, he just could not understand why they had done that because other countries still trade in slaves. My point is, that the English, in general, want to atone for what they have done."

"Stop, Kwabena! You're using another word that I don't know."

"Atone means making repayment for doing wrong. The English now want to do something to show that they are sorry for what they have done to black Africans and they are kind to us for that reason. But I think that there is another reason: you remember what Mr Blake told us when we last met that there is in England two groups of people, the rich and the poor. Labourers on the land and factory workers have to work long hours for low wages, young children are forced to work in cotton mills and coal mines, while the aristocratic landowners and wealthy industrialists live in luxury. So there is resentment among the poor and downtrodden who want a better deal while people like our friends at Moreton House try to influence the government to do something for the poor. We black Africans belong to the class of poor and exploited people.My third reason is that the English have colonies all round the world and they are very tolerant of people of other races who accept the British way of life; who learn to speak English; who dress and behave like them, maybe even learn to play cricket and football!"

"You mean like we have done?"

"Exactly that. The skin colour then ceases to matter. What matters is that we have fitted into their world; we have profited by our schooling; we speak the English of educated people, our classmates call us 'good sports' not just because we can play rugby football and cricket.We have become Englishmen with black skins. They like us for that reason."

"But suppose we had not been so successful at school, would they have liked us?"

"Yes, of course. They would have found us jobs in domestic service; you remember the black man in livery at Lord Carnarvon's who was a kind of personal servant?"

Kwame was satisfied but not completely.

"I have a deeper problem: if we accept their kindness,and don't forget, our careers are going to cost a lot of money which we couldn't possibly repay, does that mean that from now on, we have decided to live our lives in future as Englishmen in England?"

"No. Can you forget your mother and your family and the life we lived in Asante? I can't. You see, Kwame, because we have learned to live successfully in the white man's world it doesn't mean that we shall never go back to our African world. What it does mean is that if and when we qualify in medicine and law we shall be able to return on our terms."

"What does that mean, 'on our terms'?"

"It means that we can seek a post in our country as a doctor or a lawyer like any European, like Mr. Tedlie or Mr. Bowdich, for example. We won't be returning to our former life in Kumasi or Juaben but we shall be able to meet our mothers and families again. That is my secret hope. And if we do that our friends will be pleased that we have returned to help our own people. The British have made a colony in Sierra Leone and I think that they will do the same in our country. But we have a lot of learning to do before then; it won't be easy living and studying in London but Mr. Blake will be there to help us."

A further letter from the Secretary of State for the Colonies requested their personal attendance to register formally as aliens and they were coldly received by Mr. Dupuis who had not yet left to take up his appointment in Sierra Leone. He regarded them with disdain:

"You seem to have gained new influential friends. You should know that I proposed that you should return to Africa; under the so-called treaty made by Mr. Bowdich, who, I understand, has died recently in the Gambia, a stay in England was never mentioned. You were to attend school in Cape Coast only but it seems that Mr. Bowdich and Mr. Tedlie thought otherwise. The Trading Company has been dissolved so that there are no funds available for your further studies but is seems that your new friends are prepared to support you. I was overruled in my decision to send you back to Kumasi and you have both been given permission to stay a further five years to complete your education. I have to inform you that this permission by His Majesty's Government means that if you break any of the laws of Britain you will be deported. You are now registered as aliens and you are to report each year on this date in person to this office. I was tempted to register you both as enemy aliens but it seems that war between Britain and Asante has never been declared, but I warn you that if the Asante army continues its depredations on the coast, Britain may be forced into military action. I am informed that the new Asante King, Osei Yaw Akoto, has sent messengers to talk about peace. Have you understood all that I have said?" He regarded them in an aggressive way as he waited for their reply. Both answered, 'Yes Sir,' and were dismissed by a wave of Dupuis' hand.

They left the interview utterly dismayed and not a little fearful to think that officially they were unfavourably regarded by the British government. They made their slow way down Whitehall and turned into the Silver Cross tavern whose sign boasted of its origin in 1674. A part of the tavern was divided into cubicles for semi-privacy and after ordering a brown ale and a steak and kidney pie each, they took their seats in one of them. They looked at each other ruefully and Kwame asked: "Why was Dupuis so hostile? I would have thought that with the death of Edward he would have lost his animosity".

"It could only mean that because Edward sponsored us he has transferred his hatred to us. Our success is a constant reminder to him that Edward forestalled him in Kumasi and held up his personal ambitions."

As Kwabena spoke, a tall man and a young woman took seats in a cubicle nearby. They were deep in conversation and occasionally their voices were raised in anger. They listened intently, the man's voice was that of Dupuis; he addressed his companion as 'Sarah' while she used his first name 'Joseph'. After about ten minutes argument Dupuis called to the waiter for the bill and they rose to leave; suddenly Dupuis caught sight of the Asante young men and asked them angrily: "What are you two doing here?"

"After our interview we came in for a pie and a drink, Sir."

"Did you hear us speaking together?"

With great presence of mind Kwabena answered:

"We could hear voices but not clearly above the general conversation and we could not understand. We were also deep in our own discussion."

The voice of Dupuis' partner was heard: 'I am waiting', and Dupuis hurriedly made his way with her out of the tavern. They breathed a great sigh of relief and Kwame said:

"That was clever when you said that we had heard voices but that we hadn't understood; but tell me, what had you in fact understood?"

"It was clear to me that she wanted him to marry her at once because she was expecting a child, but he refused because he would be going to Sierra Leone soon. His passage was already booked. In any case, women and children were not permitted there owing to the climate. What did you understand?"

"I think that he said that he would marry her on his return and then she asked him for money for the birth and to live on afterwards. Then he offered her one hundred pounds. There was something else that I didn't catch because she began to cry."

" I'm not sure but I thought that she was asking for a marriage contract. Whether he agreed or not I can't say. He said: "It's time to go", and stood up and spotted us. What shall we do? It seems that we really have an enemy in high places."

"I think we should tell Edward's father today exactly what happened; I would feel safer if he, as our guardian now, knew. If anything takes place later it would sound like a made-up tale on our part. Remember, if the British declare war on Asante, we become enemy aliens and could be deported or imprisoned so that our word would count for nothing. But if the incident is recalled by others, it will have more force. We shall just have to live with the fact that the British government does not look on us with favour." Kwabena nodded slowly in agreement.

They set off in a subdued mood along Whitehall through the crowded city of London in a general direction eastwards. Mr Bowdich had given them a sketch-plan, Charing Cross, Strand,

Fleet Street, visit St.Paul's Cathedral, then along Cannon Street and Tower Street to the Tower and from there they should take a cab to his office in West India Dock Road. They had all afternoon before them and for the first time they wandered along famous London streets that would later become familiar to them. But their first impressions of the biggest city in the world never left them. The streets were crowded, noisy and smelly: Charing Cross swarmed with people, all going and coming in different directions; the noise came from the wheels of waggons, carts, cabs and stage coaches on the cobblestones as well as from the cries of costermongers, street traders and from the people themselves; the smell rose from the heaps of horse-dung which were trampled into a patina everywhere except where a crossing-sweeper earned a few tips by sweeping the entrance to a tavern or a public building or a part of a street clear of dung.

"Is it a festival time because of the crowds?" queried Kwame.

"I don't think so. Most of the people are poorly dressed; in fact, some of them are in rags begging; I never thought that there would be such poor white folks to be seen, some of them without shoes. Only rich men and women seem to wear fine clothes and ride in carriages. We must ask William Blake if it's always like this in London. Let's go down to the river to see what it is like there."

They made their way across the Strand into an area of mean streets and alleyways, then descended the slippery black Hungerford Stairs to the Thames itself and stood on a small landing stage built above decaying wooden piles that rose out of the black oozy mud. The tide was on the ebb and they could see and smell the waste water flowing out from a row of dilapidated wooden buildings. Across the oily water, wherries and small craft plied busily; one ferry boat was clearly making its way to the landing stage on which they stood and they realised that they were under close observation both by the ferry boat passengers and by curious onlookers, mostly youths employed in the rope-yard nearby. One of the boys called out: "Here's a pair of niggers dressed as toffs!" and they all joined in hoots of laughter. It was time to return to the relative anonymity afforded by the bustle of the Strand and Fleet Street; ahead of them the huge dome of St. Paul's Cathedral loomed up through the haze which was their next objective.

Kwame asked: "Do you remember Mr. Ferguson telling the class about the Great Fire of London that took place in the 17th century when most of the city centre was burned down?"

"Yes. He read to us from the diary of Samuel Pepys who watched the fire from a boat on the Thames. Entire streets of houses went up in flames, churches, the Guildhall and the old St.Paul's Cathedral. The roof of the Cathedral fell down like cannon balls and the fire was so hot the leaden sheets melted in the streets around. People just seized what they could carry and fled to safety, more than 250,000 people were made homeless. The fire started in a bakery and after a dry summer the wooden houses burned like a forest fire in the dry season. It must have been terrible for those who lost their homes. There was a famous architect called Christopher Wren who designed and supervised the re-building of the new cathedral which took 35 years and during this period he built 50 other churches in the city."

They were standing on the pavement opposite the cathedral looking up at the huge dome when they were accosted by a friendly man in a long black gown:

"You are important visitors from overseas I presume; may I have the pleasure of showing you round our famous cathedral?"

They nodded agreement and he asked them:

"From what country might you be from?"

"From Asante, West Africa, Sir."

When he heard the word 'Ashanti' he looked surprised and said: "I have heard that that is a powerful African nation. How came you to London?"

Kwame told him about the Bowdich expedition and how they had been sent to be educated. "We are now in London to study medicine and my cousin will study law". He then queried: "Are you the high priest of this great temple?"

Their escort laughed delightedly.

"That's a good one! No, I'm just one of the ushers, the senior one."

"You are wearing a gown like a priest. What's an usher?"

"An usher in a big cathedral like this is a man who shows people to their places and keeps everything orderly. I mean if a service has begun visitors have to be quiet; sometimes I keep them standing at the door till the choir starts singing. Can't allow any noise during the service, can we? The gown I wear is to show that I'm an official of the cathedral but the priests wear different gowns; they call them cassocks and at some services they wear a white surplice, like a shirt with wide sleeves over the gown. As for the high priest, we call him bishop or archbishop, he's the top man; he wears a pointed hat called a mitre and carries a staff curled at the top like a shepherd's crook. Everyone calls him 'Lord.' Listen, I have an hour's break at midday which I usually spend over a pint of ale in the tavern round the corner near the school; if you will join me we can have a chat and afterwards I'll show you the main parts of the cathedral. A glass of port or Madeira will cost you threepence. I don't imagine that you are gin drinkers, that's cheaper. What do you drink in your country?"

"Well, mostly palm wine made from the sap of the palm tree; it ferments very quickly and can be intoxicating. It's the same palm tree that produces the oil nuts. On special occasions we drink imported rum and other spirits from Europe."

When they were seated at a table with a view of the east end of the cathedral Kwabena asked the usher, who insisted on being called William:

"Have you worked here in St.Paul's long?"

"Man and boy these forty years! It's not so well paid, you understand, but it's secure and there's no hassle."

Kwabena interrupted:"What's hassle, William?" "It means 'bother', 'trouble' from superiors who are always finding fault and complaining about what you do. Here, so long as you perform your duties well, they don't humbug you. Then I get time off like now, and beside wages, there's tips; from foreigners mostly and at big weddings and funerals. I don't suppose you could afford a silver tip, being students," he looked at them quizzically, "but the price of a pint is always welcome!"

"We'll think it over and if we are pleased with the tour we can afford sixpence," replied Kwabena with a smile.

"A tanner for the two of you, that's half a silver shilling! Generous and gentlemanly, I assure you; for that you'll get a good shilling's worth!"

William led them into the cathedral by the choir entrance, in front of the high altar to the entrance to the crypt. "We'll start at the bottom where the building began; there's a spacious cellar under the entire cathedral, all down here survived the Great Fire, here the silver treasures are kept: wine-cups or chalices, plates, dishes, jugs with handles, all centuries old dating from the Middle Ages and earlier. Then there are graves and memorials to former bishops and famous Englishmen but I want to show you especially the memorial to the builder of this present cathedral, Sir Christopher Wren. He started in 1675 and supervised the building for the next 35 years! Later, I'll show you under the dome the place where he used to sit, there's a tablet to his honour inscribed in Latin: *Si monumentum requiris, circumspice*. I know the words by heart. Do you know what it means?"

Kwabena replied without hesitation: "If you are looking for a memorial, look around you", and William nodded with satisfaction and said: "You really have been well-educated." They came up from the crypt and read some of the memorials on the walls of the transept including that of the famous Dr. Johnson who worked for eight years on his historic dictionary of the English language which became the supreme authority on the language.

"His monument is the language we are speaking today," William told them proudly. He asked them to stand directly and gaze upwards into the Dome: "There's a gallery inside and one outside that rests on pillars, from there we shall have a wonderful view over the city and the river Thames. Inside the Dome are eight well-known paintings on the walls from the life of St. Paul. It's a long climb up the stairs but well worth the effort."

Finally he led them to the west entrance.

"Just keep on walking along Cannon Street and straight on to Tower Street and the Tower. There's so much to see there that I advise you to visit it on another day. Just walk over Tower Bridge and back, then along the riverside, you should find the Bowdich office in Wapping without difficulty. I have taken a fancy to you two lads from Africa and I wish you both well. Remember, if ever you are in trouble, call on me anytime in St. Paul's." They shook hands and said 'Goodbye.' They truly felt that they had found a friend.

According to the instructions of Uncle George Bowdich, as they called him between themselves, they should take a cab from Tower Bridge to Poplar because the drivers all knew the merchants' warehouses and offices. "Just ask for a cab going east to the docks and tell the driver where you want to go," he had said. They were lucky, the second driver they asked offered to take them.

"Coach is full inside but you youngsters can ride with me on top. It'll cost you a tanner each but I'll take you right to the Bowdich place."

They clambered up and squeezed in beside the driver who lost no time in setting the horses in motion with a deft flick of the whip. He was a non-stop talker and as they rattled along he asked them where they came from and what their business was with the Bowdich firm, and then pointed out the various workshops they passed.

"Here along they build boats and ships and make everything a ship needs: the forges heat and shape iron into nails, bolts, hooks, hoists, pulleys, anchors, chains and metal rings; the rope-yards produce thick ropes from imported hemp; the timber yards are full of pine trees imported from the Baltic to be made into masts and spars; over there they are making canvas sails from flax; there are small and large boat-builders where you smell the black, thick, oily tar, the stuff they use to fill the joints between the wooden planks to keep the sea-water out."

He pulled the horses to a halt to let two passengers alight outside one boatyard and said:

"Now sniff the tar. Wherever the ships go, they carry that pong with them! Did you know that we call a sailor by the name Jack Tar; every ship has its tar supply for repairs and preserving the timber."

Kwabena asked: "Where are the boats and ships sold?"

"Usually in the boatyard, then you have to go to the chandler to get all the fittings and supplies. Large ships have to be pulled down a sloping platform into the river and then fitted out."

"Thank you for explaining all these things. You know, we had never seen the sea or travelled in a large ship until we sailed to England."

"If you have time, go and visit the Docks; you will see sailing ships from all over the world. Here you are now at your destination." He stopped to let them come down. Kwame gave him a silver shilling and they said 'Goodbye.'

On the way home to Hampstead with Uncle Bowdich they described their first day alone in London, beginning with their hostile reception by Under Secretary Dupuis. He expressed his regret: "It is a pity that Dupuis has transferred his animosity towards Edward to you two personally. He had high hopes of his own preferment and when he knew of the expedition of Mr. Hope Smith led by Edward he must have been furious. When the merchants lobbied the Government strongly against the proposal to abolish the Africa Company and to take over the forts we were always up against Dupuis and it seemed clear to me that the abolition held special prospects of his own personal promotion. The success of Edward and Henry Tedlie was a blow to his pride that he can never forgive nor forget. What we cannot change, we must accept. At least you are now offically in England for the next five years and much can change during that time; have no doubt that I and your sponsors will do all we can in your support. I have recently heard from Blake that he has found suitable lodgings for you in Covent Garden district within walking distance of Lincoln's Inn and the College of Surgeons. He is living in Lambeth so that you can meet easily. He is very fond of you both and he looks forward to showing you the many facets of London life."

Many of these facets they saw for themselves when they moved into lodgings in James Street, a so-called 'genteel' area, in a three-storey house of yellow brick where they had a room each in the attic space. From their windows they looked down on an almost endless procession of carts carrying vegetables and fruit to and from the Covent Garden Market, and at the rear was the Opera House in Bow Street.

"Is the street always so crowded with carts and people?" Kwame asked the landlady, Mrs. Shuttleworth, who was showing them around the house.

"Maybe you find it noisy after living in Hampstead but it's because of the fruit and vegetable market that begins at the end of the street. After dark it's quiet and up here with the windows shut maybe you won't hear much except for the chimes of the Savoy Church clock. At night there's a flickering gaslight at the corner; in Bow Street there's more gaslights and there are a few shops there, a baker's, a gin shop, an eating-house, a pawnbroker's."

"What's a pawnbroker?" they wanted to know.

"Maybe you have seen the sign of three golden balls hanging above your head? That's the pawnshop, they call it 'My Uncle', that's where you go when you're really down and out; all your money is finished maybe and all that you have left is something to sell like a watch, a necklace, a gold ring, books, clothes, anything of any value in good condition. You try to persuade the pawnbroker to give you a good price. Maybe you think that your watch is worth ten pounds, Uncle will offer you two, maybe three, and if you're starving you accept. Or maybe you'll go to another pawn shop to try to get a better price. He is lending you the money and you can buy it back within a month but if you don't he can sell it. There is always people looking in Uncle's window to see if there is anything good being offered cheap. Thieves bring stolen goods to 'Uncle', so don't go out wearing a valuable watch and chain."

Mrs. Betsy Shuttleworth was a middle-aged woman with black, greying hair parted in the middle, a pale complexion, shrewd grey eyes that gave her a capable expression, at first severe but softened by her ready smile and her sympathetic disposition. At first she had been reluctant to take 'coloured' people, as she called them, but she had been persuaded by Mr. Blake that they were well-bred and well-educated young men who were related to the Ashanti royal family. Payment of the rent was guaranteed and a cash deposit of ten pounds had already been paid. In fact, as soon as she had met her new tenants she had been intrigued by their courtesy and politeness, their command of the English language and their modesty. They were easy to talk to and not at all stand-offish; while she would feel more secure to have two young men on the top floor. They were good listeners and she found herself talking to them quite easily and looking forward to their company at breakfast which she laid for them on her kitchen table: a boiled egg, a penny cottage loaf, a small portion of jam and hot tea with milk and sugar. Later on, in the evening she would invite them into her kitchen and listen avidly to their day's news over a saveloy sausage, or a piece of cheese and a glass of wine. To her neighbour across the street she called them ' my African princes.' Quite soon she related to them her family story.

"My late husband was a master handloom weaver in Chipping Camden in the west of England who employed four other weavers who made beautiful herringbone Cotswold twill. I came also from a weaving family and we had our own stone-built cottage and workshop around a vegetable and flower garden. It was all orderly and peaceful: once a fortnight a middleman supplied us with yarn and took away the finished cloth on pack-horses to London for sale here. Then with the new machines, factories were started in the north, in Yorkshire. We went there once just to see how it was: the noise in the factory was awful, you couldn't hear yourself speak and the weavers were slaves to the looms. The shuttle flew across ten times as fast as we could by hand non-stop, producing in one day more than we could in a month maybe. So it was really the end of the weaving in the Cotswolds which had been carried on for centuries. So we talked it over: maybe it would be better if we sold up and started a shop in London selling quality cloth to the tailors. And that's what we did but after three years an epidemic of cholera spread from France and spread like wild-fire in London because of the contaminated Thames water. My husband died within two days and I was left a widow; my son took over the shop and helps me to pay off the loan for this house; I let the ground floor and the attic rooms and live in the middle."

"Where do all these people come from? There seem to be crowds everywhere in London."

"They come from the towns and villages in the country from all over Britain, Ireland, Scotland and Wales. They flock to London and to the new big towns and cities in the north because the life of a farm labourer in a tied cottage is miserable; farm workers are badly-paid, their houses are little better than hovels and they are subject to the petty tyrannies of the landowners and the gentry. The new machines have made many craftsmen in the villages and country towns unnecessary, I mean weavers like us, carpenters and joiners, potters, wainwrights and wheelwrights, they've all left the country towns and gone to London or to the new factory towns. A lot of the young men don't find a proper job and become thieves; all the houses of the poor people are overcrowded and filthy without water or drainage, what we call slums. That's why London is swarming with human beings who have no proper place to live and no proper job. Don't go out at night and during the day keep any valuables or money out of sight. You both are lucky to have good sponsors who pay your rent and for your studies and to have a respectable clean house like mine to live in." She looked at them with a motherly smile.

Suddenly Kwame disappeared and returned holding his silk kente-cloth which he held out for her to see.

"This is a sample of what our weavers in Ashanti can do; they mostly live in a town called Bonwere and only men are weavers. It is silk. Often our people unravel silk cloths from Europe to make the special patterns that we like which all have a special name. The narrow strips are sewn together to make a cover cloth."

He took off his jacket to show her how it was worn by men from the shoulder and by women as a wrap-around skirt. Mrs. Shuttleworth was delighted that her lodgers from Africa knew about hand-loom weaving and she marvelled at the fact that these so-called 'backward' people possessed such skills. It became a part of the bond of friendship that grew up between them. Each morning she made for them a breakfast of a boiled egg, a penny cottage loaf, a small portion of jam, with which they drank black tea with milk and sugar and which was laid out for them in her kitchen. In the evenings about 9 o'clock they met again for a small bun and milky tea over which they recounted their day's activities to her and they listened avidly to her anecdotes and information about life in the city, how the poor people existed in insanitary slums and squalor grossly overcrowded often victims of epidemics. It was a completely different London from their experience in Hampstead and in Highfield at school and at Moreton House, the contrast could not have been greater, as though there were two Englands, one for the rich and another for the poor!

Kwame had been informed to be early for his first day at Royal College of Surgeons, Professor Dawson desired a prompt start to the first Anatomy lesson so on the next Monday at 8.30 he presented himself at the main entrance in Portugal Street. The porter looked at him suspiciously and insisted on seeing his enrolment form, then told him: "Down the stairs, second door on the left, you'll know the room by the smell!"

It was gloomy half-way underground; he knocked tentatively at the door and when no one answered went inside. The porter was right, a sweetish stink rose from a brine tank in the middle of a long narrow room at one end of which was a line of chairs facing a podium and a lectern and at the other end were two rows of dissecting tables. At one side, lying on a wooden palette made of planks and resting on trestles was a naked male corpse partly covered by a white cloth. Above it, on the wall at each side of a window that let in some light on the dead body, were a copy of Rembrandt's famous painting , 'The Anatomy Lesson', and a large chart of the human body and its organs. Kwame recognised the Rembrandt from a copy in the laboratory at Moreton House. Nearby, dangling from a coat-hanger, was a human skeleton.

Bending over the corpse busily making notes was a figure in a long, white coat who looked up and said: " Good morning, you are the first arrival and I am busy preparing for our first lesson. Put your things on a chair and wait until nine o'clock."

He was a tall, well-built man with a beard, greying hair and a gruff voice but the tone was kind and Kwame was content to wait and observe his classmates as they arrived, all seven of them. No one dared to break the silence. Promptly at 9, Professor Dawson snapped his notebook shut, stood in front of the line of new students and announced: "Before we start dissecting, tell me your names; each one of you will have blank pages in my book for my reports on your progress. Now take your jackets off and put on one of the aprons hanging up there and roll your shirt-sleeves up. Anatomy is a strenuous business as you will soon discover. Then gather around the body over there, watch me and listen and make notes in your notebooks; I speak aloud to describe every movement exactly that I make. So your complete and dedicated attention is required. We haven't a corpse for each one of you but we have a new one that came in recently. This emaciated young man was found by the roadside in Holborn quite dead. There is no record of his name and no relatives have appeared to claim him, a tragedy only too often repeated in London. According to my post mortem he died of consumption. With this scalpel, a special surgeon's knife, sharper than a razor, note how I use it and hold it, I am opening this young man's thorax and I shall point out to you the major organs of the body as they are revealed. Make notes in your books." They crowded round so as to get a good view; two of the students retched and hurriedly left the room but came back determined to overcome their nausea. How could you become a surgeon otherwise if you can't bear the sights and smell of the inside of a human body? Towards the end of the lesson they had to repeat what they had seen, from the lungs and heart to the bladder, and then they were asked in turn: "What have we not discussed?" and elicited from them the bones, the blood vessels, sinews and muscles. It was Kwame who referred to the layers of the skin and gained a word of praise from the professor.

114

"This evening you will draw in your notebooks for me to see, a human body with all the organs that we have seen in place, and tomorrow morning you will select an organ from the brine tank and begin to learn to use a scalpel. Understood?."

All eight of them nodded and filed out of the room glad to breathe the fresh air and once outside they shook hands and introduced themselves over a penny loaf and a glass of ale in a nearby tavern. They were all strangers but he was the most strange. The first step of a class camaraderie was taken; the others were curious to know about Kwame and as he spoke with them he knew instinctively that they had accepted him as one of themselves. It was a good feeling and he never forgot his first day at Surgeon's College.

So it went on day after day, they were initiated by Professor Dawson, often with grim humour, thoroughly into the mysteries of the human body; they were taught to examine every square inch critically and exactly yet to treat the human body with respect and proper regard for its superb structure and organisation. "A corpse is the house from which the soul of the owner has finally taken leave", he would say if he detected signs of levity when they 'fished' in the brine tank with the long wooden hooked stick for parts of the body to dissect, many of which had been partially cut up by other students. Just before the end of term the body of a woman who had died in Islington Workhouse of puerperal fever after a still-birth was brought. She was described as a vagrant prostitute, homeless and nameless, explained the professor, another victim of our present-day society. "This body is important for us, first because it is female with its distinctive anatomical differences from ours which we must exactly learn, and secondly because she died of a fever that we know little or nothing about, a fever that causes the death of thousands of women every year. We know the symptoms of the fever but not the cause. That's the risk our womenfolk are prepared to take to bring us into the world."

At the end of the first term their notebooks and their laboratory work were assessed by the professor. He called out:

"Mr Kwame Boating come in" as Kwame stood nervously on the threshold of his study. That's how he pronounced his name, English-style, and then welcomed him with a smile.

"You have made a very good start to your studies, what made you want to become a surgeon?"

"In Africa I got to know Dr. Tedlie quite well and I helped him to collect specimens for his materia medica. Then in England in the home of Dr. Gillman I worked sometimes with his laboratory assistant: we dissected a rabbit and a large dog so I learned to use a scalpel and a lancet. When Dr. Tedlie unfortunately died he left his medical books and equipment to me, it was a kind of challenge to try to follow in his footsteps. In any case, I admired him enormously."

"What did he die of?"

"Chronic dysentery. He was in constant pain but he never allowed it to interfere with his duties, he was totally dedicated."

"Did he ever talk to you about the cause of his illness ?"

"Yes, Sir, he did, but my knowledge of English at that time wasn't good enough to understand all that he said. What I do remember is that he said that there were microbes that lived in animal and plant decaying waste-matter and could cause illness. He was always concerned that food was boiled or fried, water was boiled, fruits were peeled and the cook's hand were freshly washed and utensils clean. He was a Christian believer. He used to say that our souls fight against sin and death, our bodies against dirt and disease."

"Did you ever see Dr. Tedlie perform a surgical operation?"

"Only once. We were staying overnight in a village and two midwives sought his help with a peasant woman who was giving birth but the afterbirth wouldn't come away. He took some boiled drinking water and scrubbed his hands clean then he reached inside her with his right hand. What he did I don't know, there was much bleeding, then he cut the umbilical and afterwards washed his hands again. He told me on another occasion how he had amputated a Fante boy's leg when gangrene had set in after a fracture. He used a catheter on an elderly man to enable him to pass water and the court treasurer in Kumasi who was badly afflicted by inguinal hernia was much relieved when Dr. Tedlie applied a padded belt."

"Did the woman in childbirth recover alright?"

"Yes. The midwives were greatly impressed that he used his right hand only in treating the woman. Among our people, Sir, the left hand is unclean, it's the hand you use when you visit the latrine. At meals we use only the right hand and when you give anything to anyone, especially money or a gift you do so with the right hand. Of course, it was pure chance that he used his right hand, but they didn't know that. He thanked me afterwards for telling him. Weeks later when he was in Kumasi she came there with a baby boy on her back and a gift to show her gratitude."

"What was the gift?"

"She gave him a wood carving of an '*akuaba*', the black Asante doll, which she had carried because she wished to be blessed with children. Its long neck and round head would help her to bear a child like it, the women believe. It was precious to her, now he should have it, maybe his wife was childless."

"How did Dr. Tedlie react?".

"He thanked her and embraced her and when she had left he sent me after her with a golden guinea coin for the child. I explained to her that the fertility spirit had already helped his wife but that he was much moved by her gesture and that, if she wished, she could give the boy the name 'Henry'. That was the kind of man he was."

"How do your people deal with illnesses and accidents?"

"Near the towns and villages there are medicine men who live in the forest and who possess a knowledge of herbal remedies that have in them a stronger spirit than the illness spirit. They have a shrine also, dedicated to strong 'abosom' or spirits, like a great tree, a river, a lake or a mountain. In times of sickness and other troubles the priest of the shrine is consulted and in an ecstatic possession-fit he is able to reveal the reason and cure for the illness."

"Do the patients benefit?"

"Not always, but they feel better because they know that the bad spirit that caused the illness or the trouble is being fought against."

"What illnesses are the commonest?"

"Very common are ulcers on the face and arms and legs that just don't heal and grow larger; there are many skin diseases that cause constant itching and don't get better; also common are griping pains in the bowels, dysentery, malaria and venereal diseases."

"How are limb fractures dealt with?"

"No one tries to set the fracture or dislocation. The limb is bound up to a splint and if the patient is lucky, the fracture heals but leaves a disability, a shorter leg or a crooked arm. If he is unlucky he dies from gangrene." The professor regarded him with great interest: "Boaten, you are one of the best informed and motivated of this year's intake; I just want to encourage you to maintain your enthusiasm. If you are in difficulties at any time do not hesitate to come to me." Kwame made his way home in the gathering darkness with this word of praise going round in his mind. How lucky he was to have earned the regard of one of the important teachers in the college!

Kwabena's enrolment in Lincoln's Inn was a more formal affair. He made his way across to Kingsway to the large area of lawn and trees to the dignified buildings of the College, containing the legal offices and chambers of the leading lawyers and barristers in England. Suddenly he found himself in a totally different London: the atmosphere was hushed and quiet, groups of black-gowned figures with wigs on their heads stood conversing together and he was glad that Mr. Bowdich and his brother-in-law were there to meet him. At the sound of a bell they made their way to the Great Hall with its ceiling of huge, carved wooden beams, its walls clad with oak panelling and the coats of arms of distinguished members. Those to be enrolled were called out by name to stand in line and shake the hand of the President. They were then prayed over by the chaplain and given instructions. Having paid their fees, they were shown around by the usher: the Library, and the Black Books which held the records of the College since 1422. He had enrolled for four years during which time he had to pass certain essential courses before the Law Society would grant permission to sit for the Practising Certificate.It was a wonderful challenge that he faced and he felt stimulated by it; how fortunate he and Kwame had been to have the continued support of Mr. Bowdich and the people at Moreton House!

At weekends William Blake took charge of their leisure time and showed them the sights of the city.

"There are two Londons," he explained to them, "there is the London of fine buildings, palaces, churches and cathedrals, monuments and memorials, but there is the London of extreme poverty, of people who live in overcrowded slums, the city of Ragged Schools and debtors' prisons, of decaying ships on the river filled with criminal offenders awaiting trans-shipment to Australia."

Usually about 9.a.m. on a Saturday morning he called for them, a slight figure in a dark frayed suit. When he took off his hat you saw his grey hair, thinning on top, but he walked with a firm step in spite of his 66 years. A warm smile always accompanied his greeting.

"We're going to visit a special kind of school this morning," he announced as he led them through the alleys and slums of Saffron Hill. "It's a school for unwanted children and it's called a Ragged School because these children have no proper clothes and are wearing tattered rags. Most of them are without a family, utterly neglected and forsaken; many of them sleep at night under bridges and porticos, in outhouses or on staircases, many have nothing to eat or to drink, nowhere to wash, no home." They went up a flight of rickety stairs in a dilapidated house to three rooms swarming with unwashed, noisy children of all ages dressed in filthy rags sitting on the floor. The fetid smell was intense. As they stepped into the first room the noise suddenly stopped when the children saw Kwame and Kwabena. A man came forward to greet them: "I'm the teacher. This boy will speak for the class." He pointed to a tall boy who looked about 11 years old who stood up and said:

"I'm the class leader; the teacher is trying to learn us some letters so's we can read." He pointed to two posters hanging on the wall, one of the alphabet and the other the Ten Commandments and the Lord's Prayer. After that, in the next room we get a slice of bread and some soup. But we have to learn those words first." The teacher queried: "And who may you be?" Mr.Blake introduced them:

"They have come from West Africa also to learn in school."

The children had stood up and were pressing forwards to see the visitors from Africa more closely, even to touch their skin, but the teacher held them back, the stench of unwashed bodies was overpowering. They said 'Goodbye' and went into the next room where soup and bread were being prepared by an elderly woman who explained:

"Miss Angela Burdett-Coutts gives us the money for the rent and the food and a small fee for our services, the teacher is my son but we also have other helpers. You appreciate that there is little that we can do". Mr. Blake pressed five shillings in her hand and they thanked her for the visit and left. Now for the questions, thought Blake, and led the way to a nearby tavern.

Kwame started off: "Where have all these poverty-stricken children come from? You said that they had no families and were unwanted. With us, every child belongs somewhere."

"England is going through an intensive and rapid period of social change brought about by the invention of the steam engine and consequent industrialisation, we have an ever-increasing birth-rate, young people are leaving their traditional work on the farms and flocking to London and to the new industrial towns, crime is on the increase, housing and sanitation are lacking, sex is free-and-easy and many unwanted children are born, while the traditional social remedies in the parishes can't cope."

"Where are the normal schools? Shouldn't these destitute children be attending them?"

"The only other schools are organised by the Church of

England and by the Noncomformist churches and they receive no money from the Government so fees have to be paid. There are many private schools and old, established Grammar Schools, and schools for the children of well-to-do parents like Eton, Harrow, Winchester and Rugby but we have no national system of education in England. Many of our children are illiterate."

"Who is Miss Angela Burdett-Coutts?" was the next question.

"She is a very wealthy woman whose family owns a bank. She gives away much money to help the poor."

"Mr. Blake, why did you take us to see this Ragged School?" asked Kwame. "Normally we show visitors only the best, the things that we are most proud of not those that we are rather ashamed of."

"That's a very good question but it will take up some of our time to answer it. It has to do with my own philosophy of life: I hate injustice and cruelty of any kind especially when it is directed against oppressed groups that can't help themselves, like slaves and abandoned children. The factory system has caused the ruthless exploitation of young children; in my poem I refer to it as 'the dark Satanic mills'. I feel the presence of evil in human life everywhere and I think of Jesus as the man sent specially by God to make this fact absolutely clear to us. But still we don't learn: there are mill-owners who go to church regularly but who underpay their workers and who employ young children; there are slave-owners who call themselves 'christian' who are quite indifferent to the cruelties and miseries imposed on slaves. In one of my poems I wrote of the parents of the wretched boy who swept chimneys but who went to church to thank God! Coleridge shares my views: he hates the materialism of our time and the so-called science of Political Economy that refers to human beings as 'hands' and thinks of them only in terms of profit and loss. He wants social and political reform and a proper school system. We both have visionary hopes for mankind, that's why we write verse, why we use metaphors and symbols a lot because that's the only way you can speak about the spiritual world which is more important than the material world we live in now. My drawings and paintings that I have shown you are full of symbolism. All this is the main reason for the great pleasure it gives us to talk to you both, you come from so-called 'darkest Africa' but you are more conscious of your ties with the spiritual world than we are. We also want you to know about 'darkest England' and not to be over-impressed by our technical and scientific achievements. Of course, there are many impressive buildings to be seen in London: we have a very long history as a people and you can learn much from us, but there is the shady side of our life and history to know about as well so that you get an objective and balanced understanding. You see, in this period of our history, there has never been deeper unrest, hopelessness, and poverty among the common people; our prisons are so full that we have to put many of the prisoners in the holds of derelict ships on the river awaiting transport to Australia. I will show them to you another time. The rich grow richer and the poor poorer so that there are really two Englands to know about!"

"Why are the prisons so full?" Kwabena wanted to know. "Why are there so many criminals?"

"Because we have so many laws against theft, many of which carry the death penalty: you can be hanged for burning a house, a hayrick or poaching fish or game, or joining in a protest for better wages or conditions, you can be transported to Australia for minor theft like stealing foodstuffs or fruit and vegetables from private gardens or shops, like purloining articles of clothing or jewellery. Most of those convicted are men and women, unemployed, destitute drifters in the towns and cities. No one thinks of changing the law; now we have a torrent of criminality and no police force!"

It was the first of the many facets of darkest England that Blake took them to see. A few weeks later on the shore of the river Thames at Deptford they gazed on the hulks, as they were called, anchored fore and aft on the sluggish, grey, opaque water in lines; some were obsolete British warships, some were French cruisers taken in battle, some had grown old in trade and commerce. Now their pride and glory had gone, but they were all serving His Majesty as floating prisons full of convicts waiting in miserable conditions for their transport to Australia. Each convict had a 14-pound iron welded to his ankle and as they watched, a chain-gang of prisoners who had been working all day for the Royal Navy in the dockyard was being rowed back to their ship, they clambered awkwardly back on board. On the decks, bedding and washing were hung out on lines, there were makeshift huts and shelters everywhere which gave them the look of an open-air market. Blake explained:

"These old ships are completely full of convicts waiting for a passage to Australia, we are sending out about a thousand every year but the crime-rate doesn't drop. Some of them you saw in Freetown on your voyage to England. I am told that the assignment system works quite well: the convict works for a farmer for seven years and then, with a good record, he is given his freedom to stay in Australia or return to Britain. Only a few return, over 90% stay. What we don't like about the system is the harshness and cruel discipline by which it is carried out. It's a problem that we can't solve." Blake wondered if it had been worthwhile bringing them to Deptford; the fact that they had seen a transportation ship in Freetown had decided him. But, as usual, the cousins brought their minds to work on the issues.

"Who pays for the upkeep of the convicts in Australia?" was Kwabena's question.

"The farmer has to pay something but the Government pays most but they both profit from the labour of the convict."

"Why, after 7 years, do the great majority stay in Australia?"

"The main reason, I think, is the fact that Australia offers the chance of a fresh life far superior to the one they had in Britain: they can own land, build their own house and become farmers. Those with artisan skills are in great demand and can make a good living. All that is far better than returning to a life of penury and uncertainty. They have a chance to improve their position in society which they did not have in England although they have paid dearly for it."

The cousins accompanied William Blake back to the city and walked slowly and thoughtfully to their lodgings. As they made their way through the slums surrounding the Covent Garden area Kwabena remarked: "I'm sure that Mr. Blake is right to show us some of the seamy side of English life as it really is: I mean, here in London when you go west you see the elegant squares and crescents with trees and parks where the rich and well-to-do people live, but if you go east you walk through a maze of streets and narrow alleys of old and new houses, swarming with people and choked with all kinds of rubbish, offal and horse dung where the poor and destitute immigrants live. Here, the sewage flows sluggishly from the houses into open drains which really stink. There are no trees, no grass, no gardens. There is no water supply and no sanitation; the cellars must be full of rats. Look at that group over there feeding on a dead cat in daylight." He spoke with some distaste. I mention it only because the English have had a long history during which they have achieved much but what they haven't succeeded in doing is to control the worst effects of the technical revolution. It seems to me that the aristocracy and the rich merchants don't seem to care at all about the persons who work for them. They are cultured with a fine life-style some of which we have thankfully experienced. It's only persons like Henry Tedlie, Edward Bowdich, William Blake, Coleridge and others whom we have met who worry about the fact that half the population of the country live deprived lives in wretched conditions. While the prosperous half is drinking its sherry and Madeira and fine wines, the other half is finding forgetfulness in gin. There seems to be a gin-shop in every street, have you seen the price, a jugful for twopence!"

They were glad to return to the sobriety and cleanliness of their rooms and to hear the ever-welcoming voice of Mrs. Betsy Shuttleworth as she welcomed them and busied herself at once to put the kettle on for tea. With her permission they could now call her Aunt Betsy but when they had explained to her that in Ashanti when you addressed your mother you used the word 'Ena' she had preferred that and told her neighbours proudly:

"My African princes use the word for Queen Mother when they speak to me!"

"You know," remarked Kwabena sententiously, "we have seen a number of things on the shadowy side of English life but we have much more on the sunny side among our friends to be grateful for: the warm welcome everywhere, the kindness and the friendship."

And Kwame responded: "I think so too, and Ena is one of the best!"

Chapter 4

Coleridge's Seminar and other Episodes

"He alone is free and entitled to the name of a gentleman, who knows himself and walks in the light of his own consciousness."
Coleridge, Letters.

Some weeks later, Blake invited them to his home in Fountain Court, The Strand, where he lived with his wife Catherine. It was clear to them that their circumstances were poor but they were welcomed warmly by Blake and his wife, seemingly insensible to the plain simple furniture and decoration of their modest home where they had lived frugally for a long time; what mattered was Blake's poetry, his paintings and engravings. He explained to them: "My father kept a draper's shop and I had to learn the trade but all that I ever wanted to do was to draw and to write. At 14 I was apprenticed to James Basire, an engraver, and afterwards I was lucky enough to study at the Royal Academy. I earned mostly from engraving metal sheets for book illustrations but my mystical approach and symbolism were not popular and we never had money to spare. I got to know Coleridge through my poems; some of them I had made illustrations for; which he admired. When we talked together we found that we had many ideas in common and I have visited him a few times in Highfield where he lives with the Gillmans in Moreton House as you know. That's when he told me about you both. Come and see some of my pictures."

He led them into a room which was chock-full of drawings and paintings, on the walls, on a long trestle table, on shelves, everywhere. An easel stood in one corner to which he called their attention. "I finished that one last week. It will form the front cover of my next book about the future of Europe. I call him, The Ancient of Days after the figure described by Daniel in the Bible (Daniel 7,9-10). God used him in the creation of the world. The idea of the golden compasses I gained from Milton's "Paradise Lost". Those pictures of Job were inspired by the book in the Bible which I have also written a book about. Job suffered much in his life but he never lost his faith in God and was rewarded later in his life. Here he is with his loving daughters." They looked closely at the pictures: how Blake decorated the borders of the pictures and included quotations and often poems which he had composed. "You understand, I see everything in symbol: in my vision, imagination and reality are joined together. I try to show an underlying meaning in all my pictures and verses. That's why to express the deepest ideas we need symbols in pictures and words. You realise that we have a thought which is invisible and immaterial; we can only convey it in a word or a picture. God thought and then He spoke and things and human beings came into existence." He smiled at them half-apologetically and they hastened to reassure him that they had understood.

"I had almost forgotten, I have a letter for you both from Mr. Coleridge, it is addressed to The Royal Boaten Cousins from Ashanti!"

The missive was quite short and invited them to take part in his seminar which was now in its second successful year. Blake explained: "It meets in Professor Green's reception room in Lincoln's Inn Fields once a week on Fridays between noon and 4 pm. He has a group of students, young men, between the ages of 19 and 25. It is a privilege for you and I urge you to accept; Coleridge is the leading humanistic philosopher in England, he has wide knowledge of literature and history, and he possesses the gift of bringing it all together in a philosophy of life which he propounds in a persuasive, eloquent manner. He is acquainted personally with most of the poets and literary figures in Britain like Wordsworth, Southey, Lamb, Keats and Shelley. I think you should attend, there will be no fee to pay."

It was an opportunity of a lifetime for them and years later they realised that the lectures of Coleridge had moulded their thinking profoundly. There were always about a dozen or more young men present, once they met Keats, the poet, there, and in the first half of the period there was a discourse by Coleridge followed, after a pause, by general discussion of the topic. Coleridge was a speaker who could hold your attention completely: his theme unfolded effortlessly, cogent arguments clothed in superb English words and phrases that pulsed with meaning and insight. They did not always understand fully but they always grasped the ideas and their attention was always held. What did he speak about? In general, it was the way in which one could interpret the problems that were much discussed, like the so-called conflict between science and religion, like the way in which morality and religion belonged together, or why the evils in English society should be eliminated. It was a spiritual world in which they lived and the materialism of the present day was destroying human values. He could dramatise his theme with his voice and gesture, he could pause to make a pensive remark in a phrase that you remembered afterwards, and he could look directly at the members of his audience in turn, his facial expression a mixture of earnestness and energy as though he had specially singled you out! During the ensuing discussion, Kwame and Kwabena were, on occasion, called upon to speak to a theme and to express the African viewpoint and that was a real challenge! But they were listened to with surprise and wonder, first because they could speak fluently with the accent of educated Englishmen, and secondly, because they could explain African points of view objectively and persuasively. It was a novel and salutary experience for their fellow students, who, for the first time in their lives were confronted with a world-view out of darkest Africa!

All the time, during this period, their studies continued but Kwame, at Surgeons' College was faced with a tremendous work load. There were lectures to attend in Chemistry, Biology, Physiology and Botany; there were detailed lessons on children's illnesses, obstetrics, bone fractures, skin diseases as well as on the scourges of epidemics of typhus, cholera, tuberculosis, and puerperal fever, as well as on tropical infections like malaria, yellow fever, yaws and ulcers. There were poisons to learn about and new afflictions that affected coal miners, textile factory workers and slum dwellers. So much to learn and to commit to memory in such a short time! There were powders, pills, unguents and aperients, tinctures and medicines all with their special healing properties and safeguards!

Then one day when Kwabena came home later than usual he found Kwame alone in his room sitting with his head between his hands; all his medical instruments were scattered on the bed. He turned a face stricken with misery and despair towards his cousin: "I can't go on. I have to find another career!"

"Tell me, what has happened?"

"I just can't be a surgeon, Kwabena. They took us today to the cutting ward at St.Bartholomew's Hospital to witness an operation for the removal of a stone from the bladder. The patient had his legs and arms tied up tight with linen strips and four strong men held his body absolutely still. When the surgeon made the first incision with his scalpel the man screamed in an agony of pain until he fainted. It was terrible to hear him. You see, Kwabena, I just couldn't be a butcher like that. When a butcher cuts up an animal, the animal is dead and feels nothing, but when a surgeon cuts a human being he is alive and suffers torments! Look at the instruments we use. There they are on the bed: see that long, thin silver one, the itinerarium, that goes through the penis into the bladder to position the stone –that's when the patient started crying out in pain. That slender one with a blunt end lets you fiddle around till you find out the size of the stone. The catheter tube also goes into the bladder to help to drain off some of the blood and fluid while the pincers grip the stone so that you can pull it out. And all this time the patient is suffering torments. And the day before we were taken to an operating theatre near St.Thomas's Hospital, the room was upstairs and the light came from roof windows. There were raised viewing stands round a wooden table where we stood to watch the surgeon cutting off a leg below the knee. A leather tourniquet was buckled tight round his thigh, then the surgeon took a razor-sharp knife curved like a sickle and sliced through the flesh in circular sweeps, then he had to saw and hack through the bone. The male patient was shrieking in agony but the men round him held quite still, then he seemed to faint. At the end the bone stump was covered with some of the remaining skin and sewn up."

He lowered his head into his hands again as if to shut out the sight and Kwabena put his arm round his shoulders:

"Kwame, listen to me. You are training to be a healer like Henry Tedlie, and sometimes he had to cause people pain to make them well again, often to save their lives. Think of that boy whose hand was crushed and he had to cut two fingers off because gangrene had set in; think of your grandfather who couldn't pass water until Henry probed through his penis with the catheter; remember that woman whose baby was delivered through a hole cut in her abdomen; remember the elder for whom he cut out that terrible swelling in his belly. All these people were already in great pain, they knew that it would be even more painful to be cured of the pain, so they endured it and were deeply grateful to Henry afterwards.

When Henry gave you his instruments he knew that you, like him, felt sorry when you saw anyone suffer but he also knew that to heal them you sometimes had to use the scalpel and the blood had to flow in order to heal them. And if they fainted from the pain, it was nature's way of dealing with the situation."

Kwame seemed somewhat comforted but not entirely:

"But if only we had something to make the patient unconscious to start with! Even a cut with a scalpel hurts, there's blood and mucus everywhere, we have to work fast knowing that the longer we take, the more pain we give, and afterwards we have to stitch the wound together again; it all takes time and the poor patient is half-dead already! Sometimes we can give the patient a soporific like laudanum or give them a strong drink like gin, rum, brandy or whiskey before the operation but not with children and not with bladder removals."

"Don't forget that people know what pain is. Think of all those who have earache, or toothache, or headache, or backache, or bellyache, sometimes continuously, or pain in the limbs. Pain tells us that something is out of order, the doctor didn't cause it," Kwabena responded.

At that point, Mrs.Betsy Shuttleworth tip-toed in; the door had been half-open and she had sensed that something was wrong as they had not come down for their supper. She had heard Kwabena's last words, her glance took in the surgical instruments on the bed and sensed that Kwame was upset. Kwabena quickly explained: "Kwame is feeling unsure about becoming a surgeon."

Betsy addressed Kwame directly and said:

"Mr. Kwame, you have seen our neighbour who has only one arm. His arm was crushed when an overloaded dray collapsed and fell on him and became gangrenous. He would have died if the surgeon had not cut his arm off; now he is full of life again." She bade him stand up and folded him in her arms as his mother would have done, and said:

"You will become a fine doctor and surgeon and we shall be proud of you." That was the medicine Kwame needed; he turned a grateful face to her, kissed her on the cheek and said:

"Now let's go and have our supper!"

It was a turning-point in their relationship: they had already begun to call her Ena or even Aunt Betsy and now they insisted that she used their birthday names. She had been instinctively aware that they had missed their mothers' love and she would be as good a foster-mother as she could!. They were her African princes and she would love them as her own! Kwabena's troubles were of a different sort: at Lincoln's Inn there was a long series of separate courses to attend, a mountain of books to read and digest, and each term there were examinations or viva voce tests to pass. A specific number of passes was required to qualify as a licensed lawyer; it could take you years to qualify but he was guided by Edward's uncle, former Governor Hope Smith, who arranged for him to be seconded during vacation periods to the magistrate's clerk at Southwark. Kwabena was also helped by a firm of Proctors who sent him from time to time to Doctor's Commons where a series of Law Courts met. There he learned how law suits were presented and decided. Sometimes English Law seemed to him to be so complicated and even absurd that he felt like giving up but he was always strengthened by the thought that Edward Bowdich had had confidence in him.

One day, on his way back on foot from Southwark he stopped for a pie and a drink at the tavern near St.Paul's School. He sat on a bench outside when, to his surprise, he was joined by two youths and a boy who held his arms fast while the boy with great skill took out the contents of his pockets, about ten shillings in coins and the silver watch and chain that Edward had left to him in his will. No word was spoken; the two released him and all three sped quickly away. It was useless to cry out for help, not another person was in sight. Then it occurred to him: he was near St.Paul's Cathedral and the usher, William, had promised his help if they met any difficulty. He ran round to the main entrance where William at once spotted him and greeted him warmly. Kwabena blurted out: "William! I've just this moment been robbed by three young thieves!"

"What have they taken?"

"About ten shillings in money, but what is more important is my silver pocket watch left to me by Edward Bowdich."

"Can you identify the thieves and the watch?

"Yes: the watch was made by Ward, London, and is engraved inside the case with the name: Edward Bowdich and the silver hallmark. There were two young men about twenty years old, one had a gap in his front teeth, the other had lost the little finger of his left hand, the boy, about ten years old had ginger hair and walked with a limp."

William smiled and said: "Very good observation! I think the chances are good that you will get your watch back. Are you prepared to pay a reward? You see, in London we have, unfortunately, an underworld; there are thousands living off crime: thieves, pickpockets, muggers, forgers and beggars. It's cash they want or anything that they can quickly turn into cash like watches, clocks, jewellery. There are pawnbrokers who are 'fences', that means, they are prepared to accept stolen goods. Now, the magistrates offer rewards for information about criminals so we have a lot of 'narks', that means people who collect rewards for information about wrongdoers. They sometimes take bribes from criminals for not informing! What I will do is to pass the word around. Often someone from the underworld comes in here to rest or to hide or to meet cronies."

"What will you tell them?"

"I will tell them that the King of England is hopping mad that a son of the King of Asante has been robbed and that if the watch isn't returned he will send soldiers after the robbers. Naturally, I will mention a reward. I think that we might find the watch in a pawnshop near by. I can't promise anything but come back to me here in a week's time."

Kwabena shook William's hand and left somewhat comforted. But he still felt bereft: the watch had become his talisman because it reminded him of Edward as nothing else did, each time he checked on the time he was conscious of Edward looking over his shoulder. A week later William had no news for him but the following week he received him with a broad smile, fished into the capacious pocket of his gown and brought out the watch and chain wrapped in a handkerchief which he handed over in triumph to Kwabena.

"It worked, you see. The underworld grape-vine worked!"

"Where was it found?"

"Like I said, in a nearby pawnshop. They had lost no time. 'Uncle' himself brought it in to me! It cost me a few bob but I had to give him something, in the underworld it's all tit-for-tat and quid pro quo!" Kwabena was so overcome with joy that he pressed two half-crowns into William's palm who protested that it was more than enough.

"It was a pleasure for me to be able to help you, I knew that you were genuine when we first met. You and your brother will go far. Don't forget, I'm always here!"

Then, in the spring of the following year, an epidemic of

cholera broke out, people, young and old, were dying like flies and one evening Kwabena was caught in its insatiable clutch. Not many days previously Kwame had been studying the disease and its symptoms, the watery stools and vomiting that so deplete the body of water and cause death within two days. Somewhere Kwabena had drunk contaminated water and the bacteria had invaded. He gave him boiled water and tea to drink, as much as he could, the fever set in and he asked Aunt Betsy to call a cab, wrapped Kwabena in blankets and drove him to Guy's Hospital in Southwark. He had worked there as a student and he knew that there Kwabena would receive the best possible treatment. A message was sent to Mr. Bowdich and to Mr. Hope Smith while he and Betsy sat continuously by his bedside. For two days he hovered between life and death but on the third day the physician spoke positively: "His strong body and his stamina will pull him through." But still they watched and waited in turns until the day came when Kwabena sat up in bed and said: "I think I must have been really ill!" And they assured him that it had been really so.

When they were all back home again, the following Sunday morning Aunt Betsy invited them to accompany her to church to give thanks to God for Kwabena's recovery. The church was quite near, it was called St.Giles in the Fields and was the centre of a parish of the Church of England. At the end of the service the minister shook the hands of members of the congregation as they left and expressed interest in his visitors from Africa whereupon Betsy invited him to call on them. His visit during the following week led to a number of discussions during which he suggested that they should be baptised and be received into membership of the church. They asked: "Is it not possible to be a member of the church without baptism?" The minister replied;

"No; it's the outward and visible sign of belonging to the fellowship of those who believe in Jesus Christ. From all that you have told me of yourselves I think that you could take this first step. Jesus himself was baptised by John the Baptist."

They discussed the matter between themselves:

"Henry was a Christian, he told me that he belonged to the

Wesleyan Church which was founded by John Wesley who was a minister of the Church of England. Henry was very pious, he tried to read something from the Bible every day. I'm not sure if I could do that," said Kwame.

Kwabena replied in his usual pragmatic manner:

"Edward was not so pious but I think that he was like most English folk who just accept Christianity as the official religion of the country. It is the religion of the King after all. If we join the Church of England it may be an advantage to us in the future; it is the established church, all the others are called noncomformist churches. Edward was married in the Church of England and was buried according to its ritual." That was how, one Sunday morning, they stood before the large font in the church accompanied by their godparents Mrs. Betsy Shuttleworth and Mr. T. Bowdich. The minister sprinkled water on their heads and blessed them with their new Chistian names, Kwame Henry and Kwabena Edward! Then they all knelt and repeated the 'Our Father' prayer.

"Our mothers would have been intrigued to see us today being baptised and getting English first-names. Something like our 'naming ceremony' of babies on the eighth day, only for adults." Kwame said.

Back at the house, they asked 'Uncle' Bowdich if there was any news from the Gold Coast, occasionally bits of information trickled through from the Government Gazette or from Mr. Hope Smith.

"There is nothing personal. You know that the new Asante King, Osei Yaw Akoto, sent messengers to Cape Coast to discuss peace terms and that the Asante army returned to Kumasi. The dispute is still continuing between Kumasi and Juaben, it seems to be almost like civil war." Kwame asked:

"Are they still feuding about the gold that Juaben warriors took from the Denkyira chief, Ntim Gyakari, at the battle of Feyiase? The Juabens will never give that up to Kumasi even if it comes to open war. In our time it seemed as though the two chiefs had become reconciled about the matter but our mothers were always uneasy."

"It seems so. The latest news is that the Ashantis are also preparing for war against Accra but no one is sure what will happen." With that they had to be content.

Kwame's final year at Surgeon's College was hectic. He still had three classes to pass before he could apply for his diploma to practise as a surgeon but he had succeeded so far so well that no one doubted that he would achieve his aim. In fact, it seemed that a post was waiting for him! One day Dr. Gillman came to see Kwame at the College and lost no time in coming to the reason for his visit: "After you qualify how would you like to work in Sierra Leone? You know about the famous judgment of Lord Mansfield in 1772 that a slave in England could not be deported or sold against his will; in effect, he was a free person. Mr. Granville Sharp had done much to provide Lord Mansfield with evidence and after the decision he came up with the plan of buying a 20 square mile plot of land from the Temne Chief and vesting it in the Crown so that it became British territory. The town called Freetown was begun and any slaves who landed there were automatically free. At first there were blacks from England and from the American colonies. You can imagine that there were many problems but when the British Government took over, Sierra Leone began to flourish. Now Sir T.F. Buxton, the M.P. and President of the powerful Anti-Slavery Society together with William Wilberforce M.P. are working hard to get Parliament to agree to complete abolition of slavery in British territories, I hope quite soon. Sir T. F. Buxton has a special interest in Sierra Leone and he would like to meet you. My second point is that the first West African doctor to be trained in Europe, Dr John Macaulay Wilson, has practised in Sierra Leone for the past two years. He desperately needs help and has written to me and I thought immediately of you, Kwame. Think it over. If you went there you would, of course, be officially appointed by the Government; we would apply for British citizenship for you. It seems also possible that the Gold Coast could well become British sometime in the future and that would open the way for you to return there at any time."

"Thank you for telling me of this possibility; please give me a little time to think it over and to discuss it with my cousin and with Mr.Bowdich." It really was an enticing prospect, mused Kwame, wasn't it time now to return to Africa, to the world where he belonged by birth? And if he couldn't get to the Gold Coast for a few years he would have made a start in his career and have established himself. In any case, there was simply no word from Ashanti or Juaben; when he did return home he needed some definite information. First, he had to talk it over with Kwabena and then with Uncle Bowdich.

When Kwame did so, they were both in favour, and when he talked to Sir Fowell Buxton he was deeply impressed by his plan for Africa.

"The Slave Trade has treated Africa shamefully and while we in Britain have abolished the trade, it still goes on. My committee is working hard to get Parliament to abolish slavery altogether in British territories and I think that might come quite soon. What is needed in Africa is to establish centres like Freetown where agriculture and commerce can develop, where there can be good schools and hospitals, and where missionaries can work. Above all, until this slavery business is wiped out, there must be centres like that where freed slaves can live and work, even if they can't get back to their own land. Such centres would have the support of the British government which would seek the co-operation of local chiefs. We've made a good start in Freetown but we need people like you with special skills. You could play an important role, not only in treating the sick but in health planning like hygiene, water supply, import of medicines from Europe, training of nurses, and so on."

Kwame accepted but he also mentioned his cousin who would soon qualify as a lawyer at Lincoln's Inn, and Buxton laughed with pleasure:

"There will be an important role for him to play in Jamaica! I think that total abolition will come soon but we are having a problem there with all the legal details.Our lawyers and the Government lawyers are working together but the planters are demanding compensation for losing their slave labour as well as firm rules as to how the slaves will be treated after they are declared to be free. What we shall need is a lawyer in Jamaica who will be a central figure in interpreting the law in the transition period. Tell your cousin to think it over!"

When Mr. Bowdich was informed he took the view that it would be preferable for Kwabena to go to Jamaica not as a paid servant of the Anti-Slavery Society but as an independent person. Some time ago he had been approached by a planter, Mr Jeremy Curtis who owned two plantations in Jamaica producing cane-sugar, cotton and tobacco which over a long period he had exported to England through the firm of Bowdich. Now he wished to retire to England and he had asked Mr Bowdich to help him to find a suitable person as overseer of the estates, the salary would be appropriate and the overseer would have full use of the Curtis house. Bowdich had put forward the name of an experienced man, by name, John Foreman, who had worked in Barbados and had been working there for two years successfully. Now, in view of the impending changes Foreman had written for help with the stewarding and the management of the estates. It was then that Mr Bowdich had had the idea of proposing Kwabena as Foreman's colleague, an African with a diploma from Lincoln's Inn and a Licence to practise English Law! A meeting was arranged between Kwabena and Mr Curtis and the post was offered and accepted. As soon as Kwabena was qualified he would sail to Jamaica! Sir Fowell Buxton was delighted and promised the full support of the Anti-Slavery Society. So it was that the stage was set for the next important episode in their lives, in Freetown, now the home of thousands of freed slaves, and in the island of Jamaica where it seemed that soon all the slaves on the plantations would be declared free. It was clear to both of them that a parting was inevitable; they both had careers to make and thanks to their sponsors the posts were demanding and worthwhile.

A passage from Liverpool had been booked for Kwame at the end of the year 1828 and in November Uncle Bowdich had invited them for the weekend during which he joyfully informed them: "I have some important news from the Gold Coast to tell you! There has been a big battle near Dodowa not far from Accra between an Ashanti army of 10,000 men and allied forces from Accra, Fanti, Akim, Denkyira together with a British group of about 100, altogether also about 10,000. The battle lasted all day and the allies were hard pressed but finally the Asante were defeated. A fresh British Governor has been appointed, Sir Neil Campbell, with the main task of making a firm peace with Ashanti, but the matter has taken so long that the British Government has decided to give the forts back to a Company of Merchants! The Company has to set up a Legislative Council to work with the Fanti and Accra chiefs to develop trade and commerce, it has to open a school in Cape Coast and keep the peace all along the coast. There will be a grant of 4000 pounds a year for this work. The Committee has already elected a Captain George Maclean as the new Governor and he will take office in Cape Coast next year. So after all, the Company comes out of all the debate quite well. I think that the developments in Sierra Leone have helped and I'm sure that everyone in the Gold Coast desires peace. It is not yet clear how the Asantehene and his people will react to the new situation but the new Company has, for the first time, a decisive social role to play on the Coast."

Chapter 5

Freetown, Sierra Leone 1835

"—with all its defects, if anything has been done for the benefit of western Africa, it has been there. The only glimmers of civilisation; the only attempt at legitimate commerce; the only prosecution, however faint, of agriculture, are to be found in Sierra Leone — And there alone the Slave Trade has been in any degree arrested."
Buxton, The African Slave Trade and its Remedy,
London, 1840, p.365.

The voyage from Liverpool had been uneventful and late in the afternoon the ship had entered the commodious harbour of Freetown. By the time the anchor had been dropped, the sun had set and disembarkation and unloading would take place in the morning. Overnight the penetrating cold chill of a European winter had given way to the all-pervading humid warmth of Africa and as Kwame looked over the rail at sunrise he had a feeling of sadness and déjà vu: it was just here that Edward, with his usual exuberance had once again demonstrated his sextant and had told them about the founding of Freetown. It was as though fate had taken a hand to the extent that he was now retracing his steps! Maybe the same destiny would bring him again to Juaben!

He gazed at the figures on the landing back stage, there were one or two whites but otherwise he saw only Africans, he was truly back in Africa again! The sun rose quickly higher and the mist cleared: nothing seemed to have changed much in the past ten years; there were more houses and buildings leading up the hill from the quay, there was a new red-roofed building with a spire, that must be the mission church that he had heard about. Now the passengers could go ashore and as he landed eager hands reached out for his baggage and there was Dr. John Macaulay

Wilson to give him a welcome in a cheerful voice: "I have a cart to take your stuff up to my house and we can walk alongside. You'll stay with me until we decide on your own quarters. I can't tell you how glad I am that at last you are here." He shook Kwame's hand warmly. As they walked, Kwame noted many changes from his former brief visit: many of the houses were built of stone; there were many more shops, stores and taverns, more wide streets had been laid out; there were new government buildings and colonial-style houses with large gardens and everywhere an air of activity and bustle was evident. It seemed that Freetown was developing fast.

When they were sitting over a drink on the shaded veranda of his house they were both full of questions. Dr. Wilson radiated friendliness and warmth, a smile hovered always on his lips and he spoke in a quiet, modest manner that commended him at once to Kwame. He asked innumerable questions about the medical training at Surgeon's Hall and if there was anything specially new in the medical field. And in turn, he put Kwame in the picture about the health situation in Freetown and what his duties would entail. Kwame asked: "How do I communicate with my patients, most of the languages of Africa must be present in Freetown?"

"The common lingua franca is called pidgin, it's a variant of Krio; that is the name given to the world-wide slang in the ports that was spoken by traders and the local people in all the large ports on the trade routes of the world pioneered by the Spanish, the Portuguese, the Dutch and the English. Pidgin has the flavour of the language of these countries as well as some local words; it was the only way of making contact. Here in Freetown it has a basic English flavour because the first inhabitants came from England and the USA and many of the freed slaves also had some experience of pidgin. You'll soon pick it up and of course you use gestures as well. For example, here is a man with abdominal pain who says: 'Belly pain me bad proper;' the word 'proper' is intensive. Or if he is constipated he tells you: 'Me no fit shit in latrine.' There are many nice phrases which we use: You give someone a letter to be delivered to the Governor's Office you say:

'You savvy dis paper, you take im go give big white man past all he live for top. Wat he give you bring my side one time, savvy?' They laughed together.

"You'll enjoy it. In any case there's always a nurse to help you in consultations. Incidentally, the Finance Officer, Mr. Dupuis, knows about you. He's called the Comptroller and was appointed in 1826 just before I arrived. He seems to have put the colony's finances in order and to be a good organiser. He mentioned your appointment to me and didn't seem too pleased. Have you had any previous dealings with him?"

"Yes. I should explain to you that ten years ago Mr. Edward Bowdich, a writer at Cape Coast Castle, was the first white man to lead an expedition to the Asantehene, my father. A Treaty of friendship and co-operation was signed by the chiefs of Asante and Juaben and Bowdich, and as a pledge of their sincerity I and my cousin, Kwabena Boaten, were entrusted to Bowdich and the surgeon, Henry Tedlie, to be educated at Cape Coast Castle. The Asantehene assumed that the Treaty was between himself and the British Government but in fact Bowdich was only the representative of the African Company. Now, at that time, Mr. Joseph Dupuis, was Under Secretary of State for the Colonies and he had high ambitions for himself. He foresaw that if and when the African Company in the Gold Coast was abolished and the British took over it might lead to promotion for him. He got himself appointed as His Majesty's Consul and Envoy for Asante, went to Cape Coast and trekked to Asante where he abrogated the Bowdich treaty, signed another official treaty, returned to England where he wrote a book, '*Journal of a Residence in Ashantee*' in 1824 in which he made it clear that he, not Bowdich, was the most important figure in negotiations with Asante and the Gold Coast. Edward Bowdich and Henry Tedlie took us, my cousin and me, to London for our education because the school at Cape Coast, at that time, was not developed. When Dupuis was back at his desk in London, the African Company was abolished and we were called in to be registered as aliens. Although, in the meantime, both Bowdich and Tedlie had died, he transferred his enmity for

Bowdich to us! He was so embittered by the fact that, as he saw it, Edward Bowdich had interfered in his promotion plans and he hated the idea that I was privy to information about his visit to Kumasi."

Dr. Wilson nodded thoughtfully and remarked: "I'm glad you've told me that. You will realise that the handful of whites and people like ourselves who have been educated in Europe or in the USA or South Africa form an elite group in the community here, together with some of the merchants and the Church of England missionaries who opened the first school twenty years ago at Fourah Bay. In 1827 they started training teachers and we are now getting a steady supply of literate children who take up jobs in commercial firms and in government, in the police force and in the schools. We are referred to as the 'aristos' and we all know one another. Dupuis is, next to the Governor, perhaps the most influential man in the country: the finances are in his hands, he is privy to all the information to and from London, all the traders get their licences through his office, development policy is mainly determined by him because he holds the purse-strings. He is not a very sociable man but we all keep on good terms with him. All these 'aristos' are my patients together with hundreds of others! You will soon have much to do!"

Full of curiosity, Kwame asked: "How was the colony started and where did the people come from?"

"Sierra Leone has a fantastic history which is bound up with certain famous names: first there was Granville Sharp who had the idea of a settlement of free slaves in Africa who would build up a self-governing community organised on the principles of English Common Law; everyone working together in a harmonious commonwealth. That was the first attempt by a group of 259 blacks from London including 60 white women married to blacks, plus a half-dozen white artisans, two surgeons, an engineer and a surveyor; commanded by Captain Thomas Thompson. They put up their tents at Granville Town on land leased from the local Temne chief, King Tom. Then disaster struck: for two months rain fell in torrents, their provisions ran out and before long they were forced to seek help from the slave traders on Bance Island and at Bullom. To make matters worse many fell sick: during July twenty-four whites and thirty blacks had died of fevers and some, including the surgeons, had deserted. When the news reached Granville Sharp he was deeply distressed and spent 900 pounds outfitting a two-masted brig, *the Myro,* to go to the rescue. On board were thirty-nine new settlers and a surgeon. The relief came in time and was effective: huts were built, some crops were sown and the death-rate had come down. The Province of Freedom, as Sharp called it, had been saved.

The second phase of the history is associated with the name of Thomas Peters who had come to London from Nova Scotia to plead for justice for the blacks who had fought and worked on the British side during the American War of Independence in the years 1775-1783. The last colonial Governor of the state of Virginia had promised complete freedom to all those slaves who reached British lines and served in some way with the forces. Thousands escaped from the plantations, altogether about 100,000 men, women and children, convinced that they would have a better future in British territory. The Mansfield verdict had become widely known. The Governor, Lord Dunmore, formed what was called an Ethiopian Regiment in which the runaway slaves enrolled by oath 'freely and voluntarily to enter the service of King George III'. Now, at the end of the war, white and black loyalists tried to get away to Canada and Nova Scotia was chosen as the main place of refuge for them; blacks and whites would live together and all would have land assigned to them. In the event, whites were given preference and most of the blacks had to be content with work as indentured servants. Peters had served as a sergeant in the army, he was illiterate but highly vocal and became the acknowledged leader and spokesman for all the blacks. When he talked with Granville Sharp in London the possibility that free blacks from Nova Scotia might go as settlers to Sierra Leone was discussed and agreed upon. In Sierra Leone there were now only sixty-four survivors but a trading company had been formed in London to support them. What was now needed was fresh support from Nova Scotia. To assist Peters in the recruiting, Lieutenant John Clarkson, younger brother of the indefatigable, life-time abolitionist, Thomas Clarkson, naval officer on half-pay, was appointed to be in charge of the expedition. He overcame opposition from authorities and white settlers in Nova Scotia and in January, 1792, a convoy of fifteen ships carrying 1,196 persons, including 383 children, set sail from Halifax and after enduring terrible winter storms landed safely in Freetown harbour after seven weeks voyage. These settlers from Nova Scotia all possessed certificates which were regarded as proof that they were free because they had been born in former British territory or born behind British military lines and they played an important part in the future development of the colony.

The third phase belongs to John Clarkson who formed a proper government system, Harmony Hall was built, the hospital that we use was put up, streets were laid out, there was a school and a proper church, the settlers were allocated parcels of land for cultivation, retail stores opened but above all Clarkson presided over a self-governing community of Africans, perhaps the only one of its kind in the world at that time. Zachary Macaulay was appointed governor in 1797 and consolidated the progress.

The last large immigrant group were the 550 Maroons transported from Jamaica who became the nucleus of the armed forces of the colony when in 1808 the Sierra Leone Company was wound up and the Crown Colony declared. Even then, it wasn't easy to satisfy all the immigrants at once: some had republican ideas, there was discontent over the distribution of plots that led to discord and envy, it took time to weld all these immigrants with different backgrounds and personal experiences but Governor Zachary Macaulay put his faith in the solid element among the settlers and it paid off. People built their houses, cleared the land, grew food crops and started to export coffee, there was a market and a few general stores while slowly Freetown was becoming a literate community and there were over two hundred children in the mission schools. The next Governor, Thomas Ludlam, a young man of 23, had problems with the dissident elements who wanted to secede and form their own colony. He used the Maroons as a military force to establish law and order and exiled over 30 settlers who had fomented rebellion. Meanwhile, the Royal Navy had made Freetown its headquarters for dealing with captured slave ships, and this helped to foster stability."

Dr. Wilson paused, smiled at Kwame, and said: "Dr. Boaten, you must be tired. That's enough history for one night!"

They said 'Good night' and Kwame was led to his room.

As he lay under his mosquito net Kwame pondered over his years in England and the task ahead of him. He was about to take an important part in a white man's enterprise whose aim was to make Sierra Leone a pleasant place for freed slaves to live in; healing their sicknesses, encouraging education, fostering commerce, and helping Christian missionaries to establish their faith firmly. Wasn't that how Buxton had expressed it in a simple equation: Commerce plus Christianity equals Civilisation? That formula had now become the accepted axiom for the betterment of Africa; it seemed clear and evident and required no discussion, the western European world was beginning to make its full impact on the African world. But after his years of study in England he wasn't so sure that the 'civilisation' aimed at was exactly right for Africa. Certainly, the Europeans lived more comfortably than Africans; truly, his education had been a tremendous experience and he could only say how grateful he was for it, he couldn't now imagine a life without it. But, and a big but it was, there were too many distasteful features of the current expression of European civilisation which made him pause: it seemed that their obsession with 'progress' had created fresh difficulties. Their inventions, for example, were always hailed as welcome steps forward in improving the quality of life but in many instances, they operated like a double-edged sword which cut wider and more brutally than you intended.

For example, the rifle that could kill and wound at a great distance had made it possible for Europeans to dominate large parts of Africa. The rifle that his father was so keen to buy from the traders which he paid for with slaves and gold dust. The huge sailing ships that could carry hundreds of chained slaves to America and the Caribbean islands to enforced labour on the sugar and cotton plantations. The steam engine that made it possible to employ young children from the age of six for long hours in huge factories, and to lower miners deep into the earth to dig coal. It was like a vicious cycle: progress was always linked to monetary gain and not necessarily to human welfare.

He had never imagined that in a civilised country like England there would be so much criminality that the prisons were crammed full and that thousands were yearly exported in chains to Australia. He had heard people speak of the horror of human sacrifice in Asante but they gave no thought to the pitiless way that convicted criminals were hanged in England. In Paris, France, they even had a machine for slicing off the heads of criminals, Madame Guillotine! He had read about the *Zong* case when 132 slaves were thrown overboard to drown so that the shipping company could claim the insurance money! In the history books he had read about Europe and its countless wars in which thousands and thousands were killed and maimed and often left to rot where they had fallen. He had read also about the brutal rawhide whip floggings suffered by recalcitrant slaves and in the navy. The Asante had no monopoly of cruelty; brutality was rife in England and Europe too; compassion did not necessarily accompany progress. All these were facets of the European world which the African world would have to absorb. And now, the European world was offering a new religion as the answer to life's problems! He remembered how on his last Sunday in England they had sung the hymn:

'How sweet the Name of Jesus sounds, in a believer's ear!'
It soothes his sorrows, heals his wounds, and drives away
his fear!'

The minister had told them that the author of the hymn, John Newton, was a sailor returning to England from a trip carrying slaves from West Africa to the West Indies. The ship was in danger of sinking in a violent storm and Newton had prayed that his life might be saved and had later composed the hymn and only then had he realised the evil of the Slave Trade! That was also an astonishing thing about the English, they very slowly became aware of things that had to be put right! How complicated the world of the white man was! Now he was back in the African world which the white man was seeking to change.His people had never thought that slavery might be wrong. After listening to Dr. Wilson he had fully realised how much it meant to Africans from all parts of the continent to be really free. At least the English with all their faults, were the first to recognise the fact that every human being, whatever his colour, was entitled to his own personal freedom and had written it into their own law. And these blacks in Sierra Leone that he had heard about had firmly believed that if you could get to a land where the British ruled, your chances of personal liberty were better. Certainly better than in America where, in spite of their own talk of freedom from British rule, they were still illegally importing slaves from Africa! With that thought, Kwame fell sound asleep, it had been a long and eventful day!

The following morning, fully refreshed, his new life began and Dr. Wilson introduced Mary Jane Pederson who presented herself promptly at 8 a.m. "Everyone in Sierra Leone has a personal history to tell but Jane's is one of the most interesting, she was brought here by a ship of the British Navy with a cargo of freed slaves but she was not really a slave!"

He turned to Jane: "Have I your permission to tell our new colleague the story?"

She smiled: "Of course", and he continued: "Her mother was an Ewe from Adidome on the Volta river, who was sold as a slave to a Danish trader called Pedersen in Keta and when she was old enough he sent her to the school in Christiansborg which the Danish chaplain H.S. Monrad organised mainly for the children of Danish traders and soldiers and their concubines. Danes serving on the coast were permitted to live with one African woman on condition that they urged her to adopt the Christian religion and paid half a month's salary into the mulatto school fund. This school had a fine record of sending pupils to Europe for further studies. Jane learned Danish and English while she picked up Ewe from her mother. Unfortunately, her mother died and her father took another woman who treated her badly. So Jane, at the age of seventeen, left home. The British naval ships frequently anchored off Keta and one day she hired a canoe to row her to a frigate flying the British flag and when they came alongside and the captain was called she convinced him that as the daughter of a slave she could justly plead to be taken to Freetown to lead a free life. So she came to work for me as a nurse and secretary and now is absolutely indispensable! She will help you for half the day until one of the nurses she is training can work for you."

Kwame regarded her, fascinated; she was tall for a woman, almost as tall as he was, her skin was the colour of the palest sand newly washed by the retreating tide, her brown eyes reflected sympathy and good humour, while her way of speaking English had an attractive lilt to it. The sailors on board the preventive ship had thought at first that she was European but her hair, her erect carriage, and the poise of her head marked her also as African. He thought, she is an ideal member of the Sierra Leone 'aristo' group. He knew instinctively that working with her would be a pleasure, and that, in a short time, proved to be so: both were modest, efficient, practised and anxious to please and with her help Kwame was relatively quickly assimilated into the African medical scene.

Later that morning, a messenger from the Government Secretariat came by and was duly introduced to Kwame by Dr. Wilson: "Come and meet Lannie. He is caretaker and a secretary at the government offices. His real name is Lance because his father was a lance-corporal in a British regiment and his mother a Bulom woman from Sherbro Island. Everyone who has reason to go to the Secretariat has to pass through his office: if you want a licence for something, or you want to travel, or you need to collect mail or parcels from anywhere, or to export something or buy a piece of land to build on, he will tell you who to see in which office. He knows everybody and everybody knows him! Sometimes he accompanies me on my trips to Mende land, we have a surgery there once a week that I want you to take over."

Kwame and Lance shook hands, it was the start of a close friendship that grew up between them. Some weeks later John Wilson and Kwame rode out in a donkey cart on the red dirt road to the main Mende village, Robana, to meet the paramount chief, the grandson of Nembana who had agreed to the lease of the Freetown land to Captain Thompson in 1787. The landscape varied: sometimes forest, sometimes grassland with scattered bushes, it reminded Kwame of his homeland except that the hills were higher and in the distance through the mist the summits of high mountains could be seen.

"I meet the chief from time to time; the Mende make up about a third of the population of the area, they spread to the hinterland of Liberia, our neighbour. There are a number of other tribes inland and I think that Britain will want to bring them together in a Protectorate but that is in the future. Many of the Mende drift into Freetown to work and to live because they feel that life in Freetown has more to offer, and when you realise that the navy brings in on average a dozen shiploads of freed slaves a year, it is inevitable that the Mende and others will be brought into the rapidly-growing, multi-racial colony of Sierra Leone. I had the idea of setting up a small clinic here in the bush a year or so ago but there is not much that we can do; the problem is the lack of personnel but now that you are here we can train more nurses. Mary Jane has made a start."

They rode on in silence for a while and then John remarked: "I have been considering what you told me about Dupuis and I think that you should know that for over a year he has been pestering me to release Jane so that she can go to him as housekeeper and of course as concubine. He has lusted after her ever since he first saw her and he has not been pleased that I have flatly refused because she is indispensable in the practice and in the setting up of a small health organisation in the colony. He has tried to induce her with offers of money but she is not at all attracted to him and much prefers the work that she is doing. Since your arrival he has been to see me on the matter, when he treated my idea of enlarging the hospital and building up a health service with contempt and went so far as to hint that you and I really wanted Mary Jane for other reasons than her work. I found his attitude insufferable and showed him the door, whereupon he went away highly offended. It would seem that in future we must both keep a low profile; such men in high places do not accept easily any obstruction of their plans." He spoke ruefully, "You see, Boaten, I had hoped this year for extra funds from him for my medical proposals."

He had used his surname, Kwame noted; that was normal in England among the educated classes, but he must still address his colleague as Dr Wilson, or Sir. Later, no doubt, they would be on first-name terms. To this fresh piece of news about Dupuis he could only respond: "I am sure that you reacted rightly. When my cousin and I had to report to him in London it was clear that he had trumped up a resentment against us because he had come to believe that Edward Bowdich had thwarted his personal ambitions. It could well be that his passion for Mary Jane will fade. In London he had a steady relationship with a young woman called Sarah Ridley who was expecting a child, the child must be six years old now. We learned that fact by pure chance."

Just then, the small, thatched roof building that did duty as a clinic, came into view and in a few minutes they got down from the cart to be greeted by a timid nurse in uniform who had been speaking to a row of women seated on the ground in front of her.

"She's one of the nurses trained by Jane and me. You see there's little in the way of equipment or medicines but the nurse can work with the traditional midwives in cases of childbirth and help a lot in first aid, cleaning and dressing wounds and generally advising. Serious cases she sends to us in Freetown. It's a start. You have already experienced most of the tropical diseases that we have, they are much the same everywhere in West Africa that Tedlie listed in Bowdich's book: ulcers and yaws that don't heal, skin disorders that itch and never get better, elephantiasis, dysentery, malaria, yellow fever, dengue that we can't really cure because we don't know how they are caused: on top of these, we get hernias, dropsy and bowel complaints by the score, as well as untreated wounds that have begun to be septic, limb fractures not set, scrofula and leprosy! I think sometimes that we are not so much further advanced in medicine and surgery than in the Middle Ages, we still have no proper anaesthetic, no real asepsis, and no cure for cholera, for typhoid or for puerperal fever! Yet people keep coming to us for treatment and nature sometimes helps us to cure someone! It's good that there are two of us in the same boat now!"

Kwame did his utmost to justify his presence and during the following year, when Dr. Wilson was on leave, he treated the Governor successfully for hernia, a leading African merchant for stoppage of urine, and two babies had been delivered by Caesarean section, as well as sustaining all the routine work of the practice. But his reputation grew when, after a weekly visit to the Mende village accompanied by Lance, they were caught in a terrible storm, the kind of tornado that only tropical West Africa experiences when the soaring clouds become black and vicious forks of lightning are so near and so intense that you feel caught up in a deadly expression of the forces of nature. You hear the rifle crack of thunder followed by a menacing roll as though to prepare you for the irrestible deluge that in minutes drenches you through and turns the ground into yellow mud. Lance urged the mule on and said: "We must try to get clear of the forest as soon as we can."

But it was too late; a great tree just ahead of them was struck by lightning and the fractured trunk toppled in slow motion across the track on top of them. In a moment they were engulfed in a maelstrom of falling branches. Lance was hit by a thick bough and fell backwards into the cart, Kwame was forced down by the sheer mass of leaves and branches, the mule had fallen sideways as one wheel of the cart had broken off. Kwame saw that Lance was unconscious, it was clear to him that the heavy branch must have injured him. His own head throbbed and he could feel blood on his cheek but he could move his legs and arms. Somehow he must get free and release Lance. He groped for his medical bag; with his surgical saw and sharp knives he made his slow way free from the debris; some twigs he could break with his hands and finally he forced his body through the tangle of branches and stood erect on the waterlogged track. In the pelting rain he managed to ease Lance's head and shoulders free and as he did so Lance's eyes fluttered and their eyes met. Urgently Kwame asked: "Where are you hurt, Lance?"

"My shoulder and I can't use my left arm."

"Lie still. I'm going to tie your left arm firmly to your body and then we'll see if with my help you will be able to walk."

Kwame used his shirt for a sling and helped Lance to his feet. He soothed Daisy, the mule, freed her from the harness and persuaded her to stand up. With his right arm round the mule's neck and Kwame at his left side, the three plodded slowly and painfully back to Robana. There they were carried to Freetown where Lance's shoulder and forearm were re-set. As he lay in hospital he thanked Kwame: "Dr. Boaten, you saved my life, what do I owe you?"

"Nothing, Lance. When I qualified I swore an oath, all doctors swear it, to heal the sick and save life whenever and wherever I can. Besides, you were helping me. Dr Wilson speaks highly of you. My reward is that you have recovered from your injuries and will be fit again."

Lance hesitated before replying: "You are a rare man, unselfish, honest, just doing good to everybody, even to me; so I consider myself to be in your debt, always. You know in my position at the secretariat, I come into contact with nearly everybody in the colony and I hear a lot of what goes on, the traders trust me because I often advise them and I am privy to private information, sometimes just gossip, sometimes not. You are a good man but even a good man can experience difficulties. So long as you are in this country I will help you; one word from you will be enough."

Kwame thanked him warmly. During the following week a young man arrived with a note from Lance that said: "The bearer is called Sam, his father was a British sailor and he lives in my house. He will call on you every morning and do any odd jobs for you. You can trust him absolutely. Teach him more English. When you need my help just tell him." After that, Sam called in most mornings and helped with the chores and was specially useful with messages and his presence was a constant reassurance that help was at hand if needed.

Slowly the friendship that developed between Jane and Kwame ripened into something deeper. For one thing, they worked so well together in treating patients and they had developed a routine which seldom needed words. She helped whenever he experienced difficulty with the pidgin, kept all the treatment records, made sure that their stock of medicines and bandages was adequate and boiled all the instruments he had used; she was, as Dr. Wilson had said, truly indispensable. Jane was deeply moved by his modesty, by his tenderness in treating people whoever they were. He used to say, 'when people are sick and ill, doctors and nurses are their last hope' and she never forgot that. His concern and care for patients and his consideration for her as his assistant, was always a source of amazement to her. At the end of a strenuous morning he would always thank her for her help and whenever anything new to her occurred he would explain carefully to her what he was going to do. She had never before in her life met anyone so compassionate and when once she referred to it he replied: " I learned that from Henry Tedlie, when patients feel that you want to cure them, that's half the battle won." So it wasn't surprising that Jane fell deeply in love with Kwame and one day, at the end of his second year, when he had delivered a baby boy after a very difficult and protracted birth and had handed the child to her to be washed, he had turned to the mother and had spoken comforting words to her. Afterwards, when they were alone and were tidying up, their eyes met and held, she opened her arms to him, they embraced each other and kissed.

"I am in love with you", Jane said softly, "I admire you and I just want to be with you always," and Kwame replied:

"For quite some time I have longed to say the same to you."

From that day it was an extra special joy to work together in the practice. Jane would have liked to tell others but Kwame persuaded her to say nothing until they were surer about how Dupuis would react. It was good advice, for the malice of Dupuis towards Kwame knew no bounds: he had proposed to the Governor that Kwame should be transferred to the Gambia but Dr. Wilson had refused; he had complained bitterly to Dr. Wilson after Lance's accident and had refused permission for Lance to accompany either of them in the future; what made the tension much worse, however, was that when Jane had once again strongly repulsed his advances, he had accused her of having another lover. The climax came when one day Kwame was called to the Comptroller's office. He had assumed that Dupuis needed medical attention but on his arrival he saw that Dupuis was sitting at his desk formally dressed. He didn't rise to welcome him and left him standing. He spoke in the manner of a judge passing a sentence: "I have finally come to the bitter conclusion, Boaten, that it is my duty to warn you that I find your presence here in Sierra Leone intolerable on account of your unwarranted interference in my affairs." He paused to take a pinch of snuff, sneezed, and gazed with narrowed eyes at his visitor. Kwame made no reply. How can you converse with a man in authority who speaks to you with spite and hatred in his voice? There was more to come.

"What Edward Bowdich said to you about me I do not know but I can make a good guess; he denigrated me in your eyes because I, on behalf of His Majesty's Government overruled his so-called Treaty with your father. You luckily benefitted from the Treaty; you were supposed to attend school in Cape Coast but Bowdich took you and your brother to England to receive an education, and now you are posturing in this Colony as an English gentleman! I have sought, so far in vain, to bring about your transfer to the Gambia but I shall not cease in my efforts, you can rest assured. On another matter, you may be aware that Miss Mary Jane Pederson is attractive to me and that since your arrival she has rebuffed my attentions, but I assure you that I shall not accept that situation much longer. I warn you to keep out of my way and to keep your nose out of my affairs."

During the last sentence, Kwame turned his back on Dupuis and walked out of the office without a word. It was abundantly clear to him that Dupuis hated him and that any attempt at conciliation would be fruitless.

John Wilson listened to his report of the interview with incredulity and regret; in recent days he had become aware of a completely different aspect of the personality of Dupuis: he had shown anger when his request to transfer Kwame to Gambia had been strongly opposed, he had sharply criticised him for allowing Lance to accompany Dr. Boaten, and had inferred that he had a hidden motive in not persuading Jane to join his household. He spoke gravely:

"We have a real problem on our hands. It could well be that our medical work may be deliberately underfunded in the future, meantime we continue our work as usual."

It was Jane who urged Kwame to seek help from Lance.

"He keeps his ear to the ground and all the traders have to get import and export licences from him, he has a close relationship with the bank manager who is in a position to make loans to people."

"Are you suggesting that Dupuis takes bribes or is dishonest?"

"I don't know. He has a good reputation for being 100% correct with Government money but if there is anything irregular Lance will be aware of it. We are utterly helpless, we don't have a single weapon in our hands."

So Kwame sent a request through Sam for Lance's help and that evening he listened attentively to Kwame's problem and at the end said: "You did the right thing to come to me, I think that I'm the only person who can help you. You understand that Mr. Dupuis is completely immune to offers of bribes but he has evolved his own system of accepting 'dashes' from anyone who has been successful in obtaining a licence or in negotiating a contract or buying or selling real estate, or in obtaining a bank loan. They pay an agreed percentage in cash anonymously into variously-named accounts in the bank that belong to him. He invested a considerable sum of money into the British Bank in Freetown which is underwritten by the Bank of England and by Barclays so that the Bank manager asks no questions. From these accounts money is transferred to accounts in London owned by Dupuis under other names. He is growing steadily richer at no risk to his reputation; how rich I can't say."

"How do you know these facts?"

"Over a period of years I have put together bits and pieces of information that have come my way. Money is always paid into these accounts in banknotes by messengers, never by the recipients of the favours. The bearers simply hand over a sealed envelope. It would be very difficult to prove that anything illegal or fraudulent is taking place."

"How can this information help us, then?"

"Have you any friends in high places who could suggest to the Government in London that an enquiry might be made? I know of certain merchants who would be pleased for the fact of these 'payments' to be publicly known."

"I owe my apointment to Sir Fowell Buxton who takes a special interest in Sierra Leone affairs and who is a friend of William Wilberforce. They are leading the movement for the abolition of slavery in Parliament."

"Do you know him well enough to write to him with your problem and to hint that the medical work is suffering because of him? If you and Dr. Wilson wrote would Sir Buxton take notice?"

"I need to think it all over again before taking any action. But I am very grateful to you, Lance, for the information that you have given me. If you learn anything more on this topic let me know." They emptied their glasses and said 'Goodbye'.

Kwame began to keep a notebook in which he wrote down everything that he knew for certain about Dupuis and from what he had learned from Lance. It was strange the Dupuis had never mentioned to anyone his relationship with Miss Sarah

Ridley in London who, it seemed from the conversation that he and Kwabena had overheard, was expecting a child and who had spoken of a marriage contract. His notebook could well serve a useful purpose if ever the animosity of Dupuis against him became public. He kept the book in a hidden pocket in the black leather bag that Henry Tedlie had given him and which held his instruments and medicaments and which never left his side.

Matters rested there for the best part of a year and Kwame began to feel that Dupuis' hatred had to some extent abated but then came the news that the Comptroller was to return to his duties at the Colonial Office in London as soon as his successor arrived. Only slowly did more details leak out: as the result of an anonymous letter to London the Governor in Freetown had been ordered to check all accounts at the bank and all transmissions of funds to England by the bank. The involvement of the Comptroller became obvious but as there was no evidence that Government grants of money to Sierra Leone had been affected, no action against Dupuis was contemplated other than demotion to his previous post.

All the hopes and ambitions of Dupuis lay in ruins and he automatically assumed that Dr. Boaten had intrigued to bring him down. Before he was transferred to London he determined to be revenged!

Ever since his arrival in Sierra Leone Kwame had taken over the responsibility for the small clinic on the edge of the large group of Temne villages in a fertile wooded valley about ten miles from Freetown on a dirt road just wide enough for a wheeled cart. Regularly, once a week he had gone there and sometimes he had been able to search around in the nearby forest for plants with a medicinal value, as he had done with Henry Tedlie. The Materia Medica, that Tedlie had compiled in the Gold Coast was his vade-mecum that he always carried with him for reference. The local people knew of his interest and some women had told him that a certain tree was in flower which was called 'okisere' in Ashanti, the bark of which could be used as powder to stop the purging in dysentery. He was alone, Sam had stayed to do a repair at the clinic. He left the footpath and made a bee-line to the tree through tangled shrubs and prickly lianas that plucked at his clothes. At one moment he had had the thought that someone was following him and then, as he bent down to scrape off a piece of bark with a knife, he heard the twang of a bowstring, felt the thud of an arrow-head in the lower part of his back and fell forward on to the ground. The pain and the flow of blood made him aware that the wound was serious but he succeeded in pulling the arrow point out of his flesh and stuffing as much of his shirt into the wound as he could. He unfastened his belt, lowered his trousers and saw that the arrow-head had penetrated his waistcoat and breeches and had made a deep incision. He fainted from the intense pain and the shock and lay helpless at the mercy of the myriad flies that hovered above him.

It was Sam who found him some hours later. He had spotted the tree and had seen the canvas of the haversack. Kwame was lying half on his back still clutching the arrow-head in his right hand. When Dr. Wilson later examined it he felt sure that it was poisoned just below the point. When he washed the congealed blood away a hard film had remained. He had given Kwame an emetic, had cleaned the wound, had sewn the incision but the patient remained in a coma. He enquired urgently of the immigration officer and asked him:

"Which people in our district would use a poisoned arrow?"

"The only group I have ever heard of in Africa are the Bushmen. They wound an animal with a poisoned arrow and then follow if for days until it collapses. Strangely enough, about two years ago we took in four of them who had been taken off with many others from a Portuguese ship off the coast of Angola. You can't mistake a Bushman; he's small, only about five feet tall, sturdy but supple, with a wrinkled face, a kind of apricot colour of skin and a sort of Mongol look, high cheek-bones, slant eyes and hair in clusters. They are the oldest race in Africa but they are now being pushed out by whites and blacks alike." He checked his file.

"They gave as their names, Nari and Nanu, for the men, and for the women Nui and Nushe. They said that they had left

Ovamboland, crossed the Cunene river and settled in Angola but the chief there had sold them as slaves. They went to live in Mende country. They carried bows with them. Wait a moment! Something quite extraordinary! They sailed to Jamaica only yesterday on the ship, *Surrey Star*, deck as passengers and paid their fare in cash. I was going to say that we might help to locate them for you."

"Have you any idea what the Bushmen used as a poison? That's my main concern at the moment, to find an antidote."

"All I know is what I heard once from a South African, they use the larvae of a beetle and sometimes venom from snake and certain poisonous plants but I can't tell you which."

John Wilson hurried back to his colleague and Jane greeted him with a smile: "Kwame awoke for a short time and spoke to me. I think that he is going to recover but he can't move his legs. He has gone to sleep again."

They stayed with him night and day until they were sure that he was out of danger; they massaged his legs but the muscles had lost their power like in a paralysis. Once he had a fever but slowly Kwame was restored to life although he could not walk and it seemed that the poison had worked its deadly effect on the nerves of his legs. Dr. Wilson was sure that someone had tried to kill Kwame with a poisoned arrow. He asked Kwame: "Had you, by chance, an enemy among the Bushman group?"

"No, I had never met them. I didn't even know that they existed."

"Then who could have had a motive to shoot a poisoned arrow at you? Nothing was stolen from your person, your haversack was lying nearby, yet only a Bushman would use a poisoned arrow, only they know how to prepare it. Did you notice anyone near you?"

"No. Once I thought that I heard a rustling but I didn't turn round to look."

When Lance came to visit and to express his sympathy, several other things became clear. He had secretly urged a number of the leading merchants and traders to write a letter to Sir F. T.

Buxton complaining of the abuse of the 'dash' custom by the Comptroller. They had not signed their names but had given their business titles intialled by each one. That had been enough to ensure Dupuis' recall as well as that of the bank manager; they were due to sail in the supply ship in a few days' time. Dr Wilson spoke emphatically to Lance about Kwame's injury: "I am absolutely convinced that the attack on Dr. Boaten was planned by Mr. Dupuis: he knew of the doctor's regular visits to the clinic and his habit of seeking herbs and roots in the bush. He was a fairly regular visitor to the Mende chief: he bought and sold plots of land from him and could easily have heard of the Bushmen and their use of poisoned arrows in hunting small game; moreover, these Bushmen paid for a passage to Jamaica in cash. I don't know how much they paid but in addition they were all wearing new clothes which they had bought in Freetown. He must have bribed them well. Don't forget how desperately poor these Bushmen are. He knew that if they took ship they would never be traced, and if they were, his word against theirs would be decisive. His own problem with the bank accounts he could, to some degree, explain away and in any case, all Government accounts were 100% in order."

"How could his involvement be proved?" queried Lance.

"I don't think that there is the slightest chance of finding proof even though I believe that it was a plot to murder Dr. Boaten."

They had no alternative but to accept the sad truth that Kwame would be maimed for life and that while the details of his injury strongly suggested a plot hatched by Dupuis there was no direct proof of his complicity. Jane convinced Kwame that he could with her help continue his practice: she had already made a plan for a chair with wheels and for broad shelves on three sides of the room for his books and instruments which the carpenter could make quickly. Sam massaged his legs and back every day and ran his errands. Kwame's life was reduced in scope but not in quality. He wrote a letter to Kwabena to be forwarded by Sir F. T. Buxton's office in London to Jamaica together with an enclosure to the man himself explaining his new circumstances but assuring him that he could still perform his duties. This is what he wrote:

"Kwabena, my dear brother! You are so far away and yet always so near in my thoughts especially now. While collecting herbs and tree bark I was hit in the back by a poisoned arrow, shot we think, by a Bushman freed slave. Only Bushmen use poison on their arrow-heads. I was desperately ill for a week but my colleague, John Wilson, and the nurse, Jane Pedersen, have pulled me through but sadly to tell you I am partly paralysed in both legs, the nerves are damaged and I cannot yet walk alone. I have a chair with wheels and I can do my work as doctor. Jane looks after me; we are in love with each other but whether I should marry in my present condition is a question. The servant of a former patient comes every morning to help me to dress and he runs errands for me. My patients collect herbs for me and I am making a list of medicinal herbs and roots in the district. So I am lucky and well looked after, do not grieve for me, one leg is already much better and I think that I shall soon be able to walk again with a stick. We plan to open a large clinic here in Freetown; we are training nurses and hoping to get another doctor for the practice. Tell me something in your next letter about your future work in Jamaica. Is it not strange that you and I will both be working to help freed slaves? You know, Kwabena, in Asante we never thought about slaves, they were not a problem, they were just inferior mortals from the north or war prisoners who didn't have the same significance or value that we had. No wonder that my father was puzzled when the British decided that trading in slaves was wrong! Now they want to abolish slavery completely but that will take a long time. Now I ask you, dear brother, if, and it is a big 'if', if you can ever find out anything about Bushmen in your island, please let me know. There were four of them who sailed from Freetown to Kingston directly, after the attack on me. The two men are called Nari and Nanu; they have wrinkled, Mongolian faces, 'peppercorn' hair, and are only about five feet in height. Only from the lips of one of them can we learn the truth; were they bribed to attack me and by whom? We suspect that Dupuis was behind the plot to kill me and once we are sure the he was involved we can decide what we can do in revenge, if anything. We are told in the Bible that we should love our enemies but I am not Christian enough to love Dupuis! Rather I should like to teach him a severe lesson."

The ministrations of Dr. Wilson and Jane together with the daily massage of his legs by Sam were so successful that one never-to-be-forgotten morning Kwame announced that he could move his toes! They redoubled their efforts and very slowly the muscles of the right leg came to life again but the left leg had suffered most from the poison and never recovered its former strength. But now, Kwame was able to walk with a definite limp and with the help of a walking stick, a disability which he soon learned to overcome. Soon afterwards, Kwame proposed marriage to Jane and to the wedding festivities came a great number of friends to wish them well. Until their own house was ready they continued to live with Dr. Wilson.

A letter arrived from London with the astonishing news that the long-standing dispute between Kumasi and Juaben over the gold of Ntim Gyakari after the battle of Feyiase had resulted in an attack on Juaben and the people had fled to Akim under the protection of Chief Ofori Atta Panyin! Kwame wondered if Kwabena had heard this news. Had their mothers left Juaben with the others? How could they get further information? He hastily penned a letter to Kwabena to go by the next ship to Jamaica. Then, just before Christmas an announcement was made from the Governor's office that Sir T. F. Buxton would be making a short visit to Sierra Leone. There was a sudden flurry of excitement as preparations were made for him and, thought Kwame, maybe he had the latest news from Juaben. On the day of Sir T.F. Buxton's arrival all the ships in the harbour flew welcome flag signals and a great crowd escorted him to the Governor's house while on the following day the church was packed to hear him speak. He praised everyone for their efforts in furthering the growth of the colony; Freetown had become a beacon of hope in the struggle against slavery. He told them of the current debates in the Parliament in London to abolish slavery altogether in British territories but there were still problems with the planters in Jamaica to be solved but he hoped that in the following year total abolition would take place. His words of encouragement stayed in Kwame's mind: "—if anything has been done anywhere for the benefit of western Africa, it has been in Sierra Leone. The only glimmers of civilisation; the only attempt at legitimate commerce; the only prosecution, however faint, of agriculture, are to be found there......and there alone has the Slave Trade been in any degree arrested."

Before he sailed away, Fowell Buxton arranged a meeting with Dr. Wilson and Kwame to thank them for their work and to assure them of his personal support. He confided to them that he was planning an expedition to the Niger river with the aim of setting up a colony there like that in Sierra Leone and that he already had gained the interest of the British Government in the project.

"It could be," he said, "that we shall need your advice and help on medical matters. I shall be in touch with you." They waved him a heartfelt goodbye as he stepped into the cutter and was rowed across the harbour to the naval frigate that was ready to sail.

Chapter 6

The Emancipation of Slaves in Jamaica, 1833

"I have been watching and waiting for a proper time and suitable circumstances of the country to raise the question of how best to provide for the moral and social improvement of the slaves, and ultimately for their advancement to the rank of a free peasantry."
William Wilberforce to Thomas Fowell Buxton in 1821. Quoted in Sherrard, Freedom from Fear, London,1959, p. 170.

After Kwabena's appointment as steward to the Witham Estates in Jamaica, Sir Fowell Buxton took an increased interest in him: he was carefully briefed about the emancipation debates in Parliament and the legal aspects of the arrangements for the slaves when they were declared officially to be free persons. After one of his visits to Parliament Kwabena wrote to Kwame.

"My dear brother,
I think that I shall be sailing soon to Jamaica. I have been sent by Sir F. Buxton to Parliament to listen to the debates on the total abolition of slavery. They meet in a former chapel in the Palace of Westminster; the members of the two parties, called Tories and Whigs, sit opposite each other on tiered benches and spectators like me sit in a gallery. There are not enough seats for all the members so it is crowded and often boisterous. Most of the members belong to the aristocracy, others are senior officers in the navy and the army, lawyers, some merchants and business men. The chairman or Speaker tries to keep order and usually when a member stands up to speak, there is quietness. When a proposal gets a majority of the votes it goes to the upper House of Lords and then to the King and if they approve, the proposal or motion, becomes law and that law must be obeyed in all British territories. In 1807 the law abolished the Slave Trade, but now the argument is

for the complete abolition and how it shall be done. The planters in the West Indies make a strong case for compensation because they will now have to pay wages to the former slaves for the work they do. There are a few who argue that slavery is in order provided that the slaves are properly treated. But Sir Buxton and his supporters are also strong and have public opinion behind them.

"Have you heard that the Juabens have all left home and have gone to Kibi? I hope that our mothers are safe, we must hope so.

In the middle of writing this letter has come your letter with the news of the attack on you as well as the fantastic news that you plan to marry Jane Pedersen! I can imagine what a fine woman she must be and how joyful you both must be! Tell me all about her in your next letter.

Of course, as soon as I get to Jamaica, I shall start looking for Bushmen and I shall enlist the services of the overseer, John Foreman, who is in charge of the work of the plantations on the estate. I shall be responsible, as factor, for all the paper-work and in particular, for the arrangements for the workers after the Abolition Law is passed. Sir Buxton tells me that it will be a very busy time for me and I shall need all my knowledge of English Law. As soon as I land in Jamaica I will write to you, that will be in a few weeks. Meanwhile, my dear brother,

Nante yiye!"

When the ship's anchors dropped with a rattle in the sheltered harbour of Kingston late one afternoon, Kwabena stood fascinated at the rail gazing at the panorama, blue sea and sky and in between golden strips of sand, rocky cliffs covered in thick green forest rising up to become mountains higher than any that he had ever seen. John Foreman stood on shore to wave him a welcome and when the formalities were over they sat in the buggy and began the slow drive up into the foothills of the Blue Mountains. He explained:

"Jamaica is beautiful so long as you live high enough away from the mangrove swamps and cactus forests, and even then we have to dodge the mosquitoes at night, on top of that we have diseases like malaria and yellow fever. But where we are going we always have a breeze and that helps a lot to keep us healthy. I worked in Barbados formerly, a small island in comparison with Jamaica, but similar in climate. There are two plantations at Witham, one called Woodhall and the other Kesteven, one grows and exports sugar, the other coffee and tobacco. In the middle is the large homestead which Mr. Curtis built, I live in one half and you will have the other half but we shall take our meals together. We have a good staff who take care of everything for us. I'm truly glad to have you with me to share the work and to have someone to talk to. I'm informed that you are a trained lawyer, just the person we need in these days. It looks as though the system of slavery will soon be abolished and this will bring all sorts of legal problems. I never liked the system personally, my boss in Barbados grew sugar but he was nearly always back in England and so I was on my own as overseer. We had to have slaves, sugar is very labour intensive, but I never used the whip, I fed them well and I organised them in family groups in decent huts. I had problems, there were thefts and runaways, but the island was small and they couldn't get far; in Jamaica it's different, you have to be stricter but flogging and the hunger weapon never produce anything but more hatred and discontent. I shall be glad when we have free, paid workers; the sugar in Europe will cost more and we shall have to provide reasonable working conditions but the entire atmosphere will be better. But I'm in a minority, there are a lot of planters who are dead against this abolition businesss, as you will soon find out."

When they reached the Witham Estates homestead, a group of all the domestic slaves, mainly women, and a smaller number of men workers on the estate lawns and gardens, were gathered to welcome Kwabena and there were audible gasps of astonishment when they saw that he was an African. Mr. Foreman introduced him and said: "Speak a few words to them, they will appreciate that."

"I've come to help Mr. Foreman to manage the plantations. I will get to know you all soon and you can tell me then about yourselves and your work. My name is Mr. Kwabena Boaten and I was born in Asante." Kwabena spoke slowly and clearly in English, in the accents of a well-educated Englishman, then he went forward and shook the hand of everyone before turning to follow Mr. Foreman up the steps to the house.

"They will respect you for those few words and for the handshake; you've made a good beginning." Foreman spoke with a smile.

"I was told by Mr. Bowdich that you are a son of a chief in Asante. I think, if it is alright with you, we can tell them that another day, it will give you status in their eyes. You see, the awful thing about slavery is that they have been completely uprooted from their African past, but they can't put roots down here. It will give them a kind of assurance, when they see and hear you that their past still exists in Africa even though their chances of ever getting back there are very slight."

"That's true," agreed Kwabena.

"My father is chief of the Juaben people. He was a close friend of the Kumasi chief, the paramount chief of Asante, but I have recently heard that there has been war between them and, to save themselves, the Juaben clan has moved away south and has taken refuge in Kibi with a neighbouring tribe. Whether my mother is safe among the refugees I just don't know yet. You see, my roots are gone too, but at least, as an Englishman with a black skin, I do belong somewhere."

During the next months and years, Kwabena rode on horseback round the plantations and wider afield, he learned to speak the creole form of English, and saw, at first hand, how the sugar cane was harvested and made to give up its sugar in the mill, how the tobacco was cured and how the coffee beans were roasted and ground. It was all labour-intensive but it seemed to him, that the hardest work of all was cutting the canes and in the mill where the juice was pressed out. The bundles of sugar cane were thrown into a machine that cut them smaller, then they had to be loaded into the steam boiler, a strenuous and often dangerous task. The juice was refined by being heated in large vats and then the boiling juice was led off into vats where the foam and scum were skimmed off. Some of the juice was cooled off in flat trays to form a crust called molasses that made rum, most of the refined juice became brown sugar for export. John Foreman had told him: "Jamaica is one of the most important trading partners for Britain: the sugar alone is worth more than the exports from the American colonies and is one of the best customers for manufactured goods. Last year Woodhall produced 150 tons, all went to Britain. The tobacco and coffee don't do as well but we make a tidy profit. You know that in Jamaica alone there are over 500 hundred plantations. It's a profitable investment: among the owners we have former sea-captains, merchants, middle class traders; some of them live here for part of the year, some hardly ever visit their plantations, they hire overseers like me because the profits can be quite large."

"What is the general attitude of the plantation owners to the campaign in Britain for total abolition of slavery?" asked Kwabena.

"Most of them regretfully accept the fact that opinion in Britain is so strong that abolition is bound to come so now they are trying to get a cash compensation from the British Government to cover their costs during the period of so-called apprenticeship of the slaves, a period of seven years for plantation slaves and five years for domestic slaves. During these periods they would receive wages and then be given their freedom. The argument is about the size of the compensation; the Government has offered 15 million pounds as a loan but the planters are not at all satisfied; they see no advantage in a loan that they would have to repay.

But there are 'hard-line' planters who say that, even after abolition, conditions on their estates will continue as before. There is bound to be trouble when the new laws are in force; you will be much in demand to explain them to the planters. I foresee a lot of problems in the future."

Not long afterwards, on the 28th August, 1833, the Act of Parliament which liberated all slaves in all British territories received the royal assent. The London Government, to bring the matter to a close, had offered the planters 20 million pounds as a free gift from the British taxpayer, which had been accepted. The process of freeing all the slaves could now begin! Hopes were high and in most cases were fulfilled but there were a number of stubborn masters who continued in the old ways and from these plantations some slaves ran away and hid in the mountains while some sought refuge with other owners. Kwabena was soon involved.

One morning, at first light, Kwabena was awakened by shouts and the barking of dogs from the grounds of Witham House. He seized his pistol and ran outside where two of the watchmen held a pair of intruders fast, they were runaway slaves seeking sanctuary. He called John Foreman and together they questioned the runaways.

"Where have you come from and who is your master?" asked John.

"Hardcrag Plantation; master be called Hardwick."

When he heard the name Hardwick, Kwabena interrupted:

"Does your boss have red hair?" He touched his own head.

"Boss, he white man with red hair," came the response, and Kwabena turned to John and said in surprise: "I think I know this man. He was in my class in Highfield School in Hampstead and was expelled for bullying."

John took up the questioning: "Why have you run away and what are your names?"

"They call we Samboy and William." Samboy continued:

"We hear slaves on other plantations get wages and then time come they go free, new Law from London say it. We ask our boss, he say, on this farm dis Law is nuttin, all be same like past time. He get mad and make us break stone on road and give us small food. William and me we run way night time."

"Why have you come to this Witham house?"

"Black man tell we at dis Witham white boss make all tings proper wid new Law from white man King in London."

"Do you want to go back to Hardcrag?"

"No, Mister, we fear him too much."

The runaways were told to wait while Kwabena and John discussed the matter; John said gravely: "We need to think carefully over what we decide to do: you see, as far back as I can remember in Barbados and Jamaica, planters have had the right and the obligation to pursue their runaway slaves and bring them back to their plantations to be severely punished. Slaves are property, they can't belong to anyone else; as proof of that they are often branded with a special mark like cattle. More than that, a runaway slave armed with a knife or a cutlass is considered to be dangerous, like a mad dog. The owner is obliged to deal with him. The only slaves I ever heard of who successfully escaped have been those who joined the Maroons in the mountains and stayed there. The notion that runaway slaves could find refuge and shelter on the plantation of another owner would be considered by everybody as utterly absurd." Kwabena replied:

"I can appreciate fully the points you make, John, but since the passing of the Abolition legislation the status of the slave has materially changed: he or she is no longer a piece of property but a human being with the same rights before the law as a citizen of Britain. He or she has the right to protest to an employer if the legal conditions of his or her employment are not being observed."

John Foreman had more to say: "There is another consideration: you must rightly inform the Kingston magistrate that we have given shelter to the runaways. So far as I know, no magistrate has ever intervened or has ever been asked to adjudicate in a case of runaway slaves. You must rightly also inform Mr. Hardwick that two of his slaves have found refuge with us. That leaves us open to an accusation that we have used 'missing' property for our own purposes if we allow them to work in the coffee-shed."

"That is an important point John. We can plead that until we have heard from the owners of the slaves as well as from the magistrate we are safeguarding Hardwick's property. I propose that the two runaways are given temporary food and shelter until we have a message from him or from the magistrate."

John nodded his agreement.

The runaways were so informed but two days later, before a reply from the magistrate came, Hardwick and his overseer, armed with shotguns, rode up to Witham House and peremptorily demanded the immediate handing-over of Samboy and William. Kwabena ordered that the runaways be brought from the coffee-shed and they stood at one side of the group looking downcast. Hardwick ordered two of the Witham workers to bind the wrists of the runaways but they hesitated and looked for confirmation to John and Kwabena. Kwabena made a sharp retort: "This matter must be discussed before any action is taken! We have been informed that you have refused to pay them wages and to give them time off to prepare for their eventual release according to the new Abolition law now in force. As you know, the Kingston magistrate has been informed of the situation."

Hardwick was livid with rage, doubly so at the realisation that the factor at Witham was none other than his former classmate at Highfield School. He spoke like someone beside himself, at the end of his self-control: "There is absolutely nothing at all to discuss especially with you. You are a bloody black bastard pretending to be an English gentleman while, in fact, you are a scheming trickster, Boaten, like you were in school."

Abusive language flowed out of his mouth like a cataract to express his intense loathing and hatred: "I will not for an instant tolerate unwarranted interference from a rascal like you and I warn you that if you poke your black nose any further into my affairs it will bode ill for you."

Kwabena took a deep breath and forced himself to remain calm: "It is not a question of interference, it is a question of the law of the land. These men have run away because you have not fulfilled the law."

"The law!" Hardwick laughed derisively. "The law at Hardcrag is what I demand to be done. I told them that nothing had changed at Hardcrag and that I did not agree with this sentimental freedom business in London. In any case, Boaten, runaway slaves are always dangerous, they must be recaptured and severely dealt with. We know in Jamaica how to deal with runaways. These two slaves are my property and I demand them back immediately."

"I suggest that you ask them if they wish to return to your service."

The mere suggestion irritated Hardwick even further:

"What they wish or don't wish is none of your business or of theirs.They are my property and they have no choice in the matter."

To which Kwabena responded:

"They have said that they do not want to return to Hardcrag."

At that moment, Samboy, who had been following the interchange of views intensively,called out in a loud voice:

"No go back to Hardcrag to work for you!"

As he heard these words defiantly spoken, Hardwick, like a man possessed, raised his gun in the direction of the voice and unexpectedly at the same instant the crack of a shot was heard and Samboy , with a cry, fell to the ground clutching his shoulder. John stepped up to Hardwick, seized the barrel of the shotgun in both hands to wrest it from Hardwick, and the two of them fought for possession of the gun. Hardwick was clearly the bigger and the stronger but John Foreman cleverly tripped him and as Hardwick fell he released the shotgun. Kwabena called out: "Leave this farm immediately! I will report this incident fully to the magistrate."

His companion helped Hardwick to his feet where he stood quivering with rage and frustration but was finally persuaded to leave. As they mounted their horses and rode away Hardwick turned in the saddle, raised his fist and shouted: "You bastard Boaten, I will be revenged on you for this!"

They turned their attention to the wounded Samboy who had received a number of leaden pellets from the shotgun in his upper left arm and shoulder. It was arranged to transport him to the doctor in Kingston. Fortunately, no one else had been injured by the pellets.

Later, over their usual drink at sundown, Kwabena said:

"It seems to me, John, that fate has given us a prime

opportunity to get this business out into the open: how would it be if Samboy brought an action in court against Hardwick for unlawful wounding under the Consolidated Slave Act of Jamaica that has been in force since 1792? According to this law anyone convicted of mutilating or dismembering a slave is liable to a fine of 100 pounds as well as imprisonment for one year. In addition, under the new Abolition Act Hardwick will be accused at Hardcrag of not fulfilling the requirements of that law. It means that the court action will compel the magistrates to adjudicate and the decision will make all recalcitrant owners tow the line."

"How can you be sure that we would win? Who would put the case for Samboy? Nothing like this has ever happened before; a black slave as plaintiff against a white plantation owner! Don't forget, some of the magistrates own slaves on their plantations while most of the whites who live here have domestic slaves."

"Let me, as a lawyer, answer your questions. The shooting of Samboy, whether by accident or by malice aforethought, took place in the presence of witnesses. We have Hardwick's shotgun as the weapon. If the pellets had gone into his head Samboy might now be dead and Hardwick would be answering a charge of manslaughter. Hardwick has only one chance in court, that is, to make the strongest plea that he can for mitigation. I, as a trained lawyer from Lincoln's Inn will personally present the case for Samboy. Of course, it is revolutionary, but the Abolition Bill is itself the cause; it is now the law of the land which we all must obey. We are moving into a future in which slaves are no longer 'property' but people with the same human rights as you and I. This is really the rub, the point at which doubt and difficulty arise for most whites, they have a built-in prejudice against blacks which sometimes goes so far as to deny the fact that blacks are truly human!"

So events took their course: Kwabena duly brought a case against Hardwick and was informed that the hearing would take place in the Court House in the capital, Spanish Town, in three months' time. The case would be heard by five senior Justices of the Peace and would be treated as a summary offence.

When the day of the hearing arrived the Court House in the Town Square of the capital, Spanish Town, was packed with spectators agog to witness the contest between the black slave plaintiff and the white plantation owner, the defendant. On such a momentous occasion, not only was the interior of the Court House crammed full but also outside around the building, people were standing in dense groups: those nearest to the wide-open louvred windows could see and hear enough to transmit brief summaries of the events to those behind them. The court room had become a theatre-stage except that this time what the audience was witnessing was a real-life drama; the characters were not actors but actual individuals whose words and decisions would have a permanent effect on the future life of all those present.

This trial had to do with the mainspring of Jamaican life: the plantation system which employed slaves imported from Africa to toil in the never-ending, back-breaking task of producing the sugar and other tropical delicacies that brought so much wealth to the plantation owners. The entire system was on trial: Parliament in London had decreed the total abolition of slavery. The minds of owners were completely preoccupied with unanswered questions: how in a few years could this drastic change take place? What would be the outcome? How could they afford to pay wages to those slaves who would be set free? Would the freed slaves be prepared to continue working in the fields? There were those who looked further into the future and who asked: when all the slaves had become free citizens would they not demand a greater say in the government of the country as the people of England had done? would not the long-established commercial and social life of Jamaica be violently affected?

Since the beginning of slavery in Jamaica, no white owner or overseer had ever stood trial for wounding a slave, but there were thousands of slaves who had tales to tell of wanton cruelty: the scars of the vicious rawhide whip that in a few strokes could take the flesh off the back whether it was wielded by the gang boss or by the professional flogger, were there to be shown. The whip was the ever-present sign and symbol of the degradation that slavery had brought. Re-captured runaway slaves were often subjected to excessive whippings or the loss of an ear but if they resisted capture and drew a knife they could be killed or hanged without any question being raised.

No wonder, then, when the five magistrates filed into their places on the dais and the senior magistrate knocked on the desk with his gavel to indicate that the trial had begun, the silence was absolute; the total attention of blacks and whites was riveted on the scene. The preliminaries to any case in English Law took place: the plaintiff, the defendant and their counsellors were introduced as they stood up in their assigned places while the Chairman addressed them:

"You have been summoned to attend this Court in the case of the plaintiff Samboy versus the defendant Alexander Hardwick in which the defendant has been accused of gross negligence and recklessness in wounding the plaintiff Samboy and further that he has been in breach of his duty toward the said slave, Samboy, according to the statutory rules of the Abolition of Slavery Act 1834. The Court will hear the submissions of both sides and will adjudicate. Before sentence is passed the defendant will be permitted personally to address the court."

The hearing was begun by the establishment of the facts in issue by Mr. Kwabena Boaten acting for Samboy. In English Law the burden of proof falls to the plaintiff because a defendant is presumed to be innocent until he is proved guilty and the proof required must be beyond reasonable doubt. When Kwabena rose to his feet and turned to address the magistrates his appearance in gown and bands evoked a few cries of admiration and hand-clapping from some black members of the audience whereupon the Chairman banged his gavel hard on the bench and peremptorily said: "During the hearing of this case there will be silence in the court; no expressions of partisanship will be tolerated."

Kwabena spoke in the assured tones of an educated English-man, each sentence slowly enunciated and the important phrases emphasised so that his arguments could more easily be followed. From time to time he turned to the spectators as if to include them in the decision-making but in the main addressed the senior magistrate in the chair:

"Your Honour, I beg to submit the case for my client, Samboy, the plaintiff. The main facts are not in dispute: my client had, unbidden, sought refuge at Whitham House. He and his fellow-slave, William, had run away from their owner, Mr. Hardwick, of Hardcrag plantation, because the provisions of the Slavery Abolition Act of 1834 in respect of the payment of wages and the free time allowance had not been observed. When they approached the defendant on the matter they were brusquely informed that no changes were planned to take place at Hardcrag. They absconded and after three days of aimless wandering they sought food and shelter at Witham House where the overseer, Mr. John Foreman, took them in and told them that their master would be informed of their presence. On the morning of the fourth day after their arrival, Mr. Hardwick the defendant, and his overseer Mr. Watson, rode into Witham House grounds each man armed with a shotgun, and without any formal announcement of their arrival demanded of two workers on the estate that the runaways be handed over to them forthwith. I, as factor, and Mr Foreman as overseer at Witham were called out; we sought to discuss the matter with Mr. Hardwick in view of the provisions of the Abolition Act but in vain. Mr. Hardwick refused angrily to discuss the incident and when the plaintiff suddenly cried out that he and William had no wish to return to Hardcrag, he grew angrier, raised his gun in the direction of the plaintiff, a shot was fired and my client, Samboy, fell to the ground clutching his upper arm which had received leaden pellets from the shotgun. Mr. Foreman struggled to wrest the gun from Mr. Hardwick. In the struggle Mr. Hardwick fell to the ground and gave up the gun. His overseer persuaded Mr. Hardwick to leave and they mounted their horses and rode away. We attended to the injured man and brought him to the doctor in Kingston. At the same time an account of the event was sent to the magistrate."

Kwabena paused, counsel for the defence had raised objections: "I object to the inference that my client was unco-operative and in a hostile mood; he had been distressed by the absconding of the two slaves and anxious to fulfil his obligation to the public by recapturing them. My client had expected instant cooperation from the factor and overseer of Witham plantation and was disappointed that the slaves were not immediately handed over; in addition he was riled by the words of the plaintiff that he and his fellow-worker would never return to Hardcrag."

After some moments thought and whispered consultation with the other magistrates, the president dismissed the objections and ordered Mr. Boaten to proceed.

"I come now to the allegation that the defendant by his negligence and recklessness has caused actual bodily harm to the plaintiff. I am able to inform the court that four leaden pellets were removed from his upper arm and shoulder. Fortunately, the plaintiff has made a good recovery but may I remind the court of the pain and discomfort that has been suffered by my client. These leaden pellets came from the shotgun of the defendant; had they struck him in the head the defendant might now be facing a charge of manslaughter. To point a gun in the direction of someone, whether the safety-catch had been set or not, is an assault in law. In this case, the gun discharged; whether by accident or intention is for the court to decide. What was the state of mind of the defendant at that moment? What was his intention in pointing the gun in the direction of the plaintiff? I put it to the court that it was a reckless act with the intent of forcing the plaintiff to obey him.

"May I now refer to the allegation of the wilful neglect to pay wages to the defendant and to make arrangements for the defendant according to the provisions of the Abolition Act. During the last decades the people of Jamaica have become aware of the overwhelming surge of religious and humanitarian opinion in Britain against the Slave Trade and against the institution of slavery itself. As a result, Parliament in London has by law prohibited the transport of slaves from, to or within British dominions from March 1st, 1808, and also by the Abolition of Slavery Act of August 28th, 1833 has emancipated all slaves in all British territories. Parliament has registered in law the expressed wish of the British people. Now, honourable Justices, we in Jamaica have a legal duty to carry out the provisions and requirements of these laws. At no time has it been permitted to exempt oneself from this duty, or to interpret the law according to one's own ideas or even to flout any particular law. I must obey the law at Witham, I cannot opt out of my legal duty, nor can the defendant. I submit to the judgement of the court that the defendant has been in breach of his legal duty towards the plaintiff."

Kwabena bowed to the Justices and walked back to his seat. There was a pause when the Chairman called the counsellor for the defendant to him and there took place a discussion between them in low voices. The counsellor returned to his seat and spoke with Mr. Hardwick who finally nodded his head and the counsellor spoke again briefly to the Chairman of Justices. John Foreman asked Kwabena:

"What is going on?"

"I think it is a case of plea bargaining. The Chairman has informally let Hardwick know that he will minimise the sentence if he pleads guilty."

"Is he allowed to do that?"

"Yes. After hearing my submission he knows that all the material facts are in our favour. I think the Justices will retire now to finalise their verdict but before they give it, Hardwick will be allowed to make a personal statement."

When the magistrates returned to their seats on the platform Mr. Hardwick was called to make a personal statement. During the interval he had closely conferred with his lawyer and now he stood up with a page of notes in his hand. Although he must have suspected that he had lost the case he seemed unperturbed and even to welcome the chance to put his point of view to such a large audience. He took time before he began speaking , looking around him confidently as though he were in charge of affairs and not the defendant about to plead guilty. He had always spoken in authoritative tones with an air of complete assurance as though the real truth of the matter was now about to be uttered! Kwabena vividly remembered his harangue in class at Highfield School when he had violently attacked the admission of blacks as pupils with the intensity and confidence of a politician presenting an irrefutable case.

"Your Honour, I welcome the opportunity to address this court in the defence of my conduct as the owner of a plantation worked by slaves. There are many of us, more than is realised, who find the recent legislation of the Parliament in London in favour of the emancipation of slaves to be unrealistic, unworkable and utterly out of touch with the reality of our situation in Jamaica. For 200 years, plantation owners have played a leading part in the commercial development of this island; with slaves we have cultivated and exported crops which have brought prosperity. Now, this development and enrichment is being put at total risk by legislators in London, who have never set foot in a plantation, who have never visited Jamaica, but who have been influenced by the religious and humanitarian sentiments of their constituents. We are fearful of the ultimate outcome: who will cultivate the farms when the freed slaves have gone elsewhere? What employment possibilities will be available for the freed slaves? What kind of social life will exist when thousands of freed slaves who have no work are roaming about in idleness?"

The Chairman rapped hard with the gavel and said:

"I remind you, as defendant, that your permission to speak does not include the privilege of proclaiming your views on the Abolition Act. You are required to keep strictly to the matter in hand."

"I apologise, Your Honour. I will speak of the slaves. Slaves cost money to buy, they have to be fed, housed and given clothing, they have to be taught the tasks they have to perform and if they run away for any reason they have to brought back and disciplined because they may be dangerous to the public. The recent legislation has created all manner of unrest in the minds of our slave workers and in the minds of the owners too. Upon hearing the news that my absconding slaves were secure in Witham I was much relieved and fully expected that they would be handed over when we arrived there. Imagine then my chagrin when I was informed that there would have to be a discussion before my property could be restored to me and moreover that the plaintiff had the temerity to refuse to return to Hardcrag. I confess my guilt in pointing my gun in the direction of Samboy but I had no intention of firing a shot at him. As I raised the gun in his direction in a gesture of frustration the gun fired. I can only surmise that the safety catch was off. I deeply regret the wounding which took place by accident; there was no malice aforethought. The unco-operative attitude of the factor and the overseer at Witham had contributed to my annoyance insofar that when they refused to return to Hardcrag it was clear to me that Mr. Boaten would continue to give my runaway slaves shelter, an attitude quite unheard of previously in this island. I rest my plea for mitigation of sentence in the hands of Your Honour and his colleagues, the Justices of the Peace."

Hardwick bowed to the Justices and to the spectators and sat down whereupon after a short interval the Chairman pronounced sentence: "We have very carefully weighed all the facts of this case and have reached a unanimous decision: we find the case proved and the defendant is found guilty as charged. We have listened to his plea for mitigation and as a result the defendant will not be sent to prison but we order as follows: the defendant is fined one hundred pounds on the first count of unlawful wounding, on the second count of failing to observe the requirements of the Abolition Act in respect of the two runaways he will give up all claim to the ownership of the said Samboy and William who are hereby placed under the guardianship of the Church of England Mission until their apprenticeship under the Act is absolved and they are declared free. To the said Church Missionary Society in Kingston the defendant will pay the sum of two hundred pounds forthwith against the costs of food, clothing and training. The defendant will also pay in full the medical and hospital costs of the plaintiff as well as his legal costs. This judgment and court order will be enforced with immediate effect. The case is closed."

The gavel was rapped on the bench to emphasise the end of proceedings.

The Justices rose and filed out and at once a storm of hand-clapping and long pent-up cries of approval of the verdict filled the hall to be echoed by the crowds outside. The unthinkable had taken place: a black slave had taken his white owner to court for actual bodily harm and neglect of duty and his black solicitor had won the case! There could be seen some gloomy faces and shaking of heads among some of the plantation owners but they were few. The majority of white owners had long since accepted the inevitable, that the overwhelming opinion and wish of the people of Britain was that slavery must be abolished. Now at a stroke, the conditions which for two centuries had operated between masters and slaves in Jamaica had been forever transformed but more than that: the black slaves had been awarded future rights as human beings and the unchecked, wilful, often wanton and inhuman treatment of slaves by owners and overseers had been bridled! In addition, within the next few years, there would be no slaves, only free men and women working for wages!

Kwabena and John, accompanied by Samboy and William, moved slowly out of the Court House into the open thronged by well-wishers; arms were stretched out to pat them on the back, hands were held out to be shaken in congratulation. Their names were on everyone's lips. All the way to their hotel in the Square jubilant spectators lined the route and as they reached the hotel, Samboy and William were bustled away by friends for their own celebration.

Over welcome drinks John asked: "Are you satisfied, Kwabena?"

They had been on first name terms for a long time and since the trouble with Hardwick their close friendship had grown stronger.

"Yes, John, I knew all along that Hardwick had no chance and I felt that his solicitor would have told him that before the

Chairman made it clear that if he pleaded guilty the sentence might be mitigated. The important thing was that justice was seen by everybody to be done. It's a real stride forward but there's a long way to go yet with the emancipation process, many owners are unsure how to go about fulfilling the requirements of the Act while the runaway situation will increase in frequency. There will be many slaves who won't wait for the end of their so-called apprenticeship, they'll run away even from Witham! Putting Samboy and William into guardianship was a neat way of solving that particular issue but it can't be made a precedent for all future runaways. I anticipate that perhaps half the slaves will stay but there's going to be a labour shortage."

"Where will the runaways go?"

"Some will join the Maroons in the mountains, others will just make new villages in remote places and live on a subsistence basis. Did you know that the authorities have already sent one contingent of 550 Jamaican Maroons to Sierra Leone as free men and that there is a proposal to recruit Kru workers for the plantations here on paid contracts?"

"How do you know these things?"

"After I was appointed but before I sailed, I learned a lot in Fowell Buxton's office, I read a lot and followed some of the debates in Parliament on Abolition. They've sent out a Dr. Richard Madden to advise and organise the apprenticeship process but he's not having much success because, as you can appreciate, every plantation presents special difficulties to the owner or overseer. I forecast that over the next few years there will be a general tendency to move towards a wage contract system. There are many complicating factors in the business of slave emancipation! The costs of production will go up; some plantations will close but the demand for our products in Europe will remain high so most plantations will survive. The Christian missions with their schools and clinics will play an increasingly important role in stabilising the situation, the slaves know that reading, writing and arithmetic are passports to jobs in our changing world; the school is a social anchor."

"Tell me more about the Maroons."

"Well, I got specially interested because many of them have links with the Guinea coast, in particular the Kormantines. The name Maroon comes from the Spanish word 'cimarron' meaning 'wild' and 'unruly'; it came to be used for the escaped slaves who fought for independence in Cuba. Here in Jamaica they established themselves permanently in the mountains under Chief Cudjoe in Ackompong and under Chief Nanny in Moore Town. They fought British troops three times and were finally granted free status so after the Abolition Act they have become a focus for runaways. Their lands in the Blue Mountains and in the upper reaches of the Rio Grande river were recognised by the Colonial government, the Maroons were given self-government and freedom from taxes. So you see, John, the Maroons have contributed to the struggle for black freedom not only for slaves but for all inhabitants of the land. That's the next big step, self-government.

"What has happened here in Jamaica is only the tip of the slavery problem world-wide; don't forget, John, that other countries are still selling slaves to Brazil, Cuba and the USA. Ships are sailing daily from European ports to the new world carrying slaves while everywhere smaller slavers will be doing a good business from smaller harbours out of the reach of the Royal Navy Squadron ships. It's going to be a long time before slavery is outlawed everywhere."

"How do you think that Hardwick will react to the verdict?"

"He will make himself scarce as soon as the fines are paid, that's what bullies do; when my brother and I brought him down on the rugby field he just walked off the field and decamped from school. But it will never occur to him that his own behaviour and temperament had caused the problem. You recall, how at Witham, he called me a 'scheming trickster like I had been at school'? People like Hardwick are never at fault, it is always other people who have been scheming to bring them down. I would love to hear the tale he tells back home!"

For some weeks afterwards Kwabena was visited by planters

and others who came for advice and when he referred them to Dr. Madden he was informed that he had left for Cuba. There were further runaways who were not admitted to Witham and slowly things returned to normal.

Then one day a message came from Spanish Town that certain Bushmen who had come from Sierra Leone had been located. Kwabena had placed an advertisement in a few local papers. He decided to send Samboy to investigate; had they really come from Freetown? What were their names? Samboy returned within a week with the information that their names and arrival time in Jamaica fitted in with the details given in Kwame's letter. A white man had given them money for their transport to Angola but they had been landed in Jamaica and all their money was finished. They were now employed as watchmen on a plantation near Spanish Town. Kwabena felt that the time had come for him to be more closely involved; he asked John to interview them and to offer them assistance to get a passge to Angola if they provided proof of their contact with Mr.Dupuis. They showed to John an old leather holdall bearing the faded inscription of a name in gilt letters: 'J—ph D-pu-s' that he had given them. It was proof that Dupuis and the Bushmen had had contact but not proof that he had bribed them to shoot a poisoned arrow at Kwame. All questioning about shooting an arrow proved fruitless. There was nothing further to be achieved so Kwabena got possession of the travelling bag in return for help with deck passages to Loanda on a Portuguese trader. What was clear in Kwabena's mind was that the suspicions of his brother and Dr. Wilson that Dupuis had been involved in the attack on his brother were fully justified. Maybe, one day in the future, Dupuis would cross their paths again.

Chapter 7

The Niger Expediton 1841

"Hitherto, we thought that it was God's wish that black people should be slaves to white people; white people told us that we should sell slaves to them and we sold them; and white people are now telling us not to sell slaves. If white people give up buying, black people will give up selling."

The Obi of Aboh, on making a treaty with the British to stop selling slaves. Quoted in Thomas, The Slave Trade, London, 1997. p.702.

Sometime before Christmas 1940, Kwame sat down one evening to write a long-overdue letter to Kwabena, maybe with luck, it might reach him in time if there was a ship bound for Kingston already in the harbour.

"My dear brother," he wrote and paused. The pen nib was rusty and had to be changed, somehow the ink had turned grey and the pressure of his hand had left a blob of sweat on the paper while the candle had burnt down and he must fetch another.

"I read the account of your successful tussle with Hardwick with great delight; how I wish I could have seen his face when he was found guilty! Do you remember how he slunk off the rugby field with a stony face after we had floored him a few times? People like Hardwick have no sense of fairness or feeling for other people, black or white. Isn't it strange that both of us have become so deeply involved with the slavery emancipation business? Isn't that the best way that we can help to uplift our African people, not just Juabens but everywhere? Recently Jane and I have become friends with Samuel Adjei Crowther, to give him his full name. He is about our age and he teaches in the CMS school here. He is a convinced Christian, like Henry Tedlie; reads the Bible every day and prays to God often. As a boy in Yoruba country in

south-west Nigeria near a town called Oyo, he was captured in a tribal war, sold as a slave and was being taken to America when the ship was caught by a naval squadron ship and he was taken to Freetown where he was educated by the mission and became a Christian. He believes that educated Africans like him must take the lead in bringing the Christian religion to Africa. He talks about the need of mission activity in Yorubaland and in Lagos where slavery flourishes. It still flourishes here too, especially in Sherbro Island where there are Spanish, Portuguese and even English traders shipping slaves to Cuba and Brazil.

Further down the coast at the mouth of the Gallinas river a Spaniard called Pedro Blanco has set up a well-organised trade on nearby islands, buys slaves for twenty dollars and sells them in Havana for 350 dollars each! He retired last year to Spain a millionaire! We all admire what the Naval Squadron does. Every month one or two captured slave ships are brought in and John and I examine the slaves; many of them are in a pitiable condition. Then they are taken to an office in Kings Yard and registered as British citizens and given a small plot of land, some clothes, a spade and a cooking pot and help to build a hut. Some are offered work for wages in your island or sign up as soldiers. There's also a special Court to deal with the prize money due to the sailors, to sell the slave ship or saw it up for sale. But, you see, Kwabena, the trade continues. So I come to the main point of my letter, the scheme of Fowell Buxton which he set out in his book, 'The African Slave Trade and its Remedy' two years ago and which has been widely read. He wants to set up a number of trading posts in the Niger river valley for legitimate trade in agricultural produce and to these areas traders and missionaries would come to set up plantations and schools. All this would be achieved by official agreements between the local rulers and the British Government. He is very persuasive and has convinced the Government to send out an expedition next year to explore the Niger and to make treaties with local chiefs. Samuel Crowther has been recruited as interpreter and I will go along as Medical Officer! It is really quite an honour and you will understand that I couldn't refuse Fowell Buxton, even if I wanted to, because he has helped us both so much.

The other main news I have is to tell you about what the Dutch are doing in Elmina. You may not know that two years ago the Dutch government sent a high-powered delegation to Kumasi where they were given a great reception. They seem to have thought out a plan to make up for the loss of the Slave Trade by recruiting male slaves in Asante to serve in the Dutch army as soldiers in Java! At the same time the Asantehene gets an income from the sale of slaves. The 'recruits' are given an advance of wages with which to buy their freedom; they leave Asante as free men but on their arrival in Elmina they are charged for their board and lodging and transport, a debt which will be subtracted from their wages in Java as soldiers. The contract as soldiers is for 15 years but it seems that the majority sign on for an indefinite period. It is a clever scheme. Incidentally, two young men, Kwesi Boachie, whose father is the Asantehene, Kweku Dua 1, and Kwame Poku whose father is Adusei Kra the warrior, but, more importantly, his mother is the eldest child of the queen-mother, sister of the Asantehene, have been sent as surety for the deal, to Holland to be educated. I just can't understand this business of making an alliance with the Dutch when the influence of the British along the coast is increasing all the time.

We hear good news of the success of Governor Maclean. He seems to have made close contacts with many of the chiefs and had persuaded some of them to accept aspects of English law. Have you had any contact with him? I think that if things develop along the coast the British might establish a colony like Sierra Leone. It would be easy for us then to go back there. A rumour has it that the Juabens have gone back but no details!

Thanks for the news of the Bushmen. We really can't expect anything more but at any rate we now have some evidence that Dupuis was involved with them. I am keeping well, I limp a bit when I am tired and if I go for a long walk I take a stick. All best wishes for Christmas and the New Year from Jane and me. Maybe by the time you read this, I shall be on my way to the Niger!"

It did not seem long before Kwame was saying goodbye to Jane and to John Wilson and making his way to the jetty in the harbour accompanied by Lance who insisted on helping with his luggage. On their way they could already see the three expedition steamers anchored in a line with smoke rising up lazily from their tall smoke-stacks set amidships and Lance remarked: "There seems to be no limit to what the Europeans can do with the steam engine! I've heard about the locomotive and the factories but now they drive ships with them! I suppose they carry enough coal for the voyage."

"I expect they do but I understand that certain ports stock supplies of coal, like Fernando Po where we shall stop," responded Kwame.

The steamships didn't look so big, about 200 feet long but they were wide with three decks, the top-deck had awnings against the sun, at the stern you could see an extra raised deck, at each side, in the middle, there were large paddle-wheels which drove the ship whatever the state of the current or tide or wind.

On board, Kwame was sharing a cabin with Samuel Crowther and James Schön, a CMS missionary, who had worked in Freetown for some years. Also on their ship were two young men from Asante, on their way back to Cape Coast after spending some years in England. They were William Quantamissah and Owusu Ansah, protégés of Rev. Thomas Birch Freeman. Freeman had been born in England of an African father and an English mother and had become a minister of the Wesleyan Methodist Church. Fired by the difficulties of the Wesleyan Mission (the first missionaries had died) he went to Cape Coast and from there in 1839 made a courageous journey to Kumasi where he was received by the Asantehene. On leave in England he raised five thousand pounds to assist the founding of a Christian mission in Kumasi and was waiting in Cape Coast for the arrival of the two Ashanti young men to make a second visit to that country taking with them a wheeled carriage as a present for the Asantehene.

Kwame lost no time in questioning them if they had any news of Juaben: "There is a rumour that the Juabens have returned from Kibi. Is that true? My brother and I are anxious for news of our mothers."

"We have no certain news, only that peace has been made between our uncle and the Juabenhene Kwesi Boaten, so it could be that a return will be possible," they replied.

The three had much to talk about especially about their sojourn in England and William, the most vocal, explained: "You see, we were not away long enough to study for a career like you and your brother in Jamaica. The Asantehene had given Rev. Freeman permission to return to Kumasi and start a school and do mission work, so we were lodged with a priest of the Church of England to learn the doctrines of the Christian religion and the practices of the Church, nothing more. Then we would be able to keep tabs on what the missionaries were saying and doing."

"Did you ever discuss Akan beliefs with the English priest?"

"Yes. Rev. Thomas Pyne would ask us occasionally about some of our beliefs and we gave the best explanations that we could but there was no real discussion. He could not for a moment seriously consider that African religious beliefs had a value of their own, what he called 'fetishism', 'human sacrifice', 'witchcraft', 'heathen customs', all had to be ruthlessly swept away and replaced by the one and only true religion, Christianity. It never occurred to him or to any others who talked to us that our social system and our religious beliefs belonged together."

"Do you belong to the church?"

"Yes, I was baptised and given the name William, and I have been to the Lord's Supper a few times, but I don't understand this business of conversion that they talk so much about. They seem to think that you must isolate yourself from your own people which no Asante would ever think of doing."

"Did you never argue forcibly with them that our traditions and beliefs simply can't be given up, perhaps they can be modified or adapted to Christian ideas?"

William replied with a proverb:

"Nea wo nsa da n'anum no, wompae n'atifi!"

(When you depend on someone, you don't antagonise him!).

They laughed together; sometimes the mother-tongue summed up the situation best.

Kwame enquired:

"What do you plan to do when you land at Cape Coast?"

"We link up with Rev. Freeman and Rev. Robert Brooking and get the carriage ready for its trip to Kumasi to be presented to the Asantehene."

"What kind of a carriage?"

"It's a four-wheeled, one-horse brougham which he can use on town visits like Queen Victoria. We shall have to widen the track in places and we shall need two large canoes to get it across the Pra river."

"What are your plans?" asked William.

"I don't know the details but I think we shall make a stop at Fernando Po island before going up the Niger to make treaties with local chiefs and to set up trading posts. I'm going as one of the medical officers, I qualified at Surgeons' College in London. My brother is a lawyer and is now working in Jamaica."

"Do you hope one day to return to Asante?"

"We belong to Juaben. That's why I am anxious to find out if our mothers have gone back there. Maybe, if things turn out well, we can go back." Kwame wanted to know more about the situation in Kumasi.

"Has your father a special interest in the Christian religion to allow the Wesleyan missionaries a permanent place in Kumasi?"

"No, his motive is quite different. After the defeat at Akantamansu and the peace agreement with the British in 1831 together with the abolition of the SlaveTrade and the way in which the British were making treaties with coastal chiefs, Asante was being cut off from direct trade with the Europeans while Denkyera and Akyem were friendly to the British. It was clear to him that the Europeans were going to play a bigger role than before, not just trading for slaves and gold to get guns and European goods. He has made a treaty with the Dutch and there's a Dutch agent resident in Kumasi who supplies one thousand male recruits every year for the Dutch East Indian Army. He lends them money to buy their freedom with so long as they sign on to serve in the army and the debt is repaid by deduction from their pay. The Dutch have already given him 2000 rifles and 800 ounces of gold. But my father thinks that the technical progress of the Europeans can help Asante and if there is a resident from Britain in Kumasi, even though he is a missionary, he is still in direct contact with Cape Coast. He likes the idea of a school but he finds the religion of Europeans unrelated to real life. He told me that when I come back I must live with them and keep an eye on them!"

"What other presents have you brought for the Asantehene?"

"The young British Queen, Victoria, has sent a fine portrait of herself and a view of Windsor Castle; the Wesleyan Missionary Society has given cutlery, a pair of elegant boots, beautiful glassware and a number of handsome ladies' dresses, cloaks and coloured muslin caps. I think he will be especially pleased with the queen's portrait."

The three packet ships of the Niger Expedition made good progress along the coastline to Cape Coast: the captains were officers who had served in the naval squadron, the engineer and stokers who fed the furnace fulfilled now an important role in keeping up steam to turn the paddle-wheels. From the bridge on the upper deck the captain could send signals by bell to the engine-room below, while from the bridge the steersman controlled the ship's direction. Their next stop before the expedition began in earnest was at the large Spanish island off the Cameroon coast called Fernando Po, about a day's sailing from the delta of the Niger river. The island was relatively healthy, its shore waters were calm in contrast with the ceaseless, pounding surf of the Guinea coast, crew and passengers could stretch their legs ashore, and most importantly, it was now used as a coaling station by British steamers. The British Foreign Secretary Palmerston, to provide the expedition with a base, had offered Spain 50,000 pounds for the island but the offer had not been accepted.

Up to now everything had gone smoothly and the members of the expedition were in good spirits; most of them were volunteers: geographers, botanists and biologists, interested in exploring a part of unknown Africa or of discovering tropical plants and animals hitherto unidentified in Europe; a few were fervent Christians fired by the notion of being involved in the grandiose plan of opening up the middle Niger region to commerce, Christianity and civilisation. All had been attracted by Buxton's bold plan and many had been recruited by him.

As they steamed westwards to Bonny, at the mouth of the river Bonny, and glided confidently through the foam of the sandbar into an inlet in which lay wrecks of old ships half-submerged, the outlook however, seemed less attractive. Around them rose dense walls of dark-green mangrove trees out of the oily-black mud of the swamp; further up the river itself lay the port where they anchored. At dinner that night the captain explained: "We shall stay here a few days to confirm the treaty that we have made with King Popple and other chiefs to encourage them to export more palm oil from the forests inland. By the treaties that we make with the chiefs we pay them a sum of money to compensate them for the loss of revenue in selling slaves."

"When shall we reach the Niger river?" Schön asked.

"Another day's cruising round the delta. The main entrance through the delta into the interior lies to the west; it was only a few years ago that it was discovered. The entire delta and the coast, all the way to Lagos is one vast swamp covered with mangrove; it's a landscape without any other visible feature for hundreds of miles. There are over twenty other river outlets and innumerable creeks where the slave traders have their barracoons and can bring out the slaves in canoes. That's the basic aim of this expedition: to get as many chiefs as possible to give up the trade in slaves and to rely on legitimate marketing but many of them are uncertain about our real intentions so that they can still sell slaves from other places in the delta which the naval squadron ships can't reach. The port of Brass, for example, has no direct outlet to the sea but has a regular slave market."

When the ships finally entered the Niger river it seemed ages before the interminable mangrove swamps gave way to the usual tropical forest and palm oil plantations. The river was twice as broad as the London Thames but relatively shallow and progress was slowed by extensive sandbanks when soundings had to be made. They dropped anchor off large settlements but were forced to wait before being allowed ashore to palaver with the chief. Each vessel was carrying two million cowries as currency for supplies as well as items for gifts like textiles, glassware, cutlery, rum and gin for the chiefs. Those members of the expedition who wished to explore onshore were often regarded with suspicion by local people. There were language problems: the former slaves brought from Freetown who claimed competence in certain local dialects were rarely successful in establishing contact and they increasingly relied on Crowther's command of Yoruba, pidgin English and signs. The constant heat and humidity enervated a number of the Europeans who had never before experienced the Guinea Coast climate and unusually during the so-called dry season a week of torrid wetness had to be endured. It was triggered off by a sudden storm when within minutes the entire sky darkened, fierce shafts of lightning shot through a massive black menacing cloud approaching them while the claps and roll of the thunder seemed to pass right through them. Then came the blare and howl of a piercing wind followed by rain that seemed to pour out from the clouds until everything and everyone in its path was utterly drenched. All that you could do was to find cover and wait until the worst of the storm had passed.

Near Igala, the capital of Idah, not far from the confluence of the Niger and the Benue rivers, was a large island market where the three steamships could anchor and most of the members of the expedition and some of the crew could go ashore. The number of canoes that thronged the ships and the number all along the shore gave an indication of the popularity of the market: on sale were yams, cassava, palm oil, gum, fowls, goats and sheep, beans and some fruits, but also, a great eye-opener for the Britishers, human beings, mainly men but some women and children, were being sold. In reply to questions it seemed that about a thousand slaves a month were bartered and transported to the coast for onward shipment. The suggestion that now was the time to give up this trade was received with complete surprise by those in charge of the slaves.

The following day Dr. Boaten sought an interview with the captain.

"A serious problem has developed and is growing worse. The number of fever cases is increasing, the sick-bay is full and I am afraid that some of the patients may die."

"What are the illnesses?"

"Mainly malaria, a few with yellow fever and some with chronic dysentery."

"Is there no cure?"

"Unfortunately not. We simply don't know the cause of malaria except that it is closely associated with tropical countries in areas of swamps and standing water. The popular view is that vapours from stagnant water cause it. What we do know is that quinine is the only effective drug: with some patients it helps them to recover, with others not. When the urine flows black there's nothing we can do."

"What about yellow fever?"

"We don't know the cause either. Some patients recover, others become jaundiced and develop kidney failure and we can't save them."

"Do black people have more resistance to these diseases than whites?"

"Not in my experience. It does seem to be the case, however, that if a person recovers from malaria he or she seems to develop a certain resistance."

"You said, Doctor, that our problem is serious and growing worse."

"Yes, Captain. The number of cases is increasing and the drug supply is rapidly diminishing. The stewards can't cope and are not trained to deal with the sick."

"Why have you not informed me before of this state of affairs?"

"For two reasons: I had to consult with my colleagues on the other two vessels, and secondly, I had to wait on the condition of my patients. No doctor likes to give up hope but now we know that some of our number are going to die."

"What in the opinion of you and your colleagues is the best course of action for me to take in view of this manifest danger to the health of the members of the expedition and the members of the crew?"

"We are all agreed that we should return as soon as possible to a healthier climate."

The following day an announcement was made by the senior captain: "In view of the increased incidence of sickness on board, the work of the expedition cannot be continued. There will be no further shore leave and the ships will return to Cape Coast, Freetown and England with all possible speed."

The same day three deaths took place but there were ten more fresh cases of persons prostrate with fever. The sick-bay was full and room had to be made for the patients in the hull where members of the expedition could look after their sick comrades. Day after day this situation was repeated until the supply of medicines was almost exhausted and the ships had become like floating clinics. Many members of the crew were unable to perform their duties and others had to be on duty round the clock. Scratch meals were taken only at intervals. Before they reached the open sea there had been more than thirty deaths and an air of deep melancholy affected everyone. Each time the ships slowed it was to commit yet further bodies to the deep. The burial service was read from the Church of England Prayer Book and as the corpses slid into the waves the first verse of the well-known English hymn by Isaac Watts would be sung:

' O God, our help in ages past, our hope for years to come,
  Our shelter from the stormy blast, and our eternal
  home'.

And then, on one never-to-be-forgotten day as Samuel Crowther and James Schön went down early to the wardroom where they had been helping to nurse the sick, one of the patients pointed to where Kwame was lying on a mattress in one corner. A wave of terrible sadness swept over them as they realised that he had died peacefully in his sleep. His bodily strength had simply become exhausted. When he had announced to them that he was going to sleep near the sick patients they had remonstrated and he had replied:

"I took an oath to heal the sick and this is where they are now. If I become sick too it is not important, my mentor, Henry Tedlie, had chronic dysentery but he still went on with his work."

As Samuel lifted the sheet he saw that Kwame's medical case was open and a sheet of paper lay inside on which Kwame had written:

"Dear Jane, Kwabena and my friends Samuel and James, I have kept my oath to care for the sick but I cannot do so much longer. Jane shall go to my brother with my bag, it has my diary in it. If my mother is in Juaben tell her that I did my best. Give my thanks to John Wilson. I cannot write more. Love, Kwame."

The signature was scrawled. Samuel silently handed over the letter to James and both men wept and James said:

"We have lost one of the finest Christians I have ever known."

When the ships dropped anchor off Cape Coast Castle there had been 41 deaths out of 200 expedition members and crew while others still lay seriously ill but were expected to recover. It was a tragedy that provoked deep reflection and comment. If you were evangelical missionaries like Crowther and Schön you never wavered in your belief that everything, good and bad, had its place in God's scheme. It is one of the impenetrable mysteries of Providence; God instructs us sometimes by prosperity, sometimes by adversity. If you were a trader in the Oil Rivers you expressed surprise that the Government in London had so hurriedly despatched an expedition with such vague aims into the interior as though by its presence the clandestine trade in slaves could be brought to a halt. If you were a politician you berated the Government for its vacillation and inconsistency in its Niger policies. Why make treaties with local chiefs that could so easily be broken? All at such cost in human life and money! If you were a surgeon you were astonished that the organisers of the expedition had so completely ignored the usual death-rate figures among those, slaves and crews, who voyaged on the Bight of Biafra and the Niger delta: 10% among slaves, 17% among crews. In the British naval squadron at least 60 sailors died each year. Had the volunteers been informed of the risk, and that there was no known cure for malaria, yellow fever and dysentery?

When they landed in Freetown, Samuel and James had the heart-breaking task of imparting the news of Kwame's death to Jane. As they entered the house her warm greeting faded as she saw their faces. She called out: "What is wrong? Why is Kwame not with you? Has he met with an accident?"

And as James spoke the words: "We are terribly sorry to tell that your husband died of malaria fever on board ship," Jane's whole body stiffened as though she had been turned to stone then she was racked with sobbing; so great was her grief. She held out her arms in appeal to them and cried:

"Help me to bear this dreadful blow."

Samuel hugged her and comforted her and James held out the black medical case and Kwame's letter for her to take and led her to a chair. Tears streamed from her eyes as they told her of the tragic voyage and how her husband had literally used up his entire strength in caring for his patients and had died peacefully in his sleep. Jane slowly became calmer, read the letter, caressed the black bag in her lap and said: "It was the last thing that he touched. You know, it went everywhere with him. Henry Tedlie gave it to him when he died and it reminded him always of Henry's devotion to his patients. And now, he wants me to take it to his brother. That I will and must do."

She began to cry again and put her head into her hands but the sobbing had ceased and it seemed to them both that her distress was beginning to ease. Dr. Wilson had entered the room silently and had heard the news. She raised her head and asked him: "You will help me to get a ship to Jamaica, won't you?"

"Of course I will, my dear Jane."

"You understand that I must fulfil Kwame's last wish and take the bag and his diary to his brother."

"Certainly I understand. We will all do everything we can to help you, be sure of that."

"I will write to Kwabena as soon as I feel more composed. Thank you, Samuel and James, for being with him and loving him right to the end." She rose to her feet, clutched the bag and the letter, and spoke through her tears:

"I am going to my room now to be alone with my grief and to thank God for the happiness that Kwame brought to me."

When the tragic news reached England Mr. Bowdich was deeply moved and went without delay to talk with Mr. Hope Smith about Kwame's untimely death and about Kwabena.

"I had thought that Kwame had a settled future in Freetown and that after a few years he and his wife would return to Juaben. What his widow will do I don't know, but I must write to her and offer my help. The brothers were very close, you know, and Kwabena belonged in a special way to our family. He was Edward's protégé and then became mine. He has made a good reputation for himself in Jamaica and I am glad that he has had that experience but is it not time now for him to get a specific post as a lawyer maybe back among his own people?"

Hope Smith took some time in replying: "Things seem promising on the coast: Maclean has made a peace treaty with Ashanti and has built up an astonishingly effective organisation among the coastal chiefs by which they accept his jurisdiction and, for the most part, have stopped fighting among themselves. He has developed a system of justice according to Akan custom but with English law mixed in it. The trade in palm-oil has increased four-fold in ten years and I have the impression that the Government is seriously considering taking over the coastal region as a protectorate. What I am coming to is this: why don't we contact Captain Maclean and suggest that Kwabena, trained and licensed in English law, a fluent spreaker of Ashanti, a member of the ruling family in Juaben, could be of great use on his staff in future developments? A top level conference at the Colonial Office is scheduled in the near future and it is certain that Captain Maclean will be attending. Could you arrange for

Mr. Kwabena Boaten to come to London so that we can arrange a meeting between the two of them?"

Bowdich nodded his head in agreement and responded:

"What a wonderful idea! I'll get a message to him to come to England. Foster can carry on alone at Witham for some time and if Governor Maclean offers Kwabena a post he can return to Jamaica for a short period to sort himself out. Will you contact the Colonial Office through your usual channels and let me know?"

Meanwhile in Jamaica Kwabena had been deeply saddened by the news of his brother's death on the ill-fated Niger Expedition and a few days ago he had received a letter from Kwame's widow Jane with the details and stating her intention of bringing certain of his personal effects including his black leather medical case and his last letter to him in Jamaica. She could now already be on her way and he had arranged for the best guest room to be made ready for her. He would have to discuss her future plans with her and offer all the help in his power.

It did not seem long before the arrival of a vessel from Freetown was signalled and Kwabena hurried down to the harbour as passengers were already being landed. Standing in line, erect in bearing, was a young woman, taller than most, her blond hair kept in place by a reddish head scarf, wearing a matching blouse and skirt. That must be she, he thought, as he recalled how Kwame had described her in one of his letters. At first glance, she looked to be European but when you observed more closely her skin colour was like pale, washed sand at low tide, and her lips and nose made you think of African ancestry. When she spoke to the sailor helping them into the landing barge, she smiled and her eyes lit up with interest and warmth, and he returned her smile. Kwabena instinctively felt that she was a person he would like to get to know. Her mother was an Ewe from across the Volta river and her father was a Dane from Keta called Pedersen and she had run away on a naval squadron ship and had been landed in Freetown where she had become the competent and skilful helper and organiser in Dr. Wilson's practice. And his brother had married her! He resolved there and then, to do everything in his power to help her to overcome her sorrow, he would be the one responsible for her welfare from now on!

And when they met and shook hands, she smiled through her tears and said: "Mr. Boaten, you look so much like your brother, I recognised you at once. I am so glad to be here in Jamaica with my brother-in-law!" And Kwabena replied:

"You are most welcome; Kwame was right to send you to me. Your room in Witham House has already been prepared and you may stay there as long as you like."

It wasn't long before Jane began to take charge of the household and to organise the office in a more efficient way, much to the pleasure of Kwabena and John. They took meals together and soon Jane began to absorb the details of plantation life and the problems of the abolition of slavery. She developed easy contacts with the domestic staff and the labourers because she quickly learned their names and took a genuine interest in them and their work. She was always friendly and cordial without being effusive and soon she had started a sick-bay in a room at the rear of the house for the treatment of minor ailments. All the records of the domestic servants and the labourers were now carefully kept by her and all the details of their final freedom were regulated.

Then, one day, a letter marked 'urgent' arrived from London written by 'Uncle' Bowdich to Kwabena requesting his immediate return to England because of the distinct possibility of a permanent appointment as a lawyer on the staff of Governor Maclean in Cape Coast. It was an opportunity too good to miss, in particular the chance to get back to his own land and to be helping there in his profession. He took the first available ship and three weeks later was sitting in a room of the Secretary of State for the Colonies being interviewed by Governor, Captain George Maclean, who was on leave in England.

From all that he had heard, Captain Maclean had built up a splendid reputation as a dispenser of justice for complete fairness, he never favoured white against black or black against white, all chiefs were treated alike, he never took bribes, he listened to every side of an issue before coming to a decision and once decided, he never changed his mind. He had brought peace and encouraged trade so that along the coast there was an air of well-being and progress. Largely through his success it seemed that the British Government was now firmly considering taking political responsibility for the coastal peoples from the Pra to the Volta. He began by asking Kwabena about his family: "I understand that you are related to the Juaben ruling family?"

"Yes, Sir, my father was the Juabenhene, my mother belongs to the Juaben Aduana clan. As a result of the conflict with the Kumasihene they fled with most of their people to Kibi."

"They have been given permission to return. The Kibi Omanhene, the Danish Governor of Christiansborg and I made an agreement with the Asantehene, Kwaku Dua 1, for them to go back. But their homecoming has been delayed. I regret to inform you that a year ago your father passed away in a village called Asaman in Akim."

"I did not know that. During my absence in England I wrote to him a few times but I never had a reply. Who was elected in his place?" asked Kwabena.

"His younger brother Kofi succeeded but within the space of three months he also died."

"Who occupies the stool now? So far as I remember there were no other brothers."

"You will be surprised to hear that their mother, Ama Sewa, has been elected Juabenhene! She was already Queenmother but she is no longer addressed as Ohema but as Juabenhene, both by her people but also by the Asantehene. She has taken the oath of fidelity to him wearing a belt of *sepow* knives, as a sign of her right of capital punishment over her subjects, she has attended the *Odwira* ceremony and she has finally led her people back to rebuild the town of Juaben which is lying in ruins! She is a very determined woman!"

"I am most interested to hear that. My mother and Ama Sewa were close friends and I am anxious to hear if my mother is still alive."

"Why not call on the Wesleyan missionary, Rev. T.B. Freeman? When he was in Kumasi he visited Juaben and spoke with Queen Ama Sewa. Call at the Wesleyan Conference Office in City Road, they will know where you can contact him. He is in London writing his Journal of his two visits to Asante and called on me in Cape Coast before he left. I was greatly impressed by him. To continue our interview; where did you study English law, Mr. Boaten?"

"I was at Lincoln's Inn and also apprenticed to the Southwark Magistrate's Clerk where I learned much of the daily routine of the court."

"Apart from your legal experience in Jamaica, you have never practised?"

"No. Recently I have begun to think that I should seek a permanent post in which my legal training would be fully used."

"You may know something of what has taken place on the coast during recent years. From the law court in Cape Coast I have sought to settle internal feuds between the different chiefs by Akan laws and customs with a leavening of English law. In the main this has proved effective and I would say, popular, insofar that we are more and more being asked to adjudicate on weighty matters like panyarring, capital punishment, land ownership, inheritance, and marriage. We are being forced to think of a basic legal system and a constitution that would be acceptable to all. I need someone like yourself who belongs to the country who can help in this procedure. You speak the language, you know English law, but above all you possess the ability which we whites only partially have of appreciating the African point of view. It is not yet decided but it is under active review whether the British Government will establish a colony on the Guinea Coast but if they were to do so a workable system of law would be desirable. You know how much of English law has developed from precedent; I think that Akan law can develop in a similar way so that the chiefs in the regions have an important role to play in it with a supreme court on the coast somewhere."

Maclean hesitated a few moments and then said: "If you were to be offered a post on my staff would you accept?"

"Yes, Sir, I should be greatly honoured and challenged."

"How soon could you arrange to leave Jamaica and report for duty in Cape Coast?"

"I need to give my present employer three months's notice during which time I must finalise a contract I have undertaken to write for Mr. Andreas Riis, the Danish missionary, who wishes to recruit some black Christians in Jamaica, mainly married couples with children, to form the nucleus of a Christian community in Akropong-Akuapem. The Swiss Basel Mission wishes to make a second start there. The recruitment is however, taking a long time.

My only other consideration is personal, namely that my late brother's widow is residing with me on the plantation in Jamaica and I must make suitable arrangements for her. Could you give me six months' grace to arrange my affairs and to allow for travelling time?"

"Before you leave London I should like to receive from you a letter of application for a post of legal assistant in my department in Cape Coast together with two testimonials, one from Lincoln's Inn, the other from Mr. Bowdich. Please send these to me care of this office. In due course you will receive an offer of the post together with details of salary and other conditions. Let us agree that you will take up the post as soon as possible after January 1st next year. I shall then be in charge of a new law department on the Coast. Meanwhile you have sufficient time to sort things out."

Captain Maclean stood up and held out his hand to shake:

"I look forward to having you as my assistant, Mr. Boaten, and to our next meeting on the Coast." He turned and left the room while Kwabena sat in a daze as he reflected on his good fortune.

A few days later Rev.T.B. Freeman, the dedicated leader of the Wesleyan Methodist mission, who had twice visited Kumasi in 1839 and 1841-2 and had persuaded the Asantehene to allow him to open a Christian mission station there, rose from his seat in the conference room of the Wesleyan Church, and held out his hand to bid Kwabena welcome.

"I understand, Mr. Boaten, that you belong to Juaben."

"Yes. When I heard from Captain Maclean that you had recently visited Juaben I wondered if you had any news of my mother. It is many years since I had any news of her."

"I regret that I can't give you any direct news but we now have a resident missionary in Kumasi, Rev.Robert Brooking, and I can pass on your enquiry to him but some time may elapse before we hear anything."

"If you should have news of my mother, Akosua Boaten, write to me care of the Colonial Office. How did you come to visit Juaben?"

"The Asante King knew that I had helped a few people with my medicines and he told me that a female member of his family was sick in Juaben and I offered to go there but although we arrived after dark and those who were carrying my camp-bed and canteen had got lost, Queen Sewa provided for me. I didn't know until then that she was the sister of the previous Ashanti King and the aunt of the present King. On the following day she sent for me. She was suffering from a severe nervous affliction which had partially paralysed her left arm and I gave her something to relieve the pain which she thanked me for, and when I left to return to Kumasi, she and her daughter accompanied me to the outskirts of the town. She seemed to me to be between sixty and sixty-five years old but full of courage and energy."

"How does the town look now?"

"About half of it is still in ruins, the house of the Juaben chief had been blown up and is not yet rebuilt but previous house-owners are busy everywhere reconstructing; some of the streets are being re-formed. During my short stay Queen Ama Sewa introduced me to her daughter Afrakuma Panyin and we spoke together at some length. In the house where she is living were a number of elderly women who seemed to be close friends of the Queen. Could it be that your mother was one of them?"

"It could be. I only hope so. May I ask, Sir, what are your plans when you return to West Africa?"

"I hope to be able to make a journey to the coast of Nigeria west of Lagos where there are a number of Allada exiles from Porto Novo who have settled at Badagry and these two towns are still much involved in the slave trade. I shall be accompanied by Mr. and Mrs William de Graft who travelled round England with me to raise funds for the Asante mission."

"I understand that the CMS also have the intention of starting a mission in Yoruba territory led by Mr. S.A.Crowther."

"That is so. They will make Abeokuta their base, much further inland. Yorubaland is large, there is room for both our Churches."

Kwabena came away from the interview in thoughtful mood. It seemed that the chances of his mother being still alive were good. Perhaps when he was in Cape Coast an opportunity would arise for him to visit Juaben. As soon as the formalities of his new appointment had been completed, he paid visits to the Bowdich family in Hampstead and to his old school; to Dr. Gillman and family, above all, to Aunt Betsy Shuttleworth who had mothered him and Kwame and nursed him after his cholera illness. She wept when he told her of Kwame's death but she was gratified that he had died so bravely. He told her of his new appointment and she said:

"I always knew that you would go far in your career. I shall pray for you and hope that you find your mother alive and well."

During the voyage back to Jamaica he read and re-read Dr. Gillman's 'Life of S.T.Coleridge' published in 1838, as well as two books on English Common Law which he thought would be useful in the future. What occupied his mind the most was Jane's position: she had made herself indispensable in the household at Witham but in addition had assisted him greatly with the records of the employees, their wages, their free time, and their health, while John found her help with ordering, storing and exporting invaluable. Her fresh environment and duties had helped her to cope with the intense sadness of Kwame's death, he thought, but what of her future now that he had accepted a post in Cape Coast? He could not simply send her back to Freetown; it had become abundantly clear to him that for her he was her nearest and only relative. In what capacity could he take her with him to Cape Coast even if she wished to go there? His return to Witham House was so festive and cheerful as the three of them sat at table to a wonderful welcome dinner prepared by Jane and he told them in detail what had happened to him in London, that he became aware of something that had been absent from his life since he had left Juaben, namely, the warmth and the affection of a home. How much in so short a time had Jane Pederson created; Witham House had become a home!

Some days later, Kwabena spoke in confidence to John Fore-man, the overseer, who asked him: "Why have you never married, Kwabena?"

"I suppose the main reason is that I was always too busy, occupied with my career and then here in Jamaica I felt that my job was a stepping stone to something else."

"Now that something else has turned up it would be an advantage to have a wife. Have you not thought of Jane in this connection? She is very a attractive and capable person, you would have to go far to find anyone her equal. She has a great regard for you, not just because you and her late husband were close friends, but for what you have achieved."

John's words took Kwabena totally by surprise; he had never before regarded Jane in that way at all and now suddenly it became obvious to him why he had felt that his return to Witham was like coming home. It was because Jane was there! How stupid he had been not to realise that her presence had begun to have that effect on him! How much pleasure he had had in telling her about his visit to London; how he had appreciated answering her questions; how she had shared his interest in his new job and in what Governor Maclean had described! But there was another important thing: how attractive Jane had looked; how her eyes had shone, how sincere her smile, when he had told her of his success! Was that not a sign of her affection for him? How dense he had been not to be conscious of that before!

He expressed his gratitude to John: "Thanks for what you have said about Jane, I never fully realised before that I had such a high regard for her. But is that love, John? Europeans seem to set so much store by love as a precondition of marriage."

John pondered a few moments over the question:

"Well, if you think of love only as doing the things that lovers do together, every couple, I would say, experiences that. But if you think of love as also having mutual respect, sharing interests, working for each other, raising children, what you do for the sake of your partner every day, year in, year out, that's the love that counts."

"But, John, how do I approach a fine woman like Jane?"

"You deal with it like you deal with a legal problem: state the facts first and then draw the conclusion as you see it. Jane is a very practical person and will appreciate your frankness. Of course, you need to start with some unmistakable token of your regard like offering her a rose or flowers, or something like that."

Some days later, when Jane sat down for breakfast, there was a vivid single red rose on her plate together with a note from Kwabena asking her to meet him in his office later. As she came in she he noticed that she had pinned the rose to her blouse; it was a good sign, he thought, and when she was seated he showed his letter of appointment with its impressive heading and red wax seal to her and then said:

"I have been reading it carefully again, Jane. You realise that at the end of this year I shall have to travel to Cape Coast and take up residence there. I should very much like you to come with me because since you have been here I have fallen in love with you. I don't want you to go back to Freetown. I mean, I would like you to become my wife and share life with me from now on."

Jane sat quite still and silent and Kwabena began to fear that he had been too blunt and had not spoken any words of praise or of his admiration for her. He hastened to add:

"I missed you very much when I was away in London and since I came back it has become quite clear to me that you have given a new meaning to my life. I have lived a solitary existence up to now and have given up everything to my career. I envied my brother that he had found such happiness with you and I have thought that fate has taken a hand in sending you to me."

Jane smiled and responded: "You should know, Kwabena, that for a woman to receive an offer of marriage from a man that she already greatly admires, is the greatest compliment that you can pay to her. I have greatly respected you ever since we met, I admire your modesty about your merits and abilities, you are patient and sympathetic towards other people and you have treated me with the utmost kindness and consideration at all times. Yes!Yes! Kwabena Boaten, I will be your wife and will be deeply honoured to be so. I will serve you and love you as you deserve."

She stood up and held out her arms for him and they embraced, gazed deeply into each other's eyes and kissed long and deep in total commitment to each other. Then he held her from him and still looking into her eyes, spoke the words that every woman needs to hear:

"And I too, will love you and serve you as you deserve!"

He took her hand and led her into the garden where they walked up and down, deep in the heart-to-heart exchange of views that lovers indulge in after their first pledge of love, oblivious to the smiles of those who observed them. It was only as John Foreman approached them with a letter in his hand, that they were brought down to earth. Kwabena smiled radiantly and said:

"John, congratulations are in order! Jane has promised to become my wife! You know, she will not need to change her name!"

John wished them every happiness and the said:

"Here is a letter from Rev. J.F. Sessing probably about the contract of service. Maybe he could officiate as the two of you tie the marriage-knot!"

Chapter 8

West Indians Sail to Akropong/Akuapem 1843

"I am convinced that although our attempt on the Guinea Coast to establish a mission has exacted a heavy toll of consecrated lives, this harvest of death......is yet a blessing to the Mission's existence. It is the most serious defect in the Mission, if no one is in a postion to face death for the sake of the Gospel. Great blessing for Basel has flowed over from Africa."
Josenhans, Basel Mission Director, Missions-Magazine.

The disturbing fact that white Christian missionaries in West Africa soon succumbed to the dreaded malaria was abundantly illustrated by the experience of the Moravians, the Wesleyans and those from Basel. The pioneer Moravians, Jacob Protten and Heinrich Huckuff at Elmina in 1737 were both in their graves within four years; a second group of five in 1767 lost three of their number within a few months while a third group of four in 1770 at Ningo, east of Christiansborg, all died of fever within two years. The first Wesleyan missionary, Joseph Dunwell, passed away six months after his arrival in Cape Coast in 1834 and his successors, two married couples Rev. and Mrs. Wrigley and Rev. and Mrs. Harrop had died within a year; Freeman's wife died two months' after their landing in 1838. In 1827 four men of the Basel Mission, Karl Salbach, Gottlieb Holzwarth, Johannes Henke and Johannes Schmidt made Ningo their base but within a year three were in their graves and Henke had taken refuge in Christiansborg Castle as chaplain where he died in 1831. Two of the three replacements from Basel, Andreas Riis and Peter Jäger, both Danes, and Friedrich Heinze, a doctor, from Saxony, had lost their lives leaving only Riis. He decided that to live on the Akwapim Ridge was healthier for Europeans and he was warmly welcomed in Akropong by Chief Addo Dankwa. Further help came from Basel with the arrival of Johannes Mürdter, Andreas Stanger and Anna Wolters, a twenty-year-old Danish bride for Riis. Stanger was dead within the year and Riis's baby daughter died in 1838 and as a result Riis decided to leave Akropong. In 1840 Riis reported the failure of the mission in Basel: twelve years had elapsed since the first attempt and eight missionaries had given up their lives while there was not a single convert to Christianity.

There was no shortage of volunteers for missionary service but it seemed wise to adopt a new strategy in view of the high death toll. The fact that from Sierra Leone Christian Africans had begun to return to their home areas in other parts of West Africa, especially Yorubas to southern Nigeria, as well as the new situation in Jamaica where there were now mission churches composed of freed slaves who were able to travel, gave rise to the plan put forward by Wilhelm Hoffmann, Director of the Basel Mission, of settling in Akropong a group of second generation liberated African slaves who had become Christian in Jamaica. This group would form at once the nucleus of a Christian congregation which would be the base and support of a renewed attempt. They would show that Christianity could be a religion for Africans and would assist the white missionaries in building and growing crops. Hoffman gained the interest of Buxton and of the Governor of Jamaica, Lord Elgin, as well as of the Danish Government in Copenhagen. The Moravian Conference at Berthelsdorf declared their agreement to the proposal that volunteers could be recruited from among their mission converts in Jamaica. The Basel mission agent, Rev. J. F. Sessing, had solicited Kwabena's help in drawing up a contract of service and now wished to finalise the arrangement and to meet him in Spanish Town.

Kwabena explained to Jane: "The Jamaican immigrants have been selected and Sessing wants me to be there to explain the contract to them before they sign. He thinks that they will feel happier when a black lawyer discusses it with them."

"What are their problems?" asked Jane.

"They are unsure about their future: in Akropong they will be living under Danish law; then most of them would like to return to Africa but the missionary aspect is a secondary aspect in their minds; they want to be certain that signing a contract will not take away their freedom."

"How long will they have to sign on for?"

"For two years during which the Mission will support them entirely, provide them with a house and land for a garden in return for which they will promise to serve the Mission in all its needs. At the end of two years they can choose to leave or to work for the Mission at a reasonable wage."

"What happens if they want to go back to Jamaica?"

"If they stay with the Mission for five years they would have their passage paid provided they had not been guilty of a moral offence during this period."

"What kind of a moral offence?"

"It's not defined in the contract but I think that only very serious matters like murder, adultery, deliberate disobedience, grave personal abuse, things like that, are meant."

Everyone at Whitham was delighted at the news of the engagement of Mr. Kwabena and Mrs. Jane, as they were called, but sad when they learned that they would soon be leaving Jamaica. The information had reached London and Freetown: Dr. Wilson sent an ivory necklace made by a Mende craftsman for Jane; from the Bowdich family a canteen of silver cutlery and a boxed set of Wedgwood crockery arrived, and Aunt Betsy had enclosed in her letter a gold signet-ring for Kwabena that had belonged to her grandfather.

When Kwabena returned from his meeting with Sessing he was bursting with information for Jane: "All went well. The Moravians have recruited six married couples who have seven children among them and two bachelors from Jamaica, another bachelor from Antigua, and a young man, George Thompson, from

Liberia, who had been brought by Sessing to Basel to be educated in the Seminary. Thompson has found a wife called Catherine Mulgrave, who at five years of age had been adopted by an Englishwoman and who later trained as a teacher. The group will be led by Andreas Riis, helped by Johann Widman and Hermann Halleur from Germany. The Basel Mission has chartered an Irish two-masted brig for 600 pounds to transport the group and their luggage, stores and equipment of all kinds as well as foodstuffs and seeds, from Jamaica to Christiansborg. The ship is called the 'Joseph Anderson' and Sessing has offered us both a passage as a recompense for the work I have done over the contract. I had mentioned the fact that you and I were engaged and he offered to marry us and bring us to Cape Coast! I told him that I had to discuss the offer with you."

"When do they plan to sail?"

"He thinks that everything will be ready at the end of January or early February next year. That would fit in with my appointment; Captain Maclean said, 'as soon as possible after January 1st.'"

"What is your reaction to the offer?"

"I am inclined to accept. When we are back on the coast it will be useful to have made contact with them. Sessing thought that they would have the chance to ask me questions about Akan life on board and I could teach them a few words and phrases. If we travel with this ship it will ease our arrangements a bit."

"I think so too. Can we inform Maclean in time?"

"We can send the information to London and to Cape Coast. Now you have to decide if you want Sessing to perform the wedding ceremony and when and where."

"Give me a day or two to think it over," Jane said with a smile.

"What sort of Christians are the Moravians? I think I was baptised by one of the Danish Lutheran Church chaplains in Keta but the only church service I ever attended was the Church of England in Freetown."

"All I know is what I learned from Sessing: they are Protestant, very pious and fervent, they read the Bible a lot like the Wesleyans. They started in Bohemia but their main centre is in Saxony and from there they send missionaries out to difficult places like India and West Africa. The Moravians are the oldest Protestant missionary society. I was baptised in London in the Church of England but I have attended church service only a few times."

"Now, Kwabena, you are using English words that I don't know! Whatever is 'pious' and 'fervent'?"

"When you study law, Jane, there is a particular word for everything so that what is intended is absolutely clear: my dictionary was hardly ever out of my hand! 'Pious' means showing or having a deep devotion to their religious belief, and 'fervent' means earnest, serious about their commitment to Christ matters more to them than anything else. But they are very nice people: honest, cheerful, hopeful, with high moral standards."

"Why don't we all live like that?"

"Because human nature is too strong: envy, jealousy, anger, pride and hate take over from time to time, even among pious groups, that's why the law courts are always kept busy!"

Jane decided that she and Kwabena would be married on a Saturday in December at Witham by Johann Sessing and all the workers on the estate should be invited; they would spend a few days' honeymoon somewhere and come back as a married couple to preside over a Christmas dinner for all the servants. It was typical of Jane to share her own happiness with those who worked on the plantations; such festivities were unheard of but Jane insisted and after discussion with Kwabena and John it was so arranged. The anticipation and excitement were intense: for the wedding the house servants and the field workers grouped themselves in a large half-circle on the front lawn with a good view of the terrace where the ceremony took place and when finally, Johann Sessing, pronounced a blessing on the couple, they broke into song:

"Kum ba yah, my Lord, kum ba yah,
Someone's crying, Lord, kum ba yah,

Someone's singing, Lord, kum ba yah,
Someone's praying, Lord, kum ba yah."
Someone's marrying, Lord, kum ba yah!"

"What are they singing?" Kwabena asked.

"It's the only hymn in pidgin English that I know," explained Sessing.

"I first heard it in Liberia; all the slaves seem to know it whatever their origin, it unites them in a real way. It can be used on any occasion to call on the Lord to take part in the situation and make it good." Then the roll of a drum was heard and the entire group began to sway to the rhythm of the song and the beat of the drum. Finally they all clapped their hands in pleasure and appreciation at being invited and pointed to one of the children who was coming forward carrying something wrapped in a strip of gold *kente* cloth which he handed over to Jane who carefully unwound the cloth to reveal an *Akuaba,* a carved, black Ashanti doll with a circular head and a long-shaped neck, a pregnancy symbol! Jane stood up and held out her arms to them in thanks, turned and took Kwabena's hand so that they stood together acknowledging the prolonged applause. Who would ever have thought that slaves would have put their meagre pence together to buy a present for the Missus!

It was the same at the Christmas Day dinner after they had come back from a brief honeymoon in the Blue Mountains and they sat together at trestle tables while the servants sat on the grass to relish their portion of Christmas pudding after a piece of roasted pork and potatoes in rich gravy: they sang again,

"Someone's feasting, Lord, kum ba yah,
Someone's feasting, Lord, kum ba yah."

There was suddenly a deep silence when Amos, their spokesman, came forward and spoke:

"Mister and Missus Boaten, we slaves and servants in this here house called Witham, we say, all of us say, we much pleased to work in this house 'cos you all and Mister Foreman, treat us right not like some white folks we know of. Soon we be free but we not forget you all." He stopped and scratched his head, having forgotten his last sentence and somebody called out; 'Merry Christmas!' Amos gave a broad smile, and said: "We all wish you all Merry Christmas and happy New Year" and held up a scroll of paper on which in bright colours their three names had been painted with the words 'Merry Christmas' and the date.

They went forward, shook his hand and thanked them all. It was a Christmas Day to remember!

On 7th February, 1843, the brigantine, Joseph Anderson, set sail with all the West Indian immigrants, the Basel missionaries and Mr. and Mrs. Boaten on board. For five days the ship struggled through a Caribbean storm, then as they reached the open ocean contrary winds hindered their progress, many passengers were sea-sick while some found the heat oppressive but by the end of the second week they had all found their sea-legs and had begun to enjoy the voyage.

Andreas Riis and Kwabena became friends and shared their experiences: "What made you select Akropong as a base for the mission?" Kwabena asked.

"The first group of four from Basel who landed at Christiansborg in 1828 were all in their graves within three years and the second group of three, of which I was one, were soon laid low with malaria and I was the only one to survive. I took up the post of chaplain at the castle but I had to wait for two years before a fresh chaplain was appointed and I was free to make a decision about the mission project. I had been warmly befriended by George Lutterodt, a trader who also had a plantation inland, who told me about the failed settlement of Dr. P. E. Isert who had signed a contract with the Chief of Akropong, Nana Obuobi Atiemo, to set up a 'plantation colony' in conjunction with missionary enterprise. He had the approval of the Danish King. Dr Isert wrote a glowing first report which he took personally to Christiansborg and there suddenly died. His successor, J.N. Flindt, seemed to have some success, but suddenly the Danish Governor abandoned the project in 1794. It seemed important to visit Akropong to check on the climate and the general situation there."

"Did you go alone?"

"No, I was accompanied by trader, George Lutterodt, and we reached Akropong in January, 1835, to be cordially welcomed by Chief Addo Dankwa. I spent an uncomfortable rainy season in a one-roomed hut but I managed to build a stone and timber house into which I moved a year later. Afterwards the locals gave me the name Osiadan or Housebuilder!"

"Did Basel accept your decision?"

"Yes. Towards the end of 1837 they sent Johannes Mürdter and Andreas Stanger, both from Würtemberg, who brought with them Anna Wolters, a twenty-year-old Danish girl from the Moravian settlement at Christiansfeld in Denmark as a bride for me! You and your wife have met her on board."

"So it seemed then that the mission work could be begun?"

"Only with the greatest difficulty. You see, in 1835, Addo Dankwa was destooled after 24 years as chief and Adum Tokori was installed in his place but the strife between their supporters was such that normal life became impossible; many people took refuge on their farms and the town was half-deserted. What made things much worse was the fact that the Danish Governor, F.S. Mörck, became alarmed at the spread of English influence through the work of Maclean, and started to enforce the rather vague Danish authority over Akuapem and Krobo. At that time the Akuapem had invaded Krobo and Mörck tried to get both sides to submit to his arbitration but the Akuapem chiefs refused. During the tribal war I was forced by Mörck to accompany the Danish soldiers who intervened and I was kept busy as chaplain attending the wounded of both sides! You see, Adum seemed to favour the Danes but the Governor assumed that I sided with the English so that from April to June in 1837 he detained me in the castle, ostensibly for my protection although I was always careful not to take sides. When Addo Dankwa took refuge with the English at James Fort, Accra, I was accused by Mörck of being involved in the affair!"

"What were you able to achieve under these circumstances?"

"We spent time learning Twi and making contacts with certain people; we improved the house and laid out a vegetable plot. But it was a bad time for us: Andreas Stanger passed away on Christmas Eve that year, Mörck banned us from doing any missionary work while Chief Adum discouraged his people from having any connection with us. Mürdter and I later managed to make two exploratory journeys to the Shai Hills, through Krobo and across the Volta into the Akwamu district but that was all. We reported to Basel and asked them to make an appeal to the Danish King against Mörck's attitude. Then came more personal tragedy: Mürdter and our baby daughter died in 1838 and my wife and I were alone."

Kwabena held the hand of Riis in sympathy and asked:

"What did you decide to do then?"

"I decided to leave Akropong, left my wife with Lutterodt in Christiansborg and went to Cape Coast en route for Kumasi."

"What was your intention?"

"You see, although Basel had given us permission to return to Europe, I was always convinced that the Christian Gospel could and should be established in West Africa. I wanted to meet Freeman and talk to him about possibilities in Asante. I wanted to be fully informed because I had suggested to Basel that instead of Akropong the main location of the mission might be Kumasi. I was warmly received by Governor Maclean: he had a positive view of the work of the Wesleyan missionaries at Cape Coast compared with the attitude of Mörck, and I was also able to meet Freeman who was hopeful of receiving permission to start a mission in Kumasi."

"I met them both in London last year. I have been appointed as assistant to Maclean as you may know. I also had the opportunity of asking Freeman if he had, by chance, any news of my mother. I belong to Juaben and most of the people have gone back there after their sojourn in Akim."

"Had Freeman any news for you?" enquired Riis.

"No. But from what he told me of his visit to Juaben I am

hopeful that she is still alive. I plan to go there as soon as I can after we land. How did you get on in Kumasi?"

"I stayed fourteen days but did not have the privilege of a private audience with the Asantehene. I reached Kumasi on 29th December, 1839 and in the following July I made my report to the Committee in Basel. After long discussions it was decided to put this new strategy with a group of West Indian Christians into effect, and to make another start in Akropong. Unlike Freeman, I was not convinced that the time was ripe for beginning a Christian mission in Kumasi."

"Why was that?"

"I thought that until the political problem with Asante was settled it would be unwise to make a commitment there. Asante was still claiming Elmina and still seeking her own outlet to the coast. I also felt that the difficulties in Akwapim and Krobo would soon be resolved and that Akropong was much nearer the coast for supplies from Europe."

Kwabena wished Andreas success this time and added:

"May I put to you a personal query that puzzles us Africans, what is the main reason for putting so much stress on religion? I mean, we can understand the traders who buy and sell for profit, we understand those who are servants of foreign chiefs and kings, but now white people come with a message about religion as though that was more important than anything else."

"It's a result of the re-awakening of many members of the Protestant Churches in western Europe through their reading of the Bible to the duty of preaching the Gospel everywhere in the world. They have a deep personal relationship to Jesus Christ that they call 'conversion' or 'being saved' or 'born again' and it dominates their lives. The Wesleyan Church and the Basel Mission are examples of this movement."

"You mean that not all Christians are missionaries?"

"They should be but they are unfortunately not. The missionaries are a minority of the members of the Churches."

"Is that why the missionaries lay so much stress on personal belief in Jesus Christ?"

"Just so. For us, the personal element is vital."

"For Africans, it is quite different. Of course, we are individuals but we never take decisions about our lives apart from our *abusua*, the total family. The idea that belief in Christ would mean that we had to separate ourselves from our family is unthinkable. I was baptised in England but it was not required of me to give up my existing African beliefs because I now, so to speak, 'belonged' to another social group called a church."

"I imagine that the minister who baptised you assumed that because you were in England you had already made the transition to European ways of thinking and living."

"I speak only as a lawyer but it seems to me that perhaps there is an error in putting European civilisation and the missionary version of the Christian religion together as though they were indispensable to each other. Africans are impressed by the material progress of the Europeans; it is somehing that they would like to have too: education, hospitals, steam engines, weapons and so on. Many people think that the God of the white man is great because he has given them so much; it would be wise to put him alongside our *Nyame!* But they would never give up their traditional beliefs. The most that I think you can expect is that some of their beliefs and traditions may be modified. You know, in all my time in England I never heard anyone speak of African religion as having any value or worth at all, it was 'primitive', 'immoral', 'superstitious', and could be dispensed with. I heard Freeman preach once what he called the Gospel or the Word of Life, it was in Cape Coast, and he got quite worked up over the state of degradation into which we had fallen especially over human sacrifices, over our ignorance of God and how we lay under the despotism of the Prince of Darkness. You know, Andreas, our people are very sensitive to ridicule but I felt that they had not fully understood him."

"What do you mean by 'civilisation' and 'the missionary version of Christianity?" queried Riis.

"I'm referring to the fact that our people are automatically attracted by the technical achievements of European civilisation:

guns and rifles in war, steamships, the ability ro read and write,their knowledge of medicine, and so on. So that when the missionaries offer schools, technical training and literacy, they will gain recruits. But the price of becoming a Christian is quite high: they are expected to repudiate most of the things that they have hitherto found indispensable in their lives, namely, their reverence for their ancestors, their innate attachment to the Earth Spirit, Asase Yaa, the close bond with the family, with the people and the chief. It's a high price to pay all at once.

"By the 'missionary' version of Christianity I am thinking of the way in which the missionaries emphasise individual conversion and separating off to join a new group that doesn't have any particular allegiance to the chief. Our social life is a unified one: from the chief down to the family there are rules that order our lives so that we know our position and our duties. When I was studying the development of English law centuries ago the feudal system had the same function; from the king to the humblest vassal everybody knew their place and their function. Now at that time there was only one religion in England and State and Church had to work together. They often quarrelled about this dual function and in the course of time the King took over the function of head of the Church in England. What I am getting at is that the missionaries should try to win the consent of the chief and the elders so that the entire community could accept Christianity. The elements that don't fit in with the Christian scheme can, in course of time, be corrected, modified or assimilated. Don't forget, Andreas, that among the Akans the chief has certain religious functions to perform for the whole community."

Riis was astonished at the way Kwabena had so clearly enunciated the issues. He was much influenced by what Kwabena had said but he knew that the overwhelming weight of opinion among Europeans was that all African indigenous religions could be dispensed with, there was virtually nothing that could be absorbed into the Christian scheme. He knew, too, that the ideal of a new dedicated, Christian group was what motivated all his colleagues. They were not impressed by the possibility of tribal conversion as had happened in Europe. Kwabena added: "You know, Andreas, that when I listened to Buxton and read Isert's book, I was much more convinced that their approach to my people was really more community-based: a mixture of agriculture, trade and religion rather than the establishment of a separate, relatively isolated religious group."

"But when you read the Bible, Kwabena, you see things differently."

"It depends upon who is reading it and what they take from it. All the Churches find the reasons for their existence, from Catholics to Quakers, in the Bible, while the Jews who wrote most of it don't accept Jesus as the Christ." Andreas smiled and felt that enough had been said for one day.

They mutually adjourned their discussion and turned in silence to lean over the ship's rail to watch the porpoises leaping and gambolling as they kept pace with the ship.

During the voyage Kwabena had spoken a few times with the immigrants about his people and their language; they were reassured by his presence. Most of them had lived for so long in Jamaica that Africa was a foreign land but all of them hoped that this new venture would mean a more secure life for them.

At length, at the end of the first week in April, the ship anchored off Cape Coast and Kwabena and Jane were welcomed on shore by Maclean who explained: "I have now been given the separate post of Judicial Assessor and we now have our own premises outside the Castle. Commander Hill has been appointed Governor so that I am free from the endless political palavers to concentrate upon the legal side of things. The British Government is working on a treaty which it is hoped that the chiefs will sign in due course, but I'll tell you all about that later. I understand, Mr. Boaten, that you have recently married and have brought your wife with you."

Kwabena duly introduced Jane and mentioned her father was Danish and her mother Ewe. Maclean bowed and said:

"Danish women have a special beauty; you would no doubt

get to know Mrs. Andreas Riis on board." He kissed her hand in welcome.

"I have been in touch with 'King' Aggrey since I returned. He is an old man now but still takes an active interest in everything that happens in Cape Coast. As a young man he served in the British navy so he is always friendly towards us. He lives in a large house not far from the Castle and he has let us have a parcel of land of about four acres not far away and we have put up an office building and two furnished houses for staff, one of which is earmarked for you, the one with a fine view of the sea and of the ships at anchor. Let me know what extra furniture you might need. The garden is not yet laid out but there will be a gardener and two watchmen. At the bottom of the plot there is accommodation for your house servants: you are allowed a cook and a housekeeper, we can help you to select them. For the next few weeks my batman will report to you every mid-morning to give you advice and help; he knows everyone locally so don't hesitate to use him. I have told him already about you. Now let's walk over and I'll present you to 'King' Aggrey."

He had been expecting them and as they approached a tall, lean figure rose to his feet, pushed his *ntama* from his left shoulder as a sign of respect and held out his right hand in greeting. He had lost one eye but the one remaining twinkled with pleasure. Seats were brought for them and they were offered palm wine to drink. He spoke English clearly and concisely: "You are heartily welcome to Cape Coast and to this domain and a happy return, Mr. Boaten, to your own land! I trust that you have not lost your mother tongue after all your years in England and that you will soon be able to visit Juaben with your wife! The wine is new and fresh, you can drink it safely."

They thanked him and drank to his health.

For Jane and Kwabena to be in Cape Coast in their own house among friends was a wonderful episode in their life together and they set about that very day making the house their home, unpacking and sorting out their belongings; and early on the following day Kwabena reported for duty. He had sensed that

Maclean was eager to discuss the legal situation with him and in Jamaica he had spent long hours trying to establish basic contact points between English law and Asante customary laws.

There were trestle tables around three sides of the room covered with files, folders and bundles of documents tied with string; on the fourth side stood a long table and two chairs. Maclean motioned him to a chair: "You need lots of table space in this kind of exercise. Tell me, from the notes I gave you in London what observations have you made?"

"When I compared your notes and the notes I made in the magistrate's court in Southwark, I was reminded of the way English law developed over six hundred years ago, I mean, the way the Common Law developed to impose a single system on the varied local customs through the work of mobile judges who supervised the local courts, and through the central Equity Court presided over by the Lord Chancellor."

"What points of contact can you make?"

"At that time, when the Common Law developed the feudal system still functioned and the holding of land was the basis: only the monarch could own land, the barons, nobles, the bishops and the abbots were tenants-in-chief and they could sub-let to lesser tenants under them. The tenants-in-chief swore an oath of allegiance to the king which involved military sevice or personal service. In Asante today, in Fante, Accra, Akyem, Akwapim for example, the position is similar: the chief allots the right to use the land but the land or plot remains the property of the stool. We have two well-known sayings:

'*Afuo ye me dea, asase ye Ohene dea , asase ye Ohene dea*' that means: 'The right to make use of the farm is mine but the land is the chief's'. When the chief handed over the farm he would say: '*Mede asase yi ma wo, hwe so ma me*', that is, 'I give you this land to look after for me'. I think that we need to plan carefully in this transition period the rules of land ownership.

The second thing is that in our customary law many household cases (*Afisem*) like thefts, slander, pawning, debts, assault and adultery, are dealt most often by the families involved who may appoint an arbitrator. Only cases that involve the state (*Oman Akyiwadie*) must go automatically to the Chief's court. I think. Sir, that we need to list cases which can be decided by customary law and which by English law."

Maclean replied: "Thank you for your interesting and useful suggestions. Recently I have listened to many cases in local courts and it has seemed to me that we need to set up a magistrate system in the large towns and to define carefully the function of local courts. For that we have to wait for Parliament in London to define the political future. What I would like you to work on immediately is to try to harmonise the customary laws; Fante, Asante, Akyem, Akuapem, Ga, and Ewe so that in the lower courts we can arrive at certain accepted generalisations."

George Maclean spoke with real warmth and enthusiasm, he was delighted that Kwabena had so succinctly grasped the essence of the problem and that at last he had an ideal colleague, one who was qualified in English law but who could, at the same time, fully comprehend the ways in which African traditions and usages could be incorporated. It was the first of many long discussions they had together and they worked in unison over the countless problems.

When, after some months, Kwabena raised the question of a short leave of absence to visit Juaben to find out about his mother, Maclean enquired: "Do you know Queen Ama Sewa personally? In any case, I can give you a note to her. Maybe, as well as contacting your mother again after all these years, you have a chance to make notes on the laws and customary usages in Juaben."

So, accompanied by two sturdy soldiers from the castle garrison and two bearers with the camp-bed and luggage, Kwabena marched back across the Pra to Kumasi where he was given a short audience by the Asantehene and then, a few days later he followed the well-beaten track to Juaben. The news of his coming had preceded him and when he announced his arrival at the Queen's house he was warmly welcomed by Ama Sewa and by a frail old lady whom he recognised at once as his dearest mother.

He held her close and she said through her tears:

"I knew you would come; so I have stayed alive! I have saved all your letters in this bag. When the war came and we fled to Akim I was glad that you were safe in Europe. Then you wrote from Jamaica and I knew that you were coming nearer. Now you are living in Oguaa and you have come to me here. My twin sister has died as well as her son Kwame in Nigeria." Later, as he said 'Good night' to her in her room, he told her about Kwame and Jane and described the work that he was doing with Captain Maclean she told him:

"That white man helped us to come back here and we are grateful to him. Ama will tell you how it is with us. I would like to come to Oguaa to you but I am too old and I am not able to walk so far. I must stay here to help Ama and her daughter Afrakuma." Her voice trailed away and she slept.

During the ensuing days Ama Sewa recounted to him the distress of the battle against the Asante army: "Your father prepared for a desperate struggle and he placed the command of our army in the hands of your uncle Kofi who took up a defensive position at the entrance to the town. But our army was only half the size of that of Kumasi. Your father brought up the rear. Time after time the attacks of the Asante warriors were repelled but we could not gain the victory and finally the order was given to retreat while our soldiers were still able to protect the people as they fled, with whatever they could carry, down the road to Akim. It was frightful as you can imagine. Fortunately, the Akim Chief accepted us and we survived there for nearly eight years until we knew that the way was clear for us to go back. But then it was all tragedy: on the journey back your father died in a village called Saman in Akim and after the burial his younger brother, Kofi, was enstooled but he too passed away within three months. There was simply no male heir, Kwabena, and everyone expected me, as Queen Mother, to give a lead. So after much heart-searching I proposed myself as Chief and the elders agreed. You are a lawyer, Kwabena, did I do right?"

"Of course you did right, because, under the circumstances,

there was no heir apparent and you, together with the elders, had to make sure that proper order and continuity was upheld. You took the customary oaths and you were set on the stool in the customary way so then you were the fully constituted ruler."

"I've been Chief now for so long that everyone accepts the fact. I carry out all the duties required of me, no one calls me Ohema (Queen Mother) but rather Juabenhene. I married the Ankobeahene but he remains an ordinary elder. The people have supported me, even those who stayed behind; they felt unsure about the peace with Kumasi and had settled down in the south. Now we are trying to bring Juaben back to normal. How is it with you personally? I think that you are fortunate to be working with Captain Maclean, he has won great respect everywhere. I think that you were treated well in England, did you encounter any great difficulties?"

"Kwame and I were lucky to be sponsored by Mr. Bowdich and his friends but we made two enemies, one of whom I still worry about."

He told Ama and her daughter Afrakuma, who had joined them, the story of their involvement with Mr. Joseph Dupuis.

"Why are you uneasy about him, is he not in London?"

"I read in a recent Gazette that he had been appointed as Consul at Bonny on the coast east of Lagos and I fear that his next move will be to Cape Coast. All his hopes are centred on promotion which he believes Kwame and I have frustrated. Once he knows that I have married Jane his hatred and resentment will know no bounds."

"Should you ever need help, don't forget that we are here."

Before he left, he promised his mother to write regularly and on his next visit to bring Jane. He was pleased that they were in contact again and that he had got to know Ama Sewa and Afrakuma; Juaben remained his home town! On the way back the heat was oppressive and twice his small group was overtaken by a fierce tornado of heavy rain and resounding thunder that reminded Kwabena of his first trek with Edward Bowdich. They were soaked to the skin on both occasions and had to take refuge in village huts overnight and when they reached a village a day's journey from Cape Coast Kwabena felt the first symptoms of malaria and hastily swallowed extra grains of quinine; his headache became more violent and the shivering began and he was laid insensible on his camp-bed. One of the soldiers hurried to Cape Coast to fetch the surgeon and a hammock with bearers, the others sat with him anxiously and,at intervals, gave him more quinine. When he finally awoke, dripping with sweat but aware that he had survived the fever, he looked up into Jane's loving face.

"You have given us all a scare, but you will be carried back home."

The surgeon nodded approvingly and they set out at once to get back before dark. It was a wonderful feeling to get his strength back in the comfort of his own home, above all, to be fussed over by a wife like Jane!

"You know, Jane, when I was ill I dreamt of Hardwick forcing me to kneel down and lick his boots but curiously, standing behind him was a tall white man with a sardonic expression on his face encouraging him. It looked like Dupuis but I couldn't be sure. I wasn't afraid so much as humiliated; it's something that has left a permanent scar on my soul. I feel that I owe it to my brother and to you to get even with him."

Chapter 9

The Bond of 1844

*"This treaty is known in Gold Coast history as the Bond of 1844.
It was signed by the chiefs of Denkyera, Assin, Abora, Donadi,
Domonase, Anomabu, and by Aggrey, chief of Cape Coast;
later on, many other chiefs in different parts of what we now
call the Colony signed as well, so that the Bond marks
the beginning of real British rule"*
W.E.Ward, A Short History of Ghana,London 1957,p.127.

A naval squadron vessel had brought the latest news from England and one morning early in 1843 a smiling Maclean entered Kwabena's office with a letter in his hand and called out: "Parliament has passed the Foreign Jurisdiction Act so we can now begin signing up the chiefs, let's start with our good friend King Aggrey!"

"What will they be agreeing to?" queried Kwabena.

"Exactly what I suggested: the introduction of a legal system in the territories of the chiefs who sign, a mixture of African customary laws and basic principles of English equity. Human sacrifices and panyarring are forbidden, all other crimes and offences will be tried before magistrates appointed by a Lieutenant Governor and the chiefs. There will be a separate government for the 'protected territory' but it will have no power over the land. It couldn't be better but we have a lot to do in a short time!"

The arrangements that Maclean had already introduced in Cape Coast were personally negotiated that year, eleven treaties or Bonds, and magistrates' courts and chiefs' courts began to function in unison. It was Maclean's greatest contribution to the unity of the 'protectorate'. For the chiefs who signed, the main motive was the sense of protection that the treaties gave against Asante ambitions. Even so, the legal reforms were a great step forward. From the mission and the fort schools a stream of literates began to flow to serve the chiefs who now conducted their correspondence with the authorities and with the courts in English on a background of agreed laws and usages. The letter-writer began to be a very important person.

Kwabena had never been so busy in his life: every day messengers arrived from chiefs who had signed and from others who had not signed, all wanted legal advice or they had cases to be solved. There were magistrates to be appointed and local courts to be organised. The Judicial Assessor's department grew in size and importance until a branch was opened in Jamestown, Accra.

Then one day in 1845 came the sad news that Sir Fowell Buxton had died. It was reported that after the tragedy of the Niger Expedition he had been dejected and had never recovered his normal good spirits. He had been made a baronet for his services and Kwabena felt suddenly bereft of yet another good friend who had helped him and Kwame. Henry Tedlie, Edward Bowdich, William Blake, Samuel Taylor Coleridge, his father and his uncle all had passed away and he thought of the proverb:

"Owuo bekum wo na wofre no agya a obekum wo, wofre no ni a, obekum wo" (Even if you call death father or mother he will still take you away). But did that matter so much? Buxton was only 59 when he died, and Tedlie and Bowdich even younger. What mattered was what good had you done with your life not the length of it. All the same, he wanted to live longer, there was still a lot to do and there was still Dupuis in the background as a threat to his peace of mind,

Meanwhile Joseph Dupuis, increasingly embittered by the boredom of his post as temporary consul in Bonny and more and more frustrated by the wait for a post on the coast in keeping with his talents, let his resentment rise as he read of the work of Maclean and his assistant K. Boaten. Just like his brother he thought, he had tricked and schemed his way into a relatively senior government appointment while he Dupuis, languished in this ugly, unhealthy backwater called Bonny! In London he had been promised an early transfer to Cape Coast or to Accra but it had not yet materialised and it seemed that he had been forgotten. He took up his pen and wrote yet another importunate letter to the Colonial Office which would go by the next ship. Since the Bond had been in force there were many new developments and certainly there must be an important position for him. It was high time he left Bonny before the next yellow fever epidemic!

Then, early one morning in May, 1847, Maclean's batman came running to call Kwabena:

"Mr. Boaten, please come quick, the Master be sick bad, he lie still in bed, he sleep fast, no hear me and no speak."

Maclean had been found unconscious in his bed and the surgeon had been called urgently but it was too late to save his life, he had worn himself out in seventeen years of devoted service and had died in his sleep.It was a terrible shock to everyone; during his time as Governor and Judicial Assessor he had brought peace and a great increase in trade, the Slave Trade had died out and he had won the confidence of the chiefs and people with his law reforms. In all the coastal areas and even across the Pra funeral customs were made for him, while for months after his death every chief who came to Cape Coast on business caused his retainers to fire gun volleys in his honour in front of the castle entrance. For Kwabena the sad news was especially personal: yet another of his mentors had passed away with his life's work unfinished. He hoped that he might be allowed to help to continue what Maclean had begun. He had not long to wait before the Governor spoke with him:

"You will no doubt have wondered what would happen to you in the future. The legal work that Captain Maclean began to which you have so ably contributed, must be continued. Until his successor is appointed, I am placing you in charge, and I want to move the legal headquarters to Jamestown, Accra. This was Maclean's plan which I discussed with him before he died. You see how the palm-oil trade has developed in the east of the country as well as trade in general and we both felt that in the future, Accra would become the main centre and the place for a Supreme

Court. Chiefs as far afield as Akuapem, Akyem and Krobo have expressed interest in the terms of the Bond."

"Are these areas not under Danish authority, Sir?"

"Only vaguely. Denmark has no official relationship with them as we have with Bonds but now that Governor Mörck in Christiansborg is aware that English influence is spreading, he has begun to exert Danish authority in these areas more openly. The arrival of the Basel missionaries with a group of English-speaking West Indians has not pleased him and he has accused Riis, their leader, of siding with the English. To return to our legal problem, I would like you to make the move as soon as possible, the merchant Cruickshank is doing well as magistrate here and I'm certain that James Bannerman in Accra will be a great standby, he seems to have made a good name for himself as magistrate. Let me know what you need for the move so that everything will go smoothly."

Kwabena felt gratified and challenged that he had been been given the responsibility and explained to Jane:

"There was no discussion of my capability. That was just taken for granted, I am now a civil servant of Her Majesty Victoria in my own right!"

"Where will we live?"

"I'm not sure yet, maybe in a hired house in Jamestown not far from the fort if not in the fort itself for a short time."

When finally all the preparations had been made, they were conveyed by ship and landed at Jamestown harbour. The acting Governor of the fort and Mr. James Bannerman, merchant and magistrate, met them and conducted them to a well-built stone house on the Winneba road with a walled garden and a balcony affording a sea-view.

There was a busy, bustling air about Accra and all along the coast and inland from the European forts there were throngs of people, petty traders lining the streets, and what was quite new were the stores of local people doing a flourishing retail business, like Bannerman, Ocansey and others who imported goods on their own account. Trading was no longer dependent on the three

European forts, James Fort(British), Crevecoeur(Dutch) and Christiansborg(Danish). Accra had become a route-centre with roads leading to Cape Coast, Kumasi, Kibi, Ada and Keta while the town stretched from the Korle Lagoon to Labadi, a distance of three miles. It was already a centre of commercial activity with people from Gonja and Dagomba in the north, from Asante, from the Fante towns, from Akyem and Krobo, and from Ada and Keta to the east, all mixing easily with the original inhabitants, the Ga tribes. The Krumen were busy all day long loading and unloading from the ships at anchor while from Ada full barrels of palm oil from the factories on the river Volta which had been floated downriver were loaded onto the waiting ships.

Two years after Jane and Kwabena had settled in, they had a surprise visit from Andreas Riis in August,1845,and as they greeted him they noticed that he looked weary and disheartened. During their conversation they asked him about the progress of the mission in Akropong.

"We have only recently achieved some stability. When we landed we had our goods head-loaded there and I, Widmann, Halleur and five of the West Indians formed an advance party but we found my house neglected and the outbuildings in ruins, while the town itself had a forsaken look because of the strife between the supporters of Addo Dankwa and Adum. We found accommodation in the town, repaired the mission house and started building a row of stone houses for the West Indians. We put up a simple building for a school and a chapel. That was the urgent thing, to get ourselves housed."

"When could you start trying to win converts?" Jane asked.

"Not at first. We began with a school composed of the West Indian children and a few boys from the town, one of whom was David Asante, a son of Nana Owusu Akyem, a prominent citizen who befriended me on my first stay there. We used English; it was the language of the Jamaicans and the use of it was spreading all along the coast owing to Maclean's influence. Widmann worked hard at the Twi with such success that after one year he preached without an interpreter and we sang the first hymn in Twi."

"We hear that you have stationed a missionary at Christiansborg."

"Yes. We had to have someone there to arrange for the supplies that came by ship so we sent Mr. and Mrs. Thompson who have started a school. But all this time the political trouble over the Akropong stool hindered everything. You see, after the battle of Akantamansu near Dodowa in 1826 and the peace made with Asante in 1831, Akwapim had become free from Asante domination, while the Bond after 1844 seemed to suggest that the British would become the most influential European country in the future. Chief Addo Dankwa had passed away in 1835 and Adum Tokori was enstooled in that year. During the funeral custom for the late chief, slaves were killed in spite of my efforts to prevent it. The Danes declared Adum destooled and approved of the installation of Owusu Akyem as vice-regent. Adum took refuge in Mampong and the bitter dispute over the succession was intensified. The Governor summoned both men to Christiansborg to settle the dispute but allowed the Osu Chief and elders, who supported Adum, to intervene in the affair, with disastrous results: Owusu, his two brothers and two of his sons, were murdered."

"I think that there was a riot at that time in Christiansborg against the Danes and that Adum was imprisoned and exiled in Copenhagen," observed Kwabena.

"You are right. The result, however, was that I was blamed by the Governor for 'interfering' in politics and of being pro-English. The entire affair was a set-back for the mission and upset the West Indians." He smiled ruefully at them both and added: "Then some of my colleagues criticised me for my undue interest in political matters and for the fact that I had bought a plantation in Abokobi and therefore wrote to Basel complaining about my leadership. So I have resigned and my wife and I will sail shortly for Europe. My visit to you is really to say goodbye. My wife's health has failed and she must return home."

"How have the Jamaicans behaved?" Kwabena asked.

"On the whole, quite well. Once we got them housed and their crops grew, they were more contented but they didn't possess a pioneering frame of mind. They found it difficult to adjust themselves to life in Akropong because they spoke only English but they were soon acclimatised; only one, David Robertson, died. What was important was that they formed an African Christian congregation and gave an example of Christian family life and steady industry on their plantations. The experiment has clearly justified itself."

"What about the contract I wrote?"

"Early this year a few wrote to Basel requesting repatriation to Jamaica but when this was refused according to the contract, a few left. Maybe there will be a few more at the end of five years but the majority have settled in well and give good help in the school and in building."

"So the mission will go on?"

"Certainly. Basel has already prepared fresh recruits."

They said goodbye to him rather sadly with the hope that his wife would soon recover and that he would build a new career in Europe and afterwards Kwabena said to Jane:

"It always amazes me how these white missionaries like Andreas Riis are prepared to face incredible privations and take the risk of an early death from malaria or yellow fever simply to convert others to their faith. They are well-educated, most of them, but poorly paid and there are few rewards in the way of converts. I can understand that when they see pupils profiting from their schooling, they feel rewarded, but to see someone become a Christian is, to me, not such a special recompense. Traders risk their lives because they get their reward in cash, and the whites in government seem to me to be well paid and to get promotion back in Europe. What do you think, Jane?"

"I recall the discussions you had with Riis on board ship when you talked about 'missionary Christianity' and he pointed out to you that the great majority of church members are not missionary-minded. The missionaries have a higher standard of personal devotion: Bible reading, prayer and what they call 'fellowship with Christ'. When I was in school in Christiansborg the chaplain was always stressing that in his lessons. I think it must be the same for the Moslems, a few take it very seriously but most are not affected so strongly. I think that the missionaries expect too much all at once from converts but I'm glad that in Akropong they have succeeded so far. What would you say if I offered to help in the school in Osu?"

"I'm sure that they would welcome you part-time. Ask Mrs. Bannermann, she will know all about the school."

Mr. James Bannerman, merchant and magistrate, educated in England, the son of a Scotsman and an African mother, married to an Asante woman related to the royal family who had been taken prisoner at the battle of Dodowa, had become the leading social and political figure in Accra. A new social class had emerged in recent years: men of mixed blood, well-educated, often in Europe, living in a European style but closely linked with the local people, who by reason of their wealth and education, held an influential place in society. There were others, Messrs. Richter and Hansen played a leading role in the Dodowa campaign, James Swanzy spoke to a Parliamentary Committee in London, William Ocansey was the leading palm oil exporter. Such men accepted an undefined leadership role in a rapidly changing society, especially Bannerman who honourably discharged the post of magistrate for many years, and who, in 1850, was appointed Lieutenant-Governor.

In that year came the astonishing news that the British had bought all the Danish forts, Christiansborg, Teshi, Ningo, Ada and Keta, for ten thousand English pounds! and, at a stroke, the chiefs of Akwapim, Akim and Krobo, would be able to sign the Bond! And one day, Kwabena returned home with even more astounding news:

"Governor William Winniett is coming to Accra from Freetown in March to make a tour with the Danish Governor Carstensen through the plain between the Volta and Christiansborg, then through Krobo and Akwapim and I am to be the chief interpreter in the Twi-speaking districts with whom he could discuss what had been said! There are others for the Ga, Adangme, Guan and Krobo areas."

"How long will you be away?"

"I think about two weeks but there is no set time table."

"Now the bad news. Dupuis has been appointed Chief Secretary to the Governor and will be here during the time that I shall be away. He knows about me but he doesn't yet know about you and I don't like the idea of you being alone."

"But I'm not alone, there's the cook and Martha keeps me company. Often we do the chores together and eat together in the evening and lock up carefully before going to bed. You don't need to worry, I shall be alright."

"You know, Jane, Governor Winniett is quite a traveller: two years ago he visited Kumasi where they gave him a lavish reception. He stayed in the Wesleyan Mission House there and now he wants to visit Akropong to meet the Basel missionaries and to pay his respects to the Chief."

At the initial meeting with Governor Winniett, Mr. Bannerman made the introductions and formally but not cordially, Kwabena shook hands with Dupuis and noticed at once that he still adopted the tone and manner of a member of the upper classes. It was clear that he had not changed and that his hatred of him was as strong as ever. When the meeting was over and the two of them were alone, Dupuis spoke in the disparaging, authoritative style of a superior to an underling:

"I am astonished to learn that you are here and that you hold a responsible position in the Law Office, I assume that you have pulled the wool over the eyes of your superiors but you should know that as I now hold a senior post in the administration I shall do my utmost to bring about your downfall. I consider you to be an upstart, like your brother who, I understand, died in the Niger Expedition. I resent your presence totally as I resented that of your brother and I warn you that I shall lose no opportunity to bring you down! Your brother had the effrontery to marry the woman I was interested in, and now, since my arrival in Accra, I have been informed that she has become your wife. Such arrogance I will not suffer! You can rest assured that the life that you are now leading will soon be put out of joint."

Hatred and contempt shone from his narrowed eyes; every word conveyed venom. Kwabena was disturbed by Dupuis' outburst but he did not show it; he had now a long experience as a lawyer and he replied calmly: " I have listened to your tirade with a patience that you do not deserve and I warn you in return that if, at any time in the future you lift a finger or say one word against me, my late brother or my wife, I will immediately inform the Governor of my suspicion that you deliberately planned my brother's death, that you were recalled from your previous post in Freetown for involvement in bribery, that you pestered the lady who is now my wife to take her as a concubine even though you had given a pledge of marriage to a woman in London who was then expecting your child! I will personally ensure that your continued service in the Government of Her Majesty here or in London will come to an untimely end! Mark my words, Dupuis!"

Dupuis was visibly shaken by Kwabena's bold reply. It was the confident answer of a man who would not be browbeaten. His face lost its colour and he muttered:

"You have no proof of your allegations."

"The proof that I have would be enough: I possess my brother's diary from Freetown, there are witnesses to your acceptance of bribes from traders, and I can show beyond doubt that you had a connection with the Bushmen. I tell you as a lawyer that there is sufficient evidence to cause you great discomfort."

Dupuis paused and then said with a sneer: "Do not imagine that because upstarts like you who have managed to get a qualification in English law and have worked with Captain Maclean that you can throw your weight about. Don't forget that I am Chief Secretary to the Governor."

He turned on his heel and strode away.

Later, Kwabena told Jane of the quarrel:

"There is nothing we can do ourselves; in Freetown he covered his tracks well and it was only with the help from Lance that he was recalled to London. We have to wait until he makes a false move against us and that may take some time, at the moment he has his hands full making arrangements for the Governor's tour."

But the anger and resentment felt by Dupuis grew to an unbearable level. When he reflected on the way in which his ambitions had been frustrated by the two youngsters from Asante his craving for revenge deepened. Not only had they damaged his career but they had robbed him of the only woman he had ever really wanted! He would not have tolerated that from a white man, let alone a black man, twice even! His lust for her grew and a plan formed in his mind, he would revenge himself on her and afterwards on him!

The first few days of Kwabena's absence passed uneventfully and when the servant girl Martha asked for leave to visit her family in Labadi at the weekend, Jane had given consent without hesitation. On the Saturday, just before sundown, as she sat on the veranda reading a book, a voice called to her from the garden and when she looked down, Dupuis stood there with a letter in his hand.

"A message has come in from Mr. Boaten."

She went down to open the door for him and he walked in to greet her effusively as he had done so many times in Freetown:

"What a pleasant house you have! I am still living in two rooms in the Castle until I get appropriate quarters. I knew Mr. Boaten was in Accra but I didn't know until recently that your were his wife."

And then suddenly his tone changed: "Mr. Boaten and I spoke together a few days ago."

"Yes, he told me."

"You know, Jane, I have never ceased to love you and I have never understood why you refused me then. I still want you and if you come to me we could have a great future together. Things are moving rapidly in the political world and I expect to be soon promoted."

Jane felt a twinge of fear. It never seemed to occur to him that a woman might find him unattractive, repulsive even.

"I beg you not to speak in that way, please give me the letter and leave" – but even as she pleaded she realised that it was too late.

"You have spurned me too often and this is the last time."

He seized her by the shoulders, ripped off her blouse and skirt, forced her down to the floor and attempted to rape her. She had heard of rape attempts but she was utterly determined that he would not succeed. He had his legs between hers and was fumbling with the belt of his trousers while trying to hold both her arms with one of his but she fought unremittingly and with one hand clawed his face until the blood ran down his face onto his shirt. She was aware suddenly that he seemed to have expended the strength of his first assault on her, and she arched her back in one last effort, tore one arm free from his grasp and at the same moment drove one knee hard into his crotch. He gasped in pain and raised his body and as he did so she rolled free, rose to her feet and ran to the bedroom where she made a barrier of a cupboard and two chairs behind the door and sat panting and exhausted on the floor in a corner listening if Dupuis had dared to follow her. It was only when she heard the front door bang shut that she felt safe but because it may have been a ruse, she put on a coat and lay on the bed until it was quite dark. Then she made sure that the house was empty, locked and barred the door, lit candles and sat on a basket chair looking at the chaos of the room where she had fought for her life. She caught sight of a key on the floor that must have fallen out of one of his pockets, she placed it carefully on a shelf. What should she do now? Whom should she tell, and if she did, who would believe her? Openly to accuse one of the highest officials in the Government of attempted rape when she had not a single witness, would only rebound on her, she would be held to have lost her reason or of plotting to blackmail Dupuis. Yet she had a compulsion to speak to someone and finally she called the cook, Henry, to accompany her to the home of Mrs. Bannerman. She had got to know her quite well and admired her capabilities; she was the sort of person who was at home with whites and blacks and who possessed a ready sympathy.

At the end of the wretched story she gave her opinion:

"I believe every word of your story, Jane, but I advise you to wait as calmly as you can until your husband returns; he is a lawyer and will know the best course of action. An open accusation at this stage would be impossible to handle and would give rise to unfriendly, even hostile gossip. But the key is a vital clue, which door in the fort does it unlock? And which white man appears in the next few days with scratches on his face? I can find that out for you without revealing the reason. What you have told me I shall keep secret. When we are sure that Dupuis is the man maybe we should consider informing my husband but let your husband first decide. Meanwhile, stay here until you feel better, I will lend you fresh clothes and we can chat together, my husband will not be back until Monday. Incidentally, what was there any news in the letter that Dupuis brought?"

"Nothing but a sheet of blank paper. It was a trick to get me to open the door and let him come in."

A week later, when Kwabena returned full of enthusiasm as he told Jane of the success of the journey and the compliments he had received from Governor Winniett, he sensed at once that something serious was on her mind, and, as she related the details of Dupuis' assault on her and her tears began to fall, he held her closely in his arms. A terrible anger and bitterness took hold of him, he realised that this man would stop at nothing to achieve his ends.

"Dear Jane, I promise you that I will be revenged on this man for his attack on you and that as soon as I can find a way."

"Do nothing rashly, Kwabena, that might jeopardise your career. Remember he did not succeed in his rape attempt and I have no witnesses. Wait a few more days until I hear from Mrs. .Bannerman about the key so that we have some proof."

"Even when we have some proof, Jane, I do not think that going to law would help us. Kwame was right. Dupuis is devilishly careful and maybe I have to seek help from friends as Kwame did."

The news from Mrs. Bannerman was indisputable: Dupuis had reported the loss of the key to his rooms in the castle and had appeared with a plaster on his face, a cut from a razor while shaving so he said.

"It is only proof that he visited you, Jane, not that he assaulted you. In a court of law it would be only your word against his. We must bide our time until a chance occurs."

The chance came sooner than Kwabena thought. Since the attack on Jane, Kwabena had arranged for a clerk to keep him informed of Dupuis' movements and it seemed that he would shortly be paying a visit to Kibi in the interest of good relations with the British. He would be accompanied by an interpreter and two servants and their route lay through Koforidua. After much thought Kwabena decided to enlist the help of Ama Sewa and Afrakuma in Juaben; he was a leading member of that community, why should they not share with him the problem of dealing with Dupuis? He was of their kindred and he had suffered the outrage of his wife being physically assaulted and he himself personally abused and slandered. Both are crimes hateful to our people and are deserving of severe punishment according to Juaben traditional law. He wrote a letter and sent it by a Juaben trader who travelled regularly between Accra and Juaben. This is what he wrote:

"Greetings from Kwabena Boaten, law officer in Jamestown, to the Juabenhene and his daughter. I wish to inform you that in my absence from home my wife suffered an attempted rape assault by Mr. Dupuis, Chief Secretary to the Governor. Previously he had abused and slandered me and my late brother. For certain reasons I do not wish to seek redress in an English court of law but I consider that he has committed two serious crimes in the category of *oman akyiwadie*, crimes hateful to our people. This man is to visit Kibi in the near future and I seek your help in this affair."

He knew that the matter would be discussed and as a son of a Chief who had passed away he had rightly referred the case to them. Although he had been away for many years, he was now back in his own land and he had never ceased to consider himself a member of their community.

Some weeks had passed and there was no news of Dupuis. The servants had returned and had told a tale of an ambush by robbers in the forest after they left Koforidua when they were in Juaben territory. They had fled for their lives but they had searched afterwards in vain for the interpreter and the white man. They had never reached Kibi and no one had been able to help them. A search party was sent out from Accra which returned without any information and it was regretfully assumed that Secretary Depuis had met with a fatal accident in the forest. Enquiries were made in Kibi and Juaben without any result, and it was recorded as accidental death from unknown causes.

When Ama Sewa passed away in the following year, Kwabena received a letter from her daughter Afrakuma:

"Salutations to the English Law Officer, Mr. Kwabena Boaten!

It is with great regret that I inform you that the Juabenhene, my mother, has gone to her village and her stool has been placed in the Stool house. I, Afrakuma Panyin, have been elected to succeed her as Juabenhene. We have heard that a certain white man has gone missing; it seems that he lost his head in the forest and I hope that this scanty piece of information will assure you that honour has been requited."

Kwabena thought deeply: justice had been done Ashanti-style and Dupuis had paid the penalty of a lifetime's inordinate hatred and resentment. Whatever had been unsuccessful in his plans had been blamed on his brother and him: they had hindered his promotion and had stolen Jane from him! What would have been the penalty in English law? Not death but certainly a long term of imprisonment for the indecent assault on Jane and for the malicious attack on Kwame. And when he came out of prison there would be no certainty that he was cured of his hatred. In Asante law what Dupuis had said and done was not considered purely on individual terms but rather that the community had been harmed, and such injury to the group must be formally expiated.

When he told Jane of the letter, he voiced his thoughts:

"At first, Jane, I had the feeling that I had brought about his death by referring the matter to the Juabenhene and the elders but I no longer think so. It was appropriate that his assault on you and his abuse of me as well as his plot against Kwame should be dealt with in our land by our laws."

"We are now free from the constant thought that we were the focus of his enmity, never knowing when his malice would strike. Justice has been done and I am personally contented that the Governor will be returning to Freetown without his secretary."

Chapter 10

Henry Dupuis and the Battle of Datsutagba

"The position of Ada, indeed, at the mouth of the Volta, marks it as the proper site of a great town. The river takes a sharp turn just at its entrance and runs at less than half a mile behind the town; canoes can therefore unload their goods without crossing the bar, and the palm nuts being carried across to Ada, and the oil there extracted, the barrels can be shipped in surf-boats to the vessels at anchor in the roads. That the place is not vastly more extensive and important than it is, is due to the constant wars and forays which are always going on....."
G.A.Henty, The March to Coomassie, London, 1874.

More than a year had passed since the presumed death of Dupuis when one morning in his office Kwabena was informed that he had a visitor, a white man. As he rose from his seat to welcome the stranger he was shocked to see standing before him a young man, the spitting image of Dupuis, the same aquiline nose, high forehead, the same shrewd grey eyes, dark-brown hair and prominent chin. The difference was that he smiled as he spoke and held out his hand:

"I am Henry Dupuis. We, my mother and I, were informed that my father never returned from a journey in the interior and that official searches had found no explanation of his disappearance. He has now been presumed dead; his personal effects have been returned to us. He kept a diary of sorts in log-book form which I have read carefully and at intervals the names of you and your brother occur. The Governor's office has referred me to you, perhaps you have some information about him unknown to the government."

It was uncanny; he spoke with the same upper class accent as his father but there was warmth in his voice. Kwabena was unsure how much information the young man might have gleaned from the diary so he replied hesitatingly:

"What kind of information?"

"It may surprise you, Mr. Boaten, to know that my mother and I hardly ever saw my father. I have a vague memory of meeting him once or twice as a boy, I only knew that he had a senior position in the government in Sierra Leone. Then he was transferred to London and later as chief secretary here but there was never any thought that we might join him. In London he had his own suite of rooms and never lived with us; it was as though he did not wish to be associated with us. Whenever I asked my mother about him she knew nothing either."

"Did he provide for you both?"

"Yes. He bought a small house in Tower Bridge Road in London for us and my mother received thirty pounds a month from one of the banks. There was an account in a certain name unknown to us from which the money was paid but the capital was not hers; the monthly sum was to be paid as long as she lived. We lived frugally but reasonably well and a place had been reserved for me at St.Paul's School. From there I went on to Cambridge. The fees were paid by the bank but the mystery was never solved. He never married my mother so she kept her own name but she gave me his. She believed that he either married another woman or had a semi-permanent concubine. So you see, when we were informed of his presumed death we were completely nonplussed."

"Was there a will and testament?"

"We don't think so but it seems that he had given the bank instructions that in the case of his death his apartment should be sold and the proceeds deposited with the account from which we live. You might say that he discharged a monetary obligation to my mother and me, but he never wanted to associate with us. That is why I am here, to try to find out something more about him and to gain an idea what he was really like."

Kwabena was put into a dilemma: either to tell some of the truth but not the whole truth or to say nothing; how could he openly assert that this young man's father had been for many years his implacable enemy and that he had finally connived at his demise? On the other hand to remain silent was impossible because Dupuis had mentioned him and his brother in his diary. He replied slowly and carefully:

"My brother and I never knew him personally, we came into contact with him officially at the Colonial Office when we had to report each year to his office in London. My brother graduated in surgery and took a post in Freetown when your father was Accounts Comptroller there. I graduated in Law and was employed on a plantation in Jamaica and then in Cape Coast and Accra where I came into contact with him twice."

"But that does not explain why, in his diary, whenever he mentions your names he does so in terms of revenge, that he sought satisfaction for damage done to him. He must have hated you both for some reason, for certain personal harm which he never states. How can you explain that?"

"My brother and I could never fully explain it to ourselves but we thought that it had to do with the fact that your father was inordinately ambitious. The high point of his career was in 1819 when he was sent to Kumasi as His Majesty's Envoy with full power to act to abrogate the treaty that Edward Bowdich, my sponsor, had made with the Asantehene. By that treaty, we were to be educated in Cape Coast, but in fact, Bowdich and the surgeon, Henry Tedlie, had privately decided to take us both to England because they had become attached to us and we to them. The treaty entered into by Bowdich was annulled by your father and after his death, the enmity he had developed against Bowdich was transferred to us. We were a constant reminder to him that the high point of his career had not lasted long and that he was back in London at his Secretary's desk."

"But you were only schoolboys at that time," remarked Dupuis shrewdly.

"That is true but we were also sons of the chiefs of Kumasi and Juaben and your father thought that we possessed private information about him. In any case, a short time later, the new treaty that he had negotiated was also annulled, yet we had somehow been linked in his mind with his failure to gain preferment."

There was a pause after which the young man went further:

"I think that there must have been another factor in his enmity towards you. There are references to a woman called Jane in the diary, the last one not long before he went missing. My mother is of the opinion that she was his lover but I am not so sure because at times he writes as though she was influenced by you and your brother."

"You are right. In the medical practice in Freetown Jane was the nurse and receptionist, she and my brother fell in love and married and when my brother died she sailed to Jamaica and married me. That focussed his hatred of us even more because in Freetown he had pestered her to live with him and she had refused."

Henry Dupuis apologised: "Forgive my curiosity. Mr. Boaten. You have made most of the puzzling parts of the diary clear and I trust that I have not offended you. I did not come with any other intention than that of clarifying the references in the diary. My father never interested himself in me or cared for my mother. In fact, when the news of his death came she said: 'The shadow over our lives has at last disappeared.' But one or two references in the diary about your brother and Jane gave me the impression that he had a plan in mind that would resolve his problem. Did your brother ever tell you anything of that kind in Freetown?"

At first Kwabena had not intended to speak of the attack on Kwame. It seemed to him inappropriate to express to this earnest young man their suspicion that his father had conspired to injure Kwame and maybe cause his death, but there was no way of avoiding the direct question. He chose his words carefully: "The answer to your question, Mr. Dupuis, is yes. While collecting herbs in the bush my brother was shot in the back by a poisoned arrow; he lost the full use of one leg and afterwards walked with a stick. The Bushmen who use such arrows were identified and a travelling bag bearing your father's name was found in their possession. Shortly afterwards, as a result of a letter to

London signed by traders accusing your father of demanding illicit payments on the issue of licences, he was demoted to his former position in London. We have no proof that your father conspired with the Bushmen but our suspicions are strong: the Bushmen, soon after the attack, took passages by ship to Jamaica and paid promptly in cash for their fares." After a pause, Dupuis said sorrowfully:

"I am appalled to hear what you have just said. It is now clear to me that my father was obsessed by the fixed idea that you were responsible for his lack of success, and the references in the diary are now clear to me. I have one last question; do you know anything about his disappearance and presumed death other than the official announcement? I ask only because the hold-up took place in Juaben territory and I have been told that you are related to the ruling family."

Kwabena disliked the necessity to lie but to tell the whole truth could lead to endless insoluble complications so he simply said: "No. The official search parties came up with nothing. The interpreter also was never located and your father never reached Kibi or Juaben. The territory you speak of is part of Kibi where some exiled Juabens happen to live. Remember that travellers in the bush are always at risk."

The interview was at an end but Kwabena was seized with the impulse to invite the young Dupuis to dinner. The longer the interview had lasted the more he had liked him. Why shouldn't Jane meet him too? Wasn't she also involved? He felt certain that she would be fascinated to hear his story. He asked: "Are you free this evening to dine with me and my wife? If so, come back here to my office at four o'clock and we'll walk over to my house together."

The dinner was a great success and it transpired that Henry Dupuis had another problem.

"I have been looking for a job for the past year. I graduated from Cambridge but although I have no specific training for a profession I am literate and a quick learner. What are the prospects here?"

"The prospects are good. We are always in need of literate people but there are health risks for Europeans and you must have the capacity to work with Africans, they soon sense whether you have a heart for them or not. I could give you a letter to the Governor, if you wish."

And that was how, Henry Dupuis, the son of the late Joseph Dupuis, was sent to the British District Commissioner in Ada at the mouth of the Volta river, as assistant to Denis Preston, a wiry, khaki-clad, bronzed former army captain who had fought against Zulus in Natal and who welcomed him with open arms: "They have been promising to send me help and now you are here! There are so many problems we are expected to solve, first to try and keep law and order with six West Indian soldiers, second, to foster agriculture and fishing, third, to wipe out the illegal slave-trade that still goes on, and fourth, to establish the British presence in the delta. They told me that you had no experience and I replied that Ada was the best place to get it. Have you ever been a soldier?"

"No, but I was a member of the cadet corps as a student."

"What else can you do?"

"I can swim and sail a boat, box a bit, play a few tunes on the flute, ride a horse, read and write; I could handle the correspondence and accounts if that would help you."

"Capital! In a week or so you will soon be familiar with the routine."

They shook hands and drank a warm beer, it was the start of a close friendship.

Later, Denis explained the problems to Henry:

"The Danish fort Prinzenstein is now ours, there is a small garrison there but the Awuna in Keta find it difficult to collaborate with us or with anyone. They have made money from the slave trade and still do. You see, since the abolition of slavery in Britain, France and Spain, the illicit trade has been continued mainly by the Portuguese and the Americans because of the huge demand for cheap labour on the plantations in Brazil and in the southern United States. They have fast ships and pick up slaves from canoes off Keta, Popo and Whydah. We even have agents from Brazil in Dutch Accra and Ada. Some years ago the Danes caught a man called Pereira Marinho and imprisoned him in the fort. This man organises most of the slave transports between West Africa and Brazil. I don't know how they caught him but they kept him a prisoner. When the Awunas heard of it they attacked the fort and rescued him. There was only a small garrison. The Christiansborg Governor came up with a large force to teach them a lesson; the Awuna waited till the troops were in the fort and then beseiged it; no food supplies were allowed in. A French ship was signalled and the Governor was rescued with difficulty. He then brought up a large force of Danish soldiers and Accra levies and beat the Awunas. The guns from the fort shelled Keta and left it in ruins."

"What is the situation now?" asked Henry.

"It's really much the same. They have been formally requested to give up their illegal selling of slaves but they refused. I would say that they are more discreet about it."

"Why are Brazil and America the main market for slaves?"

"The demand for coffee, cotton and sugar in Europe increases all the time and labour on the plantations is so intensive that more slaves are needed. Cuba also takes a lot to work on the sugar plantations."

"Do the Awuna co-operate with the Ada people?"

"No. They are sworn enemies and we hear constant reports of disagreements and skirmishes. They quarrel over fishing rights in the Volta river and over control over the towns and villages to the north. The Awuna Chief, Dzokoto, is always ready for a fight and he has trained his warriors well. He is in constant contact with the Ashanti Chief, Kwaku Dua, and it is Asante backing that encourages him to resist the Accras and the British."

"So Ada occupies an important position?"

"Very important. The local people are friendly towards the British and they have a good relationship with the Ga Mantse. The town has a good trade exporting palm oil and importing European goods and is well-placed on the river with access to the sea. That's why we are here. The Danes had an agreement of sorts with the chiefs of Akuapem and Krobo but they never exercised control over these areas and we are too short-staffed to do anything much more except that since 1850 they seem to have accepted us."

Henry learned quickly and enjoyed the varied tasks that he had to perform while a close friendship sprang up between him and District Commisioner Denis Preston. He wrote a long letter to his mother sharing with her all the information that he had gleaned from Kwabena about his father and above all that he had obtained a most satisfying job. He ended by suggesting to her that she should join him in due course! Whenever he had a few days' leave, he spent them in Accra collecting mail and supplies as well as visiting Jane and Kwabena. The coast seemed to be healthier for Europeans than inland, you could fill your lungs with fresh sea air, bathe in the sea, or sail and fish for pike in the lagoon. He got on well with the West Indian soldiers: one or both of their parents had belonged to Gonja or Dagomba and who had been sold as slaves in Jamaica where they had been born. They had helped him to fit out a local canoe with rudder and sail which they could sail on the lagoon and in return he had taught them to read and write English. Once he had been able to visit Keta that lay on a strip of sand between the ocean with its unceasing pounding surf and an extensive lagoon twenty miles long, while inland palm groves stretched and in the far distance you could see the hills of Krobo and Akuapem. A fantastic land- and seascape!

Kwabena was increasingly used by the Governor in negotiations between chiefs and the administration in Accra. It had begun with the Assin chief, Kwadjo Otibu and his private arrangement with the Asantehene.

The Governor informed him: "It has come to our ears that the Assin chief is still secretly plotting to bring Assin back into the Ashanti federation. You may not know that two years ago Otibu accepted a gift of 400 ounces of gold from the Asantehene as an inducement to bring his people into alliance with Ashanti. But his people didn't want that; the chief had signed the Bond and they were content with that so they complained to Cape Coast. Otibu was found guilty and imprisoned for a time but when he was released and took the stool again the plotting was renewed. He had taken the Asantehene's money and he felt obliged to try again. Now we are receiving alarming news: Kwaku Dua has sent a small army, led by his brother Akyeampong, to Assin with the apparent intention of taking Otibu as a hostage to Kumasi. Akyeampong has been refused passage through Assin, the Fante chiefs suspect that it is all part of a plot and have arrested Otibu and have assembled an army in defence at Dunkwa. All the while fresh troops are joining Akyeampong. So we have a tense situation. Can you go immediately to Dunkwa and try to persuade the Asante to go back across the Pra? That would be in the best interests of all the parties concerned, ourselves included."

A small group was quickly organised: Captain Gordon was in charge; with him were a sergeant and four West Indian soldiers. There were four carriers and Kwabena had one of the soldiers as his personal servant. In his baggage Kwabena had a dark-blue army officer's mess jacket with a red collar and gilded buttons together with a canary-coloured, sleeveless waistcoat to be worn under it. As headgear he had a black triangular hat to match the knee breeches and a pair of silk stockings. The Governor had said:

"When you meet with Akyeampong, appear in style. Gordon and the soldiers will naturally wear dress uniform. The Africans pay great regard to dress and I want you to observe all the traditional formalities; borrow one or two umbrellas from one of the Fante chiefs. Here is a small packet containing a silver pocket-watch, one of the latest from England, as a present for the Asantehene; show them how it is wound up. Remember that you and Gordon represent the British Government."

They marched overland from Accra to Cape Coast in two days along the track parallel to the beach about fifty yards inland, sometimes, at low tide, along the beach itself. Occasionally, the track wound further inland over rocky hills and they passed by the ruins of small forts. Palms lined the beach and then inland began the normal forest. On the third day they met the Fante

Chiefs at Dunkwa and word was sent to the Asante that a meeting place should be arranged. The two sides met at Prasu on the Assin side of the river on an open space and formal greetings and introductions were made. The Asante, led by Akyeampong, a brother of the Asantehene, made a splendid appearance in silk *ntama* with gold headbands while the British returned the compliment in their dress uniforms. The two groups sat opposite each other under umbrellas about five yards speaking distance. None of the participants carried weapons. Captain Gordon spoke first and explained the reason for their journey and their wish that the British Governor's message would be conveyed to the Asantehene. That message would be given by the Honourable Mr. Kwabena Boaten, son of the late Juabenhene and lawyer in the service of the British Governor and his official spokesman.

There were audible gasps of surprise to see that the spokesman of the British Governor was an African, dressed in the formal attire of an English gentleman who spoke fluent Asante. Kwabena spoke directly to Akyeampong like to an old friend:

"I bring greetings from the British Governor in Accra to the Asantehene in Kumasi to whom he wishes health and long life. Everybody knows that there has been peace between the Asante and Fanti peoples and that this long period of peace has brought benefits to both sides. It is also widely known that the British have signed a Treaty Bond with all the Fante chiefs including the Chief of Assin with the consent of his people. We all know that when treaties of peace and friendship are made, it means that not only do they not make war but when they are in difficulty and trouble their friends will come to help them. Now when the Fanti Chiefs and the British Governor heard that a large force of Asante warriors had crossed the River Pra and entered Assin without permission, they have become alarmed. So alarmed that the Fanti chiefs have assembled thousands of their warriors at Dunkwa in defence and have appealed to the British Governor for help. That is why Captain Gordon and I have come today to ask: what is your intention in entering Assin with such a large force? What orders have been given by Nana Kwaku Dua?

The Fante Chiefs have spoken with us and we have pledged the support of the British to them. The Governor does not wish for war and that is why he thinks that it would be better if the brother of the Asantehene led his forces back across the Pra river and take the message to the Asantehene to inform him of the situation. Captain Gordon and I will wait at Dunkwa until word comes back from Nana Kwaku Dua."

Akyeampong conferred with his captains and the gave his reply: "We have listened to the message of the officer Mr. Kwabena Boaten and Captain Gordon and we agree to return to Kumasi to inform the Asantehene."

Presents were exchanged: the silver pocket-watch and its winding-key for the Asantehene and two silk ntamas for Captain Gordon and Mr. Boaten. So the courtesies were observed. Then they watched with interest as Akyeampong and his warriors crossed the Pra, some in canoes but most forded the river chest-high with their weapons and *ntama* held up out of the water. On the third day a special messenger from the Asantehene arrived with the news that his troops would be withdrawn and peace would be preserved. They were requested to inform the Governor in Accra and to convey his greetings. There would be no war and Kwabena and Captain Gordon trekked back to Accra to receive the congratulations of the Governor.

On a subsequent occasion Kwabena was sent to Akuapem and Krobo to mediate a settlement between the two states and to arrange the appointment of magistrates in the large towns as far as Akuse on the Volta river. During the intervening years he had maintained his contacts with the Okuapemhene, Kwadade I, and with the Basel missionaries, especially after 1854 when the twenty-two-year-old Hermann Ludwig Rottmann, was appointed to Christiansborg to take control of the Mission's imports and finances. Kwabena befriended him and assisted him in the setting up of a general store which despatched up-country the requirements of the mission stations. It marked the beginning of a widespread trading enterprise which became known as the Basel Mission Trading Factory. It was the best example in

West Africa of the prevailing view in Europe in humanitarian and Christian circles that proper commerce was a vital means of the development of Africa and should always accompany the Christian mission enterprise. Kwabena remembered how Fowell Buxton had supported this idea in Sierra Leone.

He asked Rottmann once: "Was the commercial aim of the Mission ever in the forefront of their minds?"

"No. But you must bear in mind the circumstances: I have to supply the physical needs of the Mission, to transport the goods, often building materials by head-loading, then I try to sell or export any cash crops like coffee to help mission finances. In addition I stock general goods and household articles which local people need. The West Indians have been active in seeking cash crops: they brought coffee, tobacco, cocoyam, mango, avocado pear, cocoa, and bread fruit with them; they have tried rice but coffee has been the most successful so far."

"What about the training of artisans?"

"We are actively planning to open workshops for training joiners, carpenters, blacksmiths and masons. The main problem is the recruiting of suitable men in Europe, men who are in sympathy with the evangelical aim of the mission. Some of the missionaries don't care for the idea of training artisans and for trading even when the profits are used to support the religious aim of the mission and our prices are kept low."

Whenever Kwabena visited Akropong he was always sure of a cordial welcome: Dieterle and Widmann were the veterans who had founded in 1848 the Akropong Seminary for the training of teachers and catechists, while Christaller, who had been appointed in 1853 to devote himself to the Twi language and to the translation of the Bible, seized every opportunity of questioning Kwabena on precise definitions of Akan words and phrases that had to do with religion and social customs. He was the only missionary who could speak objectively about Akan ideas without giving expression to the cruelty of human sacrifice, the absurdity of 'fetishism', the tyranny of chiefs, the deception of *abosom* priests and the general description of Akan religion as depraved.

Once Kwabena asked him: "Why do your colleagues find it difficult to sympathise with Akan religion and to find points of contact with it and Christianity."

"My colleagues come from highly individualised communities in Europe in which personal self-reliance and self-discipline are stressed. This is true of the expression of their Christian faith: an awareness of their sinfulness before God and their conversion by personal commitment to Jesus Christ. In the Gospels people were converted singly so that the notion of mass conversion is unreal to them. Politically the Swiss are highly suspicious of monarchs and rulers. Their intense personal religious faith is then fostered for years in the Seminary in Basel."

To which Kwabena responded: "But according to my reading, the christianisation of most communities in Europe started by the ruler accepting the new religion and after that, during a period of many generations pagan customs and beliefs were transformed, modified, adopted or abolished. It took centuries for the leaven of Jesus' teaching to permeate the masses; imagine, you have to start loving your neighbour as yourself, to love your enemy even when he mistreats you, you must have compassion on the poor, for children, widows and orphans, you must learn that it is better to give than to receive, that the peacemakers are blessed not the warriors. Jesus brought a revolution into human ideas of morality but it takes ages before the community is influenced. In Europe, after a thousand years, the process is not complete: think of the abolition of slavery, think of the thousands who were hanged or guillotined or deported for petty crimes, while the resort to force in war is never questioned."

"That is so and that is why, according to my colleagues, mass conversion is a myth. Real Christianity exists only in small groups of dedicated believers."

"This idea will set problems here in the future because our religious beliefs do not exist in isolation from our social structure. A chief in the Gold Coast is the guardian of our religion and our traditions: he is, at *Adae* and *Odwira* times, the priest who prays for all his people. If and when a chief became Christian and his people followed him, the missionaries could then be in the front-line to christianise our beliefs and customs. The features that the missionaries find alien to the Gospel could then be slowly transformed or transmuted and the community would remain intact. In any case, when we think of the future, if and when Christianity takes root in my country, the responsibilty for the way the church develops will lie not with the missionaries but with the christianised people."

Christaller said thoughtfully: "What do you mean by missionaries being in the front line?"

"I mean that the claims of the Christian religion should first be addressed to the chief and the elders; that is where in my country the decisions are made. Our religious beliefs and our social life belong together and that is why those aspects of our religion that seem to agitate the missionaries the most: human sacrifice, polygamy, *abosom* shrines, fetishism, libation, funeral rites, drumming and dancing, can be discussed with the chief and his elders. During the centuries that followed the decisions in favour of Christianity by tribal chiefs in England, paganism continued to exist but was slowly transformed. Let the Basel and Wesleyan missionaries do what Augustine, Aidan, Columba, Cuthbert and others were able to do: the cult of the gods Woden, Thor and the goddess Frigga were relegated to one day in the week and then died out; the birthday of the god Mithras on December 25th was given to Jesus, pagan shrines were taken over by Christians, and so on. There were few references to the sense of personal sin in conversion; for us, sin consists in doing or saying anything that conflicts with the accepted traditions of the family, the chief and the nation but slowly the Christian ethic would permeate among the people. In England civil laws were slowly revised to take in Christian values. In the centuries that followed the missionaries were in the front line and played a leading part in reaching a stage when you could describe England as a Christian country."

Christaller smiled at Kwabena's enthusiasm and said ruefully: "I don't think that your theory of evangelisation will ever persuade any of my colleagues. They see no value in the traditional religion of your people and make no attempt to use it as a basis for their preaching or to combine parts of it with Christianity."

Kwabena shook his head sadly: "I'm sorry to hear that. It seems to me that to bring new religious groups into existence in direct opposition to the existing religious and social basis of our African communities, can only lead to problems in the future."

Not long afterwards, Kwabena was called to attend a conference of senior officials at which the Governor spoke:

"Our masters in London are once again considering the question of leaving the coast. The recent invasion of an Asante army and our defeat at Mankessim and the consequent withdrawal of our troops by Major Cochrane, together with the malaria epidemic that recently caused the death of hundreds of our West Indian troops at Prasu, are the reason for the hesitancy and the uncertainty of the Government. I have sent a detailed memorandum to say that we should stay here and complete the work that Maclean began and which the Bond has consolidated. I have informed them that there is a strong rumour that the Dutch will leave and we shall then be the only European nation on the coast. I have also informed them that the Fanti chiefs were so dismayed by the fiasco of the retreat of Major Cochrane, that they are seriously contemplating a confederation to protect themselves and to abrogate the Bond. My main appeal to London is that ever since Maclean's time our authority has stretched wider and wider and we have built up a legal system which chiefs on the coast as far as Akuapem, Krobo and Ada have accepted, trade is growing, the missions are building and staffing schools. We can't just give up our work here and leave the people of the Gold Coast alone. At least, not until the Asante problem is settled.

"Now I come to the point of this meeting: the only chief on the coast who has not signed the Bond on behalf of the Awunas is Dzokoto in Keta. He continues to sell slaves, he is a sworn enemy of the British, as well as the Ada and Ga people, he has been promised support by Ashanti and has organised his men into a formidable fighting force. Recently he has declared war on us and Taki, the Ga Mantse, has appealed to us for help. I am reliably informed that Kwadade, the Akuapemhene, has offered his help to Taki in the event of further hostilities by the Awuna. My plan is to send Mr Boaten to Akropong and then to Oda, first to find out if peace can be made, and if not, to assure them that a detachment of British troops will be sent in support of the allies. It seems unlikely that peace can be made but in the event of our participation in the war and an allied victory we shall have a say in the terms of peace. A victory would help our case with London."

The Governor's plan was agreed to and Kwabena left in haste to Akropong where he heard the dismal news that Ga forces had been defeated at Adidome on the Volta river and that reinforcements from Accra were on the march in support. Kwabena joined the Akuapem army but when they reached Adidome they found the Awuna camp to be deserted. After some hesitation the allied army followed the Awuna along a narrow track into the fan-palm forest and after some hours of strenuous marching they were cleverly ambushed by the Awuna warriors who had laid in wait for their enemies on the crest of a slight rise of land. All at once the air was alive with war cries, the blare of horns, the insistent pounding of the drums, followed by the staccato crackle of musket fire which poured bullets into the marching columns in the forward ranks. The terrain and the vegetation were such that the allied troops were attacked in front and on both sides and where they had no room to manoeuvre. Desperate hand to hand fighting took place as the Awuna warriors used their rifles as clubs, their cutlasses as swords, and their stabbing spears to inflict terrible wounds. But further in the rear, as it became clear what was taking place, the allied soldiers had time to form defensive squares and to give a good account of themselves. Right at the back, in company with the Akuapem led by Chief Kwadade, were Kwabena and Henry, the acting Ada District Commisioner who turned to Kwabena and said:

"Have you ever been in a battle?

"No," replied Kwabena tersely, "to tell you the truth I have no stomach for military encounters. Have you ever fought?"

"No, but I have listened often to Denis' tales of battles with the Zulus and of their ferocity. Have you the pistol ready that I gave you? It seems certain that we shall have to defend ourselves but remember we are observers and not officially combatants, so shoot only when you are personally attacked. I am wondering what Chief Kwadade will do now because we can't go any further down this narrow track."

Abruptly, Chief Kwadade gave the order to his men to follow him into the bush as he saw that he had no chance of decisively intervening in the battle unless he made a detour and came in behind the Awunas. He signalled to Henry and Kwabena to follow. The Akuapem made what speed they could in a wide half-circle through the bush, guided by the noise of the conflict on their left side and then launched a fierce, decisive attack on the rear of the Awuna army. Kwadade's plan succeeded admirably: up to that time it seemed certain that the Awunas would win another victory but the strike in the rear took the Awunas by surprise and the tide of battle began slowly to flow in favour of the allies. Still the outcome was uncertain: for a further two hours the Awunas resisted fiercely and the loss of life and the number of wounded on both sides was great. Henry Dupuis and Kwabena Boaten found some cover from the hail of bullets and spears by lying prone behind the trunk of a fallen tree while their soldier escort of four men stood guard with their rifles at the ready. Their hope of escaping the conflict, however, was soon shattered: a loud triumphant shout behind them made them aware that they had been spotted and as they turned to face four advancing Awuna warriors, two with muskets and two brandishing the vicious stabbing-spears, it was clear that they had become part of the battle and that their lives were at stake. Their escort fired their rifles in unison; two of the attackers fell, but one of the soldiers crumpled from a bullet wound and as Henry turned to help his comrade, he too was shot dead. The two remaining Awuna warriors still came forward threateningly, one was shot by one of the soldiers and as Kwabena raised his pistol the fourth launched his spear which embedded itself in Kwabena's side. The strength left his body and he fell to the ground unconscious while the Awuna fighter then fled into the relative safety of a stand of palms. The soldiers guarded the bodies and suddenly a platoon of Ga and British soldiers arrived on the scene and mercifully, soon afterwards, all was silent apart from the cries and groans of the wounded. The ammunition of the Awuna was finished; some of them had been taken prisoner but Chief Dzokoto and many of his men had escaped to fight another day. Victory had been dearly bought.

A few days later, in the cemetery at Jamestown, Henry and the West Indian soldier, were laid to rest with honours. The Governor and all the Fort staff were there and seated in the front row were Mrs Sarah Ridley and Mrs Jane Boaten. The Chaplain, in his long black gown and white neck-band presided. The British flag flew at half-mast and before the service began the military band played softly while a group of choristers sang the negro spiritual:

> 'Steal away, steal away, steal away to Jesus.
> Steal away, steal away home;
> I ain't got long to stay here.
> My Lord calls me
> He calls me by the thunder;
> The trumpet sounds within-a my soul!
> I ain't got long to stay here.'

As the plaintive melody died away in the still air, the tears rolled down Sarah's cheeks and Jane held her hand tightly in deep sympathy. The chaplain spoke in praise of Henry's life and work, of his capacity for friendship with everyone and of his modest bearing. He referred to the faithfulness and the strong sense of duty of Adam, the West Indian soldier whose forbears came from Gonja. He then read the burial sevice and the mourners sang the hymn: 'Abide with me'. Comrades carried the coffins to the graveside and in turn the mourners dropped their handful of earth into the grave: 'ashes to ashes, dust to dust, in sure and certain hope of eternal life' and then everyone stood still and silent as the bugler played the clear, plaintive, penetrating notes of the Last Post, the final tribute in the British Army to soldiers who had given their lives.

As the mourners filed away Jane asked Sarah: "What will you do now? Go back to England?"

"No. I think that I would like to stay here. You see, Jane, Henry's body lies here and his father died here and I have made more friends here than in England. I was a teacher in a school in Chelsea and maybe I can help in a school somewhere in this country."

It was then that Jane put into words what had been going through her mind ever since Henry's death and their decision to retire to Juaben.

"Sarah, you belong to the Gold Coast now, come to live with me and Kwabena in Juaben, somehow from now on, our lives are linked."

"Yes,I would love that", and the two women embraced.

Army surgeon Gordon had made it clear that Kwabena's wound was serious but not fatal, the nerves serving the muscles of his legs were completely damaged and that he would never walk again. For Jane it was an uncanny repetition of her experience with his brother Kwame, and she had already commisioned a joiner to construct a wheel-chair like the one that she had designed in Freetown. Governor Pine had visited him in hospital and had spoken warmly to him: "My dear Boaten, I am so glad that your life has been spared. The surgeon informs me that it is unlikely that you will ever recover the use of your legs but I want you to know how much we in Government have appreciated your services during the past years, especially the way in which you have successfully put Maclean's plans into practice and the contacts that you have made with the chiefs. We shall miss your services greatly but I trust that you will give your successor the full benefit of your experience. You will receive a gratuity for your services to the Crown at the recent battle at Datsutagba; although you were not a soldier you were wounded as an official observer. Moreover, I am pleased to inform you that you will be on half-pay pension for the rest of your life. That is the standard practice in Britain for serving officers who have been severely wounded in battle. Have you made any plans?"

"Yes. My wife and I have concluded that it would be best for me now to retire to my hometown of Juaben. My adopted children are now grown up and belong there. We shall build a pleasant house and I shall be in the position to offer my advice to the chief and elders on legal and other matters. You may know, Sir, that the town of Juaben is unique in this matrilineal country in having a succession of three women to occupy the chief's stool: Ama Sewa, her daughter Afrakuma Panyin and her granddaughter Akua Sapomaa. When Ama Sewa died, she was buried in the chiefs' mausoleum, and her stool and that of her daughter were placed in the Stool House."

"Were there no males in the royal clan," asked the Governor.

"There were, but not from the kindred group from which the chiefs were chosen. Akua Sapomaa is married to Asafo Agyei, the Kontihene of Juaben and it seems likely that in the course of time he will become the heir apparent. I understand that the Asantehene, Kwaku Dua has already intimated his approval to that step."

"How do you come to know all these interesting details?"

"My father was the late Juabenhene, Kwasi Boaten and my mother came from the Aduana clan and since my return to the Gold Coast I have kept in touch with Afrakuma Panyin. We shall be assured of a warm welcome. Incidentally, you may like to know that the mother of Henry Dupuis, my comrade at Datsutagba will come to live with my family in Juaben.

Finally, Sir, I want to thank you and your colleagues for all your confidence in me. I hope, from Juaben, still to be of service from time to time."

As they shook hands, the Governor responded: "Rest assured, Boaten, we shall not forget you and we shall remain in touch."

Chapter 11

The Return to Juaben

"For the first time since the days of Opoku Ware, Kumasi had been taken by an enemy. It seemed as if the Ashanti confederation was useless, and that the work of all the chiefs that had sat on the Ashanti stool was wasted. Even some of the great Ashanti stools themselves, such as Juaben, Kwahu, Mampon, Agona, Nsuta, Bekwai, and Kokofu, broke away from the Ashanti government."
W.E.Ward, A Short History of Ghana, 1957, p.167.

Kwabena and Jane together with Sarah Ridley made the move to Juaben in the autumn of 1866. They were assisted by carriers from Juaben and installed in a rented house until their own was built. When Chief Akua Sapomaa died leaving only two infant girls, her husband, Asafo Agyei, was enstooled but not with all the proper formalities and later, at a meeting with the Asantehene, on the road between Kumasi and Kokofu, Kwaku Dua installed him and presented him with an *afona*, a powder-belt and a gun, both ornamented in gold, together with a ceremonial flywhisk. In the following April, Kwaku Dua passed away having served as Asantehene for 29 years. He was succeeded by Kofi Karikari who from the beginning of his reign followed a hostile policy towards the coastal peoples and the British. An army on the west led by Akyeampong reached Axim and was marching eastwards to Komenda and Elmina; Asante forces under Adu Bofo, who had succeeded Nantwi as commander, had captured the towns of Anum and Ho in June, 1869, had burned down the Basel Mission station at Anum, and the Bremen mission station at Ho, and had taken the Swiss family Ramseyer and the German lay-brother J. Kühne, together with the French trader, M.G.Bonnat, prisoners to Kumasi. It seemed at first, that not only the political future of the Protectorate was at stake but also that of the existence of the missionary enterprise. The Fante Confederation, formed to resist the Asante and to set up an independent social order, had not proved effective.

But the taking of Europeans as hostages was alarmingly new. When the missionary Zimmermann at Odumase heard of their capture he tried to get in touch with the Ashanti camp through messengers of the Krobo chief in an endeavour to procure their release, but without success, and for a few months the fate of the prisoners remained uncertain. In September the news reached Basel and representations were made to the British Foreign Office in London which elicited the reply that the captives had been taken in territory outside British control and therefore the British Government could not assume any responsibility in the matter. J. A. Mader in Akyem received a report to the effect that the prisoners were still alive, but that the Ramseyer's baby had died on the way to Kumasi. David Asante, the son of Nana Owusu Akyem, one of the first catechists trained in Akropong and later in Basel, made his way from Begoro to the Asante border in February 1870 and managed to get a letter through to the prisoners. The Asantehene gave them permission to reply to the 'King of Europe' (the Dutch Governor of Elmina was meant), and in this way the first direct news of the captives was received in May, 1870. They were being reasonably treated and their lives were not in danger.

Remarkably, in the following October, Adu Bofo sent important persons, including his favourite son, Kwame Opoku, who had shown much friendliness to the missionaries, to Accra as a pledge of his intention to abandon hostilites and as a security for the eventual release of the European prisoners. Moreover, during the next two years, efforts to secure their release failed because the Asantehene refused to take any action until the return of Adu Bofo to Kumasi. Then, after his return the Asantehene put forward a proposal indicating his willingness to enter into peace negotiations and to free the captives against a ransom payment of 1,800 ounces of gold. Ramseyer himself counselled against accepting this proposal lest there should arise a desire among the Asante to capture more Europeans. Ramseyer recorded with astonishment the Asantehene's readiness to accept missionaries to 'pray to God'; he was allowed to preach the Gospel and even to speak against local customs and 'fetishes'. Certain abosom priests were even put to death! He was so uplifted by this goodwill that he begged the Mission Committee in Basel to consider Kumasi to be a mission station and he volunteered to return there after his release.

Asafo Agyei had lost no time in discussing these events with Kwabena whom he now regarded as the authority on British matters. He made his way out to the village of Burase on the road to Efiduase where the new house stood. They had decided to build there because most of the villagers belonged to the clan of Kwabena's mother, Aduana, and came under the Kyidomhene who commanded the rearguard in battle. So they were warmly welcomed especially as Kwabena was the son of a former Juaben chief. The advantage of the site was its position: they had a wonderful view to the south over the forest while a stream passed through the plot and in a sunken part had formed a pool so that they had a permanent water supply. The lower storey of the house was built of local stone, the upper storey of wood roofed with hardwood shingles and on all sides was a wide veranda around which Kwabena could wheel himself. A staircase gave access to the upper floor and Kwabena could receive his guests in his own study. All his favourite often-read books were accesible on low bookshelves that he could easily reach, while in the middle of the room was a large oval table of kwabohoro wood around which he and his guests could sit. His books included Blackstone's Commentaries on the Common Law of England, Granville Sharp's Memoirs, Thomas Clarkson's History of the Abolition of the Slave Trade, Hansard's Parliamentary History of England and a History of Criminal Law. On a separate shelf Coleridge's 'Ode to Relection' and Blake's 'Songs of Experience ;together with a copy of Bowdich's *Mission to Ashantee*' and a tattered school copy of the Lyrical Ballads of Wordsworth and Coleridge'. All his brother's medical books had a special place, a copy of Shakespeare, and next to them were the Bible and two copies of the English Church Prayer Book which Aunt Betsy and Uncle Bowdich had given them at their baptism. Both were inscribed with their baptismal names: Kwame Henry and Kwabena Edward. When the house was finished Kwabena had said to Jane: "I have decided that the 20th June, 1870 will also be my 65th birthday."

Whereupon Jane queried: "Do you now know certainly how old you are?"

"No. But when I retired I had to give the Government office a date of birth so I invented one. In 1820 when I went with Edward Bowdich to England I must have been about fifteen; it is now 1870 so I must be about 65. The house was finished on 20th June so it coincides with my birthday!"

Chief Asafo Agyei wanted to discuss the reluctance of the British to take positive action about the Europeans taken captive to Kumasi; but I pointed out to him:

"Don't forget that only quite recently the British have seriously debated whether they should leave the Gold Coast. If they now intervene directly in this affair it would signify not only that they intend to stay but also that they would claim sovereignty over Asante. The captivity took place in a territory over which the British have no legal control and furthermore, none of the captives is a British national. That is the legal position and the English have a great respect for the law.

"I had not realised that the Europeans are as divided as we are in Africa. My problem now is to keep Juaben independent of Kumasi. The former friendship no longer exists and I can't forget how they forced us into exile in your father's time."

"It will be impossible to detach Juaben from Kumasi, we are too near geographically. It would only be possible if you make an alliance with the British. I am convinced that the British are here to stay and I would suggest that you make an agreement with them if you are determined to maintain your independence of Kumasi."

"We have a good relationship with Akyem."

"In my opinion Akyem will sooner or later join the British and when the time comes that the British take direct action against Asante you will find that the British will consider all the former Asante federation members, including Juaben, as against them."

"You are biased in favour of the British. I think that the Dutch will pack up and leave like the Danes and that the British will soon follow."

"On the contrary, from my experience in England I have the strong impression that they will decide to stay and when they are so resolved they will invade Asante with immense force. They are stronger militarily than you can imagine with enormous resources at their disposal."

"Time will tell," concluded Asafo Agyei.

But it seemed to Kwabena that the experience of Ramseyer as a prisoner indicated an awareness on the part of the Asantehene to accept the challenge of the British not only in the political sphere but also in the religious domain. Why should it not now be possible, in spite of all the generally accepted adverse European attitudes to Asante, to suggest to the Asantehene the mass conversion of himself and his people to the Christian religion? There was good precedent in English history in the Treaty of Wedmore in the year 879, a thousand years ago, when Alfred, King of England, forced the Danish leader to retire into the so-called Danelaw in the east and north of the country. The first condition of this treaty was that Guthrum and his men who were pagans should be baptised and accept the Christian faith and thereafter live in peace with Christian Wessex. This 'christening' took time but its roots were permanent. This became standard practice: the Spanish and the Portuguese in South America baptised en bloc those they conquered. Baptism by water was the decisive act, the beginning of the long process of becoming Christian, and it seemed to Kwabena that the Asantehene, knew that for his people, politics and religion were indivisible had assumed that for the Europeans the same applied. The notion that religion belonged only to scattered groups of dedicated believers would certainly bring about an irrevocable splitting of the African community. Why don't we christen our customs like libation, naming ceremony, remembrance of ancestors, oath-swearing and the *abosom* cults? Why should not Christians join in the community festivals of Adae and Odwira?

Why should African Christians not drum and dance to God's glory? Surely God can be trusted to know and accept what we are doing? In any case, when the British took over, human sacrifice and slavery would be abolished by English law and polygamy would be regulated.

It seemed as though the British would never take action against the ever-threatening Asante. In February 1873 the Government in Accra requested those missionaries up country to retire to the coast to avoid capture. The Fante forces had been defeated at Jukwa and thousands of refugees thronged the streets of Cape Coast; British marines were strong enough to cause the Asante to retire slowly to the Pra. In October Major-General Sir Garnet Wolseley was given full power to deal with the situation. Captain John Glover raised a defence force in the east of the country among whom were 109 Basel Mission converts accompanied by two catechists. The main attack on Asante was along the main route from Cape Coast to Kumasi via Prasu and after a relatively short campaign the Asante army was slowly driven back and on 4th February, 1874, the unthinkable happened, British forces entered Kumasi, released the prisoners who had been held for four and a half years and burned the town to the ground. The Asante had lost 20,000 men and had to face a completely changed situation. A week later a treaty was signed at Fomena by which the Asantehene had to pay a large indemnity in gold, to give up his claim to Elmina, Assin, Adansi and Denkyera, to keep the trade routes open, and to cease the practice of human sacrifice. Astonishingly, however, when in the following September the Gold Coast was raised to the status of a Colony, Asante remained independent. The failure to settle the future political status of Asante was soon to have disastrous consequences.

As soon as Kofi Karikari realised that the British decision

to leave Asante independent was firm he began the process of rebuilding the confederation and called all the great Ashanti chiefs to a meeting at Manhyia near Kumasi. Many chiefs did not attend and Asafo Agyei showed his hostility by putting some Kumasi traders to death. When the Asantehene appealed to the Governor to arbitrate in the matter it was agreed that Juaben had the right to opt out. When Mensa Bonsu was enstooled at the end of 1874 he also failed to win the allegiance of a number of chiefs but the provocative action of Asafo Agyei in closing some roads and imprisoning certain men from Kumasi, brought war between Kumasi and Juaben. Again the British Governor declined to intervene and when Asafo Agyei heard that in Kumasi an army was being prepared for an attack on Juaben he rushed to seek Kwabena's advice and help.

"I repudiate forever our allegiance to Kumasi. I was never consulted about the de-stooling of Kofi Karikari nor about other important matters." Asafo Agyei spoke angrily. Kwabena replied: "I warned you about your isolation policy. If the Asantehene attacks you, who will come to your help? The British will not interfere in Asante internal affairs."

"Can you not send an urgent letter to the Governor requesting help?"

"Don't forget that I am a British civil servant on half-pay. My master has stated that he will not adjudicate in Asante internal affairs and a letter from me will not change his decision."

"Then I must at once appeal to Akim, Bekwai and Kokofu to help us."

"I am not sure that they will be so eager to take part in a civil war. You risk being blamed for the break up of the Asante confederation."

In October, 1875, Juaben stood alone against forces from Kumasi and many other divisions commanded by Awua, Bantamahene, and fighting began on the south-west approaches to the town. The Juaben army was at first so successful that a number of the Asante captains blew themselves up thinking that the battle had been lost. That was in the evening, but on the next morning reinforcements renewed the attack and the Juaben, becoming short of bullets, were completely defeated and routed. Many fled to Kibi. The stools were saved and Asafo Agyei escaped, but Yao Sapon, the young heir to the Juaben stool, and Akua Boatima were taken prisoner to Kumasi. Akosua Afrakuma fled with her father, Asafo Agyei, to Cape Coast which they entered in great state accompanied by a large number of personal servants and claimed sanctuary as refugees. When, however, Afrakuma reported to the British that her father was secretly planning an attack on Kumasi, she asked the Governor to take charge of the blackened stools until her son, Yao Sapon, was enstooled as chief. Soon afterwards, Asafo Agyei was banned to Lagos where he died.

During this upheaval, a number of people left Burase for Koforidua where some had been given land, but Kwabena and his family had remained unmolested but visitors were few and he was dejected and disappointed that Juaben had suffered so much from the failure of Asafo Agyei and the Asantehene to reach a compromise settlement as well as from the neglect of the British to profit by the Treaty of Fomena at the end of the Sagrenti War. As Kwabena explained to Jane and Sarah: "You see, the Treaty was a vital turning point which the Asantehene clearly perceived: for the first time they had been decisively defeated by the British in war. The British already had control of the coast and a wide stretch of territory inland and it was inevitable that Asante would, sooner or later, be annexed, for the simple reason that the Akans are all related. To declare the Gold Coast to be a Colony but not to include Asante was a historical blunder of the first magnitude. I just can't understand why Asante has been left independent, it is like talking about a Britain which did not include Scotland. The British seem to have forgotten their own history. The Treaty of Fomena will breed disunion: some former members of the Asante federation will break away, there will be endless appeals to the Governor which will be ignored, followed by local wars like this one in Juaben."

"What should the British have done?" queried Sarah.

"They should have done what the Asantehene and most of the chiefs expected would be done, that is, they would be taken under British control and made subject to British law. If the Asante had won the Sagrenti War the reverse would have taken place. That is why, Adu Bofo sent hostages to guarantee the safety of the white captives. That is why the prisoners were reasonably treated and why Ramseyer was so gratified and astonished that he was given permission to preach the Christian Gospel, and publicly to condemn so-called 'fetishism'. They fully expected that the British would compel them and their people to accept baptism and be 'christened' as well as to accept British law, and they were ready to comply. If Sir Garnet Wolseley, as victor, had spoken personally to Kofi Karikari on these matters and demanded his allegiance he would have got it. Now we have to face years of disorder and disunity." Kwabena shook his head sadly.

Usually, at sundown, Kwabena, Jane and Sarah relaxed on the veranda and the women would persuade him to recount some of his English experiences. One evening he produced the letter that Dr. Gillman had written to him about Coleridge's last days when he was very ill and had difficulty in breathing, how he still talked positively about 'going forward and voyaging outwards' and Gillman had quoted what Charles Lamb had written: 'When I heard of the death of Coleridge, it was without grief. It seemed to me that he had long been on the confines of the next world, that he had a hunger for Eternity.'

And Kwabena commented: "Kwame and I were so lucky to have Coleridge and Blake as mentors and friends. Both were fascinated by all the facets of human life and nature, by the victory of the spiritual over the material and the survival of the soul. Neither was a conventional Christian but they believed that you could sense God's presence every living moment. They were delighted when my brother or I described Akan beliefs to them, like our reverence for the ancestors, the various names for God, or Mother Earth, or pouring libation to the ancestors, or of Odomankoma who created death and death killed him; they said the Africans were more aware of the spiritual than the Europeans.

Blake painted his ideas and wrote a poem about them around the picture. Conversing with them made us think about Akan religious beliefs in a way that we had never done before."

One day the women had gone out to visit friends in the village and Kwabena had been carried downstairs so that he could wheel himself round the garden. He had become expert at controlling the wheelchair with his hands so long as he stayed on level ground; his room for movement was limited but he enjoyed being outside in the fresh air. He moved to watch the sunset and the way the sky slowly turned from red to yellow and the shadows lengthened and his mind was full of thoughts of those who had meant so much to him in his long life and who had passed away, dear brother Kwame, Edward Bowdich, Henry Tedlie, Uncle Bowdich and Aunt Betsy, Coleridge and Blake, his mother and Kwame's mother and Henry Dupuis, his comrade in arms, so many who had helped him and loved him! His heart was uplifted but how tired he was, how much these days his body longed for rest! His head sank forwards as blessed sleep overcame him and slowly his body slid out of the chair onto the grass. And that was how they found him on their return, he had gone to join those he had loved and his face showed a radiance and peace. He had passed away in his sleep.

At his funeral the singers sang the Akan dirge as the coffin was carried to the grave:

> "We are bereft of a leader.
> Death has left us without a leader.
> Grandsire Kwabena Boaten, who hails from Juaben,
> He has died and left us without a leader.
> We are being carried away.
> Death is carrying us all away.
> Death is carrying us all away."

And as they returned home full of sadness, Jane, Sarah, Yao and Akosua, it didn't seem the same without Kwabena, without the warmth of his voice in welcome, without his sympathy, his encouragement, his cheerfulness, yes, without his love. They stood gazing at the empty wheelchair and through her tears Jane said: "He has gone to the ancestors and they will be welcoming him with drums and horns and songs. He would want us now to live with courage without his presence, but he will always be present in our minds. We who loved him must honour his memory always. When we were building the house he once said to me: 'Jane, I feel as if I am coming back to where I started, here in Juaben, but you know, when I pass away, I shall still be going forwards.' Let his wheelchair stay in the garden as a permanent memorial of him."

That is why, ever afterwards, in their going out and their coming in, they always paused for a moment in silence by the empty wheelchair to remember him.

End.

Glossary

Words in order of occurence in the chapters

Chapter 1

writership	–	word formerly used to describe a clerk
palaver	–	discussion of a question.
kente	–	the name for costly woven silk cover cloths.
kenkey	–	a ball of cooked maize meal, the size of a fist.
protégé	–	someone protected and helped by another person.
pier-glass	–	a large, long mirror in which the entire body is seen.
guinea	–	a former English gold coin worth 21 shillings.
rub	–	the point at which difficulty arises.
Notes	–	the written agreement whereby the Europeans paid a rent for the land on which the forts were built.
okyeame	–	an important official at court who is the spokesman at all interviews with the chief.
dashes	–	presents or gifts.
mess	–	in the armed forces where they eat together.
Phew! Golly	–	English slang words expressing surprise.
Aye-aye, Sir	–	Yes. In the British Navy the response to an order.
Osbourne	–	Formerly the college in the Isle of Wight for naval officers.
H.M.S.	–	His (or Her) Majesty's Ship.
bo'sun	–	short form of 'boatswain' a senior seaman.
dormers	–	upright window built from a sloping roof.
cram	–	to study hard for an examination.

Chapter 2

dowry	–	property, money given to a daughter when she marries.
vice versa	–	Latin 'the other way round or reversed.'
Madeira	–	wine from the Atlantic island.
roasting	–	Eng. slang used when a subordinate is criticised or censured.
Gazette	–	Brit.Govt. periodical with news of official appointments.
toadying	–	used to accuse someone of flattering the boss in the hope gaining an advantage.
de-bag	–	Eng. slang: 'take the trousers off someone'.
bugger	–	Eng.slang word of abuse. In law, a sodomite.
stuffing	–	'knock the stuffing out of someone' = take away his conceit and self-confidence.
doggo	–	to lie doggo = to lie still and silent.
keep mum	–	keep silent about something.
send down	–	expel from a school or university.
good riddance	–	H's departure brought satisfaction.
blab	–	Eng. slang: tell a secret, talk indiscreetly.
swot	–	to study hard for an examination.
egghead	–	Eng. slang for persons who have superior intelligence and education. Used in envy.
highbrow	–	slang for those who have a love of learning
comptroller	–	controller of accounts.
scrum	–	or scrummage is the tight mass of forwards of both sides trying to get the ball that is thrown on the ground between them in a game of Rugby. The scrum-half puts the ball into the scrum. A try' is scored when a player carries the ball over the opponents' line and wins the right to kick a goal in front of the ' posts.

Chapter 3

tavern	–	former name for an inn or public house.
spot	–	to pick out or notice.
costermonger	–	seller of fruit and vegetables from a street stall.
patina	–	a thin layer or coating of dust on wood or metal.
wherry	–	a shallow rowing boat.
toffs	–	Eng. slang for well-dressed persons.
humbug	–	used mostly in Eng. for persons who trouble you needlessly.
transept	–	either end of the transverse part of a cross-shaped church.
pong	–	Eng. slang for an unpleasant smell.
stand-offish	–	reserved, cold and distant in behaviour.
saveloy	–	a highly-seasoned sausage.
free-and-easy	–	informal.
seamy	–	the less attractive aspects of life.

Chapter 4

chock-full	–	filled completely with, as full as possible.
dray	–	a low, flat, 4-wheeled cart.
hopping mad	–	really angry grape-vine - used metaphorically in Eng. for information which has not been made public.
bob	–	former Eng.slang word for one shilling.
quid pro quo	–	Latin phrase = something done or given in return for a service.
half-crown	–	former British coin worth 2 shillings and 6 pence.

Chapter 5

deja-vu	–	French, = already seen or experienced.
lingua franca	–	a language adopted for communication over an area in which several languages are spoken.

posturing	–	behaving in a false manner.
real estate	–	immovable property, land and buildings.
vade-mecum	–	Latin, a small handbook for reference to carry about.

Chapter 6

Tories and Whigs	–	the main political parties in Britain in the 18th and 19th centuries, conservatives and liberals.
buggy	–	a light carriage for one or two persons.
hard-line	–	stubborn in support of the old ways or ideas.
summary offence	–	in English law an offence tried before magistrates
agog	–	eager, excited.

Chapter 7

brougham	–	the name of a four-wheeled one-horse carriage.

Chapter 8

abusua	–	the family, the clan and the kindred group in Akan society.
batman	–	the personal servant of a British Army officer.

Chapter 9

equity	–	two meanings in English: the underlying principles of law; and stocks and shares.
panyarring	–	a method of enforcing payment of a debt by seizing the debtor or one of his family as hostage.
baronet	–	in England the lowest titled order.

standby	–	supporter and helper.
civil servant	–	an official in Government service.
pull the wool	–	'to pull the wool over someone's eyes' = to deceive him.
upstart	–	person who has risen to a higher social position.

Chapter 10

bar	–	one of its many meanings is here a bank or ridge of sand at the mouth of a river often hindering navigation - in the plural it means the stretch of sea near the shore where ships can ride at anchor.
foray	–	to make a raid or a sudden attack.
spitting image	–	exact likeness of someone.
ntama	–	the usual Akan word for the cloth worn round the body in Ghana.

Chapter 11

afona	–	the Akan word for the ceremonial sword.
flywhisk	–	this was often used by chiefs as a symbol of authority.

List of Books referred to in compiling the book

'They Came from Ghana'.

Contemporary

Bowdich T.E.   *Mission from Cape Coast Castle to Ashantee*, London 2nd Edition 1873.

Freeman T.B.   *Journal of Two Visits to the Kingdom of Ashanti*, London 1843.

Beecham J.   *Asante and the Gold Coast*, London 1841.

Cruickshank B. *Eighteen Years on the Gold Coast of Africa*, London 1853.

Dupuis J.   *Journal of a Residence in Ashantee*, London 1824.

Danquah J.B.   *The Historical Significance of the Bond of 1844*, in Transactions of the Hist. Soc. Ghana 1957.

Adjaye J.K.   *Diplomacy and Diplomats in 19th Century Asante*, Africa World Press, Trenton 1996.

Fage J.D.   *The Administration of George Maclean on the Gold Coast 1830-1844*, Transactions Hist. Soc. Ghana Part 4, vol.1. 1955.

Eppler P.   *Geschichte der Basler Mission 1815-1899*, Basel 1900.

Metcalfe G.E.   *Maclean of the Gold Coast*, London 1962.

Metcalfe G.E.   *Great Britain and Ghana*, Documents of Ghana History 1807-1857 London 1971.

Jenkins P.   *Basel Mission Soc. Abstracts of Correspondence*, Balme Library Univ. of Ghana, Legon 1970.

Obeng R.E.   *Eighteenpence*, ed. Kari Dako Sub-Saharan Publishers Accra 2003.

Perbi Akosua   *A History of Indigenous Slavery in Ghana*, Sub-Saharan Publishers Accra 2004.

Wilks J.   *Asante in the 19th Century*, Cambridge 1975.

Wolfson F.   *Pageant of Ghana*, (Quotations from Original sources 1471-1957 Oxford 1958

Smith Noel   *The Presbyterian Church of Ghana 1835-1960,* Ghana Universities Press Accra 1966
It Happened in Ghana Sub-Saharan Publishers 2007.

Nketia J.H.   *Funeral Dirges of the Akan People*, Achimota 1955.

Brokensha D.   *Akwapim Handbook,* Ghana Pub. Corp. 1972.

Agyemang F.   *Amu the African,* Asempa Press Accra 1988.

Adu Boahen   *Yaa Asantewa and the Asante-British War of 1900-1*, Sub-Saharan Publishers 2003

Book List (General)

Danquah J.B.   *Akan Laws and Customs,* London 1928.

Rattray R.S.   *Ashanti Law and Constitution*, Oxford, 1929.

Rattray R.S.   *Religion and Art in Ashanti* , Oxford, 1927.

Thomas H.   *The Slave Trade 1440-1870,* London, 1997.

Hughes R.   *The Fatal Shore (convict transportation to Australia)*, 1987.

Japin A.   *The two Hearts of Kwasi Boachi*, London 1997.

Edgerton R.B.   *The Fall of the Asante Empire,*New York 1955.

Holmes R: *Coleridge, Darker Reflections*, London 1998.

Stevens B.   *William Blake*, Brit. Museum Press 2005.

Picard Liza   *Dr. Johnson's London 1740-1770*, London 2000.

Tomkins S.   *William Wilberforce, a biography*, Oxford 2007

Reddie R.   Abolition Lion Hudson Oxford.